Down to the Wire

By Amber Ooley

For Barbaro,
Who will always
be greatly missed
and whose Legacy
and Spirit will
live on forever.

Part 1-The Immortal

1

Marvin sat on the paddock fence, watching the new shipment from Claiborne Farm stretch his legs. It was April 2, and the colt was scheduled to race soon. He couldn't wait to see what the two year old could do on the track. His dad, Nick was the trainer of the new colt, and Marvin was his groom. The colt was already 16 hands, and was still growing. He was jet black with a pure white blaze. His name was I'm Not Evil.

Marvin gazed at Evil, wondering what it was like to ride him. His thoughts were interrupted by a shout from the stable. He hopped down from the paddock fence and headed over to the barn to see what it was about. Looking around a stall, he saw his dad having a heated conversation with an exercise rider. It looked like his dad had the upper hand.

"I don't care if that filly was neighing from the other paddock! You almost let that horse hit the rail! That's the third time this week! I have been patient with you-"

"I sorry! I had to hold that horse back while I work him! My arms were so sore I couldn't hold him back when the filly neigh at him! He just keep pulling on bit! I sorry! Sorry, sorry, sorry! "

"Even though you're oh-so-sorry, I'm not putting you back on that horse again. I'm also taking you off that new colt tomorrow. He's got a whole career ahead of him, and I will not let him get hurt because his rider can't hold him back! Now get to work. I assigned you the first three stalls in the broodmare barn. Go! "

The exercise rider ran out of the building as fast as he could. When he was gone, Marvin came out from behind the stall and approached his dad.

"Hi, Dad, " said Marvin.

Nick looked at him casually. "Hey. "

"Who's going to ride Evil tomorrow for his work? " Marvin asked.

"Well, I was going to put Hector on him, but the idiot nearly ran a horse through the rail again this morning, so I might put Ray on him. If Ray does well, I might let him ride Evil in his first race next week, " Nick said.

"He's a jockey now? " Marvin asked again.

"He just got his license yesterday. "

"Oh. "

Marvin started to walk away when his dad stopped him.

"Marvin? "

He turned around. "Yeah, Dad? "

"Could you bring Evil in? He's not allowed any playtime once he's in my stable. "

Marvin grabbed Evil's leather halter and headed out to the paddock again. The colt was grazing on the far side of the paddock. When Marvin called his name, the colt's head came up. Marvin reached into his pocket, pulled out a sugar cube, and held it out for Evil. The colt trotted up to him and took the treat Marvin offered him. Marvin slipped the noseband over Evil's nose and buckled the halter on the side of his head. When Marvin attached the lead rope and pulled, Evil threw up his head but still followed.

When the colt was settled in his stall, Marvin did a last check on all the horses. When all were okay, Marvin jogged up to the house where Evil's owners, David and Sonya, lived. That night they were having Nick, Marvin, and all the riders over to celebrate their three year old Just Groovy's victory in the Florida Derby. His next race was the Kentucky Derby. Marvin had handled Just Groovy once, and he had almost got kicked in the head. As Marvin entered the house, he was greeted by Sonya.

"Hi Marvin! Hungry? "

"Very. "

"Good. Our cook made a delicious dinner. How's that new colt? I saw him yesterday. Gorgeous, isn't he? I know you think he is. Got any plans for him soon? I can't wait to see him run. "

Marvin heard a loud ding.

Sonya appeared startled.
"That's the cook calling for one of us. He always wants something, you know? Dinner will be ready in a few minutes, okay?"

Marvin smiled. Sonya could be very talkative at times. Just then, his dad came in.

"Hey, Marvin."

"Hi Dad."

"Did you check on the all the horses before you left the barn?"

"Yeah."

"Good. You're getting better with taking care of horses."

Marvin cringed, remembering the time when he left his pony's stall door open, allowing the pony to wander out onto the road and almost get hit by a car. He hated himself for doing that. That pony was his best friend. It died a year ago when it colicked.

Sonya's voice rang out through the hall. "Dinner!"

The dinner, as Sonya said, was delicious. Marvin went home saying to Nick it was the most delicious thing he had eaten in his life. Marvin was getting ready for bed when he heard his dad talking on the phone. He crept down the stairs to listen in.

"-------yeah, I know. But could you be here tomorrow by 5:00 AM? I've got a horse I want to put you on. Okay. Thanks, Ray. Okay. Bye." Nick hung up. Marvin crept upstairs to his bed and fell into a deep sleep.

2

Marvin's alarm went off at 4:30 that next morning. He jumped up out of bed quickly in anticipation of Evil's work that morning. He pulled on a clean t-shirt and jeans and headed down to the barn. Marvin picked up a few brushes from the tack room and headed to Evil's stall. Evil greeted him with a nicker. As Marvin brushed him, he wondered if Evil would turn out to be cheap claimer or a champion. Marvin finished grooming Evil and moved on to other horses in the training barn, skipping Just Groovy's stall. Marvin heard his dad come into the barn as he was finishing up. He put away the brushes and followed his dad. Marvin helped some other grooms tack up some horses and then went to tack up Evil. He took the bit with no trouble and didn't mind the saddling. Marvin led Evil down to the mile long training track, where he found Nick and a short man he didn't recognize. Nick took Evil's reins and gave the man a leg up. Marvin now recognized the man. It was Ray Buna, who had as an exercise rider showed enormous talent to be a jockey. Just recently he had gotten his jockeys' license.

Ray looked down at Nick. "How far do you want me to take him?"

Nick scratched his head. "Uh, let's see, why don't you take him around once at a canter to warm him

up then come back over here and
I'll tell you what we will do. "
  When Evil came back, Nick gave the
instructions. "Breeze 3 furlongs.
Slow. "

  Ray clucked at Evil, and they
set off. At the three-eighths pole,
Ray asked Evil for more. He took
off so fast, it almost unseated
Ray. He drew on all his strength as
the fast colt approached the wire.
When Evil walked back up to Nick
after a long tirade of fighting
Ray, Nick had a mouthful of words
for his rider.

  "I told you SLOW! " He held up
the watch to Ray so he could see.
"Does this look slow to you? "
  Ray looked at the time. The watch
said :34 flat, a tremendous time
for even an older horse.

  "But I was choking him! "
  Nick held up the watch again.

  "Does 34 flat mean slow in your
language? Because it doesn't in
mine. "

  "This horse, he was acting like
he could have gone around again
even faster… "

  "Oh, so now you're telling me
he's acting like Ruffian
reincarnate? No. You are very lucky
that I am a patient man. In a week
is his first race. If you show me
that you are smart enough to follow
instructions, I will put you on the
horse for that race. All right? Got
any problems with that? "

  "No, sir, " Ray said. Marvin
thought it sounded more like a
snort.

"Good. You're a good jockey. And good jockeys help make great horses."

A groom led a chestnut filly down to the track.

Nick looked at Ray with a smirk. "I hope you don't mind galloping this filly here, Speedy. After that, I've got a bay colt for you to work."

Marvin saw a groom leading the other new colt down to the track. The bay colt was sired by the horse that won the Kentucky Derby five years ago.

"I thought you said there was only one horse for me to ride!"

Marvin smiled. Leave it up to his dad to surprise someone.

Nick continued." I'll pay you 100 bucks extra to ride them two."

Ray tapped his foot. " Fine, " he said as he hopped on the filly.

Nick turned to Marvin. "Well, since you're his groom, you have the responsibility to walk him out, give him a bath, et cetera. So go ahead."

Marvin took Evil by the bridle and led him over to where a groom was standing with Evil's halter.

"Thanks, " Marvin said as the groom handed him Evil's halter. The groom nodded at him. Marvin unbridled Evil and put his halter on. He tied the colt up for a second so he could hang his bridle up in the tack room. When Marvin came back from the tack room, he saw Nick looking right into the horse's eye. His dad seemed lost,

lost in a world where no one could get him out; not even himself.

Marvin walked right up to him and poked him on the shoulder.

Nick remained unchanged. Only when Marvin began to lead Evil away did Nick speak.

"Marvin."

"Yeah, Dad?"

"That horse, what's his name again?"

"I'm Not Evil."

Nick seemed happy with the answer, then turned and walked away.

Marvin shrugged and led Evil to the washing rack for his bath.

~~~~~~~~~~~~~~~~~~~~~~

A few days later when Marvin was scooping out stalls Ray came to him. He leaned against the stall door and began chatting with Marvin.

"The black colt, Evil, is going to race tomorrow, right?"

Marvin nodded and Ray kept talking.

"Your dad officially said this morning I will ride him in that race. What kind of race is it?" asked Ray.

"Uh…." Marvin searched his brain for the answer. "Maiden Special Weight."

Ray grinned at the answer. "Your dad has high hopes for that colt, you know."

Marvin sighed. "I have hopes for him too, Ray. But it seems like every time I have high hopes for a horse, it ends up being a $4,000 claimer at Ellis Park."

Ray took a deep breath. "Marvin, no matter what has happened in the past, you can't dwell on that. You need to erase all the bad memories and move on. I remember when I had my first horse. It was my best friend. When he died of colic, I thought I would never want another horse again. My dad told me I couldn't always dwell on the past and that I need to let it all go. I took his advice and I realized I was a lot happier than I was before. I got another horse after that. I think he is still alive today. What I'm trying to say, Marvin, is that you need to keep your high hopes for Evil. Who knows? Maybe it will pay off."

Marvin nodded. At least he was willing to try.

3

The next morning Marvin jumped out of bed excitedly. Only one thought was in his head: Today was Evil's first race!

Marvin found his favorite pair of jeans in his drawer and found a bright orange t-shirt. He found out that orange was Evil's favorite color, for he was wearing the same t-shirt one day at the barn, and, for some weird reason, Evil liked the bright citrus color.

He hurried downstairs to join his dad for a quick breakfast. When he

got downstairs, his dad was pouring
himself a glass of orange juice.
Marvin grabbed himself a roll from
the basket in the center of the
table and sat down. He noticed his
dad was reading a copy of the Daily
Racing Form. Nick sat down at the
table with his orange juice and
continued reading. After Marvin had
eaten his roll, Nick asked him a
question.

"Did I tell you I was running
Happy Boy today?"

Marvin was shocked. Nick said
four days ago Happy Boy wasn't
running till August!

"But Dad, you said Happy wasn't
going to run till August! Why run
him now?"

"I didn't tell you which race I
was running him in, did I?"

A feeling of despair entered
Marvin's stomach.

"Dad! You didn't!" Marvin
exclaimed.

A smile came over Nick's face.
"Oh, yes I did."

Marvin looked his dad square in
the eye and asked for the truth.

Nick just stood there and smiled.
"I did. I entered him in the same
race as Evil. He showed me a lot in
his work the other day like Evil,
so I'd thought I'd let him take a
whack at it."

Marvin busied his flopping insides
with another roll.

After Marvin was done with his
last roll, he and Nick climbed in
the truck and set off toward the
racetrack. He and David, Evil's
owner, had taken Evil to the track

two days before. As the truck
rumbled through the gate, Marvin
wondered how Evil would tolerate a
ten-horse field. Nick parked the
truck near the backside, and Marvin
quickly hopped out. His dad walked
a few feet behind him as they
headed for Evil's stall. When
Marvin called his name, his head
popped out from over a stall door.
Evil nuzzled Marvin's orange shirt
when Marvin petted him. Nick jogged
up to Evil's stall moments later.

"His race's post time is 4:15,
for your information."

Marvin nodded. He had looked up
the approximate post time yesterday
in the Daily Racing Form. Nick had
walked away when Marvin began
talking to Evil.

"Well, Evil, I hope you run your
best today, because we all have
hopes for you."

Evil merely bobbed his head up and
down.
"Yeah, I know, buddy. But it's
fine. You'll be ok."

At last, after many hours of
waiting in the receiving barn, the
call to the paddock came. Marvin
already had Evil bridled with a
lead shank attached to the bit. As
Marvin led Evil into the saddling
paddock, the butterflies returned.
Owners, trainers, and jockeys were
standing everywhere. Marvin walked
Evil around the ring a few times,
and then he led him to the saddling
stall labeled with the number 2.
There, only Nick and Sonya were
there to greet him. David was at
Happy Boy's saddling stall with an

assistant trainer and a jockey.
Nick had just finished saddling
Evil when Ray made his way through
the crowd. He had appeared to be
running because his face was bright
red.

"Sorry I was a few minutes late!
The Clerk of Scales wanted a word
with me."

Nick looked at him skeptically.
"About what?" he asked.

"Nothing important," Ray said.

Nick boosted Ray up on Evil's
back.

"As for strategy, try to stay
near the lead. If the pace is fast,
stay in the middle of the pack, but
don't get boxed in, all right?"

"Okay," Ray said.

Marvin, Nick, David, and Sonya
all went up to their box for their
viewing of the race.

Down on the track, Ray and Evil
were making their way toward the
starting gate. Butterflies were
flying around his stomach (or so he
thought). Evil was the easiest
horse to spot on the track. At 16.2
hands already, he was easily the
biggest horse in the field. Evil
walked quietly into the starting
gate. The horse in the four stall
was giving the handler a hard time,
rearing and bucking. He was finally
walked in by using a blindfold. At
last all the horses were loaded.
Two seconds of silence, and they
were off!

Evil broke perfectly, taking off
the second the gates opened. Ray
took a good hold of him and let two
other horses pass. Evil fought the

bit, wanting to pass. Ray kept his hold on him for the first quarter mile. They passed the quarter pole. Only 2 furlongs left to go. Ray let out a notch in the reins, and Evil exploded forward.

Back in the grandstand, Marvin saw Evil make his move. The track announcer blared out the order. "Tiny Cat and Happy Boy are still battling it out for the lead, but I'm Not Evil is flying up from third! It's twenty lengths back to Wimp in fourth! It's a three horse race at this point!"

Ray knew Evil had tons of energy left. He let out the reins two more inches, and Evil was at full stride. Ray thought his stride had to be at 25 feet long. So quick and powerful, with each stride he seemed to be asking for more. Within seconds they were by the leaders, and the next second in front of them. Ray let out another notch in the reins, and Evil accelerated even more. He hit the wire seven lengths in front, and 2/5 of a second off the track record. Ray raised his whip in the air and hooted for joy.

Marvin was on his feet and screaming in the grandstand, as were his Dad and David and Sonya. Happy Boy had finished third, not even close to the brilliant performance that Evil gave. They all headed down to the winner's circle to celebrate. After getting their picture taken, Nick asked Ray some questions.

"Did he get tired at all?"

"Nope. He could have gone around again. I think he will be a distance horse. "

"Good. "

After loading Evil and Happy Boy in the trailer, Marvin realized just how tired he was. When both horses where settled in the barn at home, Marvin headed into the house. Once in his room, he didn't undress. He just climbed into bed with his dirty clothes on. He was asleep before his head hit the pillow.

4

Marvin woke up the next morning, feeling refreshed. He went to his computer and made a document, noting yesterday's events. Nick had let him sleep in that morning. Looking down, Marvin noticed that he had forgotten to change last night before he went to bed. He changed into a clean pair of jeans and a fresh t-shirt, then headed downstairs for a glass of juice.

When he got downstairs, his dad wasn't there. Marvin knew his dad usually went down to the barn around 5 AM. He fixed himself a bowl of cereal and sat down to read the Daily Racing Form. It was now April 12, and the Kentucky Derby was just under a month away. This year it was taking place on May 6. In the morning edition of the Form, there was a lot of talk about the

Run for the Roses. There was an
article about Just Groovy, where
they were recapping the Florida
Derby. The main reason why they
were still talking about it was
because the favorite broke down at
the end of the race. The x-rays
said that he had a fractured left
hind leg; broken to the point where
they couldn't save him. He was
humanely euthanized that night.
Marvin thought it was sad that such
a promising horse's life could be
ruined in the twinkling of an eye.
He shook his head. Why was he
thinking all these bad things
recently? He needed to stop this.
Marvin finished his cereal and
headed down to the barn, where his
dad was giving a horse a bath. The
bay filly was giving Nick a hard
time. She was rearing, bucking and
kicking every time she felt the
water. Nick was yelling at her.
"Get down, you loco thing!"

Marvin smiled at his dad's use of
the western word. He watched as
Nick finished the filly's bath and
led her into the shed row. Marvin
grabbed the sweat scraper and began
scraping the filly off. He chatted
with his dad for the next ten
minutes.

"How is Just Groovy doing?"
asked Marvin.

"Pretty good. I've scheduled a
work for him in three days. He only
has this work and another one
between the Derby. Every other day
he has two mile gallops, and the
days when he's not galloping or

working, he trots twice around the track. "

"Nice training schedule. What are your plans for Evil at this point? "

"I might run him in the Hopeful. Of course, he'd have a race or two between, but I'm not thinking two far ahead right now. "

"He was really fast yesterday. "

"Yeah, I know. He showed me something yesterday. "

"What? "

Nick let out a sigh. "He showed something that every good racehorse needs, and that is the will to win. You see, if a horse doesn't have the will to win, he doesn't mind getting beat. So he just keeps getting beat until he's a cheap claimer. Evil, he doesn't want to lose, so he tries to pass those horses until he's in front of them at the wire and that's what makes him a winner. "

"I see what you mean. "

Marvin walked away with a million thoughts swimming through his head.

~~~~~~~~~~~~~~~

The next few weeks seemed to go by quickly. Evil flourished under Nick's training and Marvin's care while Just Groovy prepped for the Kentucky Derby. He worked four furlongs in a quick 46 seconds, and five furlongs in a bullet :58 2/5 seconds. Evil was being prepared for an allowance race on May 18. On Kentucky Derby eve, Nick was in the barn having a serious strategy talk

with Eddie, Just Groovy's jockey.
Marvin was given permission to
listen in. They started out by
talking about the horse himself.
Nick started the talking.

"How or where does the horse
like to run? Does the horse like to
run at all? You're probably
wandering why I'm asking you this,
but I'm just checking."

Eddie began in a slight Mexican
accent, "I feel very strongly the
horse enjoys running. He usually
pulls on the reins as to say 'let's
go', so I let him run on the lead.
He usually enjoys not being
challenged, but when another horse
come up to challenge him, he pins
his ears back and pulls on the
reins really hard. In his first
race, he almost slammed himself
into another horse because it was
trying to pass. I guess you could
say he is a tough, almost violent
competitor. He can't stand being
held back."

"Shoot. Now I got to change my
strategy. I was planning to hold
him back because of the longer
distance, but if what you say is
true, then that's not a
possibility." Nick paused and
scratched his head. "I think we
should try to get out on the lead
first thing, but if it's a suicidal
pace keep a good hold on him,
Eddie. Then if the pace softens a
bit, you can let him out. Don't use
the whip. You know how he doesn't
like the whip."

Eddie nodded. He remembered how
he used the whip in the Florida

Derby. Groovy nearly threw him off when there was a furlong to go.

Nick continued on. "The 2 horse, Smagg, could have some early speed, so watch him."

Marvin decided it was time for him to turn in. He sneaked his way out of the barn and into the house. He quickly undressed and fell into bed.

Kentucky Derby morning dawned humid, muggy, and rainy. When Marvin woke up and saw what the weather was going to be like for the rest of the day, his spirits fell along with the rain. He forced himself out of bed and into a pair of jeans. The sky outside was dark and threatening. He called his cat's name, hoping Bog would cheer him up. Bog didn't come when he was called. Marvin plopped down at the kitchen table and reached for a roll, but they were all gone. Marvin slumped down in his chair. Who knew mornings could be such a drag? Nick came jogging into the kitchen from the barn and sat down at the table.

"The track will be sloppy today," Nick said.

Marvin slumped in his chair even more. "Leave it to luck…"

Nick sat up straighter in his chair. "Things will be as they were meant to be, Marvin. It's not really a matter of luck."

Marvin brightened a little. "I guess so."

"Good. I want to get to the track a little early, so we need to leave in a few minutes," Nick said.

"All right," was all Marvin had to say.

Ten minutes later they were in the truck and driving toward Churchill Downs. When they were pulling through the stable gates, Marvin was amazed by the Twin Spires across the way. Unlike when Evil was racing for the first time, Marvin walked a few feet behind Nick as they headed for the barn. Nick and a few other grooms prepped Just Groovy for the race, while Marvin scooped some other stalls. He would rather scoop stalls than have his arm eaten off. They spent the rest of the afternoon before race time like this. Finally the call came. *Horsemen, bring your horses to the paddock for the Kentucky Derby!*

Marvin brought Just Groovy's bridle to Victor, one of his groom friends that was new, so he could do the bridling. Victor apparently had made friends with the chestnut colt, so Groovy didn't snap at him like he did Marvin.

In the saddling paddock, Marvin laid the number 9 saddle blanket on Just Groovy's back while Nick approached with the saddle. He carefully laid it on top of the aqua colored blanket, tightened the girth, and he was ready to run in the Derby.

Eddie came strolling over. Nick took one look at him, admiring the red and blue-checkered silks when something caught his eye.

"Where's your whip?" he asked.

"You told me not to use one, so I didn't even bring one," Eddie countered.

"Whatever," Nick said.

Victor held Groovy while Nick gave Eddie a leg up.

Nick stared Eddie down. "Okay, we went over instructions last night. Don't do anything stupid, and don't fall off."

David and Sonya were already situated in their seats when Marvin, Nick, and Victor arrived. Among the 18 horses in the field, Groovy was the only chestnut. All the others were bay or black. As they approached the gate, Groovy started to break a sweat. The other horses were lathering themselves up. All of a sudden, Eddie heard a loud crash of thunder. It was enough to make Groovy leap into the air, almost unseating him. When Groovy came back down to earth, there was another loud rumble. Groovy reared as high as he could. This time, Eddie jumped off to safety. When he finally quieted down, an assistant starter gave Eddie a leg back up. Then the wind picked up. Someone's empty beer can came rolling behind the gate. The flash of silver spooked the 3 horse out of its mind, causing it to crow hop, buck, rear, and do just about any signs of fright it could make up. They blindfolded him when his jockey was back on and led him into the gate. Soon all 18 horses were loaded. Then, the second the starter pressed the button, heaven opened up and the rain came pouring

down. The field took off under
pouring rain, that is, except Just
Groovy. He threw up his head at the
start and missed the break by about
ten lengths. When Eddie smacked him
with his hand, he took off flying
as fast as he could.

Nick smacked his forehead with
his hand. He had seen the horrible
break and was disappointed in the
horse. He had trained him not to do
that when he was a two year old! He
knew the break had probably killed
all Groovy's chances.

Eddie couldn't see where he was
going. He could tell he was
somewhere by the outside rail, but
he didn't know how close he was.
Then he started hearing the sound
of hoof beats. He looked to his
left, and half the field was racing
right in front of his eyes! He saw
an opening toward the inside rail,
so he steered Just Groovy through
the opening. He found more
openings, so he steered him through
those, too. Then, just as quick as
it began, the rain stopped. Eddie
could now see that he was running
fifth with two furlongs to go. He
pushed Groovy into a drive and
passed the two horses in front. He
was now third with 200 yards to go.
The leaders were five lengths away,
and Eddie thought that with pure
speed he could catch them. But time
was running out, and with only 100
yards to go, he asked Groovy for
everything he had. But Groovy
couldn't give it to him. He crossed
the wire a well beaten third, when
the 20-1 shot, Smagg, had won on an

uncontested lead. Just Groovy was
the favorite, for he had won every
time he raced, with a winning
margin of over five lengths per
race; but Just Groovy had just lost
for the first time in his life in
the Kentucky Derby to a 20-1 shot.
Marvin's stomach was like a
hollow pit. Could it be that Just
Groovy had just lost the Kentucky
Derby to a 20-1 shot? Nobody had
anything to say, not even Sonya.
They loaded Groovy in the trailer
and took him home. The possibility
of Groovy being a Triple Crown
winner had just been snatched away.

5

It was raining again when they got
home. Nick had a conversation with
Eddie about the race, but it was
pointless. Everyone knew the break
had destroyed all chances of
winning. Even with that, Groovy may
have had a chance if he would've
given everything he had when he was
asked, but he was too tired from
running at full speed for the whole
race; it all traced back to the
break. The mile and a quarter had
taken a lot out of him. He would
not be raced in the Preakness or
the Belmont. They would race him
again in the late summer, possibly
in an allowance race, or he would
be retired. When they had brought
Groovy home, he seemed to be in a
distressed mood, as though he knew
what had just happened.

Meanwhile, Marvin had Evil's next race to think about, which was in just less than two weeks. The first thing Marvin did when they got home was visit Evil.

The colt's head popped out from over his stall door when he heard Marvin coming. Marvin gave Evil a scratch on the nose.

"Hey, buddy, how ya' doin?"

Evil nudged Marvin's pocket with his nose.

Marvin reached into his pocket and pulled out a sugar cube. Evil licked it up quickly.

"You know I'm spoiling you."

Evil looked toward Marvin's pocket to see if he had more.

"No, buddy, I don't have any more."

Marvin gave Evil a final pat and went to help Nick and Victor.

Victor had already backed Groovy out of the trailer and was petting him. Marvin climbed into the extra room in the trailer and grabbed Groovy's tack. There was nothing but a bridle and a few extra halters, which he left. Marvin hung his bridle in the tack room, grabbed a shovel, and began to clean out stalls. A few minutes later Victor joined him. They began talking about the race.

"What was he acting like before the race?" Marvin asked.

Victor let out a sigh. "He seemed pretty nervous. I think that had to do with the rain, thunder, and wind. But what was weird was that he didn't break a sweat until he reached the gate. That was

unusual for him. But he tried. The
mile and a quarter took a lot out
of him, since he was running as
fast as he could for most of the
time. "
   "Do you think that the not
sweating part had to do with some
health issues? "
   "I'm not sure. Maybe. But if
something was wrong he would show
it. "
Victor finished up the last stall
and put away his shovel.
   "I'm going home now, Marvin. I
promised my mom I'd be home by
eight. "
   "All right. Bye. "
   "Bye. "

~~~~~~~~~~~~~~~~~~

   The next morning Just Groovy
went lame. Nick called the local
equine vet, a man who was trusted,
especially with valuable
racehorses. He came out that
afternoon to look at Groovy. Marvin
walked in on his dad and the vet
talking about Groovy.
   "I took some x-rays, and nothing
is broken. I'm going to feel over
his legs one more time. " The vet
slowly ran his hands up and down
over Groovy's legs. He stood up and
began talking again. "I don't feel
any heat or twitching in his legs.
Trot him up and down the aisle for
me, please. "
Nick motioned to Victor, who
clipped a lead shank to Groovy's
halter. He took Groovy into the

aisle and trotted him for the vet several times. He walked him back up to the vet. He was nodding his head up and down with satisfaction.

"Well, I can't find anything wrong with him. I don't think this would have anything to do with this mysterious lameness, but he could be heartbroken because he knew he lost."

"It's a possibility," Nick said.

The vet cleared his throat. "Well, if there are no other horses for me to see, I'll be on my way."

"Okay, thanks Jim."

Victor put Groovy back in his stall and Nick swept the barn aisle. Marvin came out from behind a stall door and began helping Nick sweep the barn aisle. He struck up a conversation with Victor in the process.

"Why are you Just Groovy's groom anyway?" Marvin questioned.

Victor smiled and started sweeping. "I took an attraction to the horse. His standoffish personality made me like him, along with his chestnut coat and speed. In a way, he reminds me of Secretariat."

Marvin grinned, remembering the 1973 Triple Crown winner. He set records in the Kentucky Derby, Preakness, and Belmont. "Groovy almost bit my arm off and almost kicked me in the head multiple times."

Victor chuckled at the thought. He could just imagine Groovy trying to

bite Marvin's arm off. "Groovy
likes me, I guess."
 Marvin yawned and put his broom
up. "I guess I'll turn in.
Goodnight, Victor."
 "Night."

~~~~~~~~~~~~~~~~~

 The next few days were of the same
routine, with Marvin and Nick
getting Evil ready for his second
race, and everyone checking on
Groovy. One night Nick told Marvin
Evil was supposed to have a four-
furlong drill the next morning, and
that Ray was coming over to ride
him. Marvin's alarm went off at
4:30 that next morning. After
dressing and eating, he dragged
himself down to the barn to get the
morning chores done and to saddle
some horses. He quickly scooped
some stalls and then saddled Evil.
When he led Evil down to the track,
he saw that Ray and Nick were
already there. Nick gave Ray a leg
up and told him to drill Evil four
furlongs. At the exact right time,
Ray asked Evil. By the time they
had been running 200 feet, Ray
couldn't even see. In the corner of
his eye he saw the pole that told
him to slow down. It was hard
pulling Evil up, but Ray managed
it. He trotted Evil back to Nick,
who was staring at the watch with
his jaw wide open.
 Ray's solemn face opened up into a
grin. He new the time had been
fast, but how fast? He looked down
at Nick, who remained motionless.

Marvin took the watch and handed it
to Ray, Who stared at it in
disbelief. He knew it would be
fast, but this was ridiculous.
 The time was 44 2/5 seconds.
 Ray leaned down to listen to
Evil's breathing.
 He was barely breathing hard at
all. In fact, he looked at the
track and pulled on the reins as if
to say, "Let's go again!" Ray
hopped off Evil and handed his
reins to Marvin, who took them
quickly. He looked at Nick
expecting more horses to ride. But
Nick just said, "That's it". Ray
walked down the driveway, climbed
behind the wheel of his SUV, and
drove off. Nick, Marvin, and Evil
walked side by side as they headed
toward the barn and, for Evil, his
morning oats.

6

 Five days later, Marvin woke up on
the day of Evil's second race.
Nick, Marvin, and Victor would be
the only ones going because David
and Sonya had a filly running in
the Black-Eyed Susan. When Marvin
got to the track that morning, it
wasn't very busy. All the people
had flocked to Pimlico for the
Preakness the next day. The
Preakness, the second jewel in the
Triple Crown, had attracted a very
competitive field that year,
including the Kentucky Derby and
Santa Anita Derby winners, and also

last year's Breeder's Cup Juvenile winner.

Marvin was at the track by 5 AM that morning. He was busy giving Evil his lesser morning portions when Ray came up to talk to him.

"I was impressed with your horse in his first race. He ran effortlessly. He wanted to go around the track again. If he keeps his attitude and fitness, you could have a candidate for the Triple Crown next year."

Marvin paused to stare Ray straight in the eye. He was about to tell Ray to not get too ahead of himself when Ray spoke again.

"I know you probably think I'm getting too ahead of myself for my own good, but it's true. He loves running. You can just see it when he works and races. Evil races like a seasoned veteran does, only with a lot more speed and heart. Let's just hope he keeps that spirit."

Ray walked away, leaving Marvin deep in thought. Could Evil race in the Triple Crown next year? Marvin hoped he could.

Later that afternoon, Marvin was sitting in Evil's stall petting and talking to him before his race. "I know you have it in you to win big races. I know it. Time goes by so slow…" It seemed like it had been a million years since noon, and it had only been a half hour. Evil's race was in twenty minutes. Marvin started to doze off when the speaker crackled to life, calling the horses to the paddock for the second race. Marvin quickly bridled

Evil and led him down to the
paddock. While Marvin walked Evil
around the ring, a bay colt got a
little too close to Evil, who
reared up and pawed the air. Marvin
gave Evil's reins a quick jerk, and
he came back to earth. Marvin
thought that was enough walking, so
he led Evil to the number 1
saddling stall. Nick, Ray, and
Victor were all standing there
talking. When Marvin halted Evil in
front of Nick, he seemed pleased.
"He looks good today."
  Marvin grinned at the comment.
Nick gave Ray a leg up and patted
Evil. "By now, you know how he
likes to run. Let him run like
that, but try to conserve him."
  Marvin led Evil through the tunnel
and handed the shank attached to
his bit to the pony rider. He
walked to Nick's favorite place to
view the race, which was by the
outside rail. He found Nick and
Victor standing there.
  Out on the track, Evil was warming
up nicely. Ray pushed him into a
canter as they broke away from the
pony. Once he had cantered two
furlongs, Ray slowed Evil to a
trot, then a walk. The pony almost
had to gallop to keep up with
Evil's long strides at a canter.
They approached the gate at a slow,
quiet walk. An assistant starter
took Evil's bridle and led him in.
All the other horses loaded
quietly. When the gates opened,
Evil broke perfectly. Ray thought
if the gates had not opened just
then, Evil would have broken

through them. In a few strides,
Evil had opened up three lengths on
the field. Ray pulled on a
strangling hold. Evil shortened his
stride only a little. As they
passed the next pole, Ray thought
about how much race they had left.
The race was six furlongs.
According to Ray's calculations,
they only had four furlongs left.
Another colt, already at a drive
from his jockey, edged up beside
them. Ray looked the colt over. He
was sweating heavily, and his
tongue was sticking out the side of
his mouth. Evil saw the other
horse, and pulled hard on the
reins. Ray felt the skin on his
hands begin to rip as the reins
moved a notch. Evil accelerated as
soon as a centimeter opened up in
the reins. The other colt was
moving in the wrong direction as he
slowed down quickly, having no gas
left in the tank. Ray got a better
grip on the reins and pulled as
hard as he could. Evil slowed a few
fifths of a second. Ray looked back
and saw the rest of the field
several lengths back. The favorite
was the colt that tried to come to
him. He was in dead last. Ray
settled Evil for the last quarter
mile.
 In Nick's section for viewing the
race, Marvin watched Evil as he
cruised home under a tight hold
from Ray. He looked at Nick and
Victor and saw that both were
grinning. He grinned back as he
watched Evil open up with a furlong
to go.

Ray knew Evil had the race won.
There was a furlong to go and the
field was ten lengths behind, with
the margin increasing. He began
talking to Evil and praising him.
He glanced to the side and saw that
he had just passed Nick, Marvin and
Victor. Marvin was smiling a huge,
cheesy smile and Victor was
clapping. Nick was watching Evil's
every step, probably hoping he
wouldn't fall. Evil flashed under
the wire fourteen lengths in front.
As Ray pulled Evil up, he wondered
what was in store for him. Nick
would probably run him in the
Hopeful for juveniles in early
September, but he would have a race
before that. He trotted Evil to the
winner's circle, where he met
Marvin, Nick, and Victor.

After a quick winner's circle
photo, Ray hopped off and undid the
saddle. Nick walked up to Ray and
tapped him on the shoulder.

"Did he get tired at all?" Nick
asked.

"Not really. I think that other
horse trying to come to him gave
him an even bigger competitive
streak," Ray said.

Marvin took Evil's reins and began
walking him around to cool him off.
He pulled a sugar cube out of his
pocket and fed it to Evil. He
walked Evil to the barn where he
got tested for drugs. When the
results came back negative, Marvin
led Evil back to his stall and gave
him some oats. He watched Evil
gobble them down quickly and then
check for extras he might have

missed. About half an hour later Nick came by, ready to take Evil home. Victor had already loaded Evil's tack in the trailer. All that was needed was Evil himself. Marvin led him into the trailer and tied him up. When the trailer door was securely shut, Marvin hopped into the truck next to Victor. Nick drove out of the track gates and headed home. Marvin and Victor had a nice conversation on the way.

"Evil is a nice horse," Victor commented.

"Yeah, he is. He shows a love for running." Marvin leaned forward and tapped his dad on the shoulder. "Hey, Dad. When do you think Evil will race again?"

Nick scratched his head. "Unless he gets hurt, I'll enter him in the Hopeful. But I'm going to enter him in a race or two before that, probably the Sanford. He'd have a two-month layoff to mature some. Or I might run him in another allowance race next month before the Sanford."

Marvin thought about the grade 2 Sanford and then wondered why Nick was hesitating with Evil, putting him in these allowance races. At six furlongs, it was the same distance Evil had run that day. The purse was $150,000. If Evil ran in the Sanford, they would have to ship him up to Saratoga, where the race was held. During his layoff time, he would be trained in a way to build him up for the Hopeful, which was 7 furlongs, an eighth of a mile longer than the longest

distance Evil had run at already in
his career. That purse was $250,000
and was also held at Saratoga.

"Do you think Evil would have a
chance in the Sanford or Hopeful?"
Marvin asked.

"Marvin, if there is a horse
entered in a race, there's always a
chance it can win. I'm not sure
about the Sanford or Hopeful. But
if he's entered, he can win."

Marvin turned back to Victor. "
Well, I'm excited about Evil's
career. How's Just Groovy doing?"

"He's doing okay, except one
little thing. We aren't going to
run him anytime soon. His next
possible race if he ever races
again would be next year. He has a
hairline fracture in his pastern."

This was news to Marvin. The last
time he heard about Groovy was that
he was doing great and would race
again soon. The vet's name was Dr.
Balk. Marvin thought his last name
was funny in a way. He had come to
look at Groovy again the other day
to run some more tests and x-rays.

"He said he detected a very tiny
fracture and a bone chip in the
latest x-rays. They are small
enough that he could race again,
but Nick doesn't want to race him
any more this year. He will miss
all the major fall races and the
Breeders' Cup Classic. But I guess
it's for the best. Nick might race
him in the Pimlico Special next
year if he's healed and in shape."

Marvin grinned. His dad was the
kind of trainer that liked to plan

ahead. He wondered if Nick had
Evil's career all planned out.
 As they were pulling into the
driveway, Marvin heard Evil
stomping his foot in the trailer.
When they parked, Marvin climbed
over Victor so he could let Evil
out as soon as possible. Marvin
opened the trailer door to see Evil
looking him right in the eye, his
lead rope dangling loose from his
halter. Apparently Marvin had not
tied him up good enough or Evil had
undone the knot. He quickly grabbed
the rope and led him out of the
trailer. A whinny came from the
barn, which Evil returned. Marvin
recognized it to be Little Thang's
whinny. Little Thang had recently
come in third in the Kentucky Oaks.
She had gone off as the 9-2 second
choice and had had a troubled trip,
stumbling at the start. Her jockey
was asking her from the very
beginning, much like Groovy in the
Kentucky Derby. She finished the
same way, a closing third. It
wasn't pouring down rain like it
was in the Derby, though. She
didn't suffer any injuries and was
being pointed for the Coaching Club
American Oaks for three year old
fillies. Marvin led Evil into the
barn and into his stall. He brushed
Evil and picked out his hooves.
Marvin gave Evil a few sugar cubes
and a pat and headed out of his
stall. He was heading for the
stallion barn when he heard Nick in
a serious conversation. He peeked
around the corner of the door to
the broodmare barn and found him on

the phone. Victor was sitting on a bale of hay with a nervous expression on his face. Marvin couldn't make out the words to the conversation. He strolled in just as Nick hung up. His face was very pale as he spoke. "That was the hospital. I'm so sorry, Victor. I know this is hard for you."

Marvin was confused. "What happened?"

Nick's voice was shaky. "Victor's mom is at the hospital. She had a heart attack just a short while ago and is dangling on the bridge of life. The doctors said she doesn't have much of a chance."

Victor began crying. "I need to go see her. She needs to know I am still here for her."

7

Marvin went with Victor to the hospital. The doctors told Victor his mom was in a coma and couldn't speak to him. Victor stayed by his mom's bedside for the rest of the night. By midnight, Nick had finally got Victor to come home with him and Marvin. Victor was so tired that he finally gave in. Nick set out a cot in Marvin's room so Victor would have a place to sleep. Marvin fell asleep without even saying goodnight to Nick. Victor cried himself to sleep.

~~~~~~~~~~~~~~~~~~~~~~~

The next day was Preakness day. Marvin didn't even think about it. He looked over at Victor's cot at three in the morning and saw that he wasn't there. He pulled on a pair of jeans and went down to the barn. Marvin went through the stallion and broodmare barns and didn't find him. He looked through the training barn, waking many of the horses, including Evil. He reached his head out from over his stall door and nickered at Marvin. "Evil, not now," he said. Marvin thoroughly searched the training barn and almost gave up when he heard muffled sobs from Just Groovy's stall. He peeked in and found Victor burying his face in the horse's mane. He went into Groovy's stall without even thinking what Groovy could do to him. But now, Groovy was quiet and didn't seem to notice Marvin's entrance. Marvin stood above Victor and watched him cry. He laid a hand on Victor's shoulder and began talking to him. "Are you okay, Victor?"

Victor brought his head up from Just Groovy's mane, where there was a big wet spot from Victor's tears. "No, I'm not okay!" he sobbed. Another big burst of tears came and he buried his face again.

Marvin could feel the tears begin to well up in his own eyes. "I know what you're going through, Victor. I lost my mom over a heart attack. I thought I would never live again. Your mom is still alive. If she's a fighter, she might survive!"

Victor cried even more. "That's the thing, Marvin! She's not a fighter! She always gives in to things! I know her!" He continued to sob into Groovy's mane.

The tears were running down Marvin's cheeks now. "Don't be so negative. She has a chance." Just Groovy extended his head toward Marvin. Marvin gasped in amazement.

"He's never done that to me before! I know he agrees with me, Victor. You need to think positive."

Victor stood up, his tears lightening a little. "I know. But how can I? She hasn't been feeling well the past few weeks. I should have known something bad was coming!" The tears came heavier now than ever before.

Marvin helped Victor out of Groovy's stall, into the house, and into his cot just as the sun began its long journey into the sky above.

~~~~~~~~~~~~~~~~~~~~

That same morning Marvin took Evil out of his stall and began brushing him. Evil sniffed Marvin's pockets. He knew just what they contained. Marvin reached into his pocket, pulling out a bag of sugar cubes. He fed one to Evil and continued brushing him. Nick walked up to Marvin and Evil. " Victor isn't up yet."

"I found him in Groovy's stall at three this morning, crying. He's taking this really hard."

Nick nodded. "Of course he is. You and I were the same way when Jen died."

Marvin thought about his mom. She had loved horses, just like Marvin did. Nick didn't like horses at the time. Marvin and his mom would go on long trail rides together, just Marvin and his pony and Jen and her horse. She died of a heart attack five years ago.

Marvin finished brushing Evil and put him back in his stall. All the horses had been fed and Marvin was hungry himself. He followed Nick into the house for some lunch. His dad had made some peanut butter and jelly sandwiches for them to eat. Marvin was drooling over the sight of food, and the opening of pop cans made him thirsty.

He finished the first sandwich in a few bites and quickly began the next one,

Nick eyed him warily. "Don't make yourself sick," he warned.

Marvin didn't change his rate of eating. He downed his pop and got another one. He started eating his third sandwich. He felt full already. Oh, well. His dad had warned him. He just wouldn't let Nick know he made his stomach hurt. He went back out to the barn, where it was time for the horses' lunch. Evil was the first one to start whinnying. Evil ate the food as it was poured into his bowl. He only had a bit left after Marvin was

done pouring it in. Groovy was
next. He was more patient. He
waited as Marvin poured his grain
in the bowl. Only when Marvin left
his stall did he begin eating.
Marvin quickly finished feeding the
rest of the horses and went to hang
out in Evil's stall. Evil was
already done with his feed. Marvin
slipped him a sugar cube and sat
down in the straw. Evil nuzzled
him, asking for another. Marvin
stroked his nose. "No, buddy. No
more." Evil stared out the door,
obviously bored. Marvin thought
about it for less than a second
before it happened. Marvin walked
over to Evil's side, grabbed some
mane, and climbed aboard. Evil's
ears came up, aware of the person
now on his back. Marvin sat up
straighter and patted Evil's neck.
His head almost touched the support
beam holding the roof up because
Evil's back was so high up. He gave
Evil a light squeeze and he walked
a few steps forward. Marvin
murmured words to Evil.

"Walk on, buddy. Walk on."

Evil began making circles around
the stall. Marvin heard footsteps
approaching, so he quickly slid off
Evil's back. He plopped down in the
straw as Nick's head came into the
clear.

"I was just checking to see if
you're okay," Nick said.

"I'm fine," Marvin said with a
smile, remembering the ride. "Evil
and I here are just fine."

Nick sighed. "You and that horse
are good friends."

"Yep. He's my buddy, " Marvin replied.

"Good, " Nick said.

Marvin spent the rest of the afternoon in the barn. Evil would nicker every time Marvin passed his stall. When Marvin headed back to the house, Nick met him on the pathway.

"Victor's still asleep, " Nick reminded Marvin.

Marvin climbed the stairs to his room, where he found Victor still sleeping. His cheeks were tear-stained. His hair was messy. Marvin sighed as he undressed and climbed into bed. Victor began crying in his sleep. Marvin drifted off to the muffled crying of Victor.

8

Victor was still in his cot when Marvin woke up that morning. Marvin headed downstairs for breakfast, where he found Nick reading the Form. Marvin sat down at the table and grabbed a roll. Marvin sat at the table and ate while Nick read the Form. They were both surprised when Victor came down the stairs and sat down at the table.

Marvin watched as Victor grabbed a roll and spread some butter on it. He looked at Nick, who gave a slight nod. Marvin looked back at Victor. "Victor, are you okay? "

Victor managed the very slightest of smiles. "I guess so. I'm trying to think more positive, like you said I should. I drew this to hang

on the wall. I hope you don't mind,
Marvin."
  Marvin looked and saw that Victor
had drawn a smiley face with the
saying under it "Think
positive!". He smiled at Victor.
"I don't mind. I like it. It adds
brightness to the room."
  Victor smiled and set the picture
down. "It helps me," he said. So,
are you ready to go down to the
barn?"
  Marvin smiled back. "Yeah."
  Marvin and Victor headed down to
the barn, where the horses where
begging to be exercised or fed.
Marvin saddled Evil for his morning
gallop, and Victor checked on
Groovy. Nick had given Marvin the
exciting news last night that he
could ride Evil in his gallop that
morning under Nick's supervision.
Marvin led Evil down to the track,
where Nick was waiting. Nick gave
Marvin a leg up. Marvin felt proud
to be sitting on such a racehorse
in front of his dad. Nick smiled at
Marvin. "Gallop him slowly for one
mile. Slow. Don't be like Ray and
let the reins loose."
  Marvin grinned at his dad's
sarcastic comment. He knew Ray
didn't really let the reins loose-
Evil just ran fast under him. He
clucked at Evil and they went off
into a trot. Once he was warmed up,
Marvin chirped at Evil and they set
off into a gallop. Evil's stride
was so long, much unlike Fred's,
his stable pony. Evil tugged on the
reins, begging to be let out more.
Marvin kept a firm hold on him.

They completed the circuit of the mile training track and Marvin slowed Evil down. As they walked back up to Nick, he was grinning.

"Perfect. You did exactly what I told you to do. In a few years you could be a jockey," Nick said.

Marvin beamed at his dad's praise. He hopped off Evil and led him to the barn, suddenly feeling lighter.

~~~~~~~~~~~~~~~~~~~~~~

The next few days carried a lighter mood. Victor's mom had woken up from the coma, and Victor was a lot happier. The picture he hung up on the wall helped, too. Marvin found Victor humming to himself in Just Groovy's stall. Marvin leaned against the side of the door as he watched Victor work. Victor lifted his head up and saw Marvin standing there.

"Hi, Marvin," he said.

"Hi," Marvin replied. " How's Just Groovy doing?"

"Great. The latest x-rays show that the bone is healing. If he ever races again, it will be next year. He'll miss the Breeders' Cup."

Marvin thought it was a disappointment to miss the Breeders' Cup, after Groovy worked so hard all year. It was now May 25, and Nick had decided to race Evil in another allowance race for two-year olds in the middle of June. Nick wasn't exactly sure of the plan from there. He wasn't sure

of the Sanford any more. He was
thinking about the Saratoga Special
in mid-August. He almost doubted
about the Hopeful, though he was
considering it for Happy Boy. The
Saratoga Special, Nick thought,
seemed more like the right race for
Evil, and the Hopeful more right
for Happy.

 Marvin was thinking so deep that
he did not notice Victor get up and
leave. When he snapped out of his
thoughts, he found that he was all
alone with Just Groovy, who had
that devilish gleam in his eye that
he had when he had almost gotten
Marvin's arm.

Marvin quickly got himself out of
Groovy's stall when he thought
Groovy had decided he was hungry
and Marvin arm sounded appetizing.
He extended his head out to Marvin,
who quickly jerked away. Marvin
jogged down the hall towards Fred's
stall. He grabbed Fred's saddle and
bridle from the tack room. Fred
looked at him with a bored look,
dreading the ride ahead. Fred was a
big pony, but he was lazy. Marvin
would have to hit him hard with the
crop just to get his attention.
Evil was much more fun to ride than
Fred. Evil liked to go; Fred liked
to plod along super slow. Marvin
didn't even remember the last time
when Fred trotted. He asked Nick if
he could ride The Man, a seven-year
old Percheron gelding Nick rode
that had tons of energy. Nick said
no, explaining that Marvin wouldn't
be able to control him. He was

almost worse than Evil was in races.

When Fred was saddled, Marvin led him over to the mounting block and quickly mounted. He pointed his pony for the fields he had discovered last time out. The fields, which were just a big, open area, were deep in the woods. Marvin remembered to take the trail leading to the neighboring farm. He discovered the trail leading to the fields a few days ago when he was riding Fred. A quarter mile into the main trail there was an old trail with weeds growing over it. Marvin just barely noticed it, because Nick's Percheron had likely been through it when he got loose the day before. As he turned Fred onto the hidden trail, he wondered if the girl next door, whose dad trained jumpers, had found the trail before him. He had often seen her riding on the main trail with her gigantic hunter. She wasn't on the trail today. Fred put his head down to nibble on some grass. Marvin waved his crop in front of Fred's face and pulled his head up. Fred snorted at Marvin. They continued down the trail for some time until Fred stopped suddenly. Marvin kicked him hard. No response. He hit him hard with the crop. Still no response. Marvin tried every method he had heard of to get a horse to move, but none worked. Marvin got tired of Fred and finally hopped off. He began to try to walk him, which amazingly worked. Fred seemed to be saying,

"How do you like me now?" with
his body language and that annoyed
Marvin. He took that as an
opportunity to try to get Fred to
trot, since he seemed so full of
energy now. Marvin clucked at him,
encouraging him. Fred dropped back
into his slowest walk as if to say,
"Don't go there, buster."

Marvin grudgingly walked along
with Fred until they got home. He
unsaddled Fred and put him in his
stall, then headed up for dinner.
Nick was waiting for him when he
walked in the door.

"What took you so long?"

"I took Fred out for a ride. He
was being so slow, as usual. I wish
I had another horse to ride. A
bigger horse. Kind of like your…"

"Let's not get carried away,"
Nick warned. He knew what Marvin
was hinting at.

"Rats," Marvin said. "So,
anything new happen while I was
gone?"

"Nothing except Groovy trying to
take my arm off," Nick snorted.

"That's a bad habit he needs to
break," Marvin started.

"He'll never break that habit.
He's been doing that to people
since I got him when he was barely
two. Apparently he likes the taste
of arm," Nick interrupted.

Marvin laughed. Under all the
seriousness and years, his dad
still had a slight sense of humor.

"You any surer about when Evil
will race next?" Marvin asked.

"I think his next race will be a
small allowance race again. After

that, we might go for the Saratoga
Special. I think I'll enter Happy
Boy in the Sanford and after that
the Hopeful. But, you know, none
of this is possible if the horse
isn't training well or if he's
hurt. The Special seems more like
the right race for Evil. "
Marvin nodded. You can't push a
horse too hard. The Hopeful would
be full of the best two-year olds
of the country, and Marvin didn't
know if Evil would be up to the
challenge. He was a great horse at
his level, but against bigger and
better horses? Marvin wasn't sure.

9

 Evil galloped every other morning
that week, and had one breeze
scheduled. Ray was to ride him for
that, but Marvin galloped him every
other day for a mile. Nick was
surprised on how fit Evil got in
such a short amount of time. Marvin
woke up early on the day of Evil's
breeze so he could watch. He
quickly tacked Evil up and led him
out to the track. Ray and Nick were
already waiting. As Nick gave Ray a
leg up, he told him to breeze Evil
7 furlongs. Ray clucked to Evil and
he set off. Ray held him back with
all of his strength, even moving
his hands closer to the bit. They
crossed the line where the line
should have been and Ray struggled
to pull Evil up. Finally Ray got
his hands near the bit and pulled

hard. Evil immediately slowed.
Well, Ray thought, *I figured out
how to slow him down quick.* Evil
trotted back to Nick and Nick
seemed a little chilly. "That was
a little too fast. He went in 1:24
and 1/5 seconds. But if he's not
that tired, that's a good thing."
 Ray said he didn't seem tired and
hopped off. He started to walk
toward his car when Nick spoke.
 "You know I have more horses for
you to ride."
 Ray groaned and came back. He had
to ride a horse that didn't run
when you asked it. The horse was
also mean. He liked to do anything
he could to get Ray off his back.
 Nick turned to Marvin. "Here's
Evil. Take him and give him a bath.
You didn't give him a bath when I
last asked you to. He looked like a
light bay with all that dust and
dirt sticking to his coat." Marvin
grimaced at the memory. He HAD
looked like a light bay. Marvin
walked Evil to the wash rack, where
Happy Boy was getting a bath. His
dark bay coat was shiny. With the
attitude, looks and speed, Happy
looked like and was a great
racehorse. Would he and Evil ever
meet in a race again? Marvin hoped
so, but he didn't know who would
win.

~~~~~~~~~~~~~~~~~~~~~

The next day Marvin was out on
the trails with Victor. They both
were riding a couple of horses that
were used to pony green horses out

to the track. Marvin was so happy that he didn't have to ride Fred. He was riding Berry, the chestnut mare that loved to canter. He and Victor rode out to the fields. Victor loved the flat, open area. He and Marvin decided to have a little match race. They lined up Berry and Angel at the end of the field. They counted 3, 2, 1, Victor made a gate noise, and they both asked their horses to run. Berry got a better start, but Angel was a quarter horse and in better shape, so she soon passed Berry. She won by what Marvin estimated to be about four lengths.

Victor passed the pretend finish line with extremely loud war whoops, which brought a snort from Marvin. "My horse is too fat," he complained as he slowed Berry to a walk.

Victor rolled his eyes. "No excuses. Angel is faster."

"Whatever…" Marvin said.

Marvin and Victor trotted down the trail toward home. When they approached the barn, Marvin saw Evil cantering around a small paddock in front of the barn. Nick was casually leaning over the fence with a Coke, watching Evil with a grin over his face. Marvin decided to leave him alone, so he and Victor sneaked into the barn by dismounting and hiding behind their horses as they led them back behind the stallion barn and through the training barn's back door. As Marvin was putting Berry's bridle up, he heard Nick lead Evil back

in. He stood right by the door of
the tack room, waiting for them to
pass. He looked down at his feet as
Nick walked by. He heard a loud
whoa, so he looked up to find a big
black nose in his face. Marvin
smiled. "Hi, Evil," he said. "Go
on to your stall." Evil gave him a
look that said, "Do you think I'm
stupid?" Nick handed Evil's lead
shank to Marvin, whom Evil followed
like a puppy dog. He walked Evil
into his stall and gave him a sugar
cube. Marvin quickly walked out of
Evil's stall, remembering that Evil
was known to follow people out of
his stall. As Marvin shut and
latched the stall door, Evil's head
popped out of the open half. Nick
made it a point to leave the top
half of every stall door open so
the horse could poke his head out
and look around. All the barns
where like this except the stallion
barn. The stallion barn had no top
half, but there was a net over it.
This adjustment had been made a few
years ago, for one too many people
walking by had been bitten.

Marvin headed up to the house for
dinner. He and Nick plopped down at
the kitchen table with some TV
dinners. Nick finished his quickly
then went to take a shower before
bed. Marvin looked out the kitchen
window at the barn one last time,
then jumped the stairs two at a
time to his bedroom. He fell asleep
before he was done climbing into
bed.

~~~~~~~~~~~~~~~~~~~~

Marvin woke up the next morning
with something nagging him. He was
dying to know what Evil's goal was
beyond his next race. He pulled on
a pair of jeans and headed
downstairs. Nick was drinking a cup
of coffee and eating an orange.
Marvin skidded across the kitchen
floor and into a seat. He looked
his dad in the eye with much
seriousness and asked, "Have you
decided on Evil yet?"

Nick put down his coffee. "Nope.
I have to see what he does in his
next race. I'll let you know when
I've decided. By the way, you get
to gallop Evil this morning. I've
assigned him a seven furlong slow
gallop today. You can go ahead and
saddle him up. I'll be down in a
minute."

Marvin bounced out the door and
toward the barn. He stopped by the
tack room and grabbed a lightweight
saddle, some saddle pads, and a
bridle. He walked toward Evil's
stall, whistling. Evil heard him
coming and poked his head out over
the stall door with a nicker.
Marvin brushed him off and secured
the saddle and its pads and
fastened the girth. He easily put
the bridle on. Marvin surveyed his
work, satisfied, and led Evil down
to the training track, where Nick
was waiting. He gave Marvin a leg
up and reminded him of the
distance. Marvin cantered Evil a
furlong to warm him up and then
loosened the reins a notch. He

instantly accelerated, and Marvin
leaned forward and grabbed some
more rein for more control. Marvin
noted that Evil had a huge stride
at a slow speed, feeling that if he
didn't take another, he would hit
the ground. Even being choked, he
still covered a lot of ground in a
short time. It seemed only a short
time before the wire loomed. Evil
flashed under the wire. Marvin
stood in the stirrups, pulling Evil
up. He trotted Evil to the gap,
where Nick was standing. Marvin
looked down at Nick expectantly.
"Well? How'd he do?"
 Nick sighed. "Well, he went too
fast…again. I wanted him to go
around in about 1:26. But no, he
decided to go in 1:24 and two. You
can't change his mind, even with a
piece of metal tearing at his
mouth."
"I didn't know you were timing
him," Marvin said as he leaped
down from Evil's back, hitting the
ground hard. He looked up at his
back. Evil had gotten taller. He
had to be 17 hands. He led Evil
back to the barn and put him in his
stall. Marvin looked into Evil's
eyes and smiled. "Your name is I'm
Not Evil, but I think you have a
little bit in you. After all, which
horse doesn't?

10

The next few weeks passed by
slowly. Each hour seemed like an
eternity. But, slowly or not, they

passed. A few days before Evil's
next race he had his first serious
blowout. Ray was aboard for the
eye-opener, a full out four-furlong
work. Marvin watched as Evil ran
without Ray choking him. Evil came
back to the gap dancing. Nick was
busy staring at his watch. Marvin
sneaked a peek. The watch stated a
time so fascinating, it left Marvin
breathless. Ray didn't need to ask
how fast he went. He simply smiled
at Nick and strolled away.

After he was gone Marvin spoke.
"That should keep him on his
toes!"

Nick slowly nodded. "Yeah, it
should."

Rumors went around the barn that
Nick worked Evil too fast. Marvin
didn't think so. He knew that Evil
would soon put the rumors to rest.

On the morning of his race, Marvin
woke up in his dad's truck. He
remembered that Evil was racing at
a different track today. He walked
down the barn aisle to find Evil
sleeping peacefully. Another groom
came walking down the barn aisle
with loud stomping boots that woke
Evil up. He saw Marvin at his stall
door and stood up. Marvin decided
it was time for Evil's breakfast.
He poured a quart of grain into
Evil's bucket. He ate it quickly.
Marvin smiled and went to do his
barn chores, which were basically
scooping stalls. Marvin spent the
rest of the day with Evil, hanging
out in his stall. The loudspeaker
boomed out through the barns.
"Bring your horses to the paddock

for the seventh race. Bring your horses to the paddock for the seventh race."

That was Evil's race. Marvin clipped a lead shank to his bit ring and led him to the paddock. He had been assigned post position 5. Marvin walked him around the ring a few times, then took him to the saddling stall, where Nick saddled him in record time. Marvin continued to walk him around the ring until Ray showed up. Nick gave him a leg up. "You know what to do?"

"Yup."

"Good."

Nick walked to his usual viewing area by the rail, and Marvin, Evil, and Ray circled the ring once again, then headed out to the track. Marvin handed the end of the lead shank to the pony rider and went to join Nick.

It was starting to rain. Nick wasn't sure how Evil would handle the sloppy surface, though Marvin assured him that Evil was a good horse, and that a good horse could run on anything. Marvin looked through his binoculars at the toteboard. It listed Evil as the 3-5 favorite. The horses were beginning to load into the gate. The first four horses loaded, then it was Evil's turn. He stopped and looked at the gate to see what he was getting into, then loaded quietly. The rest of the horses loaded quietly. One split second, and then the gates opened and the race was on! Evil broke alertly and went right to the front. He seemed to be handling the sloppy track okay. Ray rated him on the front. He sneaked a peek under his arm to see how far in front he was. His mouth dropped open. He was ten lengths in front. He drew on a stronger hold, which only made him slow slightly. He watched as the next pole flashed by. There were only two furlongs to go. Evil turned into the stretch under a tight hold from Ray. The black colt coasted along easily toward the finish line, unchallenged by anything. He hit the wire twelve lengths in front of the second place horse, who was laboring on the surface. Ray pulled Evil up in the slop, who threw his head up suddenly, nearly knocking Ray off. Ray walked Evil over to the winner's circle where Nick and Marvin were waiting. Nick seemed pleased. "Good. He ran well, from what I could see. Did he cause any problems for you?"

Ray hopped down from Evil after the picture was taken. "No. This was his best race yet, in my opinion. He didn't run too fast, but he won by a lot. He did throw his head up when I slowed him down, but I think that was because he wanted to run faster, not because mud was in his face. He never got any mud in his face. He went wire to wire. I'm looking forward to riding him again." After a nod, Ray walked off with his saddle to the scales.

Marvin gave Evil a big pat and
began walking him to his stall.
"You did a good job today, Evil.
You are undefeated in three
lifetime starts. I hope you keep
performing like this." Evil bobbed
his head up and down in response.
Marvin sponged Evil off with hot
water, took his bridle off and
replaced it with a halter, put him
in crossties, and began grooming
him. Evil put his head down,
enjoying the brushing. Marvin
picked out Evil's hooves without
him noticing and gave him a pat,
which caused him to bring his head
up. Nick strolled into the barn and
picked up the tack trunk. "It's
time to go home now, Marvin."
   Marvin attached a rope to Evil's
halter and led him outside, where
it was raining hard. He trotted
Evil in hand to the trailer. Marvin
thought Evil should be given a
little more time in the barn to
relax from the racing atmosphere,
but his dad was the boss.
   Nick was standing inside the
trailer with a towel and a blanket
for Evil. He walked up the ramp
quietly and settled. Marvin loosely
tied him to the rail inside and
rubbed him dry with the towel. He
slid the blanket onto Evil's back
and fastened the straps. Marvin
picked up the towel and latched the
trailer door shut. He hopped into
the passenger seat in the truck and
shut the door. Nick started the
truck and drove through the gates.
With Evil dozing in the trailer and
Marvin resting in the passenger

seat, Nick turned onto the freeway
and headed for home.

~~~~~~~~~~~~~~~~~~~~~~~~

Marvin was woken up by Nick in
their driveway. "Marvin, we're
home. I need you to help me unload
the trailer, horse and all."
Marvin opened the door and
stumbled out. He unlatched the
trailer door and led Evil out. He
followed Marvin like a puppy to the
barn. Marvin turned him loose in
his stall that he guessed had been
fixed up by Victor. It was a foot
deep layer of fresh, golden straw.
The water bucket was full of the
best water, and his tub was full of
grain. Evil charged forward at the
first smell of it. He thrust his
nose into the grain first. Marvin
cracked up at the sight of it. He
put Evil's bridle in the tack room
and left the training barn. He
found Victor in the stallion barn,
picking stalls. A big gray stallion
was in some crossties on the other
side of the aisle. Victor came out
of his stall with the wheelbarrow
in tow. Marvin grinned at him.
"Evil loved the bed you made for
him."
Victor smiled at him. "I'll bet he
did. I made sure the water was the
freshest, the grain the healthiest,
and the straw the cleanest."
Marvin's smile grew wider. "I
knew you would. You always try to
get things done right. So, how's
your mom?"

Victor thought of his mom and lost his smile. "She's doing better, I guess. They took her off life support…"

Marvin lost his smile now. "Oops. Sorry I brought it up."

Victor was about to say more when he felt a nose on his back. He turned around to face the gray stallion. "Oh, Sour Side. You're not sour at all." Victor put him back in his stall and left the barn. Marvin was left standing there wondering if Victor was truly okay.

11

The next morning Marvin was grooming Evil when the thought again came to him. He stroked Evil's neck and wondered what was in store for him. *Maybe dad will point him for the Sanford and Hopeful series*, Marvin thought. *Or maybe the Saratoga Special.*

It was now July 1, and Nick had to decide soon. Right now, Nick was down at the track, supervising works, walks, and gallops. Marvin gave Evil a sugar cube and put him back in his stall. He jogged down to the track, where Nick was standing at the wire. There was a chestnut colt breezing easily along the rail. Marvin silently crept up to Nick. His eyes were fixed on the red horse until Marvin spoke. "Hi, Dad," he said.

"Hi, Marvin, what brings you down here?" Nick said with a scratch of the head. He continued to watch the colt out of the corner of his eye.

"Well, now that Evil is undefeated in three lifetime starts, I was wondering what you were going to do with him now." Marvin looked at his dad expectantly.

"I'm thinking Sanford and Hopeful. We are hopeful for him, right?" Nick raised his eyebrows.

"Yes, we are."

A slow smile spread across Nick's face. "I think he will be a great one. I believe the special ones distinguish themselves early."

Marvin nodded. "I hope you're right." And with that, he walked away.

Nick turned his attention back to the chestnut. He was nearing the wire with a furlong left in his breeze. He clicked his stopwatch as the horse passed. The stopwatch read 1:01 2/5 seconds. Nick smiled. *Good, exactly what I wanted.*

Nick told the exercise boy he did a good job as a groom led the horse away. The exercise rider hopped in his car and went home as Nick strolled into the barn. The vet was coming today to get more x-rays on Just Groovy. The last x-rays showed that the bone was close to being completely healed, but it was up to Nick if he was to go back into training. David made it clear that he wanted him to run again if it was possible. Even if he healed in the next week, Nick thought it was too risky to aim for the Breeders' Cup. The only race he would be able to run in would be the Classic, and he was at the very bottom of the point list. There was no chance of him getting in the list of fourteen horses that get to run. Even if he got in, the other horses would eat him alive, which would just be flat out embarrassing.

Nick was lost in these thoughts when the vet pulled into the driveway. The regular vet had an emergency call, so there was an assistant vet here to take the x-rays. He had short, dark brown hair and blue eyes that scrutinized whatever he looked at. Nick greeted him with a firm handshake. "Hi, I'm Nick Calen, the trainer of the horse that you've come to see. You must be Aiden Twine."

"Yes, I am." His blue eyes sparkled. "I'm here to see a Derby horse for x-rays?" he asked with one raised eyebrow.

"Yes. He went lame the morning after the Derby. He had a slight fracture." Nick led the way to Groovy's stall. He was taking a snooze at the back of the stall. When Nick came in, the beautiful chestnut colt picked his head up slowly. Nick slipped a halter on Groovy and led him out of the stall. Aiden set up his equipment by Groovy, who took a few sidesteps. Nick laid a hand on Groovy's neck to calm him down. After five minutes of this, Groovy finally settled down. The x-rays

were taken quickly, and when the
equipment was removed, Groovy
danced around excitedly with a
snort.

Marvin and Victor were coming
around the barn corner when Just
Groovy reared right in front of
their face. Marvin jumped back, but
Victor stayed put. Groovy came back
down to Earth with a flick of his
tail. Victor stepped forward and
laid a hand on Groovy's neck, which
made him lower his head and nicker.
Aiden mouthed "thank you" to
Victor as he viewed the x-rays.
Victor put Groovy back in his stall
and gave him some fresh water.
Aiden printed the x-rays and stood
next to Nick.

"Look at that," he said as he
pointed his finger to a spot on the
x-ray.

Nick looked at the spot and found
the bone to be completely healed.
"Wow," he said.

Aiden couldn't hide the grin on
his face. "That bone has healed
surprisingly fast. You don't see
this too often."

Nick nodded. "Thanks. That's
great. Will he need any more?"

"I don't think so, unless he has
trouble. We're done covering him on
this now," Aiden said.

"Okay. Thanks," Nick said.

Aiden stashed his equipment in his
car and drove away. Marvin thought
he was a nice guy.

~~~~~~~~~~~~~~~~~~

Marvin walked Evil the next
morning. He had looked at Evil's
training schedule before he took
him out, and he was to be trained
by means of two walks, three
breezes and a work in between
gallops. His next race was the
Sanford, and, after that, the
Hopeful. Evil was reckless this
morning, and Marvin guessed he was
feeling his oats. He walked him
around the oak tree in the paddock
nobody used. Evil suddenly threw
his head up as Marvin looked over
to see Victor walking Just Groovy a
few yards away. "Hi, Victor,"
Marvin said.

Victor smiled at him and kept on
walking. Marvin finished up Evil's
walk and took him back to his
stall. Evil sniffed his pockets and
nudged them. Marvin fed him a sugar
cube with a sigh. "You…. "

12

Over the next three weeks Evil
gained even more muscle and became
fit as ever. Just Groovy slowly
began training again, with long
walks through the paddocks. Evil
worked a few days before the race
at Saratoga. He went six furlongs
in 1:11 and two, only because Ray
was hunched over rating him with
his hands near the bit. He had
seven furlong gallops every other
day to stretch his muscles and to

prepare him for longer distances that he would run in the future.

Marvin believed strongly that Evil would win the Sanford and the races soon to follow. He also hoped that Just Groovy would race again. Victor's mood got better, and Marvin didn't ask about his mom. Sonya was excited about Evil's first stakes race, as was Marvin. Nick had decided to enter Happy Boy, the other promising two-year-old, in the Sanford with Evil. Except his first start, Happy Boy had won all of his races. Marvin, Nick, and Ray huddled in Evil's stall at Saratoga the night before the race, discussing strategy, though it was obvious what it would be.

"Evil likes to go to the front, as I know. But is it possible to rate him a little bit more during races so he can save more energy for the following one?" Nick asked.

"I doubt it," answered Ray. "He has this huge stride that eats up the ground like a starving person. I'm rating him as much as I can, but he seems to ignore me most of the time. Except for his first start, I have never carried a whip on him. If he was let out, how fast do you think he could possibly go?"

"Fast enough to break a Beyer speed figure of 130, I bet, even as a two year old. But we'll never know for sure if we don't. I don't care about time and speed ratings. What I care about is if we win. Now

we're going to use the same
strategy we use every time. Don't
let him run fast unless he needs
to. Try not to break or tie any
records, all right?"
  "All right."
  "Good. He's a good horse and I
don't want him to break a leg or
become a dud trying to break speed
records. End of discussion."
  Nick got up and left the stall.
Marvin and Ray were left to attend
to Evil for the night, which
required picking the stall out, and
for Marvin, brushing him off and
picking his feet out. They quickly
finished this and Ray went home.
Marvin turned in for the night, but
he couldn't sleep for the
anticipation of Evil's first stakes
race. He ended up going to bed two
hours late.

~~~~~~~~~~~~~~~~~~

  Marvin's mind was a blur as he
rolled out of bed and got dressed.
He remembered he was in a hotel in
Saratoga Springs, New York. Marvin
had had a dream that Evil had
gotten beat, and it felt real. He
staggered down the stairs for a
quick breakfast. Nick handed him a
paper sack and they headed out the
door. Marvin ate two rolls and an
orange on the way to Saratoga Race
Course, or commonly known as "The
Spa". As they drove through the
gates, Marvin thought if Evil would
recognize Happy Boy. They had only
met once before, in their first

start, in which Evil had easily won. But that was then. This was their first stakes race. Evil was undefeated in three lifetime starts. Happy Boy was two for three. So Evil had won one more race than Happy Boy, big deal. In a stakes race, past performances only have effect on the betting. It's how a horse runs in that race that matters.

When Nick stopped the truck, Marvin hopped out with exuberance. He walked as fast as he could to Evil's stall, trying not to run into anybody. As he neared the stall, Evil poked his head out from over the stall door, greeting Marvin, who gave him a pat and a sugar cube. He had already been fed for the day, so Marvin walked over to the cafeteria for a late breakfast. It was now 10:45. Marvin has finished his second late breakfast and went back into Evil's stall. He started grooming Evil well in advance, hoping he would make a good impression on the stakes crowd. His jet-black coat was glimmering the deepest black possible. Marvin spent the rest of the day in Evil's stall, preparing him for the race.

Shortly before the call to the paddock, Marvin gave Evil a pep talk. "All right, Evil, you're in the national spotlight now. I'm not saying this will be the biggest race of your life, but I want you to show this field who the best is. I know this will be fun for you. " The call to the paddock echoed

through the receiving barn, and
Marvin attached a lead shank to
Evil's bridle and led him down to
the paddock for the $250,000
Sanford Stakes.

~~~~~~~~~~~~~~~~

The paddock was filled with
reporters, owners, trainers,
jockeys, grooms, and fans. Saratoga
was the only racetrack in the
country where you could walk with
the jockeys as they walked over to
their mounts. The only way Marvin
could get through was because of
the monster black horse behind him.
The excitement in the air was
getting to Evil, for he jumped
around behind Marvin as he was led
to the saddling stall with the
number 7 posted on it. Nick and
Sonya were waiting there for him,
as David was at Happy Boy's stall,
saddling him. He had taken a liking
to the bay colt from day one. In a
way he sort of resented Evil,
because he had beaten his horse. He
resented Evil also because he
seemed perfect in every way, having
won all his starts by a margin of
bragging rights. Sonya liked Evil
the best, but she thought Happy Boy
was okay.
Evil was uncharacteristically
acting up in the paddock, but
Marvin thought it was just high
spirits or else he was reacting to
the flash of cameras going off
everywhere. Nick finished saddling
him and Marvin began leading him

around the paddock once again.
David had always entered Evil and
Happy Boy as separate entries.
Happy had drawn post five, giving
him a better field position than
Evil. The call for riders up came,
and Nick gave Ray a leg up. "We
know what to do, right? "

Ray nodded. "Sure do. "

"Good. Have a nice race, Ray. "
Marvin led Evil around the ring
once as the call to the track came.
He handed the lead shank to the
pony rider after walking through
the tunnel and followed Nick to his
box. Happy was throwing his head
up, for the pony rider had made an
attempt to snub his head to his
saddle horn. Evil was walking along
calmly, having escaped most of the
cameras. The field warmed up for
about five minutes then headed for
the gate. The six horses loaded up
quickly, then it was Evil's turn.
He took one quick look at the gate
and walked in without a trouble.
The announcer's voice rang out
through the grandstand. "All the
horses have loaded quietly like a
bunch of professionals, but the
twelfth horse, Watyoutalkinbout, is
giving the starters a bit of
trouble…oh, there he goes. They're
all set for the Sanford…. " The
bell rang, the gates opened, and
twelve two-year-olds leaped onto
the track; the race was on!
Marvin watched as Evil exploded
from the gate and quickly got the
lead. The 3 horse tried to go with
him, but his jockey saw that his
horse wasn't fast enough, so he

rated him five lengths behind
Evil's lead.

Meanwhile, Ray was strangling
Evil to keep his huge stride under
control. Happy's jockey saw his
chance to get close to Evil and
maybe even take the lead. He gave
the signal, and the bay colt leaped
forward. Happy Boy passed the
second place horse and gained on
Evil. If Evil would have been
wearing blinkers, he wouldn't have
seen the bay horse move up to his
flank. But he saw him, and he
caused the reins to slide through
Ray's hands. Ray nearly howled in
pain. The big black horse easily
turned down Happy Boy, who was
already trying his hardest. Evil's
lead went from three quarters of a
length into ten in just a few
strides. Happy's jockey could see
that he had no chance, so he quit
scrubbing on him and let him run at
his own pace.

Ray had regained control of Evil
and made him settle. Unknowingly,
Evil had run the half-mile in :45
flat, an astonishing pace,
especially for a two-year-old. With
less than two furlongs to go, Evil
turned into the stretch being eased
up. As he crossed the wire fifteen
lengths in front, Ray looked at the
toteboard in astonishment. Evil had
run six furlongs in 1:08 and 1, and
still had plenty left in the tank.
He was met by Marvin at the gap,
who gave him a high five and Evil a
hug. Nick had a smile on his face
for once. He stroked Evil's neck
after the winner's circle picture

was taken. "How did he run for you?"

Ray hopped off. "Awesome. I was choking him the whole way, though. When he saw Happy Boy try to come to him at the five-eighths pole, he took off and broke the skin on my hand." He lifted up his hand to show a long rip. "Even with this, I still look forward to riding him again. Thanks, Nick." He walked over to the scales to weigh in, then headed to the jockey's room.

Marvin looked at his dad expectantly. "Are we going to the Hopeful next?"
Nick looked at him with a smile. "Yes. Yes we are."

13

Marvin and Nick were to stay at Saratoga for a month, for the Hopeful was also held there. They didn't want to fly Evil all the way back to Kentucky again and then hassle him some more by flying him back up. David and Sonya decided to take Happy Boy back to Kentucky to train for his next start, which was unknown. They were definitely thinking Breeders' Cup in November, which was in four months. Marvin asked Nick about the Breeders' Cup, but Nick waved him off and said, "Of course I'm thinking about that, but I'm not planning that far in advance. We are concentrating on the Hopeful right now, and training him for that is all I'm going to think about."

Marvin bonded with Evil even more during that month, and Evil would sigh heavily as Marvin walked away. Usually he came back to reassure Evil he would not be gone for long. Ray kept winning on his mounts and sooner than usual became a journeyman jockey. He dominated the racecourse in the afternoons and all the other jockeys hated racing against him. Evil had two works during the short layoff, and he galloped a mile and a sixteenth every other day, which soon became every day. When the time rolled around for Evil to work again, Nick decided he would work six furlongs. Ray was aboard that day. With tight restraint, he went the six furlongs in 1:10 and four. Nick thought it was too fast. Ray thought he was just loping along. Marvin thought it was fun to watch. Word got back from Kentucky that Happy was being pointed for the Champagne Stakes in mid- October, and after that the Breeders' Cup Juvenile. Nick was thinking about the Champagne after the Hopeful. It would be the third race in which Happy and Evil would both be entered. Happy Boy had won two out of four lifetime starts, and Evil was undefeated in four lifetime starts with a Grade 2 win. Evil ran through his gallops quickly, and some people had to check to make sure he was not breezing. Nick knew he was something special by the way he worked and raced. He was dominant,

and Nick had always believed that
the special ones set themselves
apart from day one.

Evil was a very big colt. He was
already 16.3 hands at the age of
two. He had grown three inches
since they had gotten him. Marvin
guessed that he would mature at
17.2 or bigger. Marvin himself was
only 5' 3. Evil looked like and was
like a clone of Man O' War, only
black. Nick thought it was way too
soon to be comparing their colt to
that great horse.

On August 28, a few days before
the Hopeful, Nick and Marvin took a
trip to Belmont to learn what the
grounds of the track were like.
They visited the grave of Ruffian
and checked on some of David and
Sonya's horses stabled there. While
viewing the famous mile and a half
oval, the biggest in America,
Marvin wondered if Evil would run
in the mile and a half Belmont
Stakes, the third jewel in the
Triple Crown, a series of three
very prestigious races for three
year olds. It included the Kentucky
Derby, the Preakness Stakes, and
the Belmont Stakes. Marvin thought
if Evil continued running like
this, he had a shot to win all
three next year.

~~~~~~~~~~~~~~~~~~~~~

On the Wednesday before the
hopeful, Evil had a final work
before the race. It was his first
six furlong eye-opener before any
race. All the professional clockers

at the racetrack were watching him
as he set off at the three quarters
pole. He dashed through an opening
quarter in 22 and 1, then he sped
up even more turning into the
stretch with a half mile in 44
flat. He finished off the six
furlongs in 1: 09 and four, slowing
down just a little, for Ray took
him in hand. It was an amazing
work, though he had done it with
restraint. Racing fans all over the
country already wanted to see how
he would run as a three year old.

That night the entries for the
Hopeful were to be posted and post
positions were to be drawn. Marvin
anxiously waited as they drew
Evil's post. " I'm not Evil will
start from post three."

Marvin breathed a sigh of relief.
There were fourteen horses racing
in the Hopeful and Marvin didn't
want Evil to start on the very
outside. He and Nick headed back to
Saratoga soon after. They had
checked out of their hotel and were
staying in the barn and sleeping on
cots for the remainder of the time
that they were staying in New York.
The decision was final that after
the Hopeful, Evil would be shipped
to Belmont for the Champagne Stakes
in October. Marvin slept in a cot
outside of Evil's stall, while
Nick's was set up in the tack room.
Marvin gave Evil one final pat
before he turned in for the night.
It was September 1, and the Hopeful
was tomorrow. Marvin could barely
sleep. The Hopeful was Evil's first
grade 1 race. Marvin tried counting

sheep in his sleep, but that didn't work. He couldn't remember when he went to sleep that night.

14

Marvin was up bright and early the next morning. He grabbed an early breakfast at the cafeteria then went to feed Evil. He gave him his limited quart of grain and sat in his stall with him as he ate. Nick woke up a few hours after Marvin. "Marvin, why are you up? It's 5:30 and you didn't get enough sleep last night. Even I don't get up this early on race days, except for really big ones. I understand it's his first Grade 1, but why so early?"

Marvin grinned. "Just because," he said.

He spent the rest of the afternoon in Evil's stall, preparing him. He gave him a few sugar cubes an hour before the race. Once again the call came. *Bring your horses to the paddock for the Hopeful Stakes. Once again, bring your horses to the paddock for the Hopeful.*

Marvin and Evil were the first ones to get to the paddock. The rest of the horses came five minutes later. Evil was already saddled and walking around the paddock when the final horse arrived. He was acting calm before the cameras, apparently getting the idea. When the other horses were saddled, the "riders up" call

came. Ray was easily lifted up onto
the black Thoroughbred's back. He
and Nick didn't need to exchange
any words, for Ray had known for a
while what to do. Marvin led Evil
through the tunnel and out onto the
track, where a pony rider took him.
Marvin went to Nick's box again.
The post parade was short, only
about two minutes. Evil got warmed
up easily by cantering most of the
time. The field then approached the
gate and loaded easily without a
fuss. The announcer's voice rang
out through the sound system,
"They're all set for the Hopeful...
and they're off! I'm Not Evil goes
right out to the front as expected
as the rest of the field follows
from five lengths back."
 Out on the track, Ray was hurting.
The leather reins had ripped open
his hands again, and he was
struggling to hold Evil back. His
lead was lengthening to seven,
eight, nine, ten lengths. Ray had
to rate this horse or else Nick
would blow fire at him. He wrapped
the reins around his wrists and
pulled. That didn't hurt, and it
worked. Evil slowed down, and his
lead was shortened to five lengths.
Another horse started to come to
him, so he let out a notch in the
reins. Evil leaped at the
opportunity and lengthened his lead
to eight. Ray knew he had found his
best style of racing-getting horses
to the front and nursing them home
in the same position. As they
turned into the stretch, Evil was
ten in front. He had plenty of gas

left, but the field was tiring behind him. He hit the wire thirteen lengths in front. Ray raised his fist in the air and yelled, "Yes!"

He met Marvin and Nick at the gap and they had their winner's circle picture taken. Evil was now a Grade 1 winner, and it felt great. Nick didn't ask Ray any questions but said, "Nice race." Ray hopped down, nodded, and walked off. Marvin took Evil's reins and led him back to the barn. "You did a great job today, Evil. How does it feel to be a Grade 1 stakes winner?"

Evil ignored him. Marvin knew Evil probably had no idea what he was talking about and didn't notice any difference, just that he had crossed the wire first. He cooled Evil off by walking him around and then put him in his stall. He put a light blanket on him, for it was supposed to be cold that night. Marvin heard from Nick that they were leaving the next morning for Belmont, where the Champagne Stakes was held. Nick came back to the barn a few hours later after having a chat with some other trainers.

Marvin knew he wouldn't be able to remember all of Evil's races, so a made a note on a piece of paper:

SEPTEMBER 2
I'M NOT EVIL
UNDEFEATED IN FIVE LIFETIME STARTS
WINNER OF GRADE 2 SANFORD STAKES
AND GRADE 1 HOPEFUL STAKES

15

Marvin thought the truck ride to
Belmont was long and boring.
Halfway there, Nick stopped in an
empty parking lot so Marvin could
walk Evil around to stretch his
legs.
He put a chain on Evil's halter and
began to walk him in circles. A few
kids saw him and came running and
screaming, "Horsey! Horsey!"
Evil saw them coming, for he
rolled his eyes and danced around.
Marvin tightened his grip on the
lead shank and moved him away. He
yelled, "Don't get close!" Marvin
was lucky Nick came running out;
otherwise he would've been dead
meat. Just as the kids started to
run up, Nick held his hands out.
"Hey, guys, don't get too close.
This isn't a calm horse you'd find
at the fair. Go on back to your
moms and dads."
Somehow that set in. He deflected
the kids and they went home. Marvin
thanked him with a nod and led Evil
back into the trailer. In half an
hour they were at Belmont. Marvin
settled Evil in barn 5, stall
number 6. This would remain Evil's
home until after the Champagne.
Marvin gave Evil a fresh bucket of
water and hay. Nick stopped by
thirty minutes later to see how he
was settling in. He saw Marvin
lying in the straw, reading a book,
and Evil was laying a few inches
away. Nick decided to leave them

alone and return to the track cafeteria.

A few hours later Nick got a call from David. "Have you heard about Just Groovy?"

"No, what?" Nick was confused.

"One of your assistant trainers had him breeze six furlongs this morning. He went in 1:12 and two."

Nick literally dropped the phone. "Are you serious?"

"Very serious. He was ready. By my estimates, he could be racing soon."

"And, by your estimates… wait, what are your estimates?"

"That he continues to train well and…"

"WHAT? You've been training him the whole time I've been gone?"

"Oops. Well, he was getting too much energy built up, so we decided to put him to work."

"Did he look good?"

"He looked great! We actually had to hold him back." David was enthusiastic.

"Good. When I get back, I want to watch him run."

"Okay. Bye, Nick." David hung up.

Nick thought that if David meant what he said, Groovy could race next year. He would have a whole new shot at the Breeders' Cup next year.

~~~~~~~~~~~~~~~~~~~~

The next few mornings Evil galloped a mile. Marvin rode him

most of the time. He was good for
Marvin, though he went a tad faster
than Nick wanted him to every time.
He had a work scheduled in a few
days. It was a six furlong work
with two other horses. Marvin knew
Evil would go too fast, especially
with the other horses. He was glad
Ray would ride him. Marvin got up
early that morning to watch. Evil
did not like galloping with the
other horses to the quarter pole.
When Ray let him loose, he got away
from those horses like they were
big evil things wanting to eat him.
Ray had to take a hold of him
quick, for he had opened up a ten-
length lead in just three strides.
He galloped easily to the wire,
being pulled up. Nick stopped the
timer and gave it to Marvin to look
at. It read 1:11 and four. That was
a considerably slow time for Evil.
Ray pulled him up quickly and
brought him back. "How'd I do?"

"You did good, but that was a
slow time for him. How did he
feel?"

"He felt great! I pulled him up a
furlong before though so that he
wouldn't get too far ahead. I know
I was blazing. What was the first
quarter timed in?"

Nick searched his brain, trying to
remember. "Twenty-one and one, I
think."

"Whoa. I was right to pull him
up," Ray said with a scratch of
the head. He hopped off and handed
the reins to Marvin. With a quick
wave, he walked away.

Marvin led Evil back to the barn to cool him off. He seemed to have plenty of energy left, though he was blowing. That worried Marvin. Evil was not even blowing after he had run six furlongs in 1:09 and four! He didn't seem to be favoring any legs, so Marvin cleaned him up and put him in his stall with some fresh hay. He attacked his food, which was good. "Even if he breaks a leg, he's always hungry," Marvin said to himself with a chuckle.

16

In the weeks leading up to the Champagne, Evil's works stayed around that same margin that they had been that day. He went seven furlongs in 1:24 flat, which pleased Nick. Though his works were like that of an average horse, Marvin noticed that Evil was not himself. He wasn't as enthusiastic about his food, and after normal works he was winded. Evil never showed any signs of being injured, until the day of the race. It was October 14 when Marvin led him to the paddock under cloudy skies. He was unusually skittish, which had everyone going off the deep end, betting on other horses more. Evil went off as the 5-2 second choice. The Belmont crowd thought this would be the day that Happy Boy exacted revenge and Evil would get the first defeat of his career. Happy Boy was coming to the race off of a brilliant work, and he was

in top form. His dark bay coat
glistened, and he was on his best
behavior. Evil, on the other hand,
was lathered with sweat and acting
up. Nick saddled him quickly and
Ray leaped aboard. Evil had drawn
the number one post, and Happy the
number three. Nick always entered
Evil and Happy as separate entries,
even in their first start. The call
to the track came, and Marvin
handed Evil off. "Careful, he's a
little excited today," Marvin
warned the pony rider. He nodded
his thanks and took Evil. Marvin
went to the stands to join Nick.
 Ray could tell something had
changed. Evil was dull, and Ray
knew that if Evil didn't perk up,
he might lose. The post parade
ended and the horses made their way
toward the gate. Evil was first to
load. The starters led him in by
the bridle and shut the gate behind
him. The rest of the horses loaded,
and they were all set. Ray knew now
that there was no turning back.

~~~~~~~~~~~~~~~~~~

 Marvin crossed his fingers as the
gates opened and the race began.
Evil went right out to the lead,
which was good. He carried a three-
length lead through the opening
quarter.
 Ray knew something was wrong. He
didn't have a very strong hold on
him at all, and Evil was
struggling. Happy Boy, who was in
second, was rated three and- a-half

lengths behind. Happy's jockey could see that Evil was trying hard, and that he might have a chance to catch him. He waited another quarter to catch him. The first half mile had gone in 48 flat. At the three-eighths pole, Happy began to advance. He cut Evil's lead to two lengths, then one, then half a length. Ray saw Happy coming and began to urge Evil for the first time in the young horse's career. He responded, opening his lead to two lengths again. Happy's jockey put him in a drive as they came to the eighth pole. Happy was cutting into Evil's lead again, this time reducing it to a quarter of a length. Ray was scrubbing on Evil, but only a tiny response came. He opened his lead to half of a length as he crossed the wire.

Back in the stands, Marvin knew Evil had given a lot. Yes, he had won the race, but at what cost?

17

Marvin and Nick met Evil at the gap. He was blowing harder than ever, and he was favoring his left hind leg. The winner's circle picture was quick, and then Ray hopped off. He gave Nick the details of the race and made his way to the scales soon after. Nick took Evil's reins and led him to the vet barn to be examined. They took a few x-rays, and soon after confirmed that Evil had a hairline

fracture in his left hind ankle.
They told Nick that it didn't have
to end his career, but it would
prevent him from racing any more as
a two year old. He was being aimed
at the Breeders' Cup Juvenile, but
now he would have to pass. Happy
Boy, on the other hand, would be
trained up to it. He had come off
the Champagne in excellent
condition, and Nick had high hopes
for him. He was already the
favorite for the Juvenile. Evil's
career had a shadow cast over it.
David and Sonya had heard the news,
and they were troubled.

The next day Marvin and Nick flew
Evil back to Kentucky. He was to
stay there until the end of
November, and then be flown down to
Florida to start his three year old
training. During Evil's recovery,
Nick and Marvin supervised the
training of Happy Boy for the
Juvenile. He was coming to the race
in top form, and it was obvious
just by looking at him. It was
October 15, just a little under a
month till the Breeders' Cup. Nick
was entering three horses in all-
one in the Juvenile, and two in the
Juvenile Fillies. He had never had
a Classic horse. Even with that,
the main goal was still the
Kentucky Derby. The Triple Crown
was the second goal, and the
Classic third. Nick had never won
any of those races. They were
always the ones that got away; the
best he had was a second in the
Preakness this year. His horse was
running down the 2-1 favorite at

the top of the stretch. The eventual winner was leading by a neck at the eighth pole. He was running out of gas, but the small colt dug in and turned down Nick's horse. He went on to win by two lengths.

A few days after returning from New York, Just Groovy had a work scheduled. He was to go a slow six furlongs, preferably in 1:13 or 1:14. Just Groovy's jockey, Eddie, was aboard. Just Groovy set out at the quarter pole. Marvin, armed with his own stopwatch, caught him going the first quarter in 24 and four and the half in 48 flat. With a quarter to go, Eddie rated and pulled Just Groovy back. He flashed by the wire in 1:12 and two. Marvin heard Nick sigh and say to himself, "Well, he feels better."

Groovy had run well that day. Marvin, quite the master at eavesdropping, overheard Nick say to Victor that if Groovy continued like this, he would begin his four-year-old season early next year.

Evil was building up dangerous energy fast. He was restless and acting up every time he was led from his stall. Marvin asked Nick about this one day, and he said that Evil needed to run. Marvin now couldn't wait till the day when Evil was cleared and they took him down to Florida to begin his three year old training and Triple Crown preparation.

The Breeders' Cup tension was
building. With just a half month to
go, Happy Boy was at his best.
Nick's fillies were looking good,
too. Marvin hung out in Hahaha's
stall a few days before the World
Championships.

"You're a very good filly. I
think you have a chance of winning,
don't ya think?"

Hahaha bobbed her head up and down
in agreement.

"Yeah, I thought so," Marvin
said.

All of a sudden it was the day,
and Marvin was bouncing off the
walls with excitement. The past
three days were filled with
anticipation, but now it was
finally here. Marvin began jumping
on Nick's hotel bed yelling, "The
day is here! The day is here!"

Nick threw a pillow at him. "Go
back to bed, Marvin. It's three in
the morning and you need a lot of
rest."

"You know I won't be able to
sleep with this excitement!"
Marvin said, a little too loud.
Nick sat up and crawled into some
jeans. "I give up. Let's go to the
track."

The Breeders' Cup World
Thoroughbred Championships was held
at Aqueduct that year. It was very
close to Belmont, where it would be
held two years from now. Evil would
be four that year. Nick stopped the
truck near the barn, and Marvin was
out before it was stopped
completely. He hit the ground

running and was in the barn before Nick had a chance to speak. He went to Happy's stall first. The colt was dozing when he came up. Marvin sat a folding chair outside the stall and watched him for a while.

Nick came into the barn a while later, obviously having had his morning coffee. They stayed in the barn, giving their Breeders' Cup horses their pre-race preparation. A few hours later the call came out to bring the horses to the paddock for the Juvenile. The Juvenile Fillies was unusually a few races later. Marvin had gotten the honor of leading Happy Boy to the paddock for the race. Victor, who had stayed in a different hotel, was leading Hahaha down to the paddock for the Juvenile Fillies. The other filly had to be scratched because of a high temperature.

Marvin proudly led Happy to the paddock for his saddling. He was prancing, a sign that he felt good. As he was led through the tunnel, many whistles came up from the crowd. He met Nick at the number 11 saddling stall. Victor adjusted the shadow roll while Marvin held him and Nick put the saddle on. A few reporters came up. "What do you expect from Happy Boy today?" he inquired.

"I think he's going to run the race of the year," Nick responded confidently.

The reporter jogged off to another stall as Happy's saddle and bridle were both secure.

The jockeys came out to the paddock. Happy's regular jockey, Caleb, came walking up. Nick gave him the characteristic nod and sent him off. They knew what to do. The bugler began calling the horses to the track. It was time to see what Happy was made of.

After five minutes of warming up, the Juvenile horses headed for the gate. Stranglethebugler was first to load. He was with no question the fastest horse in the race. Munchkin was next. All thirteen horses went in quietly. The next second, the gates leaped open and they were off in the Juvenile!

The twelve horse spooked at the break and slammed into Happy. Caleb heard him grunt but he didn't go down. The other horse's jockey righted him and continued forward. Happy responded with an unreal burst of speed and jumped into fifth. He had passed horses like they were standing still. Caleb began rating as they came into third. This is where they would usually sit for the first part of the race. As they went through the first half-mile, Stranglethebugler began to tire. He had sustained a five-length lead that was quickly evaporating. He was now going the wrong way as the field gained on him. Now Munchkin was leading and Happy was second. Caleb began to urge Happy as they moved into the far turn.

Up in the stands it was pandemonium. The announcer was almost screaming. "As they move

into the far turn, it's Munchkin!
But here's the presence of Happy
Boy! And now they're turning for
home!"

As they hit the top of the stretch
Munchkin was leading by a half
length, but that lead was
evaporating like a pond in the
Sahara Desert.

The announcer continued shouting.
"With a furlong to go, Munchkin
has the lead by a quarter of a
length, but Happy Boy is closing
like a freight train on the
outside!"

Caleb flashed the whip in front of
Happy's eye, and he took flight. He
swallowed up Munchkin and took the
lead. It grew to one length, two,
three, and then four as he flashed
under the wire.

The stands went bananas. Nick
leaped out of his seat and punched
the air as he celebrated his very
first BC win. He, Marvin, and
Victor all headed down to the
winner's circle to celebrate the
win. And later, they'd be down
there again with Hahaha.

If only they knew it would be the
last time Hahaha would win.

19

The end of November was nearing.
Two days before Evil was scheduled
to be shipped down to Florida,
Aiden came over for a final x-ray.
To be safe, Victor and Marvin put
two halters on Evil and attached a

lead rope to the side of each
halter. When Aiden saw what they
were doing, he gave a chuckle.
"He's that jumpy?"

Marvin and Victor nodded. Aiden
set up his stuff and struck up a
conversation with Nick. It didn't
take very long, for the x-ray
machine was pretty fast. Marvin put
Evil back in his stall as the x-
rays were printed. After about five
minutes, they were ready; Aiden put
them under the light to examine
them. A large grin spread across
his face. He handed them to Nick.
"Well, what do you think?"

Nick studied it closely. "It
looks as if there were no fracture
at all," he said.

Aiden smiled. "Exactly. His
fracture wasn't that bad; just a
crack. I'll give him the all clear.
See you around." He took his
equipment, loaded it in his truck,
and drove away.

Nick looked at Marvin. "Well,
now he's ready for stardom."

~~~~~~~~~~~~~~~~~~~~

Exactly two days later Marvin and
Nick were heading down the freeway
with the huge trailer attached to
the back. Evil was not the only one
they were taking down to Florida.
Five horses, Evil included, were
being taken to the sunshine state.
There was Evil, Just Groovy, Happy
Boy, a filly entering her three-
year-old season, and Hahaha. Every
one hundred miles they would stop

in an empty parking lot and walk the horses. After almost eighteen hours of traveling, they made it to Gulfstream, where the horses would stay for the winter.

A few extra grooms had gone with them. One by one they unloaded the horses. Evil was settled into stall 1 and Groovy into stall 2. Happy was further on down the row.

All the horses were given a few days of rest to settle down from the trip. On December 5, Evil was walked for the first time after his injury. A few days later, on December 10, he galloped a mile easily. Nick was beaming. Evil had shown his old former self. Nick went ahead and scheduled a breeze for him on the seventeenth. He was to go a mile in about 1:37. He sure screwed that up. The colt decided he wanted to go fast, so he went in 1:34 and two. Nick was furious. He went about the stables the rest of they day taking out his anger on the poor grooms, saying that it was more like a work than a breeze.

Nick's anger disappeared when Evil began to prosper. He became racing fit again and was ready to race as a three year old. On Christmas, Marvin gave Evil a bunch of sugar cubes, a good grooming, and a new blanket with his name printed on it. Just seven days later, on January 1, Evil officially became a three-year-old. It was the start of a new year, and the start of fame.

~~~~~~~~~~~~~~~~~~~

The Eclipse Awards had come out early, and Happy Boy was named champion two-year-old. Many people didn't think he deserved that title. It had only been given to him simply because he won the Juvenile. Most handicappers thought Evil deserved the title. Hahaha was champion two-year-old filly, and that title was rightfully given.

Nick decided that Evil's next start would be an allowance race, sometime in February. Just Groovy was starting in a $47,000 allowance race the next week. He was coming into the race in his pre-Derby form. It was now January 4, and Evil's race was in exactly a month. Nick had said to him for his Triple Crown prep he would stay in Florida. The main goal while in Florida would be the Florida Derby at the beginning of April; the race that Groovy won before him. Soon after that he would go to Churchill Downs for the Derby. But for right now, he was aiming for this allowance race with a $57,000 purse. Marvin thought Evil was way too good for the competition in that race.

One day when Marvin was grooming Evil, Victor came walking down the barn aisle. "Do you think Groovy can win his race in a week?" he asked.

"Absolutely. He's a great horse, you know. He won the Florida Derby and came in third in Kentucky," Marvin said.

"Yes, but that was last year, in
his three year old season. He's
four now. He's in a whole new year
of racing now. Some horses shine in
one season and then are duds in the
next. I'm hoping he wins. I think
he can. But I'm not going to lay
any bet on him, even though he's
not facing very much competition."
Victor stated.

Marvin nodded and finished
grooming Evil. "Very well. I know
he will finish in the top three,
even if he doesn't win."

"Well, we'll find out in a
week," Victor said.

20

That week seemed to take forever.
Every hour seemed a century, and
every day seemed an eternity.
Finally race day came. Victor spent
the whole morning grooming Groovy,
getting him ready for his four-
year-old debut. Marvin spent time
with Evil.

Groovy's race was race five, the
seven furlong, $52,000 allowance
race. He would be getting his old
jockey, Eddie, on him today. Marvin
came in to check on Victor and
Groovy thirty minutes before the
call to the paddock came. Groovy's
chestnut coat shone like the sun,
and his bridle was polished. His
blue blinkers were in just the
right place. Victor looked like he
had done a lot of work.

"You got thirty minutes, " Marvin said.

"I know, " he replied. Marvin stayed with them and made short conversation until the call came.

Marvin stood up. "Ready, Groovy? " Groovy ignored him. He started to hold his head up a little higher, as if he knew what was coming.

There were not very many people at the paddock this morning, which was good. Groovy didn't like crowds. Victor took him to the 2 stall, and Marvin tagged along.

Nick quickly put the saddle on and fastened the girth. Just then, all the jockeys came out. Eddie came strolling over swinging his whip. He was glad Nick didn't say anything about it-he just gave him a leg up and nodded. Nick was not the kind of trainer that discussed strategy at the last minute.

The bugler's call came and Victor led Groovy out to the track. Nick and Marvin headed over to their favorite spot as the post parade began. Nick was armed with a pair of binoculars today, and he spent most of the time looking at Groovy through them.

"He looks really good, " he said to Marvin.

"Do you think he can win? " Marvin asked.

Nick sighed. "I think he can win, but I don't know what he'll do. He's an odd horse in the way he races and works. Some days he wants to go fast, and some days he wants to go slow. You never know. " He

continued looking through his
binoculars as the horses neared the
gate.

The first horse was giving the
starter trouble. Eddie was glad
Groovy was patient today, because
usually he would jump around and be
obnoxious. They blindfolded the
horse and finally got him in the
gate. Groovy went in without a
hitch. The rest of the horses
loaded quickly but quietly. Eddie
crouched down, preparing for the
break.

Groovy leaped at the start. Eddie
held on to his mane as the horse
sorted himself out. It was all he
could do to keep from falling off.
Groovy had only done this once
before-at the Florida Derby. When
Eddie saw that he was in last, he
waved the whip in front of Groovy's
right eye and he took off. The
jockeys who were riding closing
horses were surprised to see a red
blur flying past them. Groovy kept
moving up. He ran like this till
Eddie rated him in second; only
then did he slow. After a half
mile, the lead horse began to tire.
He began to drop back slightly.
This was all the encouragement
Eddie needed. He hit Groovy right
handed, and the colt's head came up
as he flew past. They turned into
the stretch with two furlongs to
go.

Victor grew a smile as he watched
Groovy fly down the stretch
lengthening his lead to four. As he
hit the wire in front by five, he

knew that the pre-Derby Groovy was
back.
Victor was thinking of all the
major handicap races that Groovy
could run in this year, including
the Pimlico Special, the Santa
Anita Handicap, the Whitney
Handicap, Jockey Club Gold Cup, and
the Breeders' Cup Classic at the
end of the year.
 Later that evening Marvin, Nick,
and Victor got together in the tack
room to lay out a plan for all the
horses in their barn. They were
discussing Groovy first. Marvin
brought pop and sandwiches. Nick
started the talk.
 "I was thinking the Big Cap
next," he said. "His sire won the
big one in his four-year-old
season, and I think that he can
too."
 "I agree," Victor stepped in.
"He's a great horse, and he showed
it today."
 "He sure did," Marvin agreed.
 "I've laid out a plan for him,"
Nick said. He spread out a piece of
paper on the floor. "It goes like
this- "

SANTA ANITA HANDICAP
PIMLICO SPECIAL
WHITNEY HANDICAP
JOCKEY CLUB GOLD CUP
BREEDERS' CUP CLASSIC

 "Of course, he has to do well in
these races if he goes to the
Classic," Nick commented. "I
think the June-July layoff could do

him some good. He runs pretty well off layoffs. "

Marvin took a sip of pop. "I don't know. It seems like a pretty brutal schedule to me. He just won an allowance race, facing not so good competition…"

Victor cut in. "It's perfect. He's a great horse, and I think he can handle it. "

"I'm glad you agree, Victor. " Nick said. "We probably all know where Evil's going, don't we? "

Marvin grinned. "Yep. First he'll go in this allowance race. If he does well, we'll go to the Florida Derby, and after that the Triple Crown. We're not thinking summer yet, right? "

Nick nodded. "Right. But I'm thinking and devising a schedule similar to Groovy's. As for Hahaha, I'm thinking the Filly Triple Crown, which consists of the Acorn, Mother Goose, and Coaching Club American Oaks, or CCA. Before that she might run in the Kentucky Oaks. "

Marvin started to feel tired. This was going to be a long night.

21

It was January 13. It had been two days since Groovy had won his first race back, and Evil's race was approaching. The next day he had a work scheduled. He was to go six furlongs easily. Marvin spent a long time grooming Evil the morning

before. Nick told him to walk Evil
around the shedrow a few times, and
Marvin always wanted Evil to look
good. He finished running a
polishing rag across Evil's coat
and gave him a pat. Marvin clipped
a lead shank onto Evil's halter and
led him out into the January
sunshine. It was an unusually warm
day with highs in the mid-sixties,
and Marvin didn't think Evil needed
a blanket. Groovy, like Evil, was
to walk today, only he would go
around once. Evil's jet-black coat
sparkled in the light, catching the
eyes of a few elder men walking by.
Marvin heard them mumble that he
was a good-looking horse as Evil
was led away. He had red and blue
bandages around his legs for
protection. Nick had insisted that
they be blue and red because they
were David and Sonya's colors. As
Marvin led Evil back to the barn,
he saw Groovy coming out for his
walk. He looked super-fit and his
glimmering red coat could have
doubled as another sun. He, also,
had red and blue bandages on. As
they passed each other, Marvin
noticed that Evil was a lot taller
than Groovy, who was only sixteen
hands. Evil had grown even more
over the winter. He was now about
seventeen and a half hands high.
Marvin didn't think he could get
any taller. Nick preferred to call
him "the monster " now because of
his height. Some of the grooms
compared him to War Admiral by his
color, but not his size. "The
Admiral " was much like Evil,

winning his races with authority
and grace. They looked the same
too, both being black, but not both
eighteen hands high. War Admiral
was a lot smaller.

Marvin returned Evil to his stall
and fed him some hay. He took off
the halter and wraps. Marvin
collapsed down in the straw and
sighed. He wanted to watch Evil
race. He loved watching it, but it
also made him nervous. In horse
racing, a horse could break down at
any time. Jockeys could get hurt.
It was a dangerous sport. But it
was a good one. Horse racing is the
only sport where a five-foot man
can stand ten feet tall.

Marvin was lost in thought when
there was a voice at the stall
door. "Bored?"

Marvin spun around to see Ray
standing there with his lop-sided
grin. "I saw you lead him in, so I
thought I'd stop by for a quick
chat. How's the monster?" Ray said
with a chuckle.

"You got that name from my dad,
didn't you?" Marvin replied with a
snort.

The lop-sided grin got bigger. "I
sure did. I stopped by the
cafeteria this morning and saw him.
'Everyone's peachy keen,' he tells
me. His next race is in three
weeks, right?"

"Right," Marvin said.

"Good. I love riding him." Ray
paused for a minute. "Marvin, I've
wanted to tell you for the longest
time what I thought of this horse.
I know he's special. Triple Crown

special. Breeders' Cup special. You
can tell when you ride and watch
him. He's undefeated at three years
of age in six lifetime starts. It
could have been seven if he
would've skipped that injury. I
strongly think that he could win
the Triple Crown. He's unlike
anything I have ever seen." Ray
paused again. "I hope you think
about these words in these months
leading up to the Kentucky Derby."
Ray walked away without anything
more.

~~~~~~~~~~~~~~~~~

 Marvin was very anxious. Tomorrow
was Evil's first three year old
race and the beginning of his
Triple Crown prep. He was bouncing
off the walls at the barn and many
trainers and grooms were getting
annoyed. He talked to himself all
day long. Nick tried to duct-tape
his mouth shut, but that didn't
work-it just made the sound more
annoying. Nick took him to the
beach to get his mind off it.
Marvin sat in his chair and
continued reading the Racing Form.
Evil was the morning line favorite
at even money. Nick took him back
to Gulfstream. He took away his
Form and left for lunch at the
cafeteria. Nick figured out that if
he didn't have any materials to
calculate the odds, he would stop
talking. That worked. The trainers
and grooms were glad that the groom
of the horse in the allowance race

tomorrow had finally been shut up.
Marvin used his brain now to think.
Evil's last work had gone in 1:11
flat. Marvin thought he could have
gone much faster if Ray hadn't been
strangling him with two sets of
reins and a new bit. Later that
night, in their cots in the tack
room, Marvin and Nick discussed the
race, but not for very long. All
the hype of the day had gotten to
Marvin, and he fell asleep faster
than ever.

22

Race day dawned clear and cool.
Marvin was up at what Nick
estimated to be three in the
morning. Marvin gave Evil his
limited quart of grain, and Evil
knew it was time. He polished the
quart off and looked out his stall
door out to the track. The track
had been leveled out already, and
it looked like it was ready to run
on. Evil shivered with
anticipation. Marvin spent the
whole morning grooming him and
making him look good. He even put
hoof oil on his hooves to make them
look good. He was blacker than ever
by noon. Marvin spent the rest of
the hours leading up to post time
cleaning his bridle and putting in
his old snaffle bit. The bridle
shone like new when it was put on.
Evil's race was number four, so
Marvin watched the horses from the
first race come back to the barn.

He went back into Evil's stall and
readjusted everything, making sure
it was correctly positioned. About
five minutes before the call to the
paddock, Victor stopped by to wish
him good luck. Marvin gratefully
accepted this. Just an instant
later the call came. "Horsemen,
bring your horses to the paddock
for the fourth race. Bring your
horses to the paddock for the
fourth race."

Marvin proudly led Evil down to
the paddock. He caught the eye of
many, including the older men of a
few weeks ago. Nick was waiting for
him at the number five stall. He
strapped the saddle on in record
time and Marvin began to lead Evil
around the paddock. Then the
jockeys came out. Ray was the only
jockey who displayed the blue and
red-checkered silks of David and
Sonya. Nick had almost entered
Happy in this race, but he decided
against it. Nick gave Ray a leg up
and nodded. They never needed to
discuss strategy, as Evil had his
own take on it. Marvin led him
through the tunnel and onto the
track. He handed Evil over to the
pony rider, who marveled at his
size. Marvin joined Nick at their
usual spot some time later.

Out on the track, Evil was hyper.
He was jumping around like a monkey
and trying to rear. Ray gritted his
teeth. "Sorry," he said to the
pony rider.

"No trouble," he said. "I've
dealt with worse."

After five minutes of warming up, the horses approached the gate. Evil was handed off to an assistant starter. He was unusually good as the first four horses were loaded. Then it was his turn. He paused for a minute and looked at it carefully. "You've done this before. You're okay, " Ray said. He walked in quietly and prepared himself for the break. Ray grabbed a fistful of mane, for he expected the break to be very fast. The rest of the horses loaded. The silence was overwhelming as the last horse walked in. The starter pushed the button, the gates flew open and they were off!

Evil exploded at the start. He immediately flew out to the lead and opened it up to ten lengths. Ray couldn't rate him-his pulling on the reins just made the demon horse go faster. He pulled with all his might, even though he knew it wouldn't work. Ray remembered that this race was a mile and that Evil might burn out. He began talking to him to try to slow him down. That only gave him wings on his feet. He had unknowingly blazed through five furlongs in :56 flat, a freak time. Evil turned into the stretch alone, in front by twenty-five.

And he showed no signs of stopping.

He rushed through the last furlong in 11 seconds flat. The official margin of victory, not to be found out for a week, would end up being twenty-nine lengths. The official time for the mile was 1:33 and one.

The rest of the field finished
almost six seconds later.
   Ray had trouble pulling Evil up.
He had to reach down and physically
grab the bit to slow him to a stop.
Evil pranced back to the winner's
circle with only a slight sweat
broken; he knew how well he had
done. He met Marvin at the gap.
Marvin's face was as white as white
could be-a pinched white. Ray had a
concerned look on his face. "How
fast did I go?" he asked.
   Marvin told him.
   Ray nearly fell off.

23

   Marvin led Evil back to the barn.
He was still prancing and he had
known he had done a good job. The
drug test had come back negative.
Evil had already installed himself
as the favorite for the Florida
Derby, which would be his next
race. Marvin was told to put a gag
bit in Evil's bridle to slow down
his supernatural speed. He was
undefeated in seven lifetime
starts, and they planned to make
that eight.
   All the attention was now focused
on Groovy. It was February 3 and
the Santa Anita Cap was just over a
month away. He went seven furlongs
in 1:24 and two on February 7, and
a mile in 1:36 flat, a faster work,
on the twentieth. On February 28
they flew him out to Santa Anita.
Happy Boy went with him, as he was

aiming for the Santa Anita Derby.
Nick himself didn't fly out there,
as he wanted to supervise the
training of Evil, the star of his
barn. Marvin and Nick planned to
watch the Santa Anita Handicap and
Santa Anita Derby on TV. Evil
prepped for the mile and-an-eighth
Florida Derby at Gulfstream on
April 8. Victor had gone out to
California with Nick's assistant
trainer to continue being Groovy's
groom. Groovy himself wasn't the
favorite for the Big Cap. A five-
year-old horse named
Putalil'danceinit who had won the
Breeders' Cup Classic the year
before was the even money favorite.
Nick didn't think he could win
because the horse had never won one
of his many races on the West
Coast. Nevertheless he had the
Horse of the Year title, and that
would keep him the favorite until
race time.
 Groovy was coming to the race in
top form. His coat was like the
sun, and he was perfectly healthy.
Victor thought back to when he was
in his small cast after the Derby.
But he was a four-year-old now. He
was the second youngest horse in
the Big Cap. Four of the other
horses were born just a few months
before him, and one after him of
that same year. Putalil'danceinit
was the oldest horse in the field,
being five. Just a few days before
the Santa Anita Handicap Nick had a
long talk with the assistant
trainer on the phone, talking about
strategy. Groovy was a front-

runner, like Putalil'danceinit. The
final strategy was to run with him
and hope he wore out. Victor was a
basket case the night before.

The morning of the race Victor was
up bright and early. By noon he had
Groovy's coat shining a brilliant
red. His blinkers were clean, and
his bridle was polished to look
brand new. The much-anticipated
call to the paddock came, and
Victor led Groovy out. He was
marveled at, much for his good
looks and breeding. He was hardly
remembered for winning the Florida
Derby the year before. The
assistant trainer saddled him, and
then Victor began to lead him
around the paddock. Eddie came
strolling over, swinging his whip
and whistling. He was given a leg
up. "You know what to do," the
assistant trainer told him.

Victor led Groovy out onto the
track and handed him over to the
pony rider. He went to join Mike by
the rail.

Back in Florida, Nick and Marvin
were watching the post parade
carefully. Groovy was behaving very
well, and that was good. He seemed
to love the sunny weather. As they
headed toward the gate, Groovy's
ears perked up. He knew what was
coming. Marvin was worried about
Putalil'danceinit, whose bay coat
was glimmering in the sun. He was
also behaving perfectly. Groovy had
drawn the third post, and
Putalil'danceinit the sixth. All
the horses loaded calmly except for
Putalil'danceinit. He shied and

reared and crowhopped. This was the reason he had been such a surprise winner of the Breeders' Cup Classic. They blindfolded him and made him go in. They were all set for the Santa Anita Handicap.

24

Groovy broke cleanly and alertly, and Eddie sent him out to the front. He looked behind and saw no one for a split second, then saw the rest of the field two lengths back. Putalil'danceinit had pulled up at the break with what appeared to be a slight injury, and now the race was wide open. Groovy continued running determinedly and brought his lead to five. They continued on like this until the stretch. Last year's Derby winner began to close. Groovy's lead was shortened to three lengths and continued shrinking. Eddie saw him coming and put Groovy in a drive. As the Derby winner drew within a half length, Groovy made it clear that it would not happen again. He attacked the job with a vengeance, and quickly turned him down, opening his lead again to four, then five, then six. He hit the wire seven lengths in front.

Victor jumped for joy in the air. He rushed down to the winner's circle to greet Groovy and a triumphant Eddie.

At Gulfstream, Nick was on his feet and yelling, as was Marvin. As Groovy was led into the winner's circle, Eddie pointed up to the sky with both hands. Everyone knew what he meant. The winner's circle picture was taken, and the coverage ended. Nick called Mike on his cell phone to review the performance. "It was simply brilliant! Sad news about the favorite, though," Nick yelled into the phone.

Marvin left the cafeteria and went to the barn to see Evil. The gorgeous horse was half-asleep. Marvin laid his head on the top of the stall door and watched Evil sleep. It was a beautiful sight to watch. Marvin smiled and went to clean tack.

~~~~~~~~~~~~~~~~~~~~

A few days later Evil was scheduled to work. Nick wanted to send him a mile, just to see how he went. Ray was aboard for the work. He warmed Evil up and set off. He sat chilly on him, not asking anything. Evil thought it was his chance to run fast. He lurched forward into a full run. Ray drew a strong hold on him, and with the gag bit installed in his bridle, he slowed down drastically. Ray noticed his ears were flat on his head. He threw his head up every few strides to show Ray what he thought. As they passed the wire with Evil in-hand, Ray didn't know what Nick would think. He brought

Evil back to the gap. He was
blowing, an unusual sign.
 Marvin had a weird look on his
face. "What went wrong?"
 Ray put on his "I have no idea
what you're talking about" look.
 Marvin grimaced. "Apparently
something. Dad timed him in 1:36
flat. He never goes that slowly.
And he's blowing."
 Ray shrugged. "I don't think he
approves of this bit. He tried to
run away with me, and when I pulled
him back, he kept throwing his head
up. He's probably winded from
fighting me," Ray said with his
questionable look.
 "I guess so. Dad says it was a
good work. He's got one more
heading up to the Florida Derby.
It's for seven furlongs. We'll
gallop him a mile and an eighth a
few days before that. I'll talk to
dad about the bit," Marvin said
with a nod.
 Ray hopped off and Marvin led Evil
away. He was foaming at the mouth,
a sign that he had been pulling. He
took him to his stall and unsaddled
him. Evil let out a big sigh,
letting himself expand after being
confined by the girth. Marvin
unbridled him and slipped on a
halter. He put Evil in crossties to
groom him. The colt relaxed when he
felt the brush over his back. Next
to eating, running, and sleeping,
grooming was Evil's favorite thing.
When Marvin finished, he put Evil
back in his stall. He took out
Evil's bridle to see just how
severe the bit was. It had a tall

port sticking out of the top of it. Worse, an Australian cheeker had been put on the bridle to keep it raised in his mouth. Evil was having this thing stuck in his mouth, and when they pulled back on him, this thing sticking out the top would be pushed into the roof of his mouth! Talk about painful. He took the bridle to the kitchen to show it to Nick. Nick wasn't at all surprised.

"It slows him down, " Nick said.

"Yeah, by means of pain, " Marvin argued.

" Keep the bit and cheeker on there. It slows down the speed that will eventually hurt him, " Nick said casually. He waved Marvin off like an annoying fly.

Marvin couldn't believe it.

25

Nick's advice didn't help. Evil's last work before the Florida Derby went in 1:24 and one. This was visually by far the slowest work Marvin had seen from Evil. The morning before the Florida Derby Groovy came back from the Golden State. The Santa Anita Handicap winner looked awesome off his win. His next goal was the Pimlico Special in late May.

On Florida Derby eve the excitement and nervousness started to kick in. Marvin was worried that the bit would effect Evil's performance. He fell asleep that night with a shaking heart.

On the day of the Florida Derby Marvin woke up late. He looked at his watch and realizing it was almost nine in the morning. His eyes widened and he jumped out of his cot. It was the day of the 1 million dollar Florida Derby, and he had woken up late. He hurried to get Evil his quart of oats. He was very impatient when it came to food. Evil stuck his head out his stall door as if to say, "What took YOU so long? I've been waiting forever!" Marvin poured his oats into his bowl. Within five minutes they were gone. Evil knew it was race day. Marvin got a few brushes and rags and set to work grooming him. By noon he was sparkling clean. Marvin waited in his stall the next few hours in anticipation. The call finally came. "Horsemen, bring your horses to the paddock for the Florida Derby. Bring your horses to the paddock for the Florida Derby."

Marvin led Evil out of his stall and to the paddock. When Nick saddled him, he informed Marvin that with the change of equipment, the bettors were backing off. Evil was the lukewarm favorite at only 5-2. The second choice was a bay named WhatIdidwrong. Ray came out of the jockeys' room and materialized at Nick's side. Nick gave him a leg up and a nod. The bugler began to play, calling the horses to the track. Marvin gulped. He handed Evil off to the pony

rider reluctantly and went to join
Nick.

Evil was warming up nicely. He was
prancing and arching his neck as he
trotted. They had an unusually
short warm-up that day, only about
three minutes. Evil had the 1 post
today, so he was first to load. He
went in easily, as did the other
horses. They were all set for the
Florida Derby. Ray leaned forward
and grabbed some mane just as the
gates opened. Evil broke super fast
and opened his lead to ten. Ray
cautiously drew a hold on him. He
threw his head up and lost about
four lengths. Ray kept a hold on
him as they passed the half mile
pole. WhatIdidwrong began to make a
move. The wiry bay colt moved up
into third as Evil's lead remained
at four lengths. As they turned for
home WhatIdidwrong's jockey gave
him the all-clear signal, and they
began to move up. Evil's lead was
reduced to three, two, and finally
to a length as they passed the
eighth pole. Ray peeked under his
arm and saw him coming. He took off
his hold on Evil and he only
responded a little as they passed
the sixteenth pole. WhatIdidwrong
shortened Evil's lead to half a
length as they hit the wire. Evil
had just won the Florida Derby and
had established himself as the
favorite for the Kentucky Derby.
Ray pulled him up easily after the
wire because of the gag and
cheeker. Marvin met them at the
gap, said nothing, and led him into
the winner's circle. After the

pictures were taken and the trophy received, Ray discussed the race with Nick, not mentioning the bit. Marvin had told him what Nick had said before, so Ray didn't speak a word about it. Marvin led Evil back to the barn and took off the bridle. He shook his head at it and began grooming Evil. The incredible black colt was headed to Kentucky with a cloud of questions hanging over him.

~~~~~~~~~~~~~~~~~~~

The next week was the Santa Anita Derby. Happy Boy had established himself as the favorite at 2-1. The week after the Santa Anita Derby Happy Boy would be shipped to Churchill Downs for the Kentucky Derby. Evil would be shipped during that week, maybe a day or so before Happy. Marvin had blamed the close call in the Florida Derby directly on the equipment. Evil galloped a mile and a quarter the next week, stretching his muscles for the longer distance of the Derby. Marvin and Nick stayed in Florida on Santa Anita Derby day. They watched on television as Happy Boy took the lead at the top of the stretch. They cheered him on and were the loudest people in the area. They were soon silenced as the tiny chestnut colt Ewinar passed him at the eighth pole and drew off to win by two lengths. They were disappointed, yes, but

Happy had still put in a great
effort.

He would be shipped to Churchill
the following Friday, Mike told
him. Nick planned to ship Evil this
coming Wednesday. Evil was getting
sick of Gulfstream and wanted to go
somewhere else. Nick was also
shipping Hahaha up to Churchill for
the Kentucky Oaks for three year
old fillies. Groovy was staying at
Gulfstream until after the Derby.
He would then be shipped up to
Pimlico for the Pimlico Special. On
April 19, Evil was loaded into a
trailer with Hahaha and taken to
Churchill Downs.

Marvin always loved Churchill
Downs. The Twin Spires were always
welcoming. They also reminded him
of great stakes races. Nick parked
the truck in the stable yard and
Marvin unloaded Evil and led him
around. "Well, Evil, this is where
you'll run one of the biggest races
in your life. Get used to this
place."

Nick took Hahaha out of the
trailer and took her to stall 2.
The horse in stall 1 was always the
most promising horse in their barn.
Marvin settled Evil into stall 1
and moved his tack into the tack
room. He had secretly brought
Evil's snaffle bit along. He
planned to put it in his bridle for
the Derby. Marvin went to the
cafeteria for a snack. He already
started to feel Kentucky Derby
excitement.

26

That Friday Happy Boy arrived.
He hadn't lost any of his form from
his loss. The colt that beat him,
Ewinar, had come to Churchill that
day, too. He was in a different
barn, but Marvin saw him work five
furlongs one day, and it was
amazing. They timed him in :58
flat. Marvin had only seen Evil go
faster. It was now April 25, just
10 days until the Derby. The first
wave of reporters was just starting
to come around. Nick hated
reporters. They bugged him to
death. Once when he had a horse in
the Preakness, they didn't let his
horse get any sleep, for they took
pictures of him all night. Nick
blamed his loss on them. He hired a
guard to keep watch over Evil,
Hahaha, and Happy Boy's stalls for
the week leading up to the Derby.
Hahaha was ready for the Oaks, and
every other filly in the barn knew
it. She was arguably one of the
best fillies in the country, even
though she hadn't raced at three
yet.
 Nick had never won the Derby; much
less have a horse in it. He hoped
that he could please David and
Sonya. Marvin called Victor during
Derby week and invited him up.
Victor accepted. He made a bet with
him that he could find more stupid-
looking hats than Marvin. Marvin
readily accepted this challenge.
 Marvin was hyper during Derby
week. He analyzed Evil's gallops

and works, hoping to find a
stronghold in them. Nick told him
to calm down, which didn't work. He
had never seen Marvin this hyper.
Marvin spent every waking minute
out at the barn or studying videos
of other contenders' races. On May
2, the post positions for the Derby
and Oaks were released. Marvin let
out a huge sigh. Evil had drawn
post 6, which was good considering
there was a nineteen-horse field.
Hahaha wasn't as fortunate. She
drew post 14 in the fourteen-horse
field of the Oaks. Happy Boy drew
post 11 in the Derby, and Ewinar
post 8. On May 4, the day before
the Derby, Marvin and Nick watched
sadly as Hahaha pulled up in the
final furlong of the Oaks. They
took her to the vet barn and found
out that she had fractured her left
cannon bone. After a few hours of
sorrow, they decided to retire her
to David and Sonya's farm. She
would have a happy broodmare career
there.
 Marvin got absolutely zero hours
of sleep on Derby eve. He decided
to stop trying to sleep, so he got
up and read his Racing Form. It
showed Evil's latest work in there-
a mile and an eighth in 1:47 and
four. Marvin thought that showed
Evil was willing to run, even with
the gag and cheeker.
 It was 2:30 AM. Marvin went to
Evil's stall and sat down in front
of the door. He was shivering with
excitement. It wasn't every day you
had a horse running in the Derby!
He decided to switch the gag bit

with the snaffle bit now. He
tiptoed to the tack room and
grabbed Evil's bridle. He had been
hiding the snaffle bit in his
duffel bag. He grabbed the snaffle
out of the hidden pocket and
tiptoed back to Evil's stall. This
time he went in. Marvin undid the
Australian cheeker and took it off
the bridle. He next took off the
gag bit. He put the snaffle in its
place and secured all straps. Then
the worst happened.

Nick woke up.

He came over to Evil's stall.
Marvin hid the bridle under the
straw and picked up his Form.
Nick's half asleep body came
waddling up to the door. Marvin
glanced at his watch quickly.

It was 2:45.

Nick snorted. "Why are you up?"

Marvin grinned oddly. "I couldn't
sleep," he said. He bet Nick could
see the guilt on his face.

Nick yawned. "Whatever," he
mumbled as he stumbled back to his
cot. Marvin waited till his watch
read 3:00 AM, then he quickly put
the bridle back. He stored the gag
and cheeker in his bag. He went
back to Evil's stall and read his
Racing Form till the rest of the
grooms got up. He fed Evil his
limited rations and read till 7:00.
He walked outside. Marvin
remembered last year when it was
pouring down rain on Derby day. The
field had taken off under pouring
rain and that had killed Groovy's
chances. He sported the biggest
smile at the barn when he saw that

the sun was coming up over a
crystal clear sky. Marvin was
starting to feel that he needed
sleep. He slapped himself in the
face and got his grooming box out.
At 9:30 he was still grooming. Nick
popped his head in the door.
"You're going to rub the hair off
that horse if you groom it any
more," he said with a chuckle.
    "He likes it," Marvin answered.
    "If you say so," Nick replied.
"Come to the track kitchen and
have some breakfast. You'll need
it."
    Marvin reluctantly put away his
box. "All right." He gave Evil a
pat. "Be good," he warned the
colt.
    He followed Nick to the kitchen.
It was packed with grooms,
trainers, owners, and a few jockeys
having their morning coffee. On the
TV, it was showing a handicapping
show. They were showing a tape of
the Florida Derby. Along the bottom
it said "I'm Not Evil-Winner of
the Florida Derby." The show went
to break by saying, "We'll be back
on this special edition
handicapping show of the 2 million
dollar Kentucky Derby."
    Just mentioning the purse made
Marvin's heart do a back flip. He
had a few pastries and returned to
the barn. Marvin put hoof oil on
Evil's hooves for the occasion.
This would be the only time he ran
in this grand race, and Marvin
wanted him to look good. At noon,
Marvin heard a voice. "Hey,
Marvin!"

He turned around to see Victor
standing there. Marvin laughed out
loud at his enthusiasm. Victor was
wearing a blue shirt that read
"I'm Not Evil: winner of the
Kentucky Derby" in red letters. He
had blue and red stripes under his
eyes to support the colors of David
and Sonya. The red colors matched
his red hair. Victor grinned.
"What do you think?"
Marvin laughed again. "Hilarious.
It matches your hair."
"I noticed," he said.
Marvin became serious again.
"Victor, would you do the honor of
leading Evil down to the paddock
with me?"
Victor gasped. "I'd be honored!"
Marvin smiled. "Good. Do you want
to clean his tack with me?"
Victor nodded. "Sure."
They spent an hour cleaning tack.
Soon, Victor noticed the change in
Evil's bridle after a few minutes.
"Hey, I thought he had a cheeker
and a gag bit..."
Marvin clamped his hand over his
friend's mouth, getting some blue
paint on his hand. "Shh! I did
that this morning. He wasn't
running well with that, so I
switched it. He could have won the
Florida Derby by ten or more if he
had run without the gag and
cheeker. I assume you saw the
equipment on the tape?"
Victor nodded again.
"I thought so. Don't tell anyone
I told you that, okay?" Marvin
asked.
"Okay," Victor said.

They finished up the tack just as
David and Sonya stopped by. Sonya
had a huge hat that looked like a
fruit basket on her head. Marvin
and Victor looked at each other and
both thought "Hat number 1!"
David greeted them with a smile.
"How's he doing?"
"Great! He is coming to the race
in top form. We think he'll win!"
Marvin answered jubilantly. He
glanced over to see Victor about to
burst out laughing at Sonya's hat.
Marvin barely managed to shut him
up with a smack.
"Good. He's an awesome horse. I
like your enthusiasm, Victor. See
you later," Sonya said.
Marvin and Victor smiled and waved.
Marvin turned to Victor. "I'm
going to make a bet with you that
everyone who talks to us will
comment on you."
"Bet you five bucks," Victor
said with a devilish smile.
"Deal," Marvin agreed and shook
hands with Victor.
They spent the rest of the
afternoon putting the finishing
touches on things. Marvin and
Victor waited anxiously in Evil's
stall. Marvin spoke to Evil. "Run
hard today. Run for my dad. He
deserves to win this one." The
loudspeaker crackled into the
stalls of the receiving barn.
"Horsemen, bring your horses to
the paddock at last for the Derby.
Bring your horses to the paddock
for the Derby."
Marvin and Victor clipped two lead
shanks to Evil's bit rings. Marvin

stood on the left side, and Victor
stood on the right. "Let's go,"
Marvin said in a shaky but excited
voice. As they led him through the
tunnel, the spectators whistled and
cheered. Evil began prancing, which
brought more whistles. He knew he
was being watched. Victor's outfit
brought many chuckles and giggles.
He and Marvin led Evil to the
number six saddling stall. Nick
didn't mention Victor's outfit. He
carefully placed the number six
saddlecloth with I'M NOT EVIL
printed on it. Just then Happy Boy
came through the tunnel. He, like
Evil, was also prancing. The tiny
Ewinar came next. Nick called him
" the second Seabiscuit " because
of his size. He was barely fifteen
hands. His pink blanket matched the
owners' silks and his number eight
saddlecloth. It also looked good
with his chestnut coat. Nick
carefully placed the saddle on top
of the saddlecloth and fastened the
girth tightly. He also fitted a
surcingle on the saddle, just to be
safe. Once he had a saddle slip
during a race, and he didn't want
it to happen now.
 Victor unclipped his lead shank on
Evil's right side, and Marvin began
leading him around the paddock. The
jockeys came out and stood by their
respected trainers' sides, awaiting
instruction. Marvin led Evil back
to the stall and halted him. Nick
gave Ray a leg up. "You know what
to do, Ray. Just do as you always
do. He's in your hands now. "

Ray thought, *That's just what I needed to hear…*.

The familiar bugler's call came. The pony riders took the horses and the post parade began. The traditional playing of "My Old Kentucky Home" began shortly after. This was the Kentucky Derby, the most famous race in the world, the most exciting two minutes in all of sports. Marvin went up to the stands with Victor and sat in David and Sonya's owners' box with, of course, David and Sonya. Nick was also there. He had told Victor and Marvin they could see the race better from up there. The post parade went on for ten minutes. Then all nineteen horses approached the gate. I Had a Dream was the first horse to load. Besides Evil, he was the major speed in this race. The next few horses went in. Then it was Evil's turn. He went in without a fuss. Ewinar went after the next horse. The next ten horses loaded. There was only one left. Evil pawed at the ground, eager to be off. As the last horse went in for the Kentucky Derby, a bead of sweat dripped down the side of Ray's face. *It's all in my hands now…*.

27

The next thing Ray heard and felt was the shrill sound of the gate and Evil leaping forward. He forgot all about the pressure now. It was

just he and the horse. The crowd
was a faint buzz in the background.
He encouraged Evil by shouting,
"Let's go, Evil!" and Evil flew
out to the front. Ray wanted to
conserve his energy for the last
quarter mile, so he drew a hold on
him. He kept him out in front by
three as the cavalry charge passed
the grandstand for the first time.
As they rounded the clubhouse turn,
the pressure came back on. Happy
Boy and Ewinar were running head-
to-head for second. Caleb yelled at
Ewinar's jockey, Jacob, "I got
second, man!"

Jacob yelled back, "No way, dude!
You gotta fight me for it!"

Caleb yelled back loudly, "Bring
it on!"

In the grandstand Marvin, Victor,
Nick, David, and Sonya all sat
there nervously. When Victor saw
Evil go out to the front, he
yelled, "He's going to do it!"

Out on the track, Ray's arms were
getting tired from holding Evil
back. Evil took advantage of that,
grabbing the bit and lengthening
his lead to ten, then fifteen
lengths. The wind was screaming a
challenge at Evil, and he was
answering it. He opened his lead up
to *twenty lengths*.

That same distance back, Happy Boy
was tiring. Ewinar was not. The
little horse had much staying
power. Happy didn't.

Marvin couldn't believe what he
was seeing. This had to be one of
the most brilliant performances in
the whole history of the Kentucky

Derby. Marvin leaned back and yelled to Nick, "He's going to win big, dad!"

Nick grimaced. "He's going too fast!"

Evil continued to widen his lead- to twenty-nine lengths.

He wasn't done yet.

Ray didn't know exactly how fast he was going. He figured the field couldn't stand the mile and a quarter, so he let Evil sail along with a medium hold on him. He opened his lead to thirty lengths, then thirty-one, thirty-two, and then to thirty-five as he turned for home. Ray looked under his shoulder and his mouth nearly dropped to the fast-passing track. He saw the teletimer blinking now. It was at 1:34. There was a quarter of a mile left, and Ray saw the possibility to break the track record and the race record. He saw the finish ahead. He swatted Evil left-handed and he gave him even more. Happy Boy faded back to last as Evil opened his lead to forty lengths and continued opening up. He reached the eighth pole and flew down to the wire.

Up in the stands, nobody was screaming. They were all clapping as Evil passed the eighth pole. The track announcer was amazed. " We have seen a sublime performance, ladies and gentlemen! This horse is simply not real! He can't be! This…this performance has to be the greatest the world has ever seen! He has a chance to break the track record of 1:59 and 2/5 seconds!"

Ray hand-rode him through the final sixteenth. The teletimer was blinking fast- 1:56, 1:57, then stopped in time at 1:58 seconds as Evil crossed the wire forty-nine lengths in front. The rest of the horses finished almost ten seconds later. Evil was the only horse that ran fast. The other horses had run one of the slowest Derbies ever, in a time of 2:07 and three. The distance had worn them out. Ewinar had gotten second, and I Had a Dream third. Ray punched the air as he pulled Evil up. He hooted and hollered for joy as Evil slowed to a trot, then a walk. A reporter came galloping up on her pony and the cameraman on his horse followed closely. The reporter held a microphone up to Ray. "You just broke the track record by over a full second. Do you have anything to say? "

Ray grinned his famous lop-sided grin. "Nothing but thank you God and WOO-HOO! " He raised his fist in the air when he said woo-hoo. Ray jogged Evil past the stands and traditionally doffed his helmet. He didn't stop after the first three times. The ecstatic jockey trotted Evil back to the gap and met Marvin, Victor, Nick, David and Sonya there. They led him over the turf course and into the winner's circle of roses in the center of the track, the one only used for the Kentucky Derby. Marvin and Nick laid the blanket of roses on Evil's withers. Marvin hugged Evil and said, "You are the best and most

deserving horse to ever win this
race! Your name will go down in
history." Evil's official winner's
circle picture was taken moments
later.

Ray lifted his helmet off his
head, exposing his short blond hair
and letting his head experience
some moving air. He put his helmet
back on and pointed at the sky.
David received the gold trophy and
had his picture taken with Nick,
Sonya, and once he had dismounted,
Ray joined the picture. Marvin took
Evil from them and led him to the
testing barn. When he came out
clean, he took him back to the
barn. He sprayed the little sweat
off of him and dried him off. Evil
shook the remaining water out of
his mane and let out a loud whinny.
Marvin smiled at his Derby winner's
spirit and took him back to his
stall. He put a blue and red-
checkered blanket on him and
released him in his stall with a
lot of fresh hay and water. Evil
attacked the hay first. Marvin set
to work cleaning his bridle. He
would likely be flown out to
Pimlico for the Preakness in two
weeks. Evil had never flown before,
and Marvin wondered what he would
think of it. Nick came to the barn
thirty minutes later. "Marvin, I
want to tell you something," he
said.

Marvin stood up. "What?"

Nick gave away no secrets by his
expression. "I noticed you changed
the bit on Evil's bridle."

Marvin's heart fell. "Sorry." He expected an explosion from Nick next. But it never came.

Nick gave a sympathetic smile. "It's okay. I don't think he would have won by near as much if we would've kept the gag and cheeker on. I wasn't thinking when I told you to keep it on. It caused him pain, I know. The truth is, I didn't want people making a big deal out of him before the Derby. So I put that on him to make him appear less amazing. But I guess it was pointless, huh? After all, he won the Derby by forty-nine, maybe even more when the margin becomes official. That's something unbelievable. I just wanted to tell you that. Oh, by the way, I'm pulling Happy out of the Triple Crown. He hated this distance on the dirt. I'm thinking about starting him on turf soon. He's got a little turf in his pedigree. We're flying out to Pimlico tomorrow, so I would go ahead and pack all their tack up. One more thing, we're attending a party tonight with David and Sonya. I think Victor's coming, too. So clean up in the bathroom and change. We don't want you smelling like a horse at the party."

Marvin gulped and thought out loud, "Yippee. This is going to be real fun, meeting a whole bunch of people."

Marvin hated parties.

28

Marvin grudgingly cleaned his face.
Nick knew he didn't want to go, but
he made it clear that Marvin was
going anyway.
 Marvin sat low in the back seat as
they pulled up to the estate. He
was back at the farm were he first
met Evil. They had a lot of parties
here. There were streamers
everywhere, congratulating Evil.
*Evil would rather be congratulated
with ten treats,* Marvin thought.
 The party was dreadful. Marvin
shook hands with about a million
people whose names he couldn't
remember. The only good thing was
that he got to sleep in his own
bed. He hadn't slept there in
forever. He actually got a good
night's sleep for once.

~~~~~~~~~~~~~~~~~~~~~

The next morning Nick woke Marvin
up early. Their flight left at
10:00 AM, so they had to get to the
track, get Evil, take him to the
airport, get him through all the
official stuff, and then load him
on the plane. Mike, who had come
back from Gulfstream, had already
flown Groovy to Pimlico the day
before. He had taken Happy Boy back
to David and Sonya's farm to
recuperate from the Derby. He would
rest there for the remainder of the
spring, and then be trained on the
turf. He would make his comeback in
the fall.

They loaded up all of Evil's tack
in the tack trunk. Marvin set the
trunk in the back seat. Nick
hitched up the trailer to the truck
as Marvin put traveling bandages on
Evil's legs. Evil still had his
blanket on, and Marvin left it on.
He walked Evil out to the trailer
and loaded him up. He closed the
back of the trailer and latched it.
He hopped in the front seat and
Nick drove off.

As they approached the airport,
Evil started to get restless in the
trailer. He stomped his foot. They
parked the truck. It seemed like
forever when they finally approved
Evil's flight. Marvin circled him
outside the plane while they built
a small stall for him. When it was
done he led Evil inside. They
nailed another board on the stall,
just leaving enough room for Marvin
to sit inside. The last thing he
heard was the plane taking off.

~~~~~~~~~~~~~~~~~~~~~~~~

Marvin awoke with a jerk as the
plane landed in Maryland. Evil's
head came up and he whinnied. The
plane taxied to a halt. The cargo
door was opened and the stall
broken down. Marvin led Evil down
the ramp and out onto Maryland
ground. He was fully awake now that
the jerk had woken him up. Marvin
circled him a few times as their
stuff was collected. Nick gathered
it all up and stashed it in a
rental truck. They had rented a
trailer, too. Marvin loaded Evil up

and hopped in the front seat. Nick put the truck in gear, and they drove off to Pimlico.

It wasn't very far. Nick parked the truck in the stable yard and Marvin came flying out. He unlatched the trailer door and got Evil out. Nick assigned Evil stall 1, as always. Groovy was down the row in stall 3. There was an empty stall between them. Nick gave Marvin this stall to put his cot in. Victor was in stall 4 with his cot. Marvin spent the rest of the day helping Evil settle in. He seemed to think Pimlico was okay, though his favorite track was Belmont. Groovy loved Pimlico. He had a gallop scheduled the next day to prepare for the Pimlico Special.

Nick was scared of the Preakness. So many horses had won the Derby, lost the Preakness, and then won the Belmont, being cheated the elusive Triple Crown. Barbaro, the Kentucky Derby winner of 2006, broke down in the first quarter mile of the Preakness. He was saved from certain death by being pulled up. Pimlico was also rumored to have tighter turns than most tracks, but Nick believed it untrue. The Preakness was the trick race in the Triple Crown series for many horses.

The reporters were back. Nick could find no way to get rid of them. They swarmed him like bees and honey. Nick hired two guards this time-one for Evil, and one for Groovy. That only shooed them away for a little bit. They found ways

to catch the guards on break and
snap a lot of photos. Nick was
furious. He put signs on the doors
that said, "Please don't disturb
the horse with camera flashes or
clicking shutters. Thank you" and
hired more guards. That worked. It
was like spraying fly killer on a
cabinet. They all went away.

A new horse came to Pimlico for
the Preakness. His name was Simply
Sinful, and he was fast. Marvin was
worried about him. He had drawn off
to win the Withers Stakes by
fifteen under restraint. He was a
big dark bay colt who, when looked
in the eye, would go unbelievably
fast, setting off fractions of :21
flat for a quarter mile. Marvin
believed Evil was faster, but he
wouldn't know till race day.
Meanwhile, Groovy was ready for the
Special, having gone a mile in 1:35
and two.

On May 16, the post positions were
drawn. Evil once again drew post
six. To his dismay, Simply Sinful
drew post two. Groovy drew post
three for the Pimlico Special on
May 20.

Marvin woke up on the morning of
the Preakness with a huge lump in
his throat.

Its name was nervousness.

29

Marvin groomed Evil at noon. He
had watched a Preakness
handicapping show that morning. It

made him all the more nervous
having to watch Simply Sinful's
Withers. He had one roll for
breakfast and that was all. Victor
had added onto his Derby shirt. It
said now, "I'm Not Evil: Winner of
the Kentucky Derby and Preakness
Stakes." Marvin had asked Victor
to lead Evil down to the paddock
with him. Victor agreed. Neither of
them had made five bucks at Derby
time. Nick didn't comment on
Victor, and they forgot about the
hat deal. Marvin made a new bet. He
bet Victor a dollar that Evil would
win by ten lengths exactly. Marvin
wasn't nervous anymore. He
displayed extreme confidence in his
horse now. Marvin talked to Evil
again before the Preakness. "Okay,
Evil. You're racing a horse today
that thinks he's the greatest. Show
him. You get out there and show him
you're the best. The call came.
"Horsemen, bring your horses to
the turf course for the Preakness.
Bring your horses to the turf
course for the Preakness."

Marvin and Victor led Evil
through the tunnel and into the
indoor paddock. Traditionally, the
horses were saddled on the Pimlico
turf course, but the trainers were
given the option of saddling them
in Pimlico's indoor paddock. Nick
didn't know how Evil would react to
the screaming infield. The
Preakness was more like the
Freakness because of all the crazy
people. Simply Sinful followed
Marvin and Evil to the indoor
paddock. His trainer had decided to

take him there, too. Marvin noticed
that Simply Sinful had to be only
an inch shorter than Evil. When he
was in the saddling stall, Nick
saddled him and put the surcingle
on. Marvin began leading him around
the paddock to slightly warm him
up. Simply Sinful was acting up by
rearing and dancing around, but
Evil was following Marvin like a
puppy. Once Marvin had led Evil
back out to the turf course, the
jockeys were out and ready to
mount. The riders up call came and
Ray was boosted aboard. Nick nodded
and sent him off. The bugler began
playing, and the horses were handed
off to the pony riders as the
traditional playing of "Maryland,
My Maryland" began. Nick, Victor,
and Marvin went to join David and
Sonya in their box.

 Ray was a nervous wreck. There was
even more pressure on them now that
Evil had won the Derby. As the post
parade ended, Ray let out a nervous
gulp. The pony rider showed his
sympathetic smile. The horses
reached the gate. Despite his
earlier acting up, Simply Sinful
went in calmly. The next three
horses went in quietly. Then it was
Evil's turn. He went in like a
gentleman, as always. The rest of
the ten horses went in. They were
all set for the Preakness. In an
instant Ray heard a snapping sound,
but the gates didn't come open. He
leaned forward and saw Simply
Sinful cantering down the track. He
had broken out of the gate before
the actual start. His jockey turned

him around and brought him back.
They loaded him up once again. Now
they were ready.

~~~~~~~~~~~~~~~~~~~~~~~~~

 Evil flew from the gate like
lightning. He moved in front of the
field by five. Ray thought it was
unusual when he heard an additional
set of hoof beats. He peeked over
his arm and saw Simply Sinful
running beside him. His jockey gave
Ray a little "hello there" smile
and returned to riding. Ray let out
a few notches in the reins and Evil
took off. He ran away from Simply
Sinful like he was standing still.
The colt ate up the extra rein that
Ray gave him. He turned into the
backstretch in front by five. Ray
took a hold on him. He heard hoof
beats again and looked behind. He
saw Simply Sinful again coming to
Evil. This time he was giving it
all he had. Ray yelled back at the
other jockey, "Oh no, you don't!"
and gave Evil another two inches.
He again turned down Simply Sinful
and took the lead by five. As they
left the backstretch, Simply Sinful
tried for the final time. His
jockey was laying on the whip, but
it was no use. Ray hollered at
Evil, "Let's go!" With that Evil
took flight. He opened his lead to
seven as he passed the eighth pole,
and to ten as he hit the wire. He
was nowhere close to the record,
but he had beaten an exceptionally
good horse by ten lengths.

Marvin laughed out loud as he realized he just won the bet. Evil had won by exactly ten. They all rushed down to the winner's circle for their pictures and the blanket of fake Black-Eyed Susans was laid over Evil's withers. Nick got himself an interview that was finished with the words,

"Now it's up to him to earn himself a place in immortality."

30

The next day was the Pimlico Special. It was unusually a few days late this year. Groovy was going to the post as the 2-1 favorite, and the second choice was a bay named Hellothere. Victor led Groovy down to the paddock.

"You've got tough competition today, Groovy. But you'll show them. You are the class of the field. Just get out there and show them."

Nick and Marvin were waiting for him at the three stall. Nick tightened the girth and strapped on a surcingle. It was becoming one of his favorite pieces of equipment. Victor took him and began leading him around the paddock. Hellothere was saddled and ready. The jockeys came out and strolled to their trainers' sides. Nick gave Eddie a leg up. "We're going to close," he said.

Eddie nodded and saluted Nick with his whip with a dorky smile. Nick

snorted at this. Victor handed
Groovy over to the pony rider and
followed Marvin to the owners'
boxes.

Eddie knew Groovy was the class of
the race. His chestnut coat
sparkled in the sun as the horses
made their way towards the gate.

Victor was starting to feel a bit
of nervousness. Marvin assured him.
"He'll win, Victor. Eddie knows
what to do."

It was Groovy's turn to load into
the gate. He once again looked at
the gate to see what he was getting
into. Eddie gave him a nudge with
his heels. Groovy walked in
quietly. The rest of the horses
moved into line. They were all set
for the Pimlico Special.

Groovy came out of the gate in a
bound, going right out to the
front. Eddie brought a strangling
hold on him as the front-runners
moved out. They went into the
clubhouse turn with the crowd a
faint hum in the distance. Everyone
was on his own now. Eddie sat
chilly on Groovy, enjoying the
ride. As they moved past the half
mile pole later in the race, Eddie
gave Groovy the signal to move up.
He responded, passing the third-
place horse. When they moved into
second, Eddie noticed that
Hellothere was running with him. He
asked Groovy for more, and he shot
past the leader and pounded the
turn for home.

Victor had gotten into a habit of
popping his knuckles when he was

anxious. Marvin stopped him and made him concentrate on the race.

Groovy was in full flight when Hellothere came to him at the eighth pole. Eddie waved the whip in front of Groovy's right eye, but he didn't respond. Hellothere stuck a neck in front at the sixteenth pole. His jockey waved his whip in front of his right eye, and suddenly he veered inward. Eddie hauled back on the reins to avoid clipping heels. Hellothere passed the wire a length in front, but the inquiry sign immediately flashed up on the board. Eddie posted his own objection, and Hellothere was disqualified. Groovy was the official winner after five minutes of debating. Eddie hopped back on and the winner's circle picture was taken. Victor led Groovy away to the testing barn. He would now have all summer to rest up for his next big race, the Whitney Handicap. Nick decided he might go in a small allowance race that he could easily win at the end of July. He would be shipped back to David and Sonya's farm for now.

Evil was scheduled to be shipped to Belmont for the third and final leg of the Triple Crown, the Belmont Stakes. Marvin spent the afternoon before they were leaving talking to Evil. "Evil, you are the best horse in the country right now. I know you can win your next race and prove to everyone out there that you are a horse of a different kind."

The next day Nick parked the
trailer in front of their assigned
barn. Marvin led Evil out into the
May sunshine. Nick had the trailer
already hitched up. Evil had on a
blue and red-checkered blanket, red
and blue leg wraps, and a poll
bumper. He led him into the trailer
and tied him up. He hopped out the
back and said, "Next stop, Belmont
Park!"

Marvin and Nick had a long
conversation on the way there. Nick
started it. "I hope it doesn't
happen…"

Marvin's head whipped around.
"What?"

Nick sighed. "I said I hope he
doesn't break down like Charismatic
in 1999. He broke down in the final
furlong of the Belmont. He had won
the Derby and the Preakness, like
Evil."

Marvin got mad. "Don't say
that."

Nick apologized. "Sorry. I didn't
mean to. It's just that it happens,
you know."

Marvin's anger cooled. "That's
okay. I just hate when people talk
about horses getting hurt. So, do
you think he can win?"

Nick scratched his head while he
drove with one hand. "Absolutely.
But he will have to try, unlike in
the Derby. Simply Sinful is likely
to be entered, too."

"But Evil will beat him again,
like in the Preakness."

Nick took a big breath. "I don't
know about the distance. I know
he's proved at a mile and a

quarter, but the Belmont is a mile and a half, and that's two more furlongs. I think he can do it, though. Groovy will have a long layoff, and I know that will benefit him. We're aiming for the Whitney, as you know, but I'm planning to stick him in a small allowance race at the end of July."

Marvin yawned. "Yep. I'm going to doze off here for a bit. Wake me when we get there."

Marvin stared out the window as they continued toward Belmont, the Test of the Champion.

31

"Marvin, we're here," Nick said as they pulled into the Belmont Park stable yard.

Marvin slowly opened his eyes. He then heard Evil stomping around in the trailer and then he was fully awake. He climbed out of the truck and opened the trailer. Evil was standing mildly in the back, giving no evidence of being naughty. Marvin went inside, untied him, and let him out. He would always be kept in stall 1. Marvin led him in, took off his halter, and fed him some fresh hay and water. Nick and Marvin set up their cots in stalls 2 and 3.

The next few days Evil settled into his new home at Belmont Park. For the first three days he walked around the shedrow. Then they

galloped him a mile and a half
every other day. On June 1, he went
a mile and an eighth in 1:46 and
two. Marvin noticed that since the
Derby, he was no longer a thin and
trim racehorse. He was a massive,
bulky thing that exploded when you
asked him. He was 1,200 pounds that
shook the ground when he ran. At
eighteen hands high now, he was
like a football player, only as a
horse. Most of the grooms were
afraid of him, but Marvin knew he
was just a big baby inside.

On June 6, three days before the
Belmont, Evil had one of those eye-
opener works. It was short, but
fast. He went a half-mile in :44
and three. It scared the other
Belmont contenders out of their
minds. One horse scratched, setting
an example. By the night before the
Belmont, it was only a four-horse
field, consisting of Evil, Ewinar,
the second place horse in the
Derby; Simply Sinful, and a nobody
horse named Tempus. Marvin and Nick
drank some tea to calm their nerves
the night before. They had a horse;
one horse that was about to make
history.

~~~~~~~~~~~~~~~~~~~~

Marvin woke up at 2:00 AM that
morning. He went to Evil's stall
and went in with approval from the
guard that Nick hired. He watched
Evil sleep peacefully as he peeked
up from his Daily Racing Form. He
read for what he thought to be

hours until he glanced at his watch.

It was only 2:30.

Marvin groaned and slid down in the straw. Gradually, his eyes closed, and he drifted off to sleep in Evil's stall.

~~~~~~~~~~~~~~~~~~~~

Marvin woke up to the sound of crackling. The loudspeaker buzzed. "Horsemen, bring your horses to the paddock for the first race. Bring your horses to the paddock for the first race."

Marvin jumped up, startling Evil. The race was in just a few hours, and he hadn't even started grooming! He ran to the tack room, grabbing all his grooming stuff. He set to work as Victor peeked around the corner. "Rise and shine, valentine!"

"Very funny. How long have you been here?" Marvin asked with a nagging voice.

"A couple hours. Oh, by the way, I had to make a new shirt because the old one was running out of room…" Victor trailed off.

Marvin glanced at Victor's shirt. It said, "I'm Not Evil: Winner of the Triple Crown". Marvin smiled at his friend. "Thanks for supporting us. It really means a lot."

Victor's eyes widened. "No, thank you! I get commented on this outfit so much that I'm practically a celebrity around here."

Marvin asked after a short pause,
"Would you lead him down to the
paddock with me for what will
probably be the greatest race of
his life?"
Victor smiled and nodded.
"Sure."
Marvin and Victor got Evil ready
for the next three hours. Just
before the call came, Marvin as
always spoke to Evil. "This is the
big one, Evil. I trust in you to
make us proud."
"Horsemen, bring your horses to
the paddock for the Belmont Stakes.
Bring your horses to the paddock
for the Belmont," the loudspeaker
buzzed.
Victor took the right side, and
Marvin took the left. They led him
through the tunnel with whistles,
cheering, and staring going on.
Marvin led him to the six stall,
were Nick was waiting. He put on
the saddle and surcingle. Just
before Marvin led him away, Nick
stopped him. "Wait."
Marvin halted Evil and turned
around. "Yeah?"
Nick walked up to the side of Evil
and pinned something on his
saddlecloth. As Nick moved away,
Marvin nearly let out a cry. His
mother's favorite pin was lying on
the saddlecloth right by his name.
Marvin smiled at his dad. "Thank
you..."
He began to lead Evil around the
paddock for the final time as the
jockeys emerged. Marvin led Evil
back to the stall as Victor told
him something weird. "You know

what's weird, Marvin? Evil's post
positions for every Triple Crown
race combined are 666. That's the
number of pure evil. Maybe he does
have a little evil in him after
all."

Marvin smiled. "Maybe he does,
Victor. Maybe he does."
Nick gave Ray a leg up. He
immediately told him, "Let's pray
for this race."

Marvin, Victor, Nick, and Ray all
bowed their heads. Nick led them.
"Dear God, just thank you for this
day; be with this horse in this
race. Give him wings on his feet
and safety. We love you and trust
you; in Christ's name, Amen."

The bugler's call rang out through
the paddock. Nick smiled. Marvin
could tell he had tears in his
eyes. He patted Evil's neck. "Make
us proud, Evil."

And with that Marvin led Evil away
through the tunnel and handed him
off to the pony rider. After that,
he joined everyone in David and
Sonya's box.

Evil knew that this race was
different. He could feel the
excitement and nervousness in the
air, and, luckily, was on best
behavior as they reached the gate.

Marvin noticed the weird post
positions on the gate. The only
numbers there were 1,4,5, and 6.

Evil walked into the gate calmly
after all the other horses. They
were all in line. This was the
moment of truth.

~~~~~~~~~~~~~~~~~~~~

The assistant starter hung on to
Evil's bridle for too long and he
gave the field five lengths at the
break. Ray realized this and he
strapped Evil right-handed. He grew
wings on his feet and he took
flight. He made up the lost ground
in just three strides. Simply
Sinful was out on the front by six.
The gap was evaporating as the
black giant gained on him. The
adrenaline pounded through the
veins of both rider and horse as
they flew over the Big Sandy's
surface. The lead was reduced to
three, two, one, and then they were
running neck and neck. Ray let out
five inches in the reins, and Evil
blew past. But Simply Sinful had
his pride, and he came back with a
vengeance. He cut the lead to a
length. He didn't like Evil kicking
the sandy dirt of Belmont Park in
his face, so his jockey moved him
to the outside. Ray saw him come on
again and finally got sick of him.
He let out most of the remaining
rein and Evil turned Simply Sinful
down. He separated himself by ten
lengths and almost more, but Ray
took a hold of him. He was halfway
through the race. Six furlongs
left. He sat chilly on Evil for the
next four furlongs. Suddenly,
Simply Sinful went careening toward
the outside rail. He was holding
his right front foreleg up. His
jockey had a great deal of trouble
pulling him up. Simply Sinful was
one of those great horses that had
been broken; when his body could no

longer carry him, his heart tried to take him the rest of the way. Even though there was a lot, all his heart and guts couldn't carry him the remaining quarter mile. Evil turned into the stretch in front by twenty and being eased up. In the stands, it wasn't just a race. It was a coronation of a new Triple Crown winner. It was a brilliant performance. There was no cheering; just clapping like it had been in the Derby. The other horses were slowing down and getting tired. Evil crossed the wire with a twenty-one length lead. Ray punched his fist in the air, cheering "Triple Crown, Triple Crown!"

Marvin and Victor leaped into the air. Evil was one of the immortal now. They floated down to the winner's circle, were a blanket of white carnations was put over Evil's withers. They had their picture taken. A reporter interviewed Nick. This time he gladly talked to them. The reporter held the microphone up to Nick. "At what time did you know this horse was special?"

Nick grinned. "He was special from the very beginning."

"Well, he certainly lived up to expectations. What's next for him?"

Nick scratched his head. "Well, he'll have a layoff for a while, and then we might go to Saratoga for the fall racing series there. We might aim for the Travers."

The reporter capped off. "Thank you for your time."

Nick walked over to a triumphant
Marvin and Evil. "Well, Marvin,
we've got ourselves one heck of a
horse. You can go ahead and take
him back to the barn."

Marvin and Evil came out of the
testing barn clean. He released
Evil in his stall. He put away his
halter and re-entered the stall.
Marvin gave Evil's neck a big hug.

He could have stayed there
forever.

Part 2 - The Legacy

1

Marvin yawned as they drove down the interstate towards home. The new Triple Crown winner I'm Not Evil was in the back of the trailer, resting. He would remain at David and Sonya's farm until the beginning of July. He would then be shipped off to Saratoga to be trained for the Jim Dandy, and after that, the Travers. Nick said the ultimate goal would be the Breeders' Cup Classic in November.

They pulled into the driveway and unloaded Evil. He went in stall 1, his old home. Just Groovy was next door in stall 2, and Happy Boy in stall 3. Hahaha was in the broodmare barn, living out the rest of her life as a broodmare.

Evil was by far the biggest horse that David and Sonya owned. At fully eighteen hands high and seven feet long, he was huge. Victor called him the "black giant". It was June 12, three days after the Belmont Stakes and three days after crowning Evil Triple Crown champion. Nick had already devised out Evil's race schedule for the fall:

JIM DANDY STAKES
TRAVERS STAKES
JOCKEY CLUB GOLD CUP
BREEDERS' CUP CLASSIC

Evil's winning performance in the Belmont Stakes was highlighted on every handicapping show that week. It was debated about and discussed

for two weeks afterwards.
Meanwhile, Evil had already
established himself as the favorite
for the Jim Dandy on July 28.
    Marvin spent the whole afternoon
in Evil's stall. He wasn't very
tired from his performance in the
Belmont a few days ago. Nick had
told Marvin that Evil would begin
his walks next week, then his
gallops, then finally his works and
breezes on July 1 as he prepped for
the Jim Dandy.
    Nick came walking down the barn
aisle at five. "Marvin, how long
are you going to stay down here?"
he asked in a nagging voice.
"I'm staying down here till
dinner," Marvin replied. His
stomach let out a growl. "Which
had better be soon, because my
stomach's insisting that I eat
soon," he said as he patted Evil's
neck.
"Whatever," Nick said as he went
to the stallion barn to supervise
the new groom. Marvin stood up and
checked the tack room to make sure
it was all there, for he really had
nothing else to do.

~~~~~~~~~~~~~~~~~~~~~

    Marvin spent just about the rest
of the week in Evil's stall. He was
constantly petting him and cleaning
his tack out of boredom. On June
19, Evil galloped a mile and an
eighth. He did it easily and had an
"about time!" attitude about it.
A few weeks later, on July 2, he
breezed six furlongs in 1:12 flat.

Ray was using all his strength to
hold him back, though he ran a
twelve-clip anyway. He continued
his pattern of breezing and
galloping through early July.

One day Groovy was scheduled to
work seven furlongs, and Nick put
Eddie aboard for the work. Marvin
and Victor watched as Groovy leaped
into action at the seven-eighths
pole. Eddie was rating but not
strangling him. Marvin, again armed
with his own stopwatch that Nick
had gotten him as an early birthday
present, caught him going the first
quarter in :23 and two. Victor was
staring as he accelerated at the
half pole. Eddie was not urging him
but just letting him run at his own
pace. He saw the quarter pole go by
as Groovy went into the far turn.
Eddie began to use some slight hand
urging as he turned into the
stretch and accelerated even more.
Eddie took him in hand as he
crossed the finish. Groovy was
never a problem to pull up. He
liked to please and would do
whatever you asked him. Eddie
brought Groovy back to the gap and
hopped off. "How fast did I go?"

Nick grinned. "One twenty-three
flat. Exactly what I wanted.
Victor, you can take him back to
the barn. Oh, and Marvin, I'm going
to work Evil five furlongs
tomorrow, just to warn you."

Marvin nodded. "Okay. As he
headed back to the barn, he thought
about his dad. Nick liked to work
horses according to their races.
Since Groovy raced in slower times,

he liked to work him fast. Evil, on
the other hand, raced in super-fast
times, so Nick preferred to work
him slow.

Marvin went to Evil's stall and
sat down outside the door. The
horse was sleeping, and Marvin
didn't want to disturb him right
now. He picked up the newest
edition of the Form and began
reading. There was an article
talking about the fall racing
coming up, including the return of
Evil in the Jim Dandy and Groovy in
the Whitney.

Marvin read on his Form until he
was stopped by a black nose
sniffing his head. He looked up to
see Evil's neck stretched out over
his stall door. Marvin laughed and
patted the big black nose. "Your
name sure fits you," he said.

~~~~~~~~~~~~~~~~~~~~

Later that night Marvin was in his
room when Nick came running. "Evil
got out of his stall! Come with me!
We have to find him. When you were
in the barn did you go in his
stall?"

Marvin leaped out of bed. "No…"
he said as he ran down the stairs
and out the door.

It was a warm summer night as
Marvin ran toward the barn in his
pajamas. He looked in the first
stall, and, true to Nick's word, he
wasn't there. The stall door was
wide open. Marvin checked the feed
room first, as he knew that horses

didn't know when to stop eating and
could get colic very easily if they
found the feed room door open. He
couldn't be in there, for the door
was locked with a heavy chain and
closed. He checked the broodmare
and stallion barns, and he wasn't
there either. He grabbed a
flashlight from the shed and began
scanning the grounds. He didn't see
Evil in the yard. That's when he
saw the gate to the trails left
standing open. He ran and told Nick
that the trail gate was open and
that he was going to hop on Berry
and search the trails. He saddled
her faster than ever and set off
from the stable yard at a brisk
canter, which soon turned into a
gallop as they got onto the wide
trails. Marvin scanned the
flashlight everywhere and didn't
see him. Berry knew they were on a
mission and set into her fastest
gallop as they got a quarter mile
into the trail. Marvin shone the
flashlight on the hidden trail and
saw that the brush and been
trampled. Evil had been through
here. He turned Berry on a dime and
showed her the path. Marvin was
glad that Berry used to be a
western reining horse because she
could turn quickly and come to a
sliding halt. He galloped another
mile and came to the field where he
and Victor loved to race. Just then
he heard a coyote howl and knew
that if one caught Evil, it would
very much be the end.

2

Marvin scanned the flashlight over
the field and rested it on a dark
figure. He gave Berry one hard kick
and she broke like Evil did. She
came closer to the figure with
every stride. Marvin shined his
flashlight again and saw that it
was Evil standing there, grazing.
Marvin gave Berry the signal for a
sliding halt, and she performed it
easily. It would have received a
seven in any reining class, though
Marvin nearly fell off. He nudged
Berry forward into a slow walk as
they came within ten feet of Evil.
"Evil! Come here!" Marvin said as
he stopped Berry within five feet.
He slid off and untied the rope
around his waist. He knew when he
had set off that if he found Evil,
he would need a way to lead him
back. The rope was attached to a
green nylon halter which Marvin
never used on Evil. He briefly tied
Berry to a tree as he put the
halter on Evil and secured all
fastens, straps, and buckles. He
led Evil over to where Berry was
tied and remounted. Marvin nudged
Berry into a slow walk again as
they headed home with him ponying
Evil. Marvin watched Evil as they
walked and noticed that Evil didn't
seem to be hurt in any way. He
looked good despite the dirt on his
coat. He walked elegantly and held
his head up. Marvin asked Berry to
trot and Evil pranced at the same
speed. He looked like a Saddlebred
in a saddleseat class. Marvin rode

Berry into the yard about ten
minutes later. Nick came jogging
up, out of breath. "Where was
he?"

Marvin grinned. "He was grazing
on grass in a field deep in the
woods."

Nick took him back to the barn and
put him in crossties. He ran his
hands over Evil's legs, checking
for heat or bumps. When he was
satisfied, he stood up and patted
his neck. "You were a lucky one..."

Marvin unsaddled Berry and put her
in her stall. He praised her for a
job well done and went to see Evil.
He had his head out of his stall
door and was looking at him with
bright eyes as if to say, "What? I
was only having some fun!" Marvin
patted him on the neck. "Silly,"
he said. Marvin went over him with
a brush lightly for the night. He
latched Evil's door with a chain
and went back up to the house. Now,
finally at peace, he fell asleep.

~~~~~~~~~~~~~~~~~~~~~~~

Marvin woke up the next morning
wondering what Nick thought about
still working him. He put some
jeans on and went down to the barn.
He let out a sigh when he saw that
Evil's door was still latched, just
as he had left it. He put him in
crossties and cleaned his stall.
Nick came strolling down to the
barn with his morning coffee just a
few minutes later. He set the drink
on a stool and went to Evil's side.
He ran his hands up and down Evil's

legs to check for heat. When there
was none, he commented to Marvin,
"The horse looks and feels great,
even after the escapade last night.
He's still going to work this
morning. Go ahead and get him
ready. You can finish the stalls
later."

Marvin laid his pitchfork against
a wall and went to the tack room.
He grabbed a lightweight exercise
saddle and a bridle and got Evil
ready. Ray and Nick were already
down at the training track, talking
about the future. Nick gave Ray a
leg up and nodded. They had already
discussed the distance and how to
take him. Ray took Evil to the
five-eighths pole and let him out.
The colt lunged forward,
anticipating the good run ahead.
Ray kept a good hold on him but
still let him run. He tried his
best to extend himself over the
track, but he was still running
restricted. The sun had just risen,
and he was running gloriously
across the track with the sun
shining just above the trees. Evil
crossed the wire in hand, and
slowed down unwillingly. Ray
brought him back to the gap.
"How'd I do?"

Nick shrugged. " :57 and one. You
didn't do *too* bad," he said with a
smile now on his face.

Marvin took him and led him away.
He wasn't sweating and was looking
back at the track with an eager
look. Marvin wanted to let him go
on the track so he could run for

all he was worth. But he shook his head. *That'll never happen...*

3

Evil grew more during the summer. Not in height, but in width. Nick had to get him a new girth because his old one didn't fit any more. The weeks leading up to the Jim Dandy were suspenseful and quiet in the news. Everyone knew that Evil was coming back; they could feel it. Evil was shipped up to Saratoga the Monday before the Jim Dandy. On July 25, the Wednesday before the Jim Dandy, the post positions were drawn. Evil had drawn post two. He was smack in the middle of the field, for only two other horses entered. The longshot GetAway was in the first slot. Nobody believed he could go the routing distance; he finished second-last in the Derby. On the outside was Ewinar, the tiny but staying colt that had finished second in the Derby. He was the morning line second choice at 25-1. GetAway was 70-1. Evil was at 1-20. The long-term bettors thought that if he kept running like this, he would eat this tiny field for breakfast, the Travers for lunch, the Jockey Club Gold Cup for dinner, and the Breeders' Cup Classic for dessert.

On July 26, Marvin woke up early. Evil was scheduled his last work before the race. He was to go a slow six furlongs, preferably in

1:12 and four, because Nick knew it was impossible to get him to go in 1:13. Marvin saddled Evil up and led him out to the track. Nick and Ray were standing there, waiting. Nick gave Evil a small pat and boosted Ray up. "Remember, try to make him go as slow as you can but still let him run."

Ray nodded. "Okay."

He let Evil into a gallop as they approached the three quarters pole. Ray let him gradually increase the intensity of the gallop until they reached the pole. Then he asked him to run. Evil tried to launch into a fast run, but Ray was ready for it. He kept a hold on him but still let him run at a slower pace. About a quarter mile into the workout Evil was not pleased. He thought he was going way too slow. Evil decided it was time, so he sped up immediately. Ray pulled back even more, but Evil didn't care. He wanted to run. He was running at his racing speed now. He didn't care about whoever was on his back, the metal pulling at the corners of his mouth. When Evil wanted to run, he ran. He rushed through the backstretch, leaving other horses and riders stunned in his wake. He turned the stretch for home.

Over at the gap, Nick was white-faced. Marvin had caught him going the half mile in :45 with tight restraint, and he looked to finish the work even faster. Ray tried to reach down and slow him down by grabbing more rein, but that only made him fight it. As he crossed

the wire, Ray knew Nick was
probably going to chew him out. He
leaned down, grabbed the bit, and
pulled him back. Evil threw up his
head and slowed. He brought him
back to the gap. Nick wasn't there,
but Marvin and Victor were. Marvin
gave Ray an "oh you're in
trouble" look. Ray nodded his
head. "How fast?"

Marvin handed the stopwatch up to
him. Ray couldn't believe his eyes.
It read 1:08 and 2/5 seconds. Ray
gulped and hopped off. "Where?"
he asked.
Marvin had a mock tone of death in
his voice. "The parking lot."

Victor and Marvin went to the barn
to clean stalls, as Ray would
likely be yelled at. Later on in
the afternoon Nick came back to the
barn. His face was normal-colored
again and he looked relieved.

On Jim Dandy morning, Marvin woke
up a few hours late, just like he
had on the day of the Belmont. He
knew all the racing fans in the
country were shaking in
anticipation of the return of the
newest Triple Crown winner, this
different one. Never in racing
history had a horse won the Triple
Crown with as much authority as
Evil did. No rating could hold him
back-when he wanted to go, he went.

Marvin spent the rest of the
morning giving Evil a good
grooming. He had to stand on a
stool to reach all of Evil's back.
When he was done, he put a sheet on
him and went to the track kitchen,
where Nick always hung out before

the race. There was a handicapping show on, previewing the Jim Dandy. Marvin didn't bother to watch it, so he got a snack and sat down at Nick's usual table. Nick didn't look up from his magazine. Marvin stretched and finished his snack as Nick finished whatever he was reading and put it down. That's when he noticed Marvin sitting there looking at him.

Nick jumped. "I didn't know you were there! How long have you been here?"

Marvin grinned. "A few minutes."

Nick sat up straight. "Sorry, I was too engrossed in my magazine. What time is it?" he said, remembering that he forgot his watch.

Marvin looked at his own. "Two thirty," he said with an excited tone." Post time was coming.

"You'd better go back to the barn with him," Nick said. "He knows his return time is now."

Marvin nodded and left the kitchen. He headed back to the barn. Marvin took note that it was almost 90 degrees outside and overcast. He didn't know how the conditions would affect Evil. Evil had run in warmer weather before, but never this warm. He grabbed Evil's bridle from the tack room and began cleaning it. Evil had his big black head over the stall door, watching Marvin. He stomped his foot and eagerly looked out the door toward the track. He was ready. Marvin finished cleaning the bridle and looked at his watch.

It was 3:00, an hour and a half till post time. Marvin groomed Evil again and made his coat sparkle. He could easily have scared any bystander away with his size. Marvin bridled him at four.

Finally, the loudspeaker crackled. "Horsemen, bring your horses to the paddock for the Jim Dandy. Bring your horses to the paddock for the Jim Dandy."

Marvin gulped. Saratoga was known as "the graveyard of favorites". Many great racehorses had been beaten here. Marvin quickened his steps a little and got down to the paddock first. There were many people crowded along the outside rail as Evil walked into the paddock. A few cheers and whistles rose. Nick was standing at the 2 stall, waiting. He strapped the saddle on and fastened the surcingle. Marvin led Evil around the paddock a few times till the three jockeys came out. Ray came out and materialized at Nick's side. Nick gave him a leg up when Evil came back. "Remember, don't screw up," Nick said.

Ray nodded and the bugler started to play. Marvin led his beloved horse through the tunnel and onto the track. The pony rider took him and Marvin joined Nick.

Out on the track, Ray looked at the toteboard. Evil was the heavy favorite at 1-10. Ewinar was 30-1 and GetAway 90-1. Nobody wanted to go against the colt. After about ten minutes of warming up, they approached the gate. GetAway was

blindfolded and led in. Evil walked
in without a hitch, as did Ewinar.
They were all set.

4

Evil broke like he did in the
Derby. His trademark speed had
already dominated the field on
paper, now it would show them in
life.

Evil went into the far turn in
front by four and lengthening.
GetAway was last already, and
Ewinar was having trouble with the
muddy track. Evil skimmed over the
surface like it was dry. Ray was
strangling him; he was lengthening
his lead no longer, he was running
no faster; the field was dropping
back behind him. Evil lengthened
his lead now to ten lengths. There
was a half mile to go. Evil was
under tight restraint but still
lengthening his lead to eleven,
twelve, thirteen, fourteen and
finally fifteen lengths as he
turned into the stretch alone. He
was not even sweating. Ray relaxed
for the final furlong.

Up in the stands, Marvin was
clapping. The announcer couldn't
believe it. "Brilliant! Simply
brilliant! On a super muddy track,
he has left this tiny field in his
wake! He has established himself as
the Travers favorite, and he is
just awesome."

Marvin, Nick, David, and Sonya all
headed down to the winner's circle

to meet Evil and celebrate his
victory.

   Ray pulled Evil up quickly. Evil
had not been buried in the
graveyard of favorites. He raised
his fist in the air and let out a
woo-hoo. He met Marvin at the gap,
who gave him a grin and clipped a
lead shank to Evil's bit ring.
Their picture was taken and Ray
hopped off. He quickly weighed out
and came back to the winner's
circle. He and Nick were
interviewed as Marvin took Evil to
the testing barn. He passed with
flying colors and Marvin led him
back to the barn. He rinsed him
off, even though he hadn't broken
a sweat. Marvin gave him some
fresh hay and water and Evil dug
in. He wiped his bridle off with
water and stored it away in the
tack room. The next goal was the
Travers Stakes, commonly called
the "mid-summer derby" because of
its prestigiousness. It was also a
mile and a quarter, like the
Kentucky Derby. Marvin got a piece
of paper out and began writing a
list of all the races Evil had
won.

TWO-YEAR-OLD SEASON
  MAIDEN SPECIAL WEIGHT
  ALLOWANCE
  ALLOWANCE
  SANFORD STAKES (G2)
  HOPEFUL STAKES (G1)
  CHAMPAGNE STAKES (G1)
  THREE-YEAR-OLD SEASON
ALLOWANCE
  FLORIDA DERBY (G1)

```
KENTUCKY DERBY (G1)
PREAKNESS STAKES (G1)
BELMONT STAKES (G1)
JIM DANDY STAKES (G2)
UNDEFEATED IN 12 LIFETIME STARTS
```

Marvin left the stall and went to find Nick, who never kept track of all the races he put his horses in. When he saw it, Nick would realize even more just how great of a horse he had.

~~~~~~~~~~~~~~~~~~~~~

A few days later Marvin took Evil out for a walk around the shedrow. He was outfitted in red and blue bandages. Groovy came out a few minutes later. He had the same things on. His next race, the Whitney Handicap, was in 12 days. It was August 1, and the Travers was in 24 days. Evil's next breeze was in 2 days; he would go six furlongs.

That week seemed to take forever. The days seemed like centuries. A week before the Whitney, Groovy went five furlongs in 58 flat over the Saratoga racecourse. Nick was very happy with the work. Groovy came off of it in good shape. He was at his peak, and everyone knew it. Victor was excited about the Whitney. It was all he talked about and thought about. He spent hours studying other horses' records, even though he already knew them. He made the final decision that the horse named SpeedMatters was the biggest threat.

On August 10, the post positions were drawn. Victor let out a huge sigh when he saw that Groovy had drawn post four in a ten-horse field. He galloped on August 12, the day before the race. He went easily. That time, for the first time, Nick let Victor ride him. Victor loved it and was beaming the rest of the day. He didn't forget his nervousness, though. Marvin was starting to worry about him. His friend wasn't going to get any sleep. He let Victor tire himself out and get three hours of restless sleep. Victor still woke up bright and early, at 4:00 AM. He was the first person that morning to get to Groovy's stall. Victor gave him his quart of oats and Groovy knew it was race day. He woke Marvin up at 4:15; much to the latter's dislike. Marvin fed Evil and tried to go back to sleep, but Victor kept him up with his constant chatter. Marvin decided to stop trying to sleep, so he got up and joined Victor in conversation. They talked for a few hours till Nick got up. Then all three of them went to the cafeteria for some breakfast some time later. They had fruit and pastries; they read their Racing Forms and had a few coffees, that is, except Marvin. He preferred to have a pop instead. David and Sonya met them at the cafeteria. "Are you guys excited?" David asked Marvin and Victor.

Marvin nodded and Victor whooped and hollered. Everyone in the cafeteria looked at him. He covered his face with his hand and the attention turned away from him. Victor shuddered. "Now THAT was embarrassing," he said as he left the cafeteria.

Marvin and Nick laughed. Marvin said to Nick, "I need to help him get Groovy ready."

Nick nodded, and Marvin set off after Victor.

5

Marvin cleaned Groovy's bridle as Victor groomed the horse and got him ready. Groovy had never broken his habit of nipping at Marvin, so Marvin kept his distance. They spent the rest of the afternoon doing this until the call to the paddock came. Victor clipped a lead onto Groovy's bit ring, and Marvin walked a few feet away as they headed down to the paddock. Marvin looked at the toteboard and saw that Groovy was the lukewarm favorite at 5-2. SpeedMatters was at 7-2. Victor led Groovy through the tunnel and into the paddock. Nick saddled him quickly and Victor led him around the paddock. Marvin turned to Nick. "Do you think he'll win?"

Nick looked at Marvin. "Of course I think he can win. Don't all trainers think their horse can win? He's got a great chance. The bay over there," he said, pointing to

SpeedMatters, " - has the best
chance to upset him. I think
Groovy's faster, though, " Nick
said.

Eddie came strolling over,
whistling. Nick discussed strategy
with him for a few minutes while
Victor brought Groovy back to the
saddling stall. Nick gave Eddie a
leg up and nodded. The bugler began
playing, and Marvin and Nick went
up to David and Sonya's box. Victor
handed Groovy over to the pony
rider and joined them there.

Eddie thought Groovy was warming
up quicker than usual. He was
moving very fluidly and
effortlessly. They approached the
gate after a long ten minutes of
trotting, walking, and cantering
around the track. Groovy paused and
looked at the gate briefly before
going in. The other horses loaded
quickly and quietly. They were all
set for the Whitney Handicap.

~~~~~~~~~~~~~~~~~~~~

Groovy was a little bit slow into
stride and did not break with the
whole field. Eddie let out a little
rein and Groovy lurched forward. He
caught the rest of the field in
three strides and flew into second.
Eddie let the longshot dictate the
pace until the half mile pole, then
he asked Groovy, who gave. His
chestnut flew to the leader and
went right on by. What Eddie didn't
know was that SpeedMatters was
right behind him. Groovy turned

into the stretch with SpeedMatters glued to his flank. SpeedMatters started to cut into the lead. It shrunk to a half-length, then to a neck, and finally they were running head to head as they neared the sixteenth pole. Eddie lashed Groovy right-handed with the whip, and he took a short lead of a half-length as they crossed the wire. He hadn't won by much, but he had won. Victor whooped and ran down to the winner's circle. Marvin, Nick, David, and Sonya followed him, though not as loudly.

Eddie easily pulled Groovy up. He had barely held off a charging SpeedMatters. He turned Groovy around and took him back to the gap, where Victor was standing to meet him. He had a huge smile on his face and looked happy. Victor led him into the winner's circle and their picture was taken. Eddie hopped down and weighed out. Victor led Groovy back to the barn and Marvin went with him. Victor was patting Groovy for a job well done. Marvin stayed his distance but still praised him. Groovy passed at the testing barn and Victor and Marvin settled him in his stall with fresh bedding, hay, and water. Groovy took a long drink, polished his hay off, and settled down in the straw for a nap.

Marvin was brushing Evil's coat the next day when he noticed a horrible smell in the air. It smelled like a stall hadn't been cleaned out in a while. He patted Evil and went from stall to stall, checking. He reached the four-year-old filly's stall and the smell was coming from there. He checked the stall. It was clean. He had checked all the stalls, and all of them were clean. He shrugged and went back to brushing Evil. He smelled it again. Victor came through the door. Marvin went to him. "Victor, do you smell anything?"

Victor sniffed the air. "No, I don't. I think it's just you."

Marvin shrugged and went back to work on brushing Evil. Victor went to the tack room to clean Groovy's tack. Marvin finished grooming Evil and put him back in his stall. He went over to Nick's office to find out if he had smelled anything weird lately. Nick gave him a weird look in response. "No, it's just you."

Marvin sighed and jogged back to the training barn. There were 11 days until the Travers, and racing fans were getting anxious to see the awaited return of Evil. The summer derby was getting closer by the second.

Later that week the smell got worse. It continued to come from the four-year-old filly's stall. It smelled different now, though. It was the smell of decay, the smell of death. They moved the filly to another stall to clean out her old

one. A few days later the smell was
gone from the training barn, but it
started to smell in the other
stall, where the filly was. Nick
called in the vet to check her out.
Her racing performances hadn't been
the best lately. He did some x-rays
and found nothing. He did almost
everything except an MRI. Nick
wanted to now what was wrong with
her, so he scheduled an MRI a few
days later, as Aiden hadn't brought
that equipment with him. The smell
was getting unbearable. When Aiden
finished the MRI, the worst
happened.

Aiden gulped. "She has cancer,"
he said.

Marvin, Victor, and Nick's eyes
all widened. "Cancer?" Victor
said.

Aiden nodded sadly. "Liver
cancer, stage four. It has spread
and is located along her spine and
near her heart, in places we can't
operate. I'm afraid the only humane
thing to do is put her down."

Marvin was devastated. "Can we
see the scan?"

Aiden picked it up and handed it
to Marvin, who studied it closely.
True to Aiden's word, there was a
massive growth that had spread
throughout her body and was
dangerously close to her heart.

Marvin handed it to Nick, who saw
the same thing. "I'll inform the
owners," he said. Nick left the
barn to make a call. Marvin stroked
the filly's coat, and she looked at
him with bright eyes. Nick came
back with the word. "They said

they don't want her to suffer and
that if it's the best choice to
euthanize her to do so. "
 Aiden nodded and took the
equipment back to his truck. He
came back with a small syringe.
Victor looked like he was about to
cry. This filly had been one of his
favorites, next to Groovy. Aiden
gave her the medicine, and within a
few seconds she was gone.

~~~~~~~~~~~~~~~~~~~~~~~~

 Evil had a work scheduled a few
days after the filly was
euthanized. He was to go five
furlongs at a brisk pace, but not
too fast. Marvin quickly saddled
him up and took him out to the
Saratoga track. Ray and Nick were
waiting by the gap. Ray hopped
aboard with help from Nick, nodded,
and Evil set off. The black colt
took off at the five-eighths pole.
Marvin looked through his
binoculars as Evil pounded the dirt
surface, covering more ground with
every stride. Ray seemed to
struggle to hold him back. He had
been in a tough race yesterday, and
it had taken its toll on him. Evil
skipped through a quarter in :21
and four effortlessly. This made
Marvin wonder how fast Evil would
really go if he were under the
whip. Evil flew through the stretch
and crossed under the wire without
showing any form of tiredness. Ray
brought him back to the gap, and he
was looking longingly at the track

as if to say, "Are you EVER going to let me truly run out there?"

Ray hopped down from Evil and raised his eyebrows at Nick. "Do I want to know?"

Nick shook his head. "Nope."

Ray nodded and walked away. Marvin glanced over at Nick's stopwatch. It read :55 and one. Marvin looked away quickly as if scolding himself and led Evil back to the barn.

7

The night before the Travers, Marvin busied himself reading the Daily Racing Form and looking at the field for the Travers, which was useless. Evil had scared all competitors away. The second-ranked trainer in the country decided to enter a small allowance-winning horse in the Travers just for the heck of it. After all, any horse could have a bad day. He had trained a horse that had won the Derby and Preakness, but choked in the Belmont.

Marvin woke up on Travers morning at five sharp. Evil was quietly dozing at the back of his stall, not knowing he was going to run today. Marvin checked Evil's tack to make sure it was all right and then poured a quart of oats in Evil's stall. That woke him up and he dove into the oats, now knowing what lay ahead. He polished those off and looked out his stall door at the sun that was beginning to rise and the track that horses were working on.

Marvin joined Nick for a quick breakfast at the cafeteria and strolled back to the barn. He put Evil in crossties and began grooming him. He waited in Evil's stall for the anticipated call to the paddock. There had been some other stakes races that day, and the horses were coming back from those.

The Travers was Evil's first million-dollar race since the Belmont and just as prestigious. Evil was bridled already and the bridle was polished to a perfect shine. Marvin looked at his watch and predicted the time when the call would come. "5, 4, 3, 2, 1, 1,"

"Bring your horses to the paddock for the Travers Stakes. Bring your horses to the paddock for the Travers."

Marvin led Evil down to the paddock and he was the first one there. Nick had him saddled before the other horse got down there. The other horse, named Got It, was a bay four-year-old whose last stakes race had been last year's Belmont. He had been on a sharp decline in class ever since he finished fourth in that race. Got It was coming off of a narrow win in a second level allowance race. They had just finished saddling him when the two jockeys came out. Marvin was trotting Evil around the paddock, warming his muscles up. Nick gave Ray a boost up and a nod when the

black monster had come back. The
bugler began playing and Marvin led
Evil out to the track for the
summer derby. He gave Evil's lead
to the pony rider and he went up to
the owners' boxes.

Evil was acting up, which was
unusual. He was throwing his head
up and sometimes rising up on his
hind legs. The pony rider gave a
huge sigh of relief when an
assistant starter took Evil. He
loaded into the first slot and Got
It loaded next to him. The
assistant starter smiled at Ray and
said, "I was going to wish you
good luck but I just realized you
won't need it," he said with a
small laugh.

Ray grinned lop-sidedly, then the
gates opened and the race was on!
Evil gunned out to the front,
leaving Got It in his dust. He
opened a ten-length lead on the
fast, dry track. Got It's jockey
knew it was likely impossible to
catch him, so he let his horse just
gallop along like he was in a
morning workout. Evil lengthened
his lead to twenty-five since the
other horse wasn't trying. He
continued to lengthen his lead
throughout the race. Turning into
the stretch it was forty-five
lengths. Crossing the eighth pole
it was fifty-five, and finally
sixty as he crossed the wire. He
was over a furlong ahead of the
other horse. Ray had been trying to
ease him up. The track announcer
was not surprised. "Dazzling.
Simply dazzling!"

Ray pulled Evil up easily. No records had been broken-the other horse didn't try, allowing the huge victory. He brought Evil back to the gap, where he was greeted with smiles and grins. Evil was led into the winner's circle for the thirteenth time in thirteen races. The goal in sight was the Jockey Club Gold Cup, in October. Just Groovy was also headed there, and a major rivalry would be decided.

8

On September 1, Evil was walked around the shedrow five times ahead of the Jockey Club Gold Cup. Groovy was also headed for the Gold Cup and he was walked the day before. Morning line odds indicated that Evil would be the middleweight favorite at even money, and Groovy at 4-1. Marvin thought this was ridiculous. Evil was a better horse than Groovy, and everyone knew it. They were just stupid.

Marvin had a million thoughts swimming through his head as Evil walked behind him placidly. He completed the fourth circuit and snapped back to life. There were 34 days until the Gold Cup and counting. They were going to ship Groovy and Evil to Belmont the next day.

Groovy, like Evil had the same two goals in mind-the Gold Cup and then horse racing's year-end crowning event, the Breeders' Cup

Classic. That would only mean that one horse, either Evil or Groovy, would triumph above. Marvin completed the fifth circuit and didn't realize that he walked around a few more times until Victor's head popped out from around the barn door. "Hey! How many times are you going to walk around here? I've counted you going eight times! I thought he was only scheduled for five," Victor commented.

Marvin had jumped at Victor's voice, startling Evil. The colt's head came up and he snapped into alert mode. He danced in a circle around Marvin until he was taken hold of. Marvin quickly returned him to the barn and kept his sheet on. It was getting cold and he didn't want Evil to freeze.

It was only September, and people were buzzing about the Breeders' Cup already. The Gold Cup hadn't been run yet, and Evil had already established himself as the favorite for the Classic at 3-2. He wasn't at unbelievable odds yet because of the Gold Cup and that the fact that some European champions thought that they had a chance to beat this year's Triple Crown winner. Evil had already won himself the Eclipse Award for Champion Three-Year-Old, and with a victory in the Classic he would definitely secure Horse of the Year.

Marvin got out his sheet of paper with all of Evil's wins on it and added:

TRAVERS STAKES

He thought about adding Horse of
the Year already but decided not
to. If he was beat in the Classic
by some other horse, that title
might not belong to him.
Marvin sighed and put away the
sheet of paper. He wished October 6
would just come already.

~~~~~~~~~~~~~~~~~~

It didn't come quickly. The next
few days seemed to take forever.
Marvin busied himself by writing
out what would be the perfect four-
year-old campaign.

FOUR-YEAR-OLD SEASON
 DONN HANDICAP
 DUBAI WORLD CUP
 PIMLICO SPECIAL
 JC GOLD CUP (again)
 BREEDERS' CUP CLASSIC (again)

To have Evil run in the Classic
twice would be awesome. To win the
World Cup would be even better.
Since making that list the weeks
went by quicker. Suddenly it was
the week of the Gold Cup and the
nation was fired up. On October 3
the posts were drawn. A European
horse called Proudly Wave drew post
position 1; Ewinar drew post two,
Evil post three, and Just Groovy
post four.
On October 4 Groovy and Evil were
to have their last works before the
Gold Cup. Evil went six furlongs in

1:10 under tight restraint. Later, Victor brought Groovy out for his work, and he was unusually dull. Eddie hopped aboard and they set off for the five furlongs.

Groovy was going very slow. Eddie chirped to him, but there was no response. He thought to himself, *Is it me or are we walking along here?*

Groovy plodded down the stretch and crossed the wire in what seemed to Eddie like slow motion. Eddie had no trouble pulling him up. He walked very slowly and listlessly back to the gap. His ears were lying down flat and his head hung low. Eddie hopped off as soon as Victor took the reins.

Nick looked worried. "He went in 1:07 and two for five furlongs. What was wrong with him?"

Eddie shook his head. "He didn't respond. I kicked him and chirped to him and tried everything. I really don't know."

Nick nodded and said to Victor, "Take him to the vet barn and have him checked out. This isn't like him," Nick said as he unsaddled the colt and gave Victor a halter to put on him.

Victor nodded and took Groovy's bridle off. He slipped on the halter and led Groovy away.

Nick shook his head and walked back to the barn. Marvin was in Evil's stall, reading the Form. Nick picked up his own and began reading.

9

Marvin woke up the morning of the Gold Cup excited. This was going to be Evil's last race before the Classic.

A sad thing about it was that Groovy had a fever and was quietly scratched by Nick. That left a three-horse field that would likely be dominated by Evil. Marvin groomed him to a sparkling deep black shine. Evil knew it was race day now and was excited. He eagerly looked out the barn door at the track, just waiting to go out there. Victor spent the whole afternoon making Groovy comfortable. The long-awaited call came a little bit later than usual, so Marvin had been waiting in Evil's receiving barn stall impatiently for a few minutes. He jumped at the loudspeaker and led Evil out of the barn before it was done. Marvin and Evil were the first ones in the paddock. Nick saddled the colt and Marvin began leading him around the paddock. About five minutes later Ewinar came in his pink blanket, and then Proudly Wave. The jockeys came out of the jockeys' room and mounted. Ray nodded at Nick and Marvin led Evil out to the track. He was in the safe hands of the pony rider as Marvin headed up to David and Sonya's box.

Ray knew he was on the 3-10 favorite. He knew that Evil was the greatest horse he would probably ever sit on. As they approached the gate, he leaned forward and patted Evil's neck, a move he only did at the Kentucky Derby. Evil started to prance as they came within a few feet of the gate. Proudly Wave was first to load, and then Ewinar went in. Evil was next. He arched his neck as he calmly went in. Ray leaned forward and prepared himself for the break.

When the gates opened, Evil was the first one out. He had started to run before the gates had even opened. Ray was lucky that the gate opened just then or else he would've crashed through it. Evil broke already a length in front of the field. Ray kept an unusually good hold on him, so he only was in front by three once they were in the backstretch. Proudly Wave's jockey thought that Evil was having a bad day and that he could catch him. He set Proudly Wave into a drive and he began to gain on Evil, cutting his lead to a length. Ray saw this and let out some rein. Evil lurched at this opportunity and he danced out in front again, only this time by six. Evil passed the quarter pole and turned for home in front by ten. Ewinar was making his move on Proudly Wave. He edged in front by a neck, a half-length, and finally to a full length as Evil passed the three-sixteenths pole twelve lengths ahead. He coasted along under a tight hold from Ray and flashed under the wire in front by thirteen.

Marvin, Nick, David, and Sonya took their usual route down to the winner's circle. The picture was taken and Ray hopped off. A reporter came up to Nick. "Are you aiming for the Breeders' Cup Classic next?" he asked.

Nick chuckled. "What do you think? Why wouldn't I? If I think he can win, he's going there," he said with a smile.

"What about Just Groovy? Is he still aiming for the same goal?" the reporter inquired.

Nick sighed. "He had a fever Wednesday and I had no choice but to scratch him; if he gets better he's definitely going there."

The reporter thanked Nick and went to catch Ray before he ventured back to the jockeys' room. Marvin led Evil to the testing barn soon after Ray had taken his saddle. The colt passed with flying colors, and was led back to his stall. Marvin noticed that Victor had laid a fresh bed of straw in the stall and left fresh hay and water. Marvin smiled and released Evil in the roomy, open space.

~~~~~~~~~~~~~~~~~~~

Marvin added to Evil's list of wins a few days later:

JOCKEY CLUB GOLD CUP

The Breeders' Cup was fast approaching. It was October 10, and the Breeders' Cup was on November 3. There were 24 days and counting down. Marvin had been told many times that foreign invaders whom you have never seen the likes of beat the favorites all the time. He had also been told that many horses broke down in the Breeders' Cup.

This year it was at Churchill Downs. If Evil were to win the Classic, both of his major victories would have come at Churchill-the Derby and the Classic.

On October 11, Happy Boy had his third race back at Keeneland. It was a medium-class allowance on the turf. He had already won two other allowances on turf, and he loved it. Nick didn't want to aim him for the mile and a half Breeders' Cup Turf just yet, but he was thinking about the Mile. It was a distance Happy had always loved and it was on the turf. Marvin watched as Happy was the runaway winner of the easy allowance race. Nick went ahead and pre-entered him for the Mile and pre-entered Evil and Groovy for the Classic.

Evil had a mile breeze on October 15. He had two works scheduled between the fifteenth and November 3. Marvin groomed him better every day, hoping he would look his very best on Breeders' Cup day. On October 17 Evil had a seven-furlong work. He went easily in 1:22 and three.

The next day Marvin blanketed him up and loaded him in the trailer in the slot next to Groovy. They were shipping them to Churchill early to get Groovy used to the track and to

remind Evil of how good he did on
it. There were a few people waiting
for Evil when the trailer pulled
into the stable yard. Marvin led
him out to applause. Victor led
Groovy out and some of the people
clapped. Marvin settled Evil in
stall 1 and Groovy went in stall 3.
Marvin put his cot in stall 2.
Victor finished setting up the tack
in the tack room while Marvin fed
both of the horses.

The next day, on October 19,
Groovy galloped a mile and a
quarter over the Churchill surface.
Victor was beginning to feel
confident about his horse, but
Marvin felt Evil was better. Evil
galloped on the twentieth.

The nation was buzzing with
anticipation as the Breeders' Cup
got closer by the second. Groovy
had a six-furlong work on October
22, and he went in 1:12 flat, a
sharp move for him. It was the
fastest work for that distance of
the day. On the 23rd Evil went seven
furlongs in 1:23 flat with two sets
of reins holding him back. Marvin
knew he was getting into just the
right shape at just the right time.

10

Marvin thought Breeders' Cup week
was the most hectic week of his
life. Fans and reporters were
ambushing the barn and asking to
see Evil and Groovy. Marvin wanted
to show them how good his horse

looked, but Nick would not even begin to think of allowing it. He hired guards to watch the stalls 24/7. This was worse than Triple Crown crowds because there were people from all over the world coming to see the horses.

On October 29, just five days before the Breeders' Cup, Evil had his final work before the Classic. Nick was going to send him a mile. Marvin woke up early to see that he would give the bettors that saw him for the first time something to think about.

Nick boosted Ray aboard and gave him some brief instructions before he took Evil on his own. Ray nodded at Nick and he set off.

Evil was running effortlessly, like it was something as easy as breathing. He flew through a first quarter in :21 and one, and a half in :45 and two. He finished out the mile in a blazing time of 1:33 and four.

Marvin clapped as Evil came trotting back to the gap. Ray hopped off and looked at Nick, who was smiling. Ray knew he did well and he walked off.

Marvin was about to lead Evil through the gap when a statuesque bay horse was led through towards the direction that Marvin's horse had come from. He was about as tall as Evil but not as thick. When his rider had hopped aboard and he was ridden off, Marvin led Evil back to the barn and released him in his stall. Nick came walking up with a coffee. He smiled as he watched

Evil devour his grain. "He sure
feels good," Nick commented.
 Marvin looked at his dad with
pleading eyes. "Dad, who was that
horse that passed us at the gap?"
he asked.
 Nick turned serious again.
"That's the horse Evil has to
worry about in the Classic. In
France, he's a dirt champion. His
name is I Smile Brightly. He's an
absolute monster."
 Marvin nodded and left the barn.

~~~~~~~~~~~~~~~~~

 On Breeders' Cup eve Marvin read
the history of I Smile Brightly.
Nick was right. He was a monster.
The only time he had ever lost in
his life was his first start. Ever
since then he had been dominating
the fields much like Evil. He would
try to go out on the lead and keep
it like Evil would. He would've
been a Triple Crown winner if he
lived in America a year before. He
was a four year old and this would
be his last race. Marvin truly
believed Evil was a faster horse
and with more stamina. He went to
bed or at least tried to. At around
3:00 in the morning he went to
sleep.
 He woke up an hour later, at 4:00.
Marvin decided he wouldn't get any
sleep, so he got up and gave Evil
his quart of oats. The colt
polished them off quickly and
stared out the barn door toward the
track.

It was race day.

11

It was only 4:30 in the morning and Marvin was bouncing off the walls with excitement and nervousness. He was sitting in Evil's stall, shivering. Marvin was glad it was Evil in the stall with him because any other horse would have spooked at Marvin's bouncing and would have stepped on him. Marvin pulled out his Daily Racing Form and took one last look at the Classic field. A horse from South America had drawn the #1 post. Nick said he had no speed and would probably fade early, for he was a sprinter in his home country. The #2 horse was Ewinar. He loved this distance but was not as fast as Evil. The #3 horse was I Had a Dream, the horse that finished third in the Derby. The #4 and #5 horses were both from the same barn-a very good barn, but these horses had no chance, according to Nick.

Evil had drawn the #6 post. Marvin thought this was a good thing luck wise because all of his Triple Crown post positions had been #6. The #7 horse was Proudly Wave, the horse that finished last in the Gold Cup. I Smile Brightly had drawn the #8 post. This was not a good thing because the farther away from the rail he was, the farther in front he would be. Groovy had drawn the #9 post. Nick didn't know

what to think of the drawing. There
were only nine horses and Groovy
had drawn the very outside. He was
usually not successful unless he
had an inside post.

Evil was the morning line favorite
at even money odds. I Smile
Brightly was second choice at 5-1.
Marvin glanced at his watch.

It was 5:00 AM.

Marvin picked up his Breeders' Cup
program and decided he was going to
bet. The Juvenile Fillies was the
first championship race. He got a
piece of paper out on which he
would write down his bets and give
them to Nick. In the Juvenile
Fillies, he decided to bet on the
#4 horse, a filly that had lost her
second start but then bounced back
in her last one. Marvin bet her to
show. In the Juvenile, he bet the
#2 horse. The next race was the
Filly and Mare Turf. He was a
little touchy about this race. It
was a very level playing field,
with no heavy favorites and all
horses under 15-1. He was attracted
to the #7, who had won her last two
starts in definite fashion. He put
his money on her to place.

The Sprint was next. He didn't put
anything down for this one. The
Mile was after that. He bet Happy
to place, because he didn't feel
confident about his chances against
Grade 1 competition. After that was
the Distaff. He was confident about
a filly that had won all but two of
her six starts. He bet her to win.
The Turf was full of European
invaders, of one he liked. His name

was Distinguished, and he loved the
Turf more than Happy did. Marvin
bet him to win.

The crowning event, the Classic,
was the last race on the card. He
thought it was stuck up to bet on
his own horse, so he put a blank
for it, not that he felt Evil would
lose. He knew it would be tough.
Evil hadn't seen the likes of a
certain one of these horses before,
the French champion I Smile
Brightly.

Marvin laid his program and bet
paper down on the storage bin where
Nick's hat was. It was 6:00 and he
had spent a whole hour
handicapping. Marvin was dying to
know what the weather was going to
be like. Outside, the sun was just
beginning to rise over a clear blue
sky with no clouds on the horizon.
Marvin stretched and went back to
Evil's stall, satisfied.

~~~~~~~~~~~~~~~~

Ray was nervous. In his three
years of being a jockey he had
never ridden a horse in the
Classic, especially one as good as
this. He had mounts in every race
but the Turf. Last year he had only
ridden in the Juvenile. Evil's
winning of the Triple Crown made
people notice him as a jockey. He
was riding the favorite in the
Distaff, Sprint, and Classic.

Ray showed his ID to the guard at
Churchill's gate and he waved him
through. He went straight to the

barn that Evil was stabled in.
There he found Marvin sitting at
the door of Evil's stall, polishing
his bridle and securing all the
straps. He waved hi and gave Evil a
pat. He went to say hi to all the
other horses he was riding and then
went to the jockeys' room. He was
the first one there. He grabbed
himself a glass of water and
plopped down in front of the TV,
where some famous handicappers were
giving their picks for every race.
It was ironic that his least
favorite handicapper singled I
Smile Brightly in the Classic. He
picked up a book entitled *Kentucky
Derby History* and busied himself
till the jockeys' introduction
would come in a few hours.

~~~~~~~~~~~~~~~~~~~~

Of all the people anxious for the
Classic to come, Marvin and Victor
were probably the most excited of
them all. Each spent all morning
shining Evil or Groovy's coats and
making their tack look sparkling
clean. Marvin was almost done when
he saw that his watch read 7:45.
Gates would open in fifteen minutes
and the fans would come pouring in
like Jesus Christ had come back to
earth.
Victor had made himself a shirt
supporting Groovy. It had a picture
of him on it and it said, "Just
Groovy-Winner of the Breeders' Cup
Classic" in red and blue letters.
Marvin had one too, only with his
own horse's name on it.

At 8:00 sharp the fans came pouring in. Men in polo shirts and jeans and women in flowery hats, halter tops and flowing skirts came strolling in to get to their seats, take a tour of the track grounds or get a program and snacks.

Marvin and Victor joined Nick at the cafeteria for a quick morning snack. Nick was reading his Daily Racing Form and drinking a cup of coffee. Marvin and Victor grabbed some doughnuts and joined him. A show called *Breeders' Cup Today* was playing on the TV screen, previewing the Sprint.

Victor had a short conversation with Nick about Groovy's post while Marvin watched TV. He finished up his last doughnut and headed back to the barn. Evil was still gazing out at the track, anticipating when he would go out there and show everyone he was the best.

12

Shortly before 11:30 Ray went out to the track with all the other jockeys for the jockeys' introduction. It was his turn. He jogged out onto the track waving his home country's flag as the loudspeaker announced, "From France, Ray Buna!"

He knew that over two million people were watching him. He stared at the track's surface and moved it around with his boot as the rest of the jockeys were introduced. The

loudspeaker buzzed again, "Ladies
and gentlemen, the Breeders' Cup
jockeys! "
  Clapping came from everywhere as
all the jockeys stood on the track
in front of the grandstand. When it
was over, Ray was the first one
back to the jockeys' room. He
wasn't in the first two races, so
he settled down in a chair to
mentally prepare himself for the
third race, the Juvenile Fillies.

~~~~~~~~~~~~~~~~~~~~

  Marvin was staying in the
receiving barn with Evil as the
races went off. He didn't bet on
the first two races. He had given
Nick his bet paper right before the
jockeys' introduction. Evil was
getting anxious for race time to
come. He was pacing back and forth
in his stall and he kept staring
out at what he could see of the
track. Not even Marvin's gentle
talking could soothe him. The hot-
blooded Thoroughbred had a lot of
fire in him today. Marvin took him
out of his stall and put him in a
newly-installed set of crossties.
He got his brush out and began
brushing Evil with it. This was the
only thing that Marvin could find
that would calm him down. Evil
leaned into the crossties, enjoying
the massage. Marvin just had to
keep him calm before it was time to
take him down to the track. He got
word from the loudspeaker that the
heavy favorites had both won the

first and second races. After seven
more races it would be time.

~~~~~~~~~~~~~~~~~

 Ray was given a leg up onto the #4
horse by the trainer. This filly
was a closer and was deadly fast.
The trainer told him that she liked
to run at the back, preferably in
fifth or sixth, then stun everyone
with her speed. He went to the gate
as the 7-2 second choice. She
didn't want to get in the gate at
first, but Ray eventually convinced
her it was okay. The other ten
horses in the fourteen-horse
Juvenile Fillies field loaded, and
they were all set.
 Ray let the filly have her way
near the back of the pack until
they reached the half-pole. Then he
started to ask her to move up. She
responded immediately. She had been
traveling in seventh, but as they
passed the quarter pole he was in
third and gaining. As they turned
into the stretch she had passed the
second place horse and was closing
on the leader. As they passed the
eighth pole the lead was down to a
head, and finally she passed the
other filly under a hand-ride from
Ray. She crossed the wire a half-
length in front. Ray punched his
fist in the air and pulled the
filly up. She didn't resist. He
turned her around after she had
slowed to a walk and then cantered
her back to the gap. They placed
the blanket of flowers over her

withers and took her picture. Ray
hopped off and exchanged a few
words with the trainer. Then he
headed back to the jockeys' room to
prepare for the Juvenile.

The Juvenile Fillies was the only
winning race for Ray in races 3-7.
His Juvenile horse finished off the
board after slamming into the gate
at the break. He barely finished
third in the Filly and Mare Turf,
due to a mistake by another horse's
jockey. His Sprint horse didn't
try, and his Mile horse was
scratched due to some heat in his
right foreleg. He would try to
avenge himself in the Distaff.

~~~~~~~~~~~~~~~~~~~~~

Victor led Happy Boy down to the
paddock for the Mile. He was the
fourth-longest shot in the field at
12-1. Nick saddled him in less than
two minutes and Victor began
circling him around the paddock.
The favorite, a West Coast horse
named Under the Sun, entered the
paddock to many cheers and
whistles. The Mile jockeys came out
of their room and mounted after
discussing random subjects with
their trainers. The bugler began to
play, and Victor led Happy ridden
by his regular jockey Caleb out to
the track.

Just ten minutes later, Victor was
yelling at the top of his lungs as
Happy gained on Under the Sun who
was in front by two. Happy Boy was
coming strong, but Under the Sun

held on by a length to win under the whip. Victor went down to collect Happy and take him back to the barn. He had tried hard and was blowing. Victor rinsed him off and put him in his stall filled with fresh hay and water.

The Distaff was next. Ray pushed his mare as much as she would take, but she finished second by a head as the other filly thrust her desperate nose in front as they hit the wire.

Ray didn't have a mount for the Turf, so he pulled on his blue and red-checkered silks early and waited for the crowning event.

~~~~~~~~~~~~~~~~~~~

Marvin had Evil bridled and ready to go in the receiving barn. He was full of fire again and was pacing. Down the row, Groovy was already sweating heavily. He was pounding his foreleg against the ground, throwing his head up and wanting to get out of his stall. Evil looked eagerly out at the track, waiting for the call. The Turf was over and there were five minutes till the paddock call would come. Marvin stroked Evil's neck. "This is the biggest race of your life, Evil. Maybe bigger than the Triple Crown, even.

They say that the Breeders' Cup is where champions are crowned. You get out there and show everyone how great you really are."

Victor couldn't calm Groovy down.
He got up on two legs and pawed the
air. He reached back with his left
hind leg and kicked the stall.
Victor heard the board crack.
Finally the call came. "Horsemen,
bring your horses to the paddock
for the five million dollar
Breeders' Cup Classic. Bring your
horses to the paddock for the
Breeders' Cup Classic."
Victor clipped a lead shank to
Groovy's bridle and led him out of
the barn. Marvin did the same. He
led Evil out of his stall and
grinned. "Let's go show them your
heels," Marvin said with an
excited voice. Evil began prancing
to show his agreement as Marvin led
him from the receiving barn.
Victor and Groovy were the first
ones down to the paddock. Nick was
worried when he saw how sweaty
Groovy was already. When he saw
Evil, he couldn't have been more
pleased with his behavior. He
saddled Evil first, then Groovy
after Victor had calmed him down by
leading him around the paddock a
few times. Right as the jockeys
came out, Groovy rose high up into
the air and crowhopped a few times.
He let out a buck and then jumped
up suddenly, as if he had been
spooked. Victor tried to lead him
back to his stall, but he came
slowly and was favoring a foreleg.
Nick ran his hands up and down his
right front, and he felt heat. "I
think we should scratch," he said.
Victor nodded, his heart leaping
into his throat. "We wouldn't want

to risk injury, " he commented.
Marvin could tell Victor wanted to
cry, but couldn't in front of all
these people.
Nick made a quick phone call and
Groovy was officially scratched.
Victor let Nick unsaddle him and he
led him back to the barn. The
loudspeaker boomed. "Ladies and
gentlemen, we have a late scratch.
Just Groovy is a late scratch. "
  When Groovy was back to the barn
the jockeys mounted up. Nick rarely
said anything to the jockey. This
time he spoke. " The #8 horse
should try to go out to the lead.
Try to keep it from him. Good luck
out there, Ray. "
  The bugler began to play and
Marvin led the big black horse out
to the track. He was taken by the
pony rider and ponied down the
track toward the gate. He was
moving fluidly and with purpose, as
if he were in a dressage test.
After five minutes of warming up
they were at the gate. The first
five horses went in. Then, for the
greatest and biggest race of his
life, Evil went into the gate with
enthusiasm. Then the #7 horse went
in quietly. As I Smile Brightly
went in, Ray let out a deep breath
and prepared himself for the break.
They were all set for the Breeders'
Cup Classic.

~~~~~~~~~~~~~~~~~~~~

  When the gates opened Evil thrust
himself forward so fast that it was

something Ray had never seen or
felt the likes of. He glanced to
his right and saw that I Smile
Brightly had also broken very fast.
Ray chirped to Evil and he
responded with so much speed that
it carried him in front by ten. I
Smile Brightly was trying to get to
him, but Evil was much too fast.
Marvin must have gotten some
message through to him to break
perfectly and to run like never
before. He galloped on the front by
eight as they rounded the clubhouse
turn. The crowd was a faint hum in
the distance as the horses galloped
along unaffected by them. Back ten
lengths Ewinar was stuck to I Smile
Brightly's side. The little
chestnut horse was likely thinking
'I think I can, I think I can' as
he tried to pass the huge horse
that was twice his size. Just three
lengths behind, I Had a Dream's
jockey was watching Ewinar. He had
studied the little horse's profile.
He was gutsy and had a big heart,
but the huge bay horse going with
him had a longer stride and stamina
that could take him five miles on
the front end. He didn't know how
he did if he was being challenged
by another horse and he was not in
front. He saw the half mile pole
approaching and began to make his
move.
  As they passed the half mile pole
that glue was becoming unstuck, and
I Smile Brightly was edging in
front. Ewinar was trying his
hardest, but the giant horse had a
longer stride and was trying *his*

hardest to catch Evil, who still galloped out on the front by eight. I Had a Dream had passed Ewinar and was now in third. Proudly Wave, who had had a stalking trip in fifth, knew that Ewinar was wearing down. He began to move up. What the other horse didn't know was that Ewinar had more pride than that. As Proudly Wave drew aside Ewinar, the little horse that could, the tiny chestnut found something more inside him and a new burst of confidence. He kept his neck in front and began to run away from Proudly Wave, now gaining on I Had a Dream. I Smile Brightly was in front of Ewinar, who was now third again, by two lengths as they passed the quarter pole, but none could catch Evil. I Smile Brightly was trying his hardest to make a run, but Evil was just out for a fun gallop. He coasted home under wraps. Evil seemed to hear the other horse gaining on him, so he sped up once more and drew in front by ten. Evil passed the sixteenth pole and lunged for the wire. He hit home in front by exactly eleven lengths, as I Smile Brightly had tired out behind him in second, almost being caught by Ewinar. Ray stood in the stirrups, pulled Evil up, punched the air, and let out a loud WOO-HOO!

Marvin, in the stands, let out a woo-hoo about the same time as Ray did. He high-fived Nick, David and Sonya, whose faces where also red from screaming and jubilant with victory. He led the pack down to

the winner's circle, the most
important winner's circle since
capturing the Triple Crown.

A pony horse met Ray as he turned
Evil around at the beginning of the
backstretch. The pony's rider
looked like he had just run the
same race. "That was some race,
man! How do you feel about your
horse right now?"

Ray was breathing hard from the
combination of his ride and of the
pride he felt for his horse.
"Well, I think he's the greatest
horse that was and that he will
beat anybody who thinks that they
have a chance. He's the greatest
horse I have ever sat on and
probably the greatest horse Nick
has ever trained. I know he's never
had one of his horses win the
Breeders' Cup Classic before, and
that what he's feeling right now I
will likely never be able to feel
as a trainer. I think the French
horse ran a great race, as well,
but this horse, he was just faster,
quicker, and ran with more purpose
than any horse will ever run
with."

The pony rider smiled a somewhat
familiar smile. "I don't think any
of my horses that I rode could have
beaten him myself," he said with a
look that gave it all away.

Ray's eyes widened as he
recognized his childhood hero.
"You! I've always been the biggest
fan of yours!"

The great jockey smiled. "They
all say that, but knowing where you
came from, having won the Triple

Crown and Breeders' Cup Classic and
all, I think you're a pretty good
jockey, too, " he said as he walked
his horse away from Evil as the gap
was a few feet away from the two
horses.

Ray watched as Lance Marley, the
jockey who had won the Triple Crown
thrice and the Classic five times,
trot away on his gray horse.
Meanwhile, Marvin held his hand up
and gave Ray a high-five. "That
was excellent! I don't think he
could have done any better! "

Marvin led the giant black horse
into the winner's circle. Nick and
David lifted the winner's blanket
of flowers with *Classic* imprinted
on it onto Evil's withers. The
results became official, and the
winner's circle picture was taken.
I'm Not Evil was now the official
winner of the Breeders' Cup
Classic. Ray hopped off and was
surrounded by reporters
congratulating him and asking for
interviews. He allowed some and
then headed back to the jockeys'
room to change out of his silks.

A reporter approached Nick. "That
was an amazing performance-how do
you feel about him right now? "

Nick smiled. "He's the greatest
horse I've ever trained. "

The reporter wasn't done yet.
"Will we see any more of this
amazing horse next year, or was
that his last race? "

Nick gave his honest answer.
"More is to come. I'm going to
point him for the Donn Handicap in
February. I'm not completely sure

about the Dubai World Cup yet, but
it's definitely a consideration. "
The reporter thanked Nick and went
to find David or Sonya. Marvin led
Evil to the testing barn, and as
always, he passed the test with
flying colors. He was led back to
the barn and his fresh food and
water. Marvin watched happily as
the Classic winner dove into his
oats.

13

To Marvin's relief, Nick didn't
make him attend any parties that
night. He stayed at the barn,
watching Evil. He was still awake
when Nick came back at 11:00.
Marvin had finished the page with
Evil's two and three-year-old wins
on it.

TWO-YEAR-OLD SEASON
MAIDEN SPECIAL WEIGHT
ALLOWANCE
ALLOWANCE
SANFORD STAKES (G2)
HOPEFUL STAKES (G1)
CHAMPAGNE STAKES (G1)
THREE-YEAR-OLD SEASON
ALLOWANCE
FLORIDA DERBY (G1)
KENTUCKY DERBY (G1)
PREAKNESS STAKES (G1)
BELMONT STAKES (G1)
JIM DANDY STAKES (G2)
TRAVERS STAKES (G1)
JOCKEY CLUB GOLD CUP (G1)
BREEDERS' CUP CLASSIC (G1)

Champion Three-Year-Old and Horse
of the Year^
 UNDEFEATED IN FIFTEEN LIFETIME
STARTS

 Marvin added one more thing to the
column:

FOUR-YEAR-OLD SEASON

 Marvin knew Evil had already
secured Horse of the Year by way of
his win in the Classic. He was a
runaway winner with the Three-Year-
Old title since he won the Triple
Crown. By being undefeated in
fifteen lifetime starts he equaled
the great horse Colin, and was
maybe even better.
 The next day Nick confirmed his
plans of the Donn Handicap and was
almost completely sure of the World
Cup. They planned to ship Evil to
Gulfstream the next week. For years
Nick's star horses had spent their
winters in Gulfstream, and that
tradition would continue on until
Nick didn't train any more.
 A few days later, on November 9,
Groovy had a vet check. He had
overstretched a tendon before the
Classic and the result was a
scratch. His tendon was back to
normal again, and Nick planned to
campaign him one more year, this
time as a five year old. He would
stay in America for the stakes
there while Evil would likely go to
Dubai for the World Cup. Groovy,
like Evil, was going down to
Gulfstream for the winter.

On early November 11 Victor and
Marvin loaded Evil and Groovy into
the trailer in two separate stalls.
Both horses were wearing blue and
red-checkered blankets in the
chilly weather. Groovy plodded into
the trailer like an old pony horse,
and Evil walked in with the grace
and elegance of the Thoroughbred
that he was. Once he and Groovy
were secure, Marvin closed the
trailer door and hopped in the
passenger seat. They began the long
drive to Gulfstream in South
Florida.

~~~~~~~~~~~~~~~~~

"Marvin, we're here," Nick said
as he parked the car in
Gulfstream's stable yard.
Marvin yawned and sat up. He
glanced at the clock and saw that
it read 10:15 PM. They had left
around 6:45 AM, so it had been
about eighteen hours and thirty
minutes since they had left
Kentucky. Nick got out of the truck
and shut the door. Marvin opened
his and scrambled out. He joined
Victor at the back of the trailer
and opened it up. Evil rolled an
eye back and stomped his foot as if
to say, "Finally! What took you so
long?"
Marvin led him out of the trailer
and took him to his old stall in
the security barn that he had
stayed in when he was turning into
a three year old. He released Evil
in it and gave him some hay and
water. Marvin saw to it that Groovy

had been settled in and he sat at the door of Evil's stall and read the newest edition of the *Bloodhorse*. He was glued to it for an hour till he was finally done with it. He needed to go to sleep soon, or else he would be very tired the next day.

Evil settled in easily to his old stall at Gulfstream in Nick's barn. He had spent last winter there and he was very familiar with it. Groovy remembered being down at Gulfstream in the past, and he also liked it.

Nick had confirmed the day before that Groovy would stay in the United States for the spring while Evil traveled over to the United Arab Emirates for the Dubai World Cup. He was just recently invited over there along with a few other horses from around the world. Groovy would follow a plan much like that of the year before. His overstretched tendon was almost completely healed, as it had been enough to scratch him from the Classic but not enough to take him out of training for months.

After finishing second in the Mile, Happy Boy was shipped back to David and Sonya's farm. He had no definite target for the next three months, though his year-end goal was the Breeders' Cup Turf. He had come out of the Mile in excellent shape and in perfect form.

Nick had also decided that this was both Evil and Groovy's final year of racing. Both would likely once again travel to the Breeders'

Cup for the Classic at year's end,
and then they would be retired to
stud. David and Sonya had
syndicated Evil at the end of his
two year old season; they also
decided as long as they paid the
breeding fee, anyone could bring
their mares to Groovy.

Marvin peeked over the edge of
Evil's stall door. The giant black
horse was dozing peacefully, not
knowing what lay ahead of him.

14

Two weeks later, on November 25,
Evil had his first breeze since the
Classic. He easily went a mile as
if it was as easy as breathing.
Groovy cautiously had his first a
few days later. When he went
without a hitch in front of the
vet's eyes, he gave him the all
clear, and Groovy went back into
serious training.

When December rolled around, Evil
was at his full height, weight, and
width. He was eighteen and a
quarter hands high, almost 1,300
pounds, and nearly four feet across
in width. He was perfectly fit,
healthy, and gorgeous.

What was different about him in
December was that he had gotten
more pushy and stallion-like. He
was very docile as a two-year-old
and earlier in the spring, but now
he was becoming more aggressive,
which wasn't good. With his size,
Evil could bulldoze anything in his

path. Under control, he was a great
horse, but if he ran wild, he could
seriously hurt someone or
something.

 On December 10, Evil had a seven-
furlong work. He went in his usual
quickness, timing in 1:22 and
three. As usual, it was faster than
Nick wanted, but Ray thought it
didn't challenge him at all. Evil
wasn't winded afterwards and he
likely felt like he could do it
again.

 Later that day Marvin sat at the
door of Evil's stall, writing a
biography about him. He described
Evil's 15 lifetime wins that kept
him undefeated and his personality.
Evil was standing at the front of
his stall looking at a water bucket
that must have been interesting,
for he stared at it with his ears
up. Marvin noticed the black horse
looking at it so he picked it up
and brought it over to Evil. He
sniffed it and then lost whatever
interest he had in it. Marvin
chuckled at this and went back to
writing.

             ~~~~~~~~~~~~~~~~~~~~~

Two weeks later Evil was woken up
at around midnight as Marvin burst
into his stall chanting 'Merry
Christmas'. He handed Evil five or
six sugar cubes and a pat. He
pulled Evil's old sheet off and
laid on a new one that was blue and
red-checkered with his name on it.
He checked all the straps, gave

Evil another pat, and left the
barn.
 Just a few hours later Marvin came
back to the barn. Evil was sleeping
again, and this time Marvin decided
not to disturb him. He plopped down
onto a bay of hay and started to
read the Form.

~~~~~~~~~~~~~~~~~~~~

 It was January 4, and the Donn
Handicap was a little under a month
away. Nick had made the decision to
pre-enter Groovy for the Sunshine
Millions Classic on the twenty-
sixth. He was training nicely and
Nick thought the race would suit
him perfectly. He had a little bit
of an idea of where he would go
after that, but it wasn't for
certain. Evil almost had a rock-
solid plan for the year, consisting
of all stakes races. Marvin was
certain that no horse could beat
Evil or even get close to him. In
Groovy's next race, the Sunshine
Millions Classic, Nick thought that
the main threat was a Uruguayan
horse named All For You. The
chestnut horse closed like a
freight train when no other horse
was in his way.
 Evil was done growing in size, but
still young in mind. One day a new
groom came to work in Nick's barn.
He was only 14 and did not have a
lot of experience. He walked a
little too close to Evil's stall
one day and Evil thought the
groom's orange shirt looked

delicious. He jumped forward and tore off a large chunk of the groom's sleeve. The groom yelped as Evil accidentally caught a little bit of flesh in his teeth. Marvin happened to be standing across the aisle cleaning a bridle when it happened. "Be careful around him," Marvin warned. "He can be nippy."

The groom examined the torn skin. "That's okay," he said. "Worse has happened before. My mom's Saddlebred took off half a finger once. Oh, by the way, I'm Tim."

Marvin shook his hand. "I'm Marvin, and that's Evil," he said, pointing to the black horse that stared at the groom's shirt like he wanted another bite.

Tim put a finger on his chin. "I'm Not Evil?"

Marvin nodded.

Tim turned to face Evil. "Before I came here I watched that horse and stared at his profile on the Internet. He's a lot bigger than he looks on TV. I wonder what Ray feels when he's on his back…"

"You might be lucky, in March he's not going to be here," Marvin said.

"Why?" Tim asked with a question in his voice.

Marvin gave Evil a pat. "He's going to Dubai for the World Cup."

Tim nodded. "When is he leaving?"

Marvin scratched his head. "I'm not sure, probably at the beginning of March. The track is a little weird over there and Nick, um, my

dad, wants him to be able to handle
it well. "

Tim nodded again. "Oh. Well, I
should probably get back to work.
See you around. "

15

A week later, on the 17th, Evil and
Groovy had a work scheduled on the
same day. Groovy was going six
furlongs, and Evil was going seven.
Tim finished all his barn chores
early to watch Evil, who was going
first. Nick gave Ray a leg up and
nodded. Ray made a clicking noise
at Evil and he began jogging. After
a furlong of warm-up, Evil exploded
into a run. Tim watched in awe as
the giant moved so effortlessly and
quickly over the Gulfstream track.
Ray let out a little in the reins,
and Evil gave more. He was moving
at almost a ten-clip when he
crossed the wire. Ray stood in the
short exercise stirrups and slowed
Evil to a trot. Evil fought the bit
but eventually cooperated. As Tim
watched Evil come back, he heard
hoofbeats come up behind him at a
walking pace. He turned around and
saw Victor leading Groovy, who was
also fitted with an exercise
saddle, up to Nick. Victor gave a
quick glance around and looked
confused. "Where's Eddie? " he
asked.

Nick turned to Victor. "Eddie
wasn't available to work him this
morning, so I'm going to let Ray do

it. You can trust him. By the way, this is Tim. He's a new groom I hired to help out with some of the new three-year-olds. Tim, this is Victor. He's the personal groom of Just Groovy. Oh, and Marvin, he went in 1:22 and four."

Victor nodded and shook Tim's hand as Evil pranced up to Marvin, who clipped a lead rope to his snaffle bit ring. Ray hopped off Evil and then leaped onto Groovy with Nick's help. Nick mumbled "six furlongs" and Groovy set off. Victor noted that Groovy was being a little rambunctious this morning. When Ray asked for him to run, he tossed up his head and refused for a brief moment, then took off at a blistering run. Ray kept a decent hand on him to keep him from going out of control.   Groovy's long stride covered the ground in quick time as he finished the work out in a brisk 1:11 and two. The chestnut horse slowed into a quick trot as he neared the gap. Nick was talking to one of the official clockers on his cell phone. "I got him in 1:11 and two. What'd you get him in? 1:11 and one? Okay."

Victor took a hold of Groovy's bridle as Ray halted him. The blond jockey hopped off. "Well, what do you think?"

Nick nodded. "Good, good. I'll give him one more before the Millions Classic. It was satisfying."

Ray thanked Nick and jogged off to the jockey's room to hang out before the afternoon's races.

~~~~~~~~~~~~~~~~~~~~~~

A short week later, Groovy had his
last work before his five year old
debut, a five furlong slow work.
Eddie was back aboard for it and
Groovy was on his best behavior.
The official clocker timed him in
1:02 and two, but Nick got him in
1:02 flat. The Sunshine Millions
Classic was just two days away, and
Groovy benefited off of works that
were scheduled right before his
races.

Evil was galloped two miles every
day, to keep his muscles in tone.
Nick often let Marvin ride, for
Evil was always on his best
behavior for him. The Donn Handicap
was in 8 days, and Evil was ready.
Groovy had drawn the number 2 post
position for the Millions Classic,
which was a little closer to the
rail than Nick had wanted, but it
was probably going to change where
Groovy laid on the pace a little
bit. Nick now wanted Groovy to be a
little to the outside of the
pacesetters and a couple lengths
back, instead of right up there.

On the 25th, the night before the
Millions Classic, Groovy got
special treatment from Victor and
Marvin, only this time he didn't
try to take Marvin's arm off.
Victor gave Groovy a bath in the
dwindling rays of the Florida sun
as Marvin cleaned his tack extra
carefully. Groovy relaxed and put
his head almost on the ground. When
Victor turned off the hose,

Groovy's dark chestnut, fiery red coat glimmered in the sun's final goodnight. Marvin partially dried him off with a towel, then put his blanket on him. Back in the barn, Victor released him in his stall and whispered only in Groovy's ear:
"Tomorrow's the day…"

16

Victor was surprised he didn't wake up earlier than 5:00 AM. He rose at 5:13 and fed Groovy his quart of grain. He polished it off and looked at Victor as if to say, "Is that all this mighty fine horse gets?"
A few hours later Victor joined Marvin in the track kitchen for a hearty breakfast of pancakes, chocolate milk, sausage, and waffles. When Marvin and Victor strolled back to the barn, they literally felt that just the tiniest speck of food would make them explode. The Sunshine Millions Classic was just under 7 hours away. Nick had told Marvin to walk Evil around the barn a few times in the morning to give him some form of exercise. Marvin put a thick leather halter on Evil and attached a lead shank with a chain to it. He led Evil out of the barn and into the little sun that was shining that morning. The forecast for the day was rain, and the worst was to come around post time for the Classic. Evil bowed his neck and

walked stiffly. Marvin clucked at
him and he moved into a regular
trot. He slowed him down after a
few strides, and he started to walk
normally again. Marvin guessed that
he just wanted to stretch his legs.
He didn't give Evil much walking
time, just three times around the
barn. He put the black horse back
in his stall and went to see how
Victor was doing with Groovy.

Victor had him finished just a
few minutes before the time to
bring the horses to the receiving
barn came. Much later, when the
call to the paddock blared through
the receiving barn, Victor leaped
up and made sure he was the first
one to the paddock. As Victor led
Groovy through the tunnel, Groovy
gave a little buck. Victor smiled
at him, knowing that he felt good.
When Nick had him saddled in the
paddock, Victor could only lead him
around just once, for he kept
bucking. Soon the jockeys
materialized at their trainers'
horses' stalls. Victor asked Nick
about the bucking.

Nick scratched his head. "He
seems full of energy today…"

Nick gave Eddie a leg up and
nodded. Victor led Groovy out to
the track as the bugler played.
Nick headed up to the owners' boxes
where Marvin, David, and Sonya were
already standing.

Eddie felt the familiar smooth
trot of Just Groovy beneath him as
the 10 horses approached the
starting gate. Groovy let out a few
crowhops as he was led up to the

number 2 stall. Eddie gave him a little swat with his whip, and he moved into the gate.

~~~~~~~~~~~~~~~~~

 Groovy exploded like lightning from the gate, a few steps in front of every horse. When the pacesetters caught up, Eddie had a hard time restraining him. He was very headstrong today, which was unlike him. Eddie moved him to the outside of the leading horse and took a good hold on his mouth. Groovy threw his head up and lost a bit of momentum. In the backstretch, when they had passed the half-mile pole, Groovy took the bit in his teeth and began pulling Eddie along the track and closer to the lead. He had almost full control as they passed the quarter pole. Groovy was finally given his head by Eddie as they turned for home in the Sunshine Millions Classic. Groovy shot past the tiring leader and dominated the race down to the wire. He came home three lengths in front, with All For You a fast closing second.
 Eddie pulled him up and gave him a pat on the neck as a reward for hard work. He trotted him back to the gap for the winners' circle picture. He was blowing heavily, almost giving the race everything. Marvin helped Victor take him back to the barn and cool him off. When he was released in his stall, the thought came to Marvin:

The Donn Handicap was in a week.

17

Marvin led Evil down to the track the next morning for a gallop. Nick had given him permission to ride him, and Marvin loved it. When they reached the gap Nick and Tim were standing there. Tim was wisely not wearing Evil's favorite color today. He clasped a hand on Evil's bridle as Nick helped Marvin aboard the huge horse. Nick muttered "take him two miles" and Marvin clucked to Evil. He moved into an effortless gallop down the track into the rising sun. Marvin was glad he wore dark goggles to allow him to see through the sun's rays. Evil floated over the ground in an effort as easy as breathing. Marvin thought Evil behaved better for him than for Ray. He did get a little headstrong as he galloped past other horses, though.

When Evil finished his gallop, he cantered back to the gap and stood perfectly still for Marvin to get off. Nick was standing a few feet away from Evil staring in amazement. "He hasn't behaved that well since the beginning of his three year old season!" he said.

Marvin led Evil back to the barn and turned him loose in his stall. He gave him some fresh hay and water and went to the track kitchen for some breakfast.

A short five days later, it was the eve of the Donn Handicap. Evil had drawn post six and had been assigned the high weight of 135 pounds. Nick thought this was too harsh a weight for him, but Marvin thought he would be an even greater horse if he continued to win his races with domination under heavy weight. Marvin was once again analyzing every other horse's gallops and races like he did on the eve of the Derby. The only horse that Marvin thought could be a threat was a gray horse with the intentional name of Powdered Snow. He was fast, but not always consistent. But anything could happen in horse racing.

Marvin woke up at 6:00 sharp on Donn Handicap day. He poured a quart of oats into Evil's food tub and watched him devour it. When it was gone the gigantic black horse looked out the barn door to the track.

The champion was back.

~~~~~~~~~~~~~~~~~~~~~~

Nick still insisted that morning that if Marvin groomed or even brushed Evil any more his hair would fall off. Marvin didn't think so. Evil's black coat shined in the deepest, richest black Marvin had ever seen. It was so black it almost highlighted a shade of blue. His coat was much darker than his number 6 saddlecloth.

There were originally 7 horses in the field, but by noon on the day

of the race, it was just a three
horse race with the remaining post
positions being 2, 6, and 7. The
number 2 horse was the familiar
Ewinar, Evil was the 6, and 7 was
Powdered Snow.

When Marvin took Evil to the
receiving barn before the call to
the paddock, he was followed by an
Arabian-looking man that appeared
to be in his late twenties. As he
walked a little closer, Evil threw
his head up and snorted. Marvin
gave Evil a little tug on his lead
to hurry him away from the strange
man. When Evil was settled in his
stall in the receiving barn, Marvin
parked a lawn chair in front of it
and sat down. The call would come
in a few hours.

Just a few hours later the
loudspeaker crackled. "Horsemen,
bring your horses to the paddock
for the Donn Handicap. Bring your
horses to the paddock for the Donn
Handicap."

Marvin collected Evil from his
stall and led him down to the
paddock, which was swamped with
reporters for such a small field.
Most of them were hovering around
Nick, who was desperately trying to
shoo them away. All of them in
Evil's way jumped aside as the big
horse parted them like the Red Sea.
Nick saddled him as quick as ever
and Evil began walking around the
paddock. The gray horse, Powdered
Snow, was the second horse to begin
walking and Ewinar the last. All
three jockeys came out to the
paddock and were given help up onto

the Thoroughbreds. The familiar
bugler's call came as the three
horses were led out to the track by
their handlers. Marvin reluctantly
handed off Evil, then went to join
David, Sonya, Nick, Victor, and Tim
in the owners' boxes.

Ray thought Evil felt better than
ever. Nick had him in top form, and
the glossiness of his coat and
speed showed for it. After around
eight minutes of warming up, the
horses approached the starting
gate. Ewinar went in with his usual
calmness, then Evil strolled in
like it was so easy, and not scary
at all. As Powdered Snow walked in,
Ray prepared himself for the break
by leaning forward. Evil's final
season was about to begin.

~~~~~~~~~~~~~~~~~~~

Evil launched himself out of the
gate lightning fast. He snatched
the possibility of an early lead
away from the other horses as he
took a five-length advantage. As
they headed into the clubhouse
turn, Evil was beginning to pull
Ray along. Ray's arms were not in
top rating strength at the time
because he hadn't ridden Evil in a
while. Evil pulled him through an
opening half mile in :46 and four,
and kept getting faster. He seemed
to fly through the first part of
the race. When he passed the half-
mile pole, that flying turning to
soaring as every furlong was at
least a fifth of a second faster

than the previous one. At the
quarter pole, after he had gone
seven furlongs, his total time was
1:22 and 1/5 seconds. Evil turned
for home in the Donn Handicap nine
lengths in front and widening. He
glided by the sixteenth pole twelve
in front, and finally hit the wire
fourteen lengths in front of
Powdered Snow. Ray held his fist in
the air and hooted. Evil had run
that final eighth in almost ten
seconds, which was unbelievably
fast after he had already gone a
mile. Ray realized he had probably
broken the track record for a mile
and an eighth at Gulfstream. He
pulled Evil up to a trot and turned
him around. He clucked at Evil to
move him into a canter towards the
winner's circle. He headed toward
the winner's circle sort of
lackadaisically. Marvin high-fived
Ray and led Evil into the Donn
Handicap winner's circle. Evil
looked at the track as if the time
for his next race was now. Marvin
looked into the horse's eyes.
  His next stop was Dubai.

18

  Evil came out of the race very
well, like it was merely an act of
fun. Nick was busily in the process
of finding a flight for Evil to
Dubai. The flight there and back
would be the longest trip of his
life.
  He was very playful these days.
Often he would dance around Marvin

as he walked him. He still liked to try to get a bite out of Tim's shirt as he walked past. Nick told Tim to swat him on the nose, but Evil kept to his little ways.

A few days after the Donn win Marvin wrote down under the four year old season column:

DONN HANDICAP (G1)

Marvin wasn't going to write down Evil's starting record until he was retired at the end of the year. If all stayed well and Evil kept winning, his final race would likely be the Breeders' Cup Classic at the end of the year.

Just Groovy was being aimed for the Santa Anita Handicap again. If he won again this year, he would be the fourth horse in history to win the Big Cap two consecutive years. The horses that did that before him were John Henry, Milwaukee Brew, and Lava Man. It was at the beginning of March, in about a month. Nick always liked to get his horses there early if he could, so he was looking for a flight.

On February 12, he successfully found a flight for Evil to Dubai. It was a trip from New York to England for a fuel stop to the airport closest to Nad Al Sheba, the place where the World Cup and a few other big races were held. The flight left on February 20th. A few other contenders were flying on the same plane for some big races over there, like the Duty Free and UAE Derby.

Nick had also found a flight for
Groovy to California. It was a
FedEx flight that went from Miami
International Airport to Los
Angeles International Airport. He
would likely be the only horse on
the flight. That plane left in a
few days, on February 17th.

Nick would not fly out to
California with Groovy; he was
going to Dubai to supervise Evil's
training. Victor, Tim, and Nick's
assistant trainer would fly out
with him. Marvin would go to Dubai
with Evil and Nick.

On the 15th, two days before Groovy
would leave for California, Marvin
and Victor packed most of his tack
that he would need for his stay in
California. All of his tack was
stored in a few tack trunks and
loaded onto the trailer. He would
not need any of it the next day,
for he was just walking. Marvin and
Nick would pack Evil's stuff a few
days later.

The day before Groovy's flight
left, Marvin joined Victor as he
walked the chestnut horse around
the shedrow. He was walking with
his head up, looking at all the
happenings around him. Victor had
obviously groomed him very well,
for the irregular white blaze on
his forehead was gleaming against
his chestnut coat. The last time
Groovy had gone to California was
for last year's Big 'Cap, and he
seemed to love the sunny weather.
Nick thought that maybe he would
base Groovy in California for the

rest of the year if he continued to flourish in the sunny weather.

Victor and Marvin talked as they walked Groovy. Marvin started the conversation. "Are you going to watch the World Cup on TV?"

Victor gave him a sarcastic look. "You know I will. What about you? You'll watch the Big Cap on TV if you can, right?"

"If I can," Marvin said. "I try to watch the race every year if I can, whether one of our horses is running or not."

"That's good…" Victor commented. "How do you think Evil will handle the plane trip to Dubai?"

Marvin scratched his head. "I don't know. When he was a three year old, he handled the plane trip to Pimlico, but I don't know how he'll travel to another country overseas! There will probably be other horses on the plane whinnying really loud, and that might scare him."

Victor nodded. "Maybe. Groovy handles flights really well."

Victor and Marvin finished walking Groovy and put him back in his stall. Victor gave him a pat. "This is the last day of your life you'll be in Gulfstream's barn, Groovy," he said with a tone of farewell in his voice.

Groovy looked at him like he didn't care.

19

The next morning Victor and Marvin
got up extra early to collect
Groovy from the barn and take him
to the airport. Groovy felt the
change in the minds of the people
around him and danced in circles on
the end of the lead rope. Victor
shortened the rope, and Groovy
showed his displeasure by throwing
his head up. They got him into the
trailer with a little work, and
hopped into the truck.

When the truck was given
permission to go back by the
planes, Victor began to bounce up
and down in excitement. The plane
would take off in half an hour.
Nick halted the truck so Victor and
his assistant trainer could get out
and unload Groovy. Marvin loaded
the tack trunks onto a baggage
carrier as Groovy pranced out of
the trailer. He had thick traveling
bandages around his legs and a
blanket on. He was on his best
behavior for Victor as he was led
toward the plane. Victor led Groovy
up the ramp and into the area where
he would be for the flight. As
Groovy was halted in a certain
spot, some airport workers came and
built a small box stall around him
so he couldn't move. Groovy didn't
make a move as the stall was
completed and Victor joined him in
it. The assistant trainer had a
seat reserved in first-class, so it
would be Victor and Groovy alone
for almost four hours in the one
area of the plane. The workers
began to close the door of the
plane. Marvin gave a big, cheesy

smile, jumped up and down, and
waved as he got a last glimpse of
his friend and the horse.
 Victor waved bye to Marvin. It
would probably be the last glimpse
of him for a few weeks, or for a
long while.

~~~~~~~~~~~~~~~~~

 Half an hour later, in midair,
Victor was sitting upright in
Groovy's stall, bored. The chestnut
horse had dozed off into a lazy
sleep. Victor was counting the
hairs on his arm to keep himself
occupied. Suddenly, the plane hit
some turbulence and it woke Groovy
up. He pricked up his ears and
moved a little uneasily. Victor
stood up and went to his side.
"It's okay, Groovy. It's just
empty air that's making the plane
bounce."
 Groovy calmed down a little bit
when the turbulence was over. He
lowered his head and began to go
back to sleep. Groovy did, in fact,
handle flights very well.

~~~~~~~~~~~~~~~~~~~

 Back at Gulfstream, Marvin was
packing some of Evil's tack for
Dubai. Extra bits, reins, and
saddle pads might be needed in
Dubai if something were to break.
Evil himself was hanging his head
over the stall door, watching
Marvin. It was two in the afternoon

and he was bored. He'd already had
his walk, his morning grain and his
grooming time. Evil pawed at the
straw on the floor of his stall,
trying to get Marvin's attention
again.

The flight for Dubai left in three
days. The approximate departure
time was about noon, so Marvin
figured they should be at the
airport at about 11 AM. Marvin
wondered if Evil would like the
sunny, hot Middle Eastern weather.

Marvin finished packing extra tack
and left the barn to get a snack.
Evil watched as he left the barn.
When he was out of sight, Evil
stomped his foot on the ground as
if to say, "HELLO? Did you forget
about me? "

~~~~~~~~~~~~~~~~~~

Victor was woken up by the
screeching of jet engines and tires
on the runway. They had landed in
California already. Victor did not
know when he had fallen asleep, but
it had made the time go faster.
Victor listened as the plane taxied
to a stop at the terminal. Groovy
was stomping his foot, sick of
being in the plane. When the door
was opened up, Victor could see
that it was sunny outside. The
workers came and broke down
Groovy's stall so he could stretch
and move around. As soon as the
ramp was let down, Victor led
Groovy off the plane. It was hot in
California today, and Victor was

still wearing his sweatshirt from
the chilly Gulfstream weather.
Victor began walking Groovy in
circles as he waited for a trailer
to arrive and take him to Santa
Anita Park. Nick's assistant
trainer hadn't shown up yet. Victor
wondered if he had gotten lost.

Groovy still had his blanket on in
the hot weather, so Victor took it
off and laid it on the ground a
short distance away. Groovy was
checking everything out, looking
everywhere with his ears pricked
up.

Finally the assistant trainer
showed up. He was driving a truck
with a trailer attached. He stopped
the truck and opened the trailer.
Victor walked Groovy in one more
circle, then led him up the ramp.
Some airport workers unloaded the
tack trunks from the plane and put
them in the storage section of the
trailer. One picked up the blanket
and put it in with the tack trunks.

Victor made sure that every latch
on the trailer was fastened, then
hopped into the truck. Nick's
assistant trainer started the truck
and drove through the airport
gates. They were on their way to
Santa Anita.

20

The next two days at Gulfstream
Marvin spent packing Evil's things
and grooming him. Evil had a few
slow gallops on the main track. He

would never run at Gulfstream
again.
On February 19, the day before the
flight left, Marvin called Victor
in California to see how he and
Groovy were doing. Victor sounded
happy but worn out. "The flight
over here was stressful, but it was
worth it. The weather over here is
perfect, and Groovy loves it!"
Marvin half-wished he could be
over there with the warm weather.
But he would soon be in warm
weather too, in Dubai. "I'll be in
warm weather soon, too," Marvin
said.
"Yeah, you will," Victor
replied.
Marvin heard Nick calling him.
"My dad probably wants me to help
him pack some more tack, so I'd
better go," Marvin told Victor.
"All right. I guess I'll talk to
you later or see you on TV next
month. Bye."
"Bye."
Marvin hung up the phone and went
to help Nick, who was busy packing
the exercise saddles and Evil's
bridle. A thought came to Marvin as
he was helping. "Is Ray coming
with us?"
Nick put down a saddle. "Yeah. He
won't be on our same flight. He's
coming over here sometime in the
middle of March because he still
has a couple of stakes horses to
ride in other races."
Marvin nodded. "Oh."
Marvin went to bed that
night…barely. He was literally
bouncing up and down in his cot in

the barn. After all, they were going to Dubai the next day for the 6 million World Cup in March! Nick scheduled the flight early because the Dubai surface was a little bit different, and he didn't know how Evil would handle it.

~~~~~~~~~~~~~~~~~~~~

Marvin turned over in his cot, waking up. He pulled his watch over to him from his packed bag.

It was 3:00 AM.

Marvin rolled out of bed and went to Evil's stall. The eighteen hand horse was quietly dozing in the back of his stall. Marvin quietly entered the stall and collapsed in the straw. He accidentally let out a yawn and woke Evil up. The great horse looked down at him with a look that said, "What was that for? I was sleeping! "

Marvin gave him a pat. "Sorry, " he said as he sat up. Marvin decided he wanted to groom Evil, so he left the stall to get a brush. When he came back Evil was dozing again. Marvin decided not to disturb him again, so he went back to his cot and, somehow, fell asleep.

After only about two more hours of sleep, Marvin woke up again at 5:15. This time Evil had his head out from over the stall door, wanting breakfast. He nudged Marvin as he walked by towards the feed room. Marvin smiled, watching the big horse nicker at him and try to get his attention. For most horses, first priority was food, then sleep, then work. Marvin carefully measured out Evil's grain, then dumped it in his feed bowl. Evil gobbled it up without acknowledgement of Marvin.

Meanwhile, Nick sleepily staggered out of his cot and checked the time on his watch, which was lying a few feet away on the packed tack trunks.

The watch read 6:13.

Marvin has probably already fed the horses, Nick thought. He walked the shedrow, checking all his horses' feed tubs. All were empty. Evil was dozing in the back of his stall, so he had obviously been fed. Evil would always come to attention at 5 sharp, wanting to be fed. He would not go back to sleep until everything was gone.

Nick searched the barn that morning for Marvin, who was avoiding Nick on purpose to frustrate him. Nick finally caught him in Evil's stall. Marvin was reading a list of all the horses invited to the World Cup. Evil had his head on Marvin's shoulder. He almost looked like he was reading off the list of competitors that couldn't beat him. Marvin looked up at Nick with a grin that stretched across his whole face.

At 8:00 the predawn frost glimmered on the grass like diamonds as the February sun began to sizzle over Gulfstream Park. It was unusually warm today, warmer than the weatherman predicted.

Marvin's excitement was growing
like a tornado that destroyed
everything in its path. Nick had
blurted out that they would leave
at 11:00. He also informed Marvin
that the plane would have to stop
in England for a fuel stop, which
Marvin had forgotten about. Nick
hit himself for letting Marvin know
that. He was so excited that he
would probably go around telling
all the reporters and it would end
up on the 6:00 news. He managed to
catch Marvin before that happened
and sent him to Evil's stall to
bandage him up and get him ready.
Marvin happily accepted this task
and hauled his enormous grooming
trunk to Evil's stall. Nick was
surprised that the bulk of pointy
grooming things didn't spook Evil.
 Marvin loved spending time with
Evil. He loved to know that the
huge, powerful black horse wouldn't
hurt him. He thoroughly groomed
Evil and picked out his hooves.
Then he knelt at Evil's feet and
began putting ultra-thick traveling
bandages around his legs. Marvin
was grateful that Evil wasn't like
Groovy, who would tear his bandages
off with his teeth and fling them a
distance away.
 At 10:30 Marvin had Evil
completely ready. He was outfitted
in a red and blue-checkered stable
sheet, thick white traveling
bandages, and an extra-strong
leather halter with a thick chain
on it. Nick had the trailer backed
up near the barn, ready for Evil to
be led in. Nick himself was nowhere

in sight. Marvin figured he had probably gone to the track kitchen to get some more food and make himself even fatter. Marvin plopped himself down on the ground and let Evil graze. One of his favorite things to do besides grooming and riding was to sit in the grass and let a horse graze by his feet.

About ten minutes later Nick showed up, carrying a slice of pizza. He slightly grinned at Marvin and let the trailer ramp down. Marvin led the big colt up into the trailer and tied him to one of the bars. Evil stomped his foot, sick of all the traveling. Nick smiled. "Just one more year of this, Evil, then you'll be retired to stud duty."

The words hit Marvin like a speeding car. Not once had he thought of Evil's retirement. He couldn't imagine racing without the black horse, and he was sure that no other racing fan in the world could, either. If he could be just as good as a stallion as he was on the track, he would be remembered as the greatest sire in history.

But Marvin was getting ahead of himself. Evil was not going to be retired until the middle of November, after the Breeders' Cup. He would likely run in the Classic again. The five million dollar race would be his last. If all things went well, he would NOT dodge Groovy again.

And Groovy always meant business.

21

Nick drove the rental truck and
trailer through the Miami airport
gates and back towards where the
planes were. The plane would take
off in thirty minutes, and another
of the other Dubai-bound horses was
arriving, too. A three year old
gray colt that was running in the
UAE Derby was unloading from his
trailer. He was giving his handler
a hard time by rearing and bucking.
He had obviously never been around
a plane before. The airport crew
helped to haul him up the ramp and
into the underside of the plane. He
had probably already been in
quarantine. Nick barely convinced
the airport officials after a full
health check back at Gulfstream
that his horse was healthy and
didn't need quarantine. Marvin
circled Evil outside as they built
a small wooden stall around the
gray colt, which showed its dislike
by throwing his head up and down.
When they had him under a decent
amount of control, they gave Marvin
permission to take Evil up the
ramp. Marvin halted him inside the
plane a distance away from the
other colt. The airport workers
built another small stall around
him. Nick waved bye to Marvin as
they closed up the area.
 Marvin and Evil were in a stall
about a hundred feet away from the
gray colt and his handler. As the
plane's engines roared to life, the
other colt began to get uneasy. He

shifted from side to side and
looked about the airplane. As the
plane taxied toward the runway, the
colt pawed at the ground. The plane
was now on the runway. It began to
pick up speed, which startled the
gray and caused him to rear. The
plane was almost at takeoff speed
now. Right before the plane lifted
off, the colt reared in the air as
high as his short frame would
allow. His young handler tried in
vain to settle him by yelling
"Easy! Easy!" but it was no use.
The colt continued to paw the air,
screaming like a stallion. Even the
mild-mannered Evil began to whinny
nervously. The handler of the gray
colt was almost crying in his
pleading as he tried to yank him
down. Not even the chain on the
colt's nose was taking him down.
For a few seconds he seemed to have
never been tamed. When the other
handler yelled, Evil let out the
loudest scream Marvin had ever
heard from a horse. There was a
glint of wildness and fire in his
eyes. As the plane slowly lifted
off the runway, the gray colt's
handler took his belt and looped it
around the horse's nose to bring
him down. The colt was down to
Earth for the few seconds that the
plane needed to lift up into the
air and level out. When the plane
was stabilized in the air, the
handler of the gray colt took his
belt off the colt's nose and put it
back on. The young horse in his
moment of fright had ripped a
bloody opening across his nose. He

had been so scared that he had ignored the sharp chain and ripped his skin open. Marvin had never heard Evil scream before, and he never knew it could be so loud.

After an hour in the air both horses had settled down. The gray colt was covered in sweat but settled, and Evil was slightly dozing. Marvin picked at his nails, bored. He figured he could sleep a little until they got to England. Marvin leaned his head against the back of Evil's stall and closed his eyes. He didn't fall asleep slowly.

~~~~~~~~~~~~~~~~~

The next thing Marvin heard was the screeching of the plane's wheels on the runway and the anxious whinny of the colt one hundred yards away. He glanced up and saw that the landing had just woken Evil up, too. The black horse gazed out of his stall and towards the other colt. Marvin looked over and saw the colt's handler standing up and talking to him. "Are we in England? "

The young boy turned to look at him. "Yeah, probably. It's been about twelve hours or longer since we took off and I have gotten absolutely zero sleep thanks to *him*, " he said, looking at the gray colt. "Is that I'm Not Evil in the stall with you? "

Marvin nodded. "Yup, the one and only. He handles plane rides pretty well. Not the case with your colt,

I see," he said with a hint of
sarcasm. "Who is he?"
The handler scratched the colt on
the neck. "This is Home Free. He's
going to run in the UAE Derby. I
think the owners want to try and
cram as many stakes races into this
horse as possible. They're going to
try and run him in the Triple Crown
when he gets back in April. The sad
thing is, his trainer agrees with
them. But going back to the subject
of the champion in the stall with
you, is he normally as well-behaved
as this?"
Marvin nodded. "Usually. He's a
real devil on the track in the
mornings and especially the
afternoons, but if I'm in his stall
with him he's perfect."
"Home Free is the same way,
though he does have a lot of temper
tantrums," the boy said. "By the
way, my name is Peter," he said.
Marvin nodded. "I'm Marvin, the
personal groom of the greatest
racehorse that ever lived," he
said.
Peter nodded. "He *is* great."
Marvin heard the plane's wheels
squeak as they started onto the
runway again. This time Peter had
control of Home Free from the start
of takeoff. And, this time, Home
Free was quiet. Evil barely made a
move as the plane lifted up off the
runway and headed toward Dubai.

~~~~~~~~~~~~~~~~~~~~~~

Marvin didn't know how long he was asleep or how he had fallen asleep under the circumstances, but all he knew was that the plane was landing again.

He glanced over at Peter. "How long have I been asleep?"

Peter stared at his watch like a hawk. "Since we took off, so approximately nine and a half hours."

Marvin let out a big yawn and a stretch. He looked up and saw Evil gazing at him with his dark eyes. Marvin and Peter stood up in their horses' stalls as the plane taxied to a stop. Marvin checked Evil's blanket, bandages, and body to make sure nothing had slipped or that he wasn't hurt. When he passed the test, Marvin untied the loose quick release knot and stood at the front of the stall, eager to be let out. Peter was doing the same thing.

The Dubai airport workers let down the ramp, revealing the world of Dubai to Marvin and Evil.

22

Marvin was the first to leave the airplane. He led Evil behind him, who stopped a few times to look everywhere. Peter and Home Free were next. They came down the ramp much quicker.

Lucky for Peter, a trailer had already arrived to take Home Free to Nad Al Sheba, the racetrack where all the big-money races were, like the World Cup. Peter circled

Home Free a few times before loading him into the trailer. The gray colt walked quickly up the ramp and was tied up in the trailer. Marvin guessed Home Free's trainer had gotten him out of quarantine somehow. Marvin didn't know how his dad got Evil out of quarantine, but somehow he did. Peter shut the back door and climbed into the truck. That was the last Marvin would see of him for a little while.

As Marvin circled Evil around, he looked at the surroundings. It was very hot over here in Dubai, much different from the slightly cooler Florida. Sand was everywhere, along with tall, skyscraper-looking buildings and tan people wearing turbans. Marvin removed Evil's blanket and folded it under his arm. Finally a trailer pulled up and Nick hopped out. "What do you think of Dubai?" he said.

Marvin looked around again. "I like it," he said.

Nick opened the back of the trailer and Marvin led Evil in. The big black horse was perfectly calm as Marvin tied him up. He hopped in the passenger seat next to Nick as they drove towards Nad Al Sheba.

Halfway there, Marvin saw bouncing, running figures out in the sand. "Dad, are those horses out there exercising on the sand?"

Nick took a look and nodded. "They do that a lot here. I think we'll exercise Evil on the sand while we're here, you know, to see if it helps his training any."

Marvin scratched his head. *His training is already perfect, he's undefeated,* he thought.

Nick drove into the Nad Al Sheba stable yard a while later. Marvin noticed the track looked very dry and sandy. He wondered how Evil would handle it. But, then again, it's like his dad always said, "A good horse can run on anything."

When the rental truck and trailer were parked in the stable yard, Marvin was the first one out of the truck. He immediately went to the trailer and unloaded Evil. Nick went to the tack compartment and began unloading Evil's things. Marvin took off Evil's traveling bandages and stuffed them in a tack trunk Nick had unloaded onto the ground. The big black horse lifted his head up and sniffed the wind. His breed ancestry originated from here, and he knew it. He let out a loud whinny and followed Marvin to the barn.

Evil was always assigned stall 1. Always. The giant horse loved to look outside at all the happenings. He was like the person who knew about everything, all the gossip. Nick probably always assigned him stall 1 because he was aware of this.

Marvin turned Evil loose in stall 1. He stored the halter in the tack room then went to the feed room to get Evil's lunch. He poured the grain into his feed tub. Evil polished it off in record time. Marvin chuckled as the oversized horse nosed around the feed tub to

make sure he hadn't missed any. He
turned and looked at Marvin with a
look that said, "Is that ALL I
get?"

~~~~~~~~~~~~~~~~~

Marvin, Nick, and Evil spent the
next week getting used to Nad Al
Sheba. Evil started galloping over
the racecourse by the end of the
week, and he didn't seem to mind
the new surface.
On March 3, Evil breezed four
furlongs over the course. The
official clocker caught him in :47
and two, but Nick caught him in
forty-seven seconds flat. Evil
seemed to like the sandier surface
at Nad Al Sheba, which would be to
their benefit in the World Cup.
Later that day, Marvin and Nick
tuned in to the TV to watch Groovy
run in the Santa Anita Handicap. He
was breaking from post five under
his regular jockey Eddie. Marvin
was nearly screaming in joy as
Groovy overtook the tiring
pacesetter at the top of the
stretch and took the lead by a
length. Eddie didn't see a fast
closer coming at him, but he heard
one. He waved the whip in front of
Groovy's right eye, warning him not
to lug out into a horse that could
possibly be there. Groovy sped up
to avoid the bullet closer from the
back of the pack. He hit the wire a
length in front of the other horse.
Marvin called Victor to
congratulate him after the race.

The morning of March 5, Nick woke Marvin up earlier than usual. "We're going to take Evil out into the desert for his gallop today," Nick said.

At that, Marvin leaped out of bed and into some jeans. He grabbed his exercise riding helmet from the tack room and Evil's tack. He loaded it in the trailer and then brought Evil out. The big horse loaded into the trailer easily. Nick drove the truck out to a flat, open area where other people sometimes exercised their horses. Nick parked the truck and Marvin unloaded Evil. He walked him around a few times and then tacked him up. The black colt looked about curiously, surveying his surroundings. Nick gave Marvin a leg up. "Take him around this area a few times and see how he handles it," Nick told him. "Not too fast," he warned.

As Evil slowly walked away Marvin murmured to himself, "I think I'll go gallop him off at full speed into the desert…"

Nick turned around. "What?"

Marvin grinned behind his dad's back. "You didn't hear that," he said.

Nick snorted as Evil began his medium gallop around the area. Evil pricked his ears up, enjoying the new environment. After just two times around the area Marvin had broken a sweat on his forehead. He was not used to the extremely hot weather yet, but it was making him fatigued. The only force that was

helping him on was the swinging
strides of Evil's gallop. After
just a few more times around the
large, sandy area, Marvin pulled
Evil up and came back to Nick.
"Whew! It's hot out here today!"
 Nick nodded. "It is. That's
probably enough for today. We
wouldn't want you to collapse up
there on his back," he said
flatly.
 Marvin hopped off and wiped his
forehead with his shirt. He
untacked Evil, who had also broken
a light sweat in the hot weather.
Nick opened the trailer back up
after Marvin had thoroughly walked
him out. The black colt was still
looking around everywhere.
Marvin walked Evil up into the
trailer and tied him. He would
probably hose him off when they got
back to Nad Al Sheba.

23

 Nick parked the truck and trailer
in the stable yard as Marvin hopped
out. He quickly unloaded Evil from
the back and took him to the barn.
He loosely tied Evil to a post
outside the barn and began hosing
him off. Evil let out a big sigh in
relaxation as the cool water rinsed
over him.
 When Evil was thoroughly rinsed
off, Marvin grabbed the sweat
scraper from his grooming kit and
began scraping the water off of
Evil, who seemed to enjoy it.

After Evil was completely groomed
and clean, Marvin put him in his
stall. The colt was asleep almost
one full minute after he was turned
loose. Marvin sat at his stall door
cleaning tack the rest of the day.

On March 7, Evil had his first
blow-out since arriving in Dubai.
Ray had flown in a few days before
so that he could still work Evil
and possibly pick up some other
potential mounts.

Ray himself had never been to,
much less ridden in Dubai. He knew
it was a lot hotter here and that
you could lose your strength
quickly. That was not good if you
were riding Evil, who was unaware
anyone was on his back until they
started pulling on his mouth.

Nick gave Ray a leg up. "Take him
five furlongs. Don't strangle him,
now. I want to see how fast he'll
run over this course," he said.

Ray collected Evil's reins and
turned him onto the track. The colt
knew he was going to run. Ray
warmed him up at a canter till they
reached the five-eighths pole. Then
Ray lowered his hands on Evil's
neck and he took off. Evil bounded
along, gaining speed like a plane
flying down the runway and taking
off. Ray could feel almost a week's
worth of coiled up energy being put
forth in the effort. He wouldn't
take the risk of possibly allowing
Evil to get injured, so he drew a
snug hold on him.

Evil didn't like the tight hold
that restrained from doing what he
was born to do. He grabbed a

portion of the bit in his teeth and began picking up speed. Soon he was flying down the homestretch out of control. He didn't feel the small jockey on his back or the bit in his mouth anymore. All he felt and heard was the pounding of his legs on the track, the steady rhythm of his gallop, and the joy that came from running.

Ray didn't feel like Evil was out of control but he knew it would be hard to stop him. As he flew under the wire Ray stood in the stirrups and hauled back with all his remaining strength. Lucky for him Evil dropped the bit after he saw Marvin standing at the edge of the racecourse. He lost interest in his work and slowed to a walk. Ray still had no control, but Marvin did. The huge horse approached Marvin and nudged his pockets, checking for treats. Marvin grabbed his rein and Ray hopped off. His face was as red as a cherry. "How fast?" he asked with a grim look on his face.

Marvin checked his stopwatch. "Well, the time for the total work was :56 and three, but the final quarter mile was timed in almost twenty seconds flat," he informed Ray.

Ray gritted his teeth. "What did the boss say?"

Marvin tapped his forehead. "I remember him saying, 'Well, we won't have any problems with him handling the track'."

Ray's face turned grim. "I'll see you later, Marvin."

"See you later."

~~~~~~~~~~~~~~~~~~~~~~

A few days later Marvin walked
down the barn aisle towards Evil's
stall. The colt had been bugging
him for treats lately and now
Marvin was going to give him some.
As he looked into the stall his
adrenaline went up sky-high.
The stall was empty and the door
was wide open.

~~~~~~~~~~~~~~~~~~~~~~

Evil was not in his stall, but his
food was polished off and all his
tack was in the tack room. Marvin
went into the stall and examined
it. There were no signs of foul
play, no weird liquids or anything.
Marvin went to the front of the
stall and realized what had
happened. The stall door latch was
covered in horse slobber. Evil had
somehow unlatched his stall door
and walked out easily. Marvin had
to find him.
First he checked the feed room.
When Marvin saw that no grain was
missing and Evil wasn't there, he
breathed a sigh of relief. He was
somewhere on the Nad Al Sheba
grounds.
Marvin checked every barn and
shedrow on the backside. Evil was
not there. Then he remembered the
most obvious place to look: the
track! He headed that way with a

halter and lead rope. Marvin got
there just in time to see Evil walk
through the gap and onto the track.
Marvin released the shrillest
whistle he could manage. The big
colt turned his head and saw Marvin
dangling a carrot from his
fingertips. Food was all the
temptation that Evil needed. He
trotted over to Marvin with his
ears pricked up, looking at the
treat. As Evil crunched the carrot,
Marvin slipped the halter over his
nose and buckled the side strap.
Marvin led Evil back to his stall
and turned him loose. This time he
restrained the treats from Evil
until he was calm and had forgotten
about his little adventure. Marvin
plopped down in front of Evil's
stall and read the other World Cup
contenders' works back in the
United States and elsewhere. The
biggest threat so far was a
European horse named Maximum
Strength who was as fast if not
faster than the speed they had seen
from Evil in his career. He was a
freakish-looking dark bay that was,
like Evil, big as he was fast. He
was beaten in his first race this
year due to a bad break, but he
still showed gameness. Maximum
Strength was a tremendous closer,
so Ray wouldn't have to worry about
a speed duel at the beginning but
would have to watch for him in the
last quarter mile.

Another horse was Smagg. The
medium-sized bay horse was the
winner of the Derby that Groovy had
finished third in. The other horse

already working for the World Cup was Powdered Snow, the gray colt that was second to Evil in the Donn Handicap.

A horse that Evil hadn't seen since the Triple Crown was Simply Sinful. The large bay colt was second in the Preakness and pulled up with a tendon injury in the Belmont. He had gone to France after that to recuperate. His injury healed by the fall and he had come back with a few wins. The Dubai World Cup itself was expecting a five to six horse field, depending on how some of the other horses trained in the next half-month.

Marvin was observing the works at the track one morning when he saw a familiar gray colt sprint past him. He recognized Home Free, the colt that had been on the plane with Evil. Home Free was blazing along. Marvin whipped out his stopwatch and timed his last quarter mile. He caught him in :23 and two, a pretty good clip. He spotted Peter hunched over the rail a distance away. Marvin called out to him, "He looks great!"

Peter smiled back. "Thanks!"

Nick came and joined Marvin at the rail. "Remember Happy Boy?" he inquired.

Marvin did. "Yeah. He's still a turf horse, isn't he?"

"He is. Did you hear about his California race, the Sunshine Millions Turf?" Nick asked with a hint in his voice.

Marvin stared at him. "No," he said.

Nick tilted his head. "January. I never told you, and you never watched? He won by ten lengths under restraint. He's really taken to the turf nicely."

Marvin raised his eyebrows. "He'll always be on turf, right? He'll never move back to dirt?"

Nick nodded. "He has made his home on the grass."

The trainer walked away towards the barn. Marvin followed him but went to Evil's stall. The colt sniffed his pockets, knowing exactly where the treats were. Marvin laughed and said to the colt, "You know, you are a real monster on the track, but you are the perfect angel when it comes to begging, you know that?"

24

The next week and a half went by lightning fast. On March 26, the entries for the race were drawn. This year's Dubai World Cup had drawn a ten horse field. Among the entries were Evil, Powdered Snow, Simply Sinful, Maximum Strength, Smagg, and a few Asian horses that Marvin had never heard of before. Marvin's excitement about the race was once again gathering like a tornado picking up steam.

On March 27, Evil had his last work before the race. A four-furlong eye-opener over the fast

track would be Evil's last serious
run before he ran in the richest
race in the whole world. Ray was up
for the work. Marvin watched as
Evil took flight, his legs barely
touching the ground before they
came up again. Ray was hunched over
his back, rating him for the last
furlong when he would let Evil run.
At the furlong pole, Ray let out
three inches in the reins, and Evil
leaped forward. He was not given
much time to run, as his long
strides ate up the ground for only
a furlong. He flashed under the
wire and tried to keep going, but
Ray took so tight of a hold on him
that his head was practically
pulled against his chest. Evil
slowed down drastically and tried
to throw his head up, but Marvin
was already there to grab his
reins. Evil nudged Marvin's pockets
for carrots, but Marvin didn't give
him any. Ray hopped down from Evil
and very slowly turned toward Nick.
Nick was tapping his foot on the
ground, and he didn't look too
happy. "I got him in :44 flat…"
he said with a serious look.
 Ray gritted his teeth. "Got any
other horses for me to ride?" he
asked rather nonchalantly.
 Nick slowly shook his head, and
Ray briskly walked to his rental
SUV and drove off to a hotel
somewhere. Marvin led Evil back to
his stall and gave him his
breakfast.
 The next day post positions for
the World Cup were drawn. Evil had
drawn post 3, on the inside of most

of the horses. Maximum Strength had
drawn the far outside post 10,
which Marvin didn't think would
affect him. Simply Sinful drew post
5, and the Japanese horse named
Tough Luck drew the very inside
post.

On the eve of the Dubai World Cup,
Marvin was walking towards the barn
when, all of a sudden, Evil emerged
without anyone at his side. He saw
Marvin and came toward him with his
ears pricked. Marvin greeted him
with a pat. "Evil! Did you undo
your stall latch again?" he asked
the big horse.

Evil just looked at him like he
hadn't said anything.

Marvin managed to coax Evil back
to his stall by dangling a carrot
in front of his nose. Evil would do
anything for food. When Evil was
back in his stall with a lock on
the latch, Marvin set up his cot at
the door of his stall so Evil
couldn't get out and no one else
could get in. He didn't exactly
know how, but somehow Marvin
managed to fall asleep peacefully
that night.

~~~~~~~~~~~~~~~~~~~~~~

Marvin woke up at 6:00 sharp the
next morning. Evil was dangling his
head out the stall door, looking at
Marvin with that hungry look.
Marvin barely pulled himself out of
his cot and went to the feed room
to get Evil's quart of grain. He
had still not gotten used to the

major time change. When he came
back with the grain, Evil was doing
the tappy-toe dance at the front of
his stall. Marvin regretted making
Evil wait so long for his
breakfast. That sound was so
annoying.

Evil polished off his oats and
looked out his stall door to the
track. He knew it was race day.
Here he was, in this strange
country, taking over their track
and showing them who was boss.

Just several hours before post
time, Marvin had Evil looking his
very best. His black coat was so
black that it highlighted a silvery
shade of blue. Marvin took Evil's
bridle from the tack room and
carefully placed it on his head,
making sure all straps fit
perfectly. He softly clipped the
lead shank to one of Evil's bit
rings and waited for Nick to show
up. Nick was going to walk behind
Evil to ward off spectators that
might get a little too close as
they made their way to the
receiving barn.

Finally his dad came to the stall
door and accompanied him out. The
path to the receiving barn was
lined with fans. A little boy
rushed out of the crowd and nearly
bumped into Evil's legs. Nick
quickly intercepted him with one
hand and turned him back to the
crowd. "Stay back, please," he
said.

The black colt did not like the
crowds. He skittered next to Marvin
as they finally reached the

receiving barn. Evil was put in the
third stall, near Maximum Strength.
The dark bay, almost black horse
looked at Evil with what was almost
a sneer. Marvin put himself next to
Evil so he couldn't see the other
contender.

The next hours spent in the
receiving barn were short. The
loudspeaker crackled. "Horsemen,
bring your horses to the paddock
for the six-million dollar Dubai
World Cup. Bring your horses to the
paddock for the World Cup. "

Marvin took a deep breath and let
it out slowly as he led Evil alone
to the paddock. Nick was already
there with the saddle and
equipment. He saddled Evil
carefully and checked him. He was
in perfect shape, he looked good,
and his equipment was perfectly
aligned. Marvin began walking him
around the ring.

Soon the jockeys came out. They
looked like all different kinds of
birds in their silks. Ray jogged
over to Evil's saddling stall for a
quick chat with Nick. Marvin led
Evil back to the stall. Nick
boosted Ray on board when the
'riders up!' call came. "Don't
screw up, and don't fall off, "
Nick told Ray as the bugler began
to play and the horses began to
make their way out towards the
track. Marvin handed Evil to the
experienced hands of the pony rider
and followed Nick up to the owners'
boxes. David and Sonya had flown in
the previous day. They did not want
to miss this big race. Evil was

carrying 133 pounds, giving him at least 18 pounds to every horse.

Ray didn't think Evil would ever be more fit. Nick had conditioned him perfectly, and it showed. For ten minutes they warmed up their horses under the blistering heat. They were seen all over the world on TV, some people criticizing them and some staring in awe. They began their way towards the twenty-ton metal starting gate. The Japanese horse Tough Luck loaded into the first slot. The next horse loaded, and then it was Evil's turn. He loaded in without flinching. Ray swiped at the sweat on his forehead. He figured the sweat was the result of the heat and nervousness mounting up inside of him. Evil patiently waited for the rest of the horses to join him in the gate. As the last horse walked into the gate, a bead of sweat dripped down Ray's face and landed in Evil's mane. *Here we go*, Ray thought. They were all set for the richest race in the world.

25

Evil broke perfectly the second the gates opened. The other horses broke about a half-step later, but Evil was already out to the front, were he would remain. Simply Sinful came out running in second, vainly trying to catch Evil and hoping that he would get tired. But Evil didn't get tired. He romped out on the front end as he turned into the

backstretch. He was dancing along
on the lead, out for fun. Evil was
one of those horses that could run
all day.

The race rapidly unfolded behind
Evil on the clubhouse turn. Maximum
Strength unusually moved up into
second, pressing Simply Sinful to
pick up the pace. Simply Sinful
sped up to try to avoid the other
horse, but Maximum Strength was
giving him no time to relax. He was
pushing Simply Sinful along the
turn and into the backstretch.
Powdered Snow waited in behind them
as he hoped a hole would open on
the rail. A few of the other
closers trailed about five lengths
behind.

Ray thought Evil was galloping to
the beat of twelve, but the horse
was dragging him along. The first
three-eighths were timed in :34 and
two, and the first half mile in :45
flat. The colt was getting faster
as he went along, and Ray was
barely aware of it. He was running
against his only competitor, the
clock. The first five furlongs were
caught in :57 and two, and still
Evil showed no signs of backing
down.

Simply Sinful was tiring behind
Evil. The heat was taking its toll
on him along with the pressure put
on him by Maximum Strength. He
slowly began going in the opposite
direction, forcing Powdered Snow to
swing out and go three wide.
Simply Sinful labored and tried to
go on, but there was no energy
left. He faded back to last as the

rest of the field moved into the far turn, that is, except Evil. He was completing the far turn and was running for home. He was running alone, with no one to challenge him. His time for the mile-and-an-eighth was 1:45 and three, amazing. Ray saw the finish ahead and didn't yet understand that he was just 220 yards away from a world record for the mile and a quarter. Ray knew how fast he was going now, and he tried to restrain him.

 Evil would have none of that. He sped up his pace even more and lunged for the wire.

 The timer stopped at 1:57 flat. It was a new world record for a mile and a quarter. It was faster than his Derby by a full second, and faster than the old record by a few fifths of a second. Ray lifted his fist in the air and made a face at all the flashing cameras around him. He was sure that the pictures they took would end up on the nightly news. He stood in the stirrups and let Evil gallop out an extra eighth. When Evil turned around and headed for the gap, Ray leaned forward and gave the black giant a hug around his neck. Evil ignored him and headed toward the gap where Marvin was standing with one of the most cheesy, triumphant grins you ever saw. When the horse was within a few feet of the winner's circle Marvin reached out and gave him a hug. Evil didn't mind one bit. Marvin clipped a lead shank to his left bit ring and led him into the winner's circle. Evil

stared straight into the camera
with his dark eyes. After that
picture was taken, Ray hopped off
and joined David, Sonya, and Nick
for the picture with the World Cup
itself. Marvin was busy leading
Evil to the testing barn. After he
came out clean, Marvin took him
back to the barn to hose him off.
He had used a good amount of effort
in the World Cup, breaking the
world record for the mile and a
quarter. Marvin ran the cool water
over Evil's head, which startled
him. He threw his head up and shook
the water off. Marvin gradually
eased the water onto his head, and
this time the colt didn't budge.
Marvin scraped him off and turned
him loose in his stall with a feed
tub full of oats. Evil let out a
squeal and dove into them. Marvin
laughed at his enthusiasm.

~~~~~~~~~~~~~~~~~~~~

Evil came out of the race well, so
they were going to go ahead and fly
him out of Dubai the day after the
World Cup. Nick was barely able to
convince the flight management for
to let him fly on their plane with
only a day's notice. Nick knew that
he would never bug these officials
or fly on their airline again.
The day they were leaving Dubai,
Marvin packed all of Evil's tack.
When he was done, he carefully
checked the room to be sure that he
hadn't left anything behind. He
stashed the tack trunks by the barn
door and bandaged Evil up. He

didn't throw a blanket on him this time. Evil would be in quarantine with a full routine vet check for a few hours. Nick convinced them for the last time that his horse didn't need a three day quarantine.

This flight was going to go from Dubai, to England, and back to Marvin's native home of Kentucky. Evil would be kept at David and Sonya's farm for a few weeks, and then be shipped wherever his next race was. Nick was thinking about the Metropolitan Handicap, more commonly called the Met Mile or the Stamp of Stallions, in May.

Groovy was going to stay in California for the rest of the year. He would go through their summer classic series, fall stakes races, and then would like be flown back up to Belmont for the Breeders' Cup.

Nick came towards the trailer and let down the ramp. Marvin guided Evil up the ramp and tied him securely. He slipped Evil a sugar cube and gave him a pat. Now they were ready to go home. Marvin hopped in the passenger seat of the truck as Nick started it up. Marvin turned around in his seat and got one last glimpse of Nad Al Sheba. When it was out of sight, Marvin turned back around and closed his eyes.

The next thing Marvin felt was Nick's hand on his shoulder, gently shaking him. "Marvin? We're here. We're finally going home."

Marvin rolled out of the truck and back to the trailer. He slid the

door open and scrambled inside.
Evil had his head turned around,
looking at him. Marvin untied Evil
and led him out of the trailer. The
sudden blast of hot air from the
Dubai airport hit him like a car.
Marvin was awake long enough to
lead Evil up the ramp and into the
airplane. When the stall was built
around him, Marvin unclipped his
lead shank and gave Evil his head.
The plane took off about half an
hour after Evil was settled. The
jet engines kept Marvin up for four
hours after the plane took off.
Marvin didn't seem to hear the
noise around him. He was so
overcome from the excitement of
Dubai and the World Cup that he
virtually collapsed on the near
side of Evil's stall. The big black
colt stood watch over him while he
slept.

~~~~~~~~~~~~~~~~~~~~

Marvin was woken up by the
screeching of jet engines and
patter of rain on pavement after
all was quiet. He looked up and saw
his faithful colt watching him to
make sure he was all right. Marvin
heard the airport crew opening up
the hold, so he figured they were
back in Kentucky. True to his
thought, he saw the familiar green
pastures and stone stallion barns
that made up his home state. The
airport crew broke down Evil's
stall and Marvin led him out into
the light Kentucky rain. Evil

lifted his head and sniffed the
air. Besides the World Cup, all of
Evil's greatest triumphs had come
here in Kentucky. The Kentucky
Derby and the Breeders' Cup Classic
victories had come at Churchill
Downs. His first race was at
Keeneland. Marvin loaded Evil into
the very first trailer he had
ridden in, David and Sonya's
personal trailer. Evil sniffed his
old surroundings and relaxed.
 Nick drove his own worn-down truck
down the freeway. A couple of miles
away was his home, to which he had
come close to but hadn't been in
for almost a year. Marvin realized
just then how terribly homesick he
was. He was so close, but yet so
far away! His dad turned off the
freeway onto an exit. A few minutes
later, he turned onto the familiar
dirt road that he had been up and
down so many times in his life.
Marvin could see the training track
now, the barns, David and Sonya's
house, and finally his own home as
Nick parked the truck in the dirt
driveway. Marvin launched himself
out of the truck and to the back of
the trailer. He shoved the door
open and Evil looked at him in
surprise. Marvin took the black
horse to stall 1, in which he lived
in as a two-year-old, and turned
him loose. There was fresh grain in
the feed tub, which Marvin guessed
had been placed there by David. The
stall was super-clean. Marvin
figured that Evil had been the last
horse in it, and it had been
cleaned a long time ago. He

unloaded the tack trunks from the trailer and stored them in the tack room. Marvin decided he would unpack them tomorrow. When he made sure that everything and every being was out of the trailer and settled in the barn, he ran up to his house and burst through the door. Marvin dashed up the stairs in record time and sprinted into his room. He threw himself face down on the bed and mumbled into the covers,

"It's good to be home again... "

26

Marvin awoke to the sound of bacon sizzling on his dad's skillet. The very thought of the food pulled him up out of bed and dressed him. He clumped down the stairs and parked himself at his dad's side, staring at the food with his tongue nearly hanging out like a dog's. Nick turned at grinned at Marvin.
"Sorry, this is all mine!"
Marvin gave his dad a sarcastic look.
Nick's grin turned to a smile.
"Just kidding!" he said as he put a few pieces of bacon on Marvin's plate.
Marvin snorted as he sat down and began eating. Nick sat down and joined him. Marvin thought about Evil. "What's Evil's next goal?"
Nick chewed on a piece of bacon.
"Well, I was thinking about the Met Mile in May. I think we'll probably leave him here this month

and let him rest. Plane rides take a lot out of a horse, even horses like him, " he commented.

Marvin finished his bacon and went down to the barn. Small particles of water from the light rain the day before dotted the grass, creating a display of sparkling diamonds across the Kentucky bluegrass. Marvin went to the familiar training barn. He assumed that Nick had already given the horses their morning feed. Evil came to the front of his stall with a nicker.

Marvin would never get sick of the horse's enthusiasm. He went to the tack room and unloaded the tack trunks. All the bits, bridles, and everything in between were in place, except for the leg wraps he had stuffed messily into one in Dubai. When all the tack was back in its old place, Marvin went into Evil's stall with a soft face brush and sponge and plopped down. The big black horse rested his head on Marvin's shoulder. Marvin used the face brush on Evil's white blaze, perfecting every curve and angle. He went over the rest of his head quickly and then got out the sponge. He smoothed the hairs in all the right directions.

Evil liked the face massage. He leaned his head into Marvin's hands and dozed off.

~~~~~~~~~~~~~~~~~~~~~~

Marvin enjoyed being home at the
farm in those next April weeks.
Evil was hand-walked for a week to
give him a light form of exercise.
Nick didn't want to put too much
strain on the colt following his
massive effort in the World Cup. In
the middle of April he would start
jogging again, and at the end of
April into the beginning of May he
would resume his regular training
schedule.

On the morning of April 17, Marvin
tacked Evil up for his first jog
around the track since being in
Dubai. Nick was going to watch him,
just in case. He had some of his
other horses galloping that day on
the training track, and Nick didn't
want Evil to take off after the
other horses with Marvin still
clinging to his back!

Marvin led Evil out to the track.
Nick helped him up and sent him on
his way. The black colt was
behaving perfectly for Marvin as
they began trotting around the
outside rail. Marvin peered at the
passing track between Evil's black
ears. Even at the trot, Evil
covered a lot of ground. He made
the trot of the training track seem
short, and before Marvin knew it,
it was time to get off. He slid off
the tall colt's back, careful to
bend his knees when he hit the
ground. He led Evil back to the
stable and turned him loose in his
stall. As he was putting Evil's
tack away Marvin saw the piece of
paper that contained each of Evil's

wins on it. He lifted a pen out of an old tack trunk and wrote:

DUBAI WORLD CUP (G1)

 The reality of the Dubai win still had not sunken in, even after eighteen days. Marvin put the pen and paper back and went through the barn, looking at every horse and checking their stalls to make sure nothing was broken or needed spiffing up. All stalls were fine except an unoccupied stall that needed painting. Marvin was only checking the maintenance because he was bored. He wished Victor was there. The bright, red headed boy always knew how to put a smile on everyone's face. Thinking of Victor made him think of Just Groovy. The chestnut horse was staying in California until the Breeders' Cup at the end of the year. Marvin went to Nick's office, were his dad was studying a Daily Racing Form.
 Marvin sat on the desk that Nick was reading on, who tried to swat him off with a newspaper. He didn't budge, so Nick looked at him sarcastically. "Do you mind?" he asked in an obnoxious tone.
 "I just wanted to know when just Groovy's next race was," he said, adding a look that probably made him look uninterested.
 Nick turned the page of the Form. "His next start will likely be in the Hollywood Gold Cup in June,"

Nick answered. "Why do you want to
know?"
 Marvin wriggled his foot. "Just
wandering…"

~~~~~~~~~~~~~~~~~~~~~~

 When late April rolled around,
Evil was in top shape again. His
thick muscles rippled under his
glossy coat, which was super-shiny
as a byproduct of his exercise,
grooming, and overall health. On
the twentieth, Evil was scheduled
to have his first work since the
World Cup. Nick decided that Evil
was more behaved for Marvin than he
was for Ray, so he let Marvin ride
him for the work. It was a slow
five furlong work. Nick thought
that if Marvin did well here, he
could ride him in the faster works.
 Marvin lowered himself in the
saddle at the five-eighths pole,
and he felt Evil leap forward
instantly. Marvin was glad he wore
gloves to help him hang on to the
reins. Ray didn't believe in gloves
because he thought that it
interfered with the communication
between rider and horse. Marvin
wore them almost always when he
rode, except for when he was riding
Fred.
 Evil was a powerhouse in control
under Marvin. The oversized horse
rounded the far turn and turned
into the stretch. Marvin let out
half an inch in the reins, and Evil
responded with more speed. He did
not go out of control like he did

with Ray. Marvin guessed it was a
respect issue. He let one more tiny
notch out in the reins and Evil
accelerated at they reached the
sixteenth pole. Marvin still didn't
feel like they were going too fast
as Evil dived for the wire. Marvin
patted Evil on the neck as he
pulled him up. Evil slowed down
quicker, trying to get more praise.
Marvin turned him around and walked
him back to Nick, ignoring Evil's
efforts to get more praise and
possibly a treat.

Nick was looking at the watch
with a bored look on his face. "I
got him in :59 and three. You
didn't do *too* bad," he said with a
smirk.

Marvin leaped off Evil and led
him, laughing, back to the barn.

26

Nick thought Marvin was doing so
well that he was going to let him
ride Evil in his faster works.
Marvin was bouncing off the walls
on the night of April 22. The next
day, on April 23, Evil was
scheduled a fast six furlongs, and
Marvin was going to ride him.

Nick had told Marvin the day
before that they were going to ship
Evil up to Belmont by trailer
instead of plane. Nick thought Evil
had gotten enough plane rides in
the past year, so he wasn't going
to put more stress on the gallant

black colt in his last year of
racing.

Nick was going to drive Evil up to
Belmont on May 3, the day before
the Kentucky Derby. David and Sonya
didn't have any horses in the Run
for the Roses, but they had another
horse in the Woodford Reserve Turf
Classic the same day. Evil was
aiming for the Grade 1 Metropolitan
Handicap on May 27, a Monday. This
would be the first time in his life
Evil would race on a weekday, which
Marvin knew would have no effect.

When Marvin woke up on April 23,
he was dressed in record time and
out to the barn without breakfast.
Nick had been in the kitchen
drinking coffee, so he wouldn't be
down for at least another half
hour. Marvin went to Evil's stall,
where the black colt was doing a
tappy-toe dance. Marvin gave him a
sugar cube and began brushing him.
He next saddled him carefully and
bridled him. As Marvin was putting
the bit in Evil's mouth, the colt
began sidestepping and looked
outside the stall. Marvin barely
slipped the bit into Evil's mouth
before he turned and saw Victor
standing right there with a big,
cheesy grin on his face. "Hi! I
was missing home, so I thought I'd
come back and visit for a few days.
I haven't been here in so long, and
I haven't seen you in so long! And
Evil! That world record for a mile
and a quarter was fantastic! I
never knew you were so fast! "
Victor exclaimed.

Marvin grinned. "He was a good boy. How has California been?"

Victor's grin went ear to ear. "Wonderful. There has only been one rainy day since I've been there, and it's so warm! Groovy loves it too."

Marvin patted Evil. "I hope California is not as hot as Dubai was when we were over there. It was scorching hot and Evil came back every day after his works with a heavy sweat on him."

Victor yawned. "It looked like it was blazing hot there by just watching the World Cup on TV," he said.

"Pictures don't tell lies. I get to ride him in his work today," Marvin said, referring to Evil. "A fast one."

Victor's eyes got big. "Really? I never get to ride Groovy. Anyway, I'm going to go outside and watch you, okay?"

Marvin nodded. He led Evil after Victor outside to the training track, where Nick was standing watching a gray filly work. She was giving her rider a hard time. Nick turned for just a moment to lift Marvin up onto Evil and send him through the gap while the filly finished.

Evil walked eagerly out onto the track as the gray filly was halted in front of Nick. Marvin watched the ground pass between Evil's ears as the black horse trotted past the seven-eighths pole. He then eased him into a canter for the next furlong. As the three-fourths pole

passed by, Marvin lowered himself
in the saddle and Evil began
flying. He kept a snug hold on the
reins as the powerful colt hurdled
himself across the track. The
chilly April air stung Marvin's
face, but he didn't feel it in the
joy of riding Evil around the
track. Marvin realized then what
Ray meant when he said that Evil
had a huge stride. It was like
sailing along. Marvin felt that
Evil would hit the ground if he
didn't take another stride.

Evil swung into the stretch under
no urging from Marvin. He was
working all by himself as his rider
let out a notch in his reins. He
picked up speed flying past the
eighth pole and dove for the wire
like he had done in the World Cup.
Marvin let him gallop out an extra
eighth before slowing him gradually
down to a walk. He circled Evil and
brought him back to the gap, where
Nick was standing staring at the
stopwatch in his hand. Marvin
leaned forward and patted Evil's
neck. "How fast?" Marvin asked.

Nick gulped. "Fast. I got the
first quarter in 23 and two, the
first half in 45 and three, and
finally the whole six furlongs in
1:08 flat." He began tapping the
watch, thinking it would give him a
more realistic time.

Marvin looked at Evil, who was
pulling on the reins in an attempt
to get back to the track. The black
colt didn't seem to be tired from
his run. He grabbed a good hold on
the reins and slid off the horse.

Victor gave Marvin a pat on the back. "Good job, Marvin!"

Marvin grinned at Victor and led Evil back to the barn. The black colt was breathing easily and looking forward to his breakfast. If you took away the unreal racing brilliance, Evil was just another regular horse.

~~~~~~~~~~~~~~~~~~~~~

Sadly, Victor had to leave for California on the 25th. Marvin accompanied him to the airport to say goodbye. Unless he took another plane trip back, Marvin would probably see him at the Breeders' Cup at the end of the year since Groovy was in California the whole year.

On May 1 Nick gave Marvin rare permission to take one of the horses in training out on the trails. Marvin picked Foreign Luck, a five year old gray mare that was usually calm and reserved. Nick prevented him from taking Evil. He didn't know what that crazy horse would do if he was on a trail.

Marvin placed his English saddle on Foreign Luck's back and tightened the girth. She didn't like the strange leather girth that felt different from the elastic one she wore all the time. The gray mare pawed the dirt in her stall floor and snorted. Marvin soothed her with a pat and bridled her with ease. She seemed to calm slightly as Marvin led her out into the

stable yard. He mounted up with
ease as the mare started to walk.
She held her head up high and blew
heavily as Marvin guided her onto
the trail. As they went deeper into
the woods, the mare's breathing got
quicker and more labored. Marvin
began to turn her onto a trail when
she stopped dead-cold. He looked up
into a tree and saw an owl perched
on the branch. It had cold, mean
looking eyes that had a tint of red
in them. Marvin usually was not
scared of much, but now a tingling
sensation went up his spine as the
creepy bird stared him in the eye.
Before Marvin had quit school, he
had learned the adrenaline rushes
through your blood when you are
scared to prepare you to defend
your life or run for it. Marvin
couldn't stand the cold eyes of the
owl anymore, so he whirled Foreign
Luck and gave her a BIG kick. The
mare was spooked at the owl and she
lurched into a wild, crazy run.
Marvin grabbed some of her mane and
struggled to hang on. This run was
nothing like the controlled gallops
when he rode Evil. This was a
scared bolt in which the mare felt
like she had to run for her life.
Foreign Luck zigzagged across the
trail, unseating Marvin. Finally
the gray mare leaped over thin air
before Marvin could get a hold of
her. He could no longer keep his
seat. As the gray mare leaped a
second time, Marvin felt himself
falling off the right side of the
mare. He no longer saw the blowing
gray mane in his face, but instead

saw the dusty ground rushing up to meet him. Marvin was falling at an angle where, if he didn't break the fall somehow, his whole body weight would land right on the weaker bones of his neck. He stuck his left arm out in front of him in a desperate attempt to break his fall.

The next thing Marvin heard and felt was his full body weight being thrown down on his arm with momentum from the horse. He heard a bright snapping sound, like the breaking of a twig, as he collapsed onto his arm. The arm was surely broken badly as he felt extreme pain and sizzling feelings up the whole left side of his body. Marvin watched as Foreign Luck galloped off towards the farm with no rider. He struggled to turn and lie on his back without causing much pain, but that was impossible. The arm felt like one of those loosely attached Barbie doll arms that swiveled like a Tilt-a-Whirl. Marvin looked at his arm, which was already beginning to swell. No bone was protruding through the skin, but it was close. The whole underside of his left arm was purple. Marvin looked up through the trees at the little sky that showed. Foreign Luck's hoofbeats could no longer be heard, so Marvin guessed she was a few miles away now, maybe even back at the farm. Marvin glanced at his arm again. There was a tingling feeling in his head, spine, and arm as he slowly closed his eyes. The next thing he felt was a feeling of

freefalling, and then total
blackness.

27

Marvin woke up surrounded by the
white-washed walls of a hospital
room. His arm was heavily wrapped
in a thick white cast that went up
to his elbow. His arm was not as in
as much pain, but Marvin guessed he
was under a very heavy dose of pain
medicine. He scanned the room,
looking for any evidence of someone
he knew. Nick's denim jean jacket
was hanging on a chair close to the
bed, and there were a few "Get
Well Soon!" balloons by the
window. The best thing Marvin saw
in the whole room was not the
jacket or balloons, but it was a
simple piece of paper on the walls.
Marvin recognized it from two years
ago. It was a plain white paper
with a yellow, smiling face in the
middle that said "Think
positive". Marvin remembered
Victor making it to help him get
over his mom's heart attack and
coma. The rest of the room was
mostly white, except for a small
color TV hanging from the ceiling
across the room, perfect for
Marvin's viewing. The Weather
Channel was on, showing some
working horses and the forecast for
the Kentucky Derby. The Derby was
that Saturday, and the horse Marvin
had chosen to win was Home Free,
the gray colt he met on the plane
to Dubai that was third in the UAE

Derby. The fast colt showed no signs of tiredness from Dubai and had won the Blue Grass Stakes at Keeneland.

Marvin looked for anything to eat. He hadn't had anything to eat since breakfast that morning, and it was almost 8:00 at night. Marvin didn't see anything so much as a pickle. He used his good arm to reach into his dad's jacket pocket to check for any mints or anything. The closest thing he could find to food was a training schedule for one of the older horses in the barn.

Marvin watched the Weather Channel for the next ten minutes. Finally Nick came in with some fast food. The sight literally made Marvin's mouth water. Soft drinks, burgers, fries, and all that good-tasting stuff that was bad for you.

Nick caught sight of Marvin staring at the food. He let out a small chuckle. "I figured you'd be hungry, so I got us some food. I heard the cafeteria food wasn't the best, so this will have to do."

Marvin didn't say a thing. He reached out with his good arm and grabbed a soft drink from the tray. Nick and Marvin didn't converse for the next few minutes as they stuffed their faces.

Nick was the first one to break the silence. "How'd you fall off?"

"She spooked at a bird, an owl, actually, and bolted. She began zigzagging across the trail and leaping over thin air. At the second leap I fell off. Oh, by the

way, how is the horse? " Marvin
asked.

Nick took a couple of fries and
shoved them in his mouth. When they
were gone, he commented, "She ran
out of the yard and down the road,
where the neighbor's horses were
eating. She thought she was going
to join them for a little extra
breakfast. Luckily the neighbor saw
her and brought her back. "

"How'd you find me? " Marvin
asked.

"After you didn't come back for a
while, I started to get worried.
When I saw Foreign Luck running
towards the neighbor's farm without
a rider, I knew something had
happened, " Nick said. "I saddled
up my Percheron and took Evil with
me. I let him be a kind of
detective, letting him sniff the
ground. He led me to you. "

Marvin winced for two reasons. The
first was because he moved his arm
weirdly and a heavy amount of pain
came, even with the medicine still
in effect. The second reason was
that he had forgotten about his
beautiful black horse. Evil had
helped find him and maybe saved his
life. Marvin didn't know what kind
of creatures were out there in the
woods, and he didn't want to know.

~~~~~~~~~~~~~~~~~~~~~~~

Marvin was in the hospital without
complaining for the next three
days. He was really missing Evil,
and he was sure Evil missed him.

The big black horse always did his best when Marvin was around. Besides him, Evil's only other friends were his blazing-quick speed and his food.

Nick had told Marvin a few days before that he might have to have another surgery, which Marvin did not want. He wanted to go home and see the horses, but that would not be allowed. Nick said that another one of his assistant trainers was managing the horses at the barn. Marvin thought Nick was the best trainer in the world and that nobody could take his place.

The sad thing, Marvin found out a day later, was that he did need another surgery to insert a few more screws. He didn't know how he would manage his schoolwork. Marvin had been home schooled every day of his life since age 10. He was 14 now, and he had been doing his work at home when he wasn't down at the barn. Even when he was out of state or the country his work was e-mailed to him, and he e-mailed back the answers.

The surgery was to take place the next day. Marvin had not known he had even had surgery the first time, so he didn't know what it was like consciously knowing you were going to go through it. The thought of people digging in your body just didn't sound right to Marvin.

On the morning of the surgery Nick told Marvin that as soon as the doctors gave clearance, he could go home and see Evil. But he couldn't ride, that was a fact. Ray would

ride him for all his works and fast
breezes. Evil was probably
wondering where his best friend had
gone.
 Marvin had to be moved onto a
portable bed to be moved into the
operating room. The worst thing
about having surgery that Marvin
discovered was that you couldn't
have anything to eat or drink 12
hours before surgery. What was even
worse was when your dad was
drinking an ice cold pop in front
of you and you couldn't have any.
Marvin was taken into the operating
room, still conscious. They were
beginning to give him some
anesthesia, and he felt sleepy. He
was tired from all the hype in the
hospital, not to mention he
couldn't get any sleep at night.
The next thing Marvin was conscious
of was a growing sense of
blackness, and then emptiness.

28

 Marvin woke up in the recovery
room. His eyes were barely open,
but he managed to sneak a peek at
his arm. It was wrapped up more
than ever before in a thick, white
gauze. It didn't hurt, but Marvin
knew that was because he was under
heavy pain medicine and that the
arm was still. The nurses weren't
aware that he was awake until five
minutes after he had woken up. One
of them stood up and began pushing
Marvin back towards his hospital
room. Marvin forgot how long the

endless white hallways of the hospital were. When he was back in his room, Nick wasn't there yet. Marvin half-guessed he was at the barn checking on all the horses. The nurse made sure Marvin could get into the hospital bed safely, and then she left. Marvin was very hungry and thirsty. He hadn't eaten or had drunk anything in almost 18 hours.

How relieved Marvin was when his dad walked through the hospital room door with some fresh food. By looking at the bag, Marvin could tell it had come from his favorite fast food place. Nick began dangling the bag in front of his face, and Marvin slapped him with his good arm. Nick began laughing and handed the bag over to Marvin, who reached into the bag with his good arm and grabbed a handful of French fries. Boy, fries had never tasted so good. Considering the circumstances, they were probably the best fries he had had in his life. Marvin slurped down the drink in record time and it didn't hurt. He guessed it was probably some slight euphoria that kept it from hurting when he ate so fast. He glanced at the TV, which Nick had switched to the broadcasting station of the Kentucky Derby. There were five minutes to post, and the TV was showing a glimpse of Home Free warming up. The beautiful gray colt looked in top form despite his heavy racing schedule. Marvin got a few glimpses of some of the other horses before they

field began loading. Home Free was
loaded in the 8 post after several
horses were in. The Derby field
this year was a full 20, leaving no
room for mistakes by any horse or
jockey. When all the horses were
loaded, the crowd was so loud that
it was an overwhelming sound from
the TV. Then the gates broke and
the Kentucky Derby field was off!
Marvin watched as Home Free's
jockey took a medium hold on him,
settling him in fourth as the early
pacesetter went out to the front,
going through the opening quarter
mile in a fast :22 and one. Home
Free was enjoying the outing,
flicking his ears back and forth as
he glanced around. In front of him
the race rapidly began to unfold as
the second and third place horses
went up to challenge the early
leader. Home Free's jockey kept the
snug hold on him as the gray colt
was tempted to join the battle
early. The leader turned down the
challengers with a quick burst of
speed as the field approached the
half mile pole. The six furlongs of
the race had been run in 1:12 flat,
a perfect twelve clip. As the Derby
horses approached the far turn and
began it, the cavalry charge of
closers began to come up from the
back of the pack. Home Free's
jockey looked back and saw them
coming. There was a fine art of
riding a horse perfectly in a race
like this, and he had no intention
of doing it wrong. He began to
slightly move his hands with the
horse's stride, slowly at first,

but then faster as they reached the midpoint of the far turn, driving him. The leader was fatigued after setting a twelve clip after seven eighths of a mile. On his outside, the easy-to-spot light gray colt led all the closers.

Home Free flew past the pacesetter at the top of the lane.

Close behind him were the furious closers pounding the ground. The fastest one, Monday Madness, a *filly*, was emerging from the wave. At the three sixteenths pole Monday Madness moved to Home Free, matching strides with him. Home Free's jockey glanced over at the chestnut filly matching the climbing strides of his gray colt, who was trying to get a better hold of the surface. At the eighth pole, Monday Madness stuck her desperate nose in front of Home Free. Now Home Free's jockey went to the whip, and that was all he needed. The gray colt pushed his head in front of the filly who was giving her all. Monday Madness was beginning to see her hope fade away as she called on all of her class for a final try. Her jockey was going to the whip over and over again as she came back and matched strides with the colt once again. Their heads were bobbing in perfect unison as they came within fifty yards of the wire. Home Free pushed his full body weight into the ground and shoved himself forward a few inches farther than his regular stride. The filly had done the same. Her jockey had been yelling

at her to try to get her to extend
herself even more. The twosome
swept under the wire in the closest
photo finish Marvin had ever seen.
Both horses had given all of their
effort and more. What the world had
just witnessed was one of the most
exciting Kentucky Derbies, probably
more exciting than Evil's.

The results hadn't come even five
minutes after they had been pulled
up. Then the photo was posted up on
the board with the numbers, and the
crowd came alive after moments of
dead silence. The whole place
erupted as the saw that it was the
filly who had won by the slimmest
fraction of the nose. The photo
looked like the two noses were a
centimeter apart. The jockey on
Monday Madness whooped and hollered
as he saw that his filly had won.
Not by much, but she had won.

Marvin was clapping on his cast
for the very game filly. Home Free
had given his all, but it was
destined that the filly would give
more. In that moment, in the
hospital bed watching the winner's
circle ceremony, Marvin knew that
his arm was going to be okay, and
the very thing that had given him
hope was the sport that he had
loved his whole life —horse racing.

~~~~~~~~~~~~~~~~~~~~~

Both horses came out of the race
in good health, but both were very
tired. The connections of Monday
Madness were going to gallop her a

few days later and see how she went. If she had enough energy in her she would run in the Preakness. Home Free would not run in the Preakness, but he would likely run in the Belmont.

It was May 7, two days after the Derby and six days after Marvin was hospitalized. The doctors had given Marvin permission to go home the next day. Marvin was constantly bugging Nick with questions about the horses at the farm, particularly Evil. Nick said the black colt was missing him terribly. Marvin said his arm didn't hurt anymore, but Nick knew Marvin was probably fibbing.

On May 8, Marvin was put in a wheelchair and wheeled out of his room into the elevator. He was almost bouncing up and down, eager to get out of the whitewashed rooms and hallways and into the open freedom of the Kentucky bluegrass.

The elevator dinged and Marvin was pushed out onto the main floor towards the exit. If Marvin's arm had been healed, he would have jumped out of the wheelchair and ran out the door to David and Sonya's farm. But that would not happen. The nurse slowly wheeled him towards the automatic door and it opened. Marvin took a deep breath as the smell of antiseptic quickly turned to the smell of spring air. Nick's truck was parked right by the exit, so Marvin didn't have to go far to get to his escape source. Nick helped Marvin out of the wheelchair and into the truck.

He thanked the nurse and climbed into the driver's seat. Nick started up the truck and drove away from the hospital. Marvin hoped it was the last time he had to go in there. Of course, he had to go to the orthopedist's office for checkups until he was cleared, but not to the hospital.

Nick turned the truck into the familiar driveway about ten minutes later. Marvin was about to jump out of the truck on his own, but he really didn't want a tongue-lashing from Nick. When the truck was stopped, Marvin crawled out and waddled toward the barn holding his arm, with Nick close behind. Marvin waddled as fast as he could to Evil's stall. He couldn't get there as fast as he wanted, so he called out the colt's name. "Evil!" Marvin yelled.

He heard a high, loud whinny from the training barn and some kicking of hooves against a stall. Marvin jogged as fast as he could without hurting his arm. The black Thoroughbred was stretching his neck out towards him. Marvin slowed when he came within a few feet of the colt. He reached out with his good arm and gave Evil a hug. The colt nuzzled his head with his nose and then caught sight of his cast. As Marvin revisited with Evil, something important caught his mind. If Evil was going to run in the Met Mile at the end of the month, how was he going to go with him if Nick said Marvin would have to have regular doctors' checkups?

Either Marvin was going to Belmont with Evil, or Evil was leaving without him.

29

The next day Marvin went to Nick's office, where he was reading news about another Met Mile contender. He sat in the chair in front of his dad. "Dad, what are we going to do about the Met Mile? If I have to stay here, will Evil go without me? Or will I go with you?"

Nick turned a page. "I've already arranged that. The doctor that did your surgery simply said that you can get checked out by a hospital up there and send the doctor's comments back to him through the mail."

Marvin's eyes widened. "Really? Oh, thank you! Thank you so much! Now I never have to leave Evil!" he said as he rushed out the door back to the barn.

Nick sat at his desk shaking his head. "I have never seen a kid so crazy about a horse," he mumbled.

~~~~~~~~~~~~~~~~~~~~

On May 11 Evil was scheduled to be shipped up to Belmont for the Met Mile. He was originally going to be shipped up eight days before, but nick put that off because of Marvin's injury. Marvin packed all of Evil's tack with both arms the day before. He was under heavy

doses of pain medicine, though.
Marvin was able to control Evil on
the lead rope with one hand, and
Evil followed him like a puppy. The
black colt had no interest in the
big white cast on Marvin's arm,
which was good.

The day that Evil was scheduled to
be shipped, May 11, finally came.
Nick had the trailer in the
driveway, ready for Evil to step
into it. Marvin led the big black
horse into the trailer and securely
tied him. Evil let out a big sigh,
not looking forward to the long
ride. The only thing he would be
looking forward to in his near
future would be the Met Mile.

Marvin shut the trailer door and
hopped in the passenger seat of the
truck. Nick was just now walking
from the house, carrying a cup of
coffee and a doughnut. Marvin knew
that food was always the first
thing on Nick's mind. His dad
crawled into the driver's seat, put
the doughnut and coffee on the cup
holder, and started the truck.

The ride up to Belmont was long
and boring. Nick preoccupied
himself by listening to the radio,
and Marvin stared out the window
for most of the time. He was
imagining what Evil would probably
think of being retired to stud
duty. Marvin was sure he would miss
racing and everything that came
with it - the hype of race day, the
seriousness of workouts, and the
competition that never caught him
on a good day. His colts and
fillies would be the only physical

thing that was evidence of him on the racetrack. In the colt's mind, though, he would be at the track running every day.

Marvin soon began to think about the competition for the Met Mile, Evil's eighteenth lifetime start. The Met Mile was often called the Stamp of Stallions because so many great stallions had won this race. There were some pretty good horses in there, but none compared to his. The first and biggest threat was Maximum Strength, the horse that had run second to Evil in the World Cup. He was the only horse that had the speed to go along with Evil, but only for perhaps a quarter mile. The positive thing for his connections was that he was a much better miler than he was a mile and a quarter horse. Maximum Strength was capable of taking a mile in 1:33 and change, but Marvin felt that Evil could do it better and faster.

The horse that could possibly beat Maximum Strength was Smagg. The horse that had beaten Groovy in the Derby was also a spectacular miler. He was a true distance horse, but he was also a true front-runner. He would have to take on a stalking position with Evil in the race. There was no way he was going to steal the lead from Evil early on. The race was, of course, Evil's to lose.

~~~~~~~~~~~~~~~~~~~

Marvin was woken up by his dad's
hand shaking him. "Marvin, we're
here. I need you to, if you can
with your arm, help me unload the
horse and trailer."
Marvin thought his arm hurt a
little, but he wasn't about to tell
his dad that. He crawled out of the
truck. He opened the trailer,
ignoring the slight pain in his arm
as he led Evil out towards the
security barn. The colt was holding
his head up high in the air,
sniffing the air around him.
Belmont would most likely also be
the place of Evil's final race,
which would probably be his second
consecutive Breeders' Cup Classic.
It would be the scene of the grand
black Thoroughbred's final act on
the racing stage.
Marvin led Evil into his stall at
the security barn and turned him
loose for a short while. The colt
paced what he could of the stall
and then turned to Marvin. Evil
pushed his nose near Marvin's
pockets, looking for treats. Marvin
chuckled and pulled one out of the
depths of his pocket. "You know
where they are, don't you?" Marvin
said as his horse crunched the
treat with satisfaction.

30

On May 17, Evil had his first work
since arriving at Belmont. It was a
four-furlong slow work, and Ray was
aboard. Marvin felt a little

resentment toward Ray because it was Marvin himself who had ridden Evil successfully in his works. Since his arm was still broken, Marvin was going to be away from riding for a while.

Nick gave Ray a leg up. "Easy as you can with it still being a fast enough run to be registered as a work," he mumbled.

Ray nodded and moved the horse out onto the track. He liked the way the horse was moving underneath him this morning. He was coiled up like a spring, ready to be set loose. At the half mile pole, Ray dropped to a crouch in the saddle and was nearly unseated by the powerful horse exploding from beneath him. He was not fully in control as Evil began the far turn. The colt was blazing along, and Ray knew he was going to have to find some way to get a hold on this demon if he didn't want to pull a Secretariat in the 1973 Belmont in a regular work. He leaned forward more than usual, grabbed more rein, and rode hunched over the colt.

Evil didn't like how the tight hold pulled his head near his chest. His kept his mind on his feet but began shaking his head. The black horse soon stole a large amount of rein from the helpless rider on his back. He began rolling across the ground, picking up steam like a locomotive. He was like an iron horse, and no bit pulling on his mouth was ever going to stop him. He was opening up daylight on the invisible competitor. Evil

roared down the stretch with Ray
trying in vain to pull him up. The
outrider was on alert just in case
that the colt would go completely
out of control. But Evil eased up
as he passed the wire, just like he
would have in a real race. Ray
snagged the reins from the
Thoroughbred and pulled him to a
quick halt. He whirled Evil around
and cantered him back to where Nick
was supposed to be standing, but he
wasn't. Marvin was there holding a
stopwatch and twitching his eyebrow
at it. Ray said in a shaky voice,
"Do I want to know?"
  Marvin told him, covering Evil's
long ears. Ray wiped his forehead
with a sigh and slid off. "Do you
know if he's got any works between
now and his next race?"
  Marvin looked at the stopwatch
again. "If he comes out of this
fine, I think he'll have one more
before the Met Mile, but I'm not
sure. I'll have to ask my dad."
  Ray nodded and walked away. Marvin
held the stopwatch in front of
Evil's face. "Was this time good
enough for you?"
  Evil ignored the stopwatch, which
held an unreal time of :43 flat,
anything but slow. If Marvin was
thinking correctly, that would be a
new world record for four furlongs.
He hung on to Evil reins and bent
down to feel his legs for heat,
bumps, or any deformities. When his
hands touched the colt's legs, they
were perfectly cool and normal.
This horse was a freak, he was
simply not real!

~~~~~~~~~~~~~~~~~~~~~~

A few days later Marvin was hanging out in Evil's stall, waiting for Nick to get up. The trainer was going to reveal the rest of Evil's schedule for the remaining week leading up to the Met Mile.

While he was waiting for his dad, Marvin thought about the things going on in the racing world. It was May 22, and the filly Monday Madness had won the Preakness. The chestnut was on the verge of being the very first filly Triple Crown winner. Her main competition in the Belmont was Home Free, and the other few horses were longshots.

Marvin's thoughts were interrupted by Nick, who had just come up to the stall door. He motioned Marvin out of the stall and to a folding chair. He started off with the words, "This horse is the greatest horse that ever lived, to start out. We all know that by now. What I wanted to ask you was, do you want to help me train the greatest horse that has ever lived?"

Marvin was shocked. Him? Train Evil? "Sounds like fun to me," he responded.

Nick nodded and pulled out a sheet of paper. "Write down what you think would be a good training schedule after the Met Mile."

Marvin took the paper and scribbled down what Evil had mostly had during his layoffs. He handed the paper back to Nick, who shook his head in satisfaction. "You think like me," he said, beginning a long conversation that would take them until the late afternoon.

On May 24 the entries for the Met Mile were drawn. There were only four horses in the race, which were Evil, Maximum Strength, Smagg, and a horse Marvin had never heard of. Of those three horses, Marvin knew that not one posed a threat. Evil was unbeatable, and the world knew it. Able to rip off incredible fractions at any distance, he never got tired. Marvin didn't know if it was a gift or determination at first, but after a year of his Derby win, Marvin came to the real realization-he ran so fast for so long because of only two reasons. He was born and bred to run, and he loved running. When Evil was on the track, that was the only rule – no horse was allowed to pass. Never.

31

On the night before the Metropolitan Handicap, Marvin spent three hours grooming Evil for his first start since the World Cup. Racing fans across the country were anxious to watch him.

The big black colt loved to be groomed. It was one of his all-time loves, under running. Evil knew he was the best horse ever on the track. He was a very smart horse and knew what he wanted to do. In his horsey mind, he figured that he was the boss around there, and all were supposed to run behind him and not in front of him. He was the ruler of the dirt oval.

Marvin woke up at 4:30 sharp. He stumbled sleepily over to the feed room, half asleep, and scooped out Evil's single quart of oats. Evil ate them quickly and looked out his stall door. It was race day once again, and once again time to remind everyone why he was the best.

The hours after 7:00 AM Marvin spent grooming Evil again. Even though Nick still insisted that his son was going to groom the hair off the horse, Marvin didn't stop. He spent all of his time with Evil until it was time to take him to the receiving barn several hours before the Met Mile.

Nick had to send some extra grooms with Marvin to guard Evil as he was taken to the receiving barn. Fans had learned some way to crowd the pathway, and Nick didn't want them messing with his champion horse. The big colt walked calmly to the receiving barn next to Marvin, ignoring the spectators around him. They clapped and cheered and hollered, but Marvin hustled Evil along to keep him from being distracted.

When Evil was settled in his stall, Marvin looked around at the other horses in the barn. Most of the Met Mile horses were there, except for Smagg. He had a reputation for always being to the receiving barn later than the other horses. Maximum Strength was a few stalls down, which was good. Marvin thought that when the dark bay colt looked at Evil, he was sneering.

Finally, after long hours of waiting, the loudspeaker crackled to call the horses to the paddock for the Met Mile. Marvin made sure that Evil was the first horse there, so he walked Evil quickly past the handler who was taking Maximum Strength.

As the black colt pranced through the tunnel, loud cheers rose from the spectators. Evil loved being cheered. The big Thoroughbred had never been booed, as he was perfect. Nick was waiting for Marvin and Evil in the paddock. He placed a few thin pads on Evil's back, and then the saddlecloth and saddle, which was weighted down heavily from the track handicapper. Marvin began circling him around the walking ring as the other three horses began to get saddled. Marvin thought the plain racing snaffle bridle looked good on Evil, especially on his straight white blaze. The colt had never needed any gadgets, such as blinkers or a figure-eight noseband. The only time he had ever worn them was in the Florida Derby and in the workouts before.

The jockeys emerged from the jockeys' room in their bright, colorful silks. They were a standout compared to the four dark horses in the paddock, followed by the grooms in their t-shirts and the trainers in their gray and black suits. Ray approached Evil's number 4 saddling stall. Marvin had

walked Evil around for the final
time and halted him in front of
Nick and Ray, who nodded. "He
looks really good," the jockey
commented.

At the "riders up" call, Nick
gave Ray a boost up and his
trademark nod. The bugler began
playing from out on the track, and
Marvin led Evil behind the other
horses. He was the last horse to
walk onto the track, but the crowd
was on its feet and roaring as the
black giant made his way past the
grandstands. The colt's movements
were fluid and powerful, which was
what Ray liked.

The wind was picking up. The
clouds were darkening and
threatened rain at any moment. Off
in the distance Ray saw a small
flash of lightning. As the horses
finished their warm up and began
loading, the wind blew an empty
soda can near the horses. Evil
became afraid of this and reared up
high. From the fans' view, he could
have been the Black Stallion. Ray
turned him and he softly floated
back down to the ground. As the
wind blew, Evil became even more
keyed up as they loaded him into
the gate. He was pacing back and
forth, ready to run from the
blowing air that scared him. Smagg
was the last horse to load, and
they were all set for the
Metropolitan Handicap.

~~~~~~~~~~~~~~~~~~~~~~

Ray had never seen nor felt such a
fast break in his life-not even
during the Triple Crown last year.
Evil exploded like his feet were on
fire and flying was the only way to
escape it. He ran out to the lead
within two strides and opened it up
to ten lengths with furious speed.
Ray drew a good hold on him and
tried to reserve something for the
last quarter mile, but the powerful
horse pulled through his hands and
kept on running. He wasn't running
tame now. He was running as if he
had to run for something. He wasn't
running as fast as he could, Ray
could tell, but he was going at an
excellent clip, somewhere around 10
and 3/5 for the first furlong and
21 and 2/5 for the first quarter
mile. Ray knew that Evil had never
actually run this fast in a race,
but Smagg was running just a second
slower a few lengths behind Evil.
Ray didn't think that Smagg could
keep pace with Evil for the whole
mile, so he let him sail along.
    Turning into the backstretch also
meant turning into the wind. All
four horses were running against
the wind. Evil was running at a
good enough clip to keep himself in
front by five lengths, but Smagg
was dropping back. The ultra fast
first quarter was already too much
for him, and it had drained most of
the reserved energy for the mile.
The wind wasn't helping him,
either.
    Evil was enjoying his chance to
run. His ears were pricked up and
he was dead on in the bridle. He

had rushed through the first six
furlongs in 1:08 and two. As he hit
the top of the lane, he pricked up
his ears again and picked up even
more speed. Ray hunched over him,
trying to slow him down, but it was
no use. Much of his coiled up
energy from his layoff was being
released in his huge stride, and he
wasn't laboring. Evil passed the
eighth pole and joyfully galloped
to the finish. He hit the wire
fifteen lengths in front of Maximum
Strength, who had outdueled the
longshot for the place. Smagg had
finished last, about another
fifteen lengths behind the show
horse.

Ray managed to finally slow Evil
down after the wire. He turned the
big black Thoroughbred around and
headed towards the winner's circle.
Out of the corner of his eye, he
saw the teletimer reading a final
time of 1:31 and 4/5 seconds.

It was a new world record for a
mile, and also a new track and
stakes record. What was the most
impressive about it was that he did
most of it against the wind. Ray
halted Evil at the gap to the
winner's circle as Marvin gave him
the biggest hug he could manage
with his arm. He led the happy colt
into the circle so he could have
his picture taken. His ears were
pricked up as they had been during
the race. Marvin laughed at the
oversized horse's enthusiasm.

He knew he was in the winner's
circle.

32

The Met Mile had drained some of Evil's built up energy, but it didn't exhaust him. The black horse was back to himself the next day, nosing Marvin's pockets and bugging the other grooms. He enjoyed his walks the next few days.

It was June 1. Evil stuck his head out over his stall door, looking for his favorite person. It was way past time for his so called "afternoon treat" and Marvin was nowhere in the huge horse's sight.

Meanwhile, Marvin was in the track kitchen enjoying a croissant, chatting with Nick about the horses in the barn and other horses they hadn't talked about in a while.

Marvin took a drink of chocolate milk. "How's Happy Boy doing? I haven't heard anything about him in a while," he inquired.

Nick took a sip of coffee. "Well, he's in California right now. He's won a couple of low-graded stakes races. We're trying to stretch him out to the distance of a mile and a half on the turf, and it's going along pretty slow. We're thinking about running him in the Charles Whittingham Memorial Handicap, but we're not sure yet. We do have to decide soon, because the race is in a week."

Marvin picked up his other croissant. "What's Evil's next start going to be?"

"Probably the Whitney in July. That's one of the reasons that we're not going home until he's done for good. The Whitney is at Saratoga, which is not too far away," Nick said.

"Are Evil and Groovy both aiming for the Breeders' Cup Classic at the end of the year?" Marvin asked. He knew the answer, but he wanted to keep Nick talking.

"I already told you that."

"I know."

Marvin talked with Nick till the evening, and then Marvin went back to the barn to check on Evil. The horse sniffed his pockets right away. Marvin gave him a treat and said, "I know, you've missed me." A few days later, on June 6, Marvin got a phone call from California. It was Victor, telling him he was sorry that he broke his arm and some stuff about Groovy. His next start would be the Hollywood Gold Cup on the 30th. The conversation was short, but full of information.

Marvin got on the computer that night and looked up pictures of Groovy. There was a picture of him winning the Santa Anita Handicap. It was a head on shot, and the chestnut horse was shining with sweat, but his ears were up. The good-sized horse looked like Secretariat. What disturbed Marvin was the look in his eye. There was a look of authority in his eye, unlike any he had ever seen, not even from Evil. Evil always had a playful look in his eye, like he was toying with his competition.

Evil had many kinds of looks and
personalities - playful, clumsy,
but never serious like this. The
chestnut looked completely serious
about his look. In that moment,
Marvin felt as though he had never
felt before, a feeling of neglect
for his horse.
  He felt Groovy could beat Evil.

~~~~~~~~~~~~~~~~~~~~~~~

Under Nick's training, Evil became
in the perfect shape. At 18.2 hands
tall, almost three and a half feet
wide at the chest, and about seven
feet long, the huge black colt
could seriously almost not fit in
the starting gate. Starting gates
were bigger now than they used to
be, but Evil could still almost not
fit. He was now fully grown. Marvin
wondered if his colts and fillies
would be just as big.
  The month of June flew by like
Evil on the track, who had a couple
of slow-turned fast works to keep
him fit, and up to 2 ½ mile
gallops. In the Triple Crown, the
Belmont was a shootout between Home
Free and Monday Madness. The
Belmont was very similar to the
Derby in the way it was run, but
finally, the filly buckled. Her
stamina gave out in the final
sixteenth and Home Free won by a
neck.
  Marvin was glad his dad was Evil's
trainer. He had incredible stamina
because of Nick's superb training,
but Marvin believed that it was the

Thoroughbred's love of running that propelled him through his workouts and races.

On the night of June 27, Marvin once again logged onto the Internet and looked at the picture of Groovy. It still sent chills up his spine when he looked the horse in the eye. He went to NTRA.com and discovered that the post positions for the Hollywood Gold Cup were posted. Just Groovy had drawn post six, which was smack in the middle of the field. Eddie would have to hustle him out of there in order to keep at least a few lengths off the pacesetters.

Word got back from California through trainers that Groovy was lame in his left front leg. Nick's assistant trainer denied this, but rumors still spread. Marvin knew that if the horse was truly lame, Nick would be blowing his top about it.

Victor called Marvin again the night before the Gold Cup. "Have you heard the lame rumors?"

"Yes," Marvin said.

Victor had a confident tone. "They're not true."

Marvin chuckled. "I never thought they were."

What Victor said next reminded Marvin of Groovy's serious look.

"He is unstoppable. Not even Evil can beat him."

33

Marvin was tuned into the hours
of prerace in the track cafeteria.
He didn't really think that any
other horse in the race had a
chance to beat Groovy, except for
Ewinar, the infamous tiny chestnut
colt who ran second to Evil in the
Derby. He was compared to
Seabiscuit because of his small
size but big heart. He didn't win
the big dance, but was always in
the money. He was always the
bridesmaid and never the bride.
Nick joined him as the post parade
began. The horses were sweating in
the early summer sun, the coats
glimmering. Groovy was the fittest-
looking of them all. He moved with
definition and grace, as if he was
performing a dressage test for the
queen of Britain. The chestnut
horse was moving towards the gate
very fluidly, and Eddie looked like
he was enjoying the ride so far.
As the horses began loading into
the gate, Marvin saw Eddie ask the
assistant starter holding Groovy a
question. He watched as the starter
pointed Groovy's head straight
towards the sixth slot, letting him
get a good look. When it was his
turn, Groovy actually lunged
forward into the gate eagerly,
ready for the race to begin.
Finally, they were all set for the
Hollywood Gold Cup.
Groovy broke perfectly, but, to
Nick, Marvin, and Eddie's dismay,
he was slammed into by another
horse coming out of the gate. Eddie
heard the horse give out a grunt as
the outside horse squeezed him in.

He felt him scramble for footing
and almost go down, but,
thankfully, the chestnut horse
righted himself on the surface.
Eddie looked around and saw that he
was at the back of the pack, along
with the stragglers and very late
closers. Groovy began his move at
the clubhouse turn. It was hard to
tell when it began, for it was so
slight; that change in speed was
barely detectable.

 Heading into the backstretch
Groovy was gaining ground on the
other horses, but he was still
second last. Eddie called out
encouragement to his mount, and he
soared past the next small group of
two horses. He was now in ninth
place. Eddie continued to urge him
on. The chestnut Thoroughbred was
beginning to get heavy in the
bridle and ask for more rein. He
was floating across the Hollywood
Park surface, which he handled
easily. Eddie knew his horse was
starting to pick up even more speed
as they passed some more horses.
Unknown to Eddie, every furlong
that Groovy had run had been faster
than the previous one. He ran the
first furlong in a lackluster :13
and 4/5 seconds, but the next few
were gradually faster. Entering
into the far turn, Groovy had just
run his quickest furlong yet, in a
time of :12 flat. He was in fourth
now, as the pacesetter had begun to
tire after setting a very fast
pace. Groovy moved into second,
passing the third and second place

horses, who had just been locked in a speed duel.

Groovy moved to the leader at the top of the lane.

He was followed closely by another closer, unknown to Eddie until Groovy passed the leader. The horse was roaring down the stretch, drawing away from the other closer. They wouldn't catch him today. He was unstoppable, just like Victor had said, but Marvin believed that was only meant to be in the Golden State, like the champion Lava Man was.

The reporters for the TV station followed the post race into the winner's circle, where Marvin saw Groovy try to take a bite out of his winner's blanket. He saw Victor slap him on the nose and that was that.

~~~~~~~~~~~~~~~~~~~~~~

On July 2, Marvin led Evil up into the trailer and tied him up. Nick had rented an extra large trailer, perfect for an extra large horse. They were taking Evil to Saratoga, where the Whitney Handicap was scheduled to be run later that month. After that race, he was likely to run in the Travers again, according to Nick. Evil was likely going to run in the Jockey Club Gold Cup after that, and then the world famous Breeders' Cup Classic would be his last race.

The Whitney Handicap had been Groovy's Classic prep last year.

Looking back in history, Marvin knew that various Classic winners had come out of the Whitney, like Invasor, who surprised everyone when he defeated the even-money favorite by about a length in the 2006 Classic.

As Nick drove along the road, Marvin looked at all the other cars passing by, hoping to see another horse trailer. In the short ride to Saratoga, Marvin only saw an empty, beat-up trailer.

Nick drove the truck into the Saratoga stable yard a short time later. Marvin was already out the side before the truck had come to a complete stop. He unlatched the trailer door, opened it, and saw Evil standing right there, waiting to be led out. It was a trick he had learned as a two year old; he had learned to untie the knot with his teeth.

Marvin led him out of the trailer and into the receiving barn, where he was expected.

A small crowd of had gathered near the barn, waiting for him. Cheers and clapping rose up from the group as Marvin led Evil into the barn and towards his stall. The black colt pranced past the spectators and got them to whistle.

Marvin laughed at his horse. Evil was, in fact, a camera ham.

34

A few days later, Evil was scheduled to breeze six furlongs in

a perfect twelve, or at least
close. Nick knew it was probably
going to be faster, like it always
was. Ray was aboard for the move.
If Ray didn't keep a hold of this
horse, he might not have working
duties anymore. He might only ride
him in races.

It was July 4. At 6:30 on
Independence Day Nick gave Ray a
leg up onto the huge horse. "I
know he's hard to control, but
still try!"

Ray saluted Nick with his right
hand and moved Evil out onto the
track. He was calm and behaved this
morning, not keyed up as usual. Ray
felt the horse stretch out
underneath him as he began
cantering. The three-quarters pole
was approaching as Ray grabbed a
handful of Evil's mane to prepare
himself for the explosion of
fireworks that would soon come.
Evil felt Ray's hands move forward
a little and he knew it was time.

As Ray began to ask the horse for
run, Evil responded almost too
eagerly. He lurched forward at the
instant slight drop of the reins.
Ray leaned back in the saddle,
putting his weight against Evil's
mouth, hoping to rate him.

Evil hated that dreaded pull on
his mouth. He just wanted to run
free-that's all he asked for. Lucky
for Evil, his brute size helped him
fight the rider's commands. If he
would have been smaller, his rider
would have more control over him.
That was not to be. He grabbed the
bit in his teeth and began running

faster. Ray tried to hold him back,
but the oversized Thoroughbred was
ignoring the pulling on the reins.
He yanked the reins away from Ray
to the point were Ray could only
hang onto them for balance as Evil
completed the far turn and hit the
top of the lane. The colt was
rolling now, his long strides
becoming quicker every second. As
he crossed the wire, Evil began to
ease up. He was a very smart horse
and he knew it was probably time
for him to slow down. Ray wished
Evil could be smart enough to know
how fast his works should go.

 Ray immediately seized control of
Evil as the horse slowed to a
canter, then a trot, and finally to
a walk as Ray turned him around.
The horse still had plenty of
energy left-Ray could tell-and he
probably could have gone a lot
faster if he was being pressured by
another horse.

 Nick was once again not standing
at the gap when Evil came back. Ray
cut Marvin short before he could
start talking. "I don't want to
know," the jockey said briskly and
flatly. He hopped off the horse and
strolled off in the direction of
the parking lot.

 Marvin slowly moved his eyes
towards the watch again. Evil's
final time for the six furlongs was
caught in a suicidal time of 1:07
and 2/5 seconds. Nick wanted him to
go in a time like 1:12, but Evil
had always been an overachiever.

~~~~~~~~~~~~~~~~~~~

On July 13, two weeks before the
Whitney Handicap, Evil breezed five
furlongs in :59 flat. Nick switched
the bit on his bridle the day
before. The colt was not going to
race with the new bit, which was a
kind of gag, but he was going to
wear it in his workouts and breezes
to help Ray keep better control of
him and to slow him down.

Groovy had come out of the
Hollywood Gold Cup in prime shape,
and was being pointed for the Grade
1 Pacific Classic in August. Evil
was likely to race in the Travers a
week after that. That race had
originally only been for three year
olds, but the New York Racing
Association wanted to spice it up
by adding four and five year olds
to the mix that year. If all went
well, Groovy's last races would be
the Pacific Classic, Goodwood
Handicap, and then the Breeders'
Cup Classic.

Marvin was not looking forward to
either horse's retirement from
racing. With Evil gone, a huge,
gaping hole would be left in the
Classic division. That division
would miss Groovy, as well. His
beloved black colt would leave his
spirit at the racetrack, but it
would never be seen.

Bright and early on the morning of
July 16, Evil was having a dream in
his sleep. He was running in his
final race, leading by two lengths.
They were at the top of the lane,
and one horse, a *chestnut* horse,

was catching him. Passing the three-sixteenths pole, the older horse had collared Evil and stuck his head in front. Evil was trying hard but still not gaining. *He would have to call on all of his class…*

~~~~~~~~~~~~~~~~~

It was 4:30. Marvin rose to his feet and plodded to the feed room, where Evil's breakfast was stored. He had to hurry or else the colt would start calling and would wake every horse and human in the barn. Marvin scooped out Evil's rations and took them to his stall. The big black horse was standing at the front of his stall expectantly, waiting for his true love-food.

The morning dragged on. Grooms shouted through the shedrow, horses whinnied to people passing by, trainers timed their horses' works, and life went on as usual at the racetrack.

What was unusual was that Nick did not get a call from his assistant trainer in California. He was supposed to get a progress report that day early in the morning, but it didn't come. Either something had gone wrong, or something had gone wrong. Marvin didn't want to choose.

Finally, word came on July 18, at 3:30 in the morning. There had been a training accident and Victor, who had been riding Groovy, had fallen off. He had hit the ground hard and

twisted his leg. Further x-rays
revealed that his right leg was
broken. It didn't need surgery, but
Victor would be in a cast for a
long period of time. Groovy was
okay; a pony rider had caught him
after he had run off.

Marvin wondered if Groovy had
thrown Victor. It would've been
very much like the horse.

35

Victor was still in the hospital
the week of the Whitney Handicap,
but he could watch it on TV. He
would be away from his favorite
horse for a while, but at least he
wasn't dead.

Back on the East Coast, at
Saratoga, the Whitney Handicap had
become a three-horse field. Evil
had drawn the number one post
position. The other two horses were
longshots whose owners thought that
they could catch Evil on a bad day.
All horses had a bad day, and Evil
had had his as a two year old.
Marvin didn't really think that
Evil would ever have a bad day in
the remainder of his races.

On the eve of the Whitney, Marvin
looked over the conditions for the
race again. Evil was obviously the
highweight at 136 pounds, but it
didn't really worry Marvin. He
thought Evil was big and strong
enough to still win with that
burden.

The big black colt had his nose on Marvin's shoulder as he read. It almost looked like Evil was reading the list of the horses who would try to beat him the next day.

Marvin lay down carefully in his cot an hour later, making sure his arm wouldn't get squished. He was already keyed up for the race tomorrow, which was a bad thing. He wouldn't get any sleep.

~~~~~~~~~~~~~~~~~~~~

The birds were calling when Marvin woke up. He rolled over and looked at his watch on the floor, which read 8:15. Marvin had overslept by a long time, and his horse was probably starving. He rolled out of bed and stumbled over to the champion colt's stall. When he looked in, Evil was dozing peacefully, his head hanging low. Marvin was surprised that he was not looking out his stall door to the track. On race day, he would stare at the track for most of the day until it was time to go to the receiving barn. Today, Nick had probably already fed him. He never went to sleep unless he had been up in the night for a while. Marvin felt bad about oversleeping and neglecting his horse.

A few hours before it was time to take Evil to the receiving barn, Marvin put Evil in the crossties and groomed him as quickly as he ever had in his whole life. A few minutes before Nick came to escort

him to the receiving barn, Marvin
had the colt sparkling at his
deepest black. The white blaze on
his face shone like snow when the
sun was out. When Nick arrived, he
approved of his son's grooming.

Marvin led Evil out of the barn
and along the pathway to the
receiving barn. The Saratoga path
was crowded with fans. The young
women of the crowd were dressed in
their wide-brimmed hats, short
skirts, and halter tops. The men
were wearing bright-colored polo
shirts and jeans. Nick followed
Evil closely, ready to intercept
any mischievous kid that might
charge unknowingly at the
Thoroughbred. Elderly people were
looking enthusiastically at the
young, powerful horse like they
hadn't seen one in years. Marvin
led the colt into the safeties of
the receiving barn while the people
applauded him.

Evil relaxed in his stall several
hours before his race. Marvin
stayed with him. He never went
anywhere else when Evil was in
there. He was way too protective of
his champion horse to leave him in
the barn unattended.

Finally, after long hours of
waiting, the loudspeaker crackled
and buzzed. "Horsemen, bring your
horses to the paddock for the
Whitney Handicap. Bring your horses
to the paddock for the Whitney. "

Marvin clipped a lead shank to
Evil's left bit ring and gave him a
pat on the neck. He led the
enormous horse down to the saddling

paddock, where owners, trainers, and other people associated with the horses were standing.

Nick saddled Evil slower than usual today. Maybe it was the heat. When he was finished, Marvin began walking Evil briskly around the walking ring. Soon the tiny jockeys came out of the jockeys' room and materialized at their respective trainers' sides. Grooms led the horses up to the trainers so they could help the jockeys up onto the big Thoroughbreds. Some of the trainers also did a final tack check.

Nick boosted Ray up onto the oversized horse and gave his signature nod. Ray gathered up his reins and stuffed his toes in the stirrups as Evil began walking again. The bugler began playing the familiar tune that called the horses to the racetrack as Marvin led Evil out in front of everyone else.

The weather at Saratoga was warm, but high wind gusts made racing in consistent times hard. Evil's red #1 saddle cloth fluttered in the breeze as he made his way towards the starting gate. The colt was already throwing his head in the air, fighting Ray's control. Marvin had switched Evil's bit again that morning and Evil felt the obvious difference when Ray pulled. A snaffle bit, like the one Evil was wearing, gave a horse more freedom to move than other bits and is not as severe. It also didn't have the

weird functions of a gag or port
bit.

As the horses approached the
gate, Evil began doing his tappy
toe dance. He was keyed up to run
today, like he always was. An
assistant starter led the colt up
to the gate, and he went in with a
small leap. The two longshots
loaded on the outside, and the
small field was ready for the
Whitney Handicap.

36

The shrill sound of the gates
opening and three Thoroughbreds
leaping out onto the track was a
very quiet noise compared to the
roar of the crowd. The fans were on
their feet, some chanting Evil's
name. Ray simply sat on Evil as he
coasted along on the Saratoga
racecourse. The two longshots were
behind him, struggling to keep up.
The big black horse danced into the
clubhouse turn in front by four
lengths. One of the other horses
had been taken into hand and rated
a few lengths behind the other
horse.

Ray knew that was not the way to
challenge Evil. His horse would
easily turn down any closing
efforts, and he would do it in
style. It was Evil's special
dancing style of running that
mirrored the style of the great
filly Ruffian. He would run fast
quarters on the front and wear the

field out, then draw away. He just
never got tired.

As they passed the half mile pole,
Evil was in front by eight and
still gaining ground. He rounded
the far turn and turned for home
under tight restraint, and the
other two horses were battling it
out for second money.

Marvin knew his horse had the race
won. He also knew that the next few
races would not be as easy. Nick
was already standing up and getting
ready to head down to the winner's
circle for the picture.

Ray was easing Evil up. At the
eighth pole, He was ready to joke
that he had pulled the horse up to
a walk. Evil was moving easily
underneath him, out for a fun day.
He galloped over the wire thirteen
lengths in front of the second
place finisher, an older horse
named The End. Ray let the colt
gallop out an extra eighth before
finally slowing him to a walk and
turning him around. Evil pricked
his ears up and pranced back to the
winner's circle in a very animated
trot.

Marvin met the horse at the gap.
He was barely sweating and looked
in prime condition to go around for
another lap. He led the champion
colt into the winner's circle for
his picture. Nick, David, and Sonya
were standing there, smiling
happily next to the winning horse.

When the winner's circle
ceremonies were completed, Marvin
led Evil back to the backside and
the testing barn, where he would

get his routine drug tests. He
passed with flying colors, and
Marvin took him back to the barn.
He hosed the large colt off with a
wide stream of lukewarm water.

Evil enjoyed the bath. After
Marvin had scraped the remaining
water off him with a sweat scraper,
Evil nearly pulled him back to the
barn to get to his stall, where his
true love awaited-his oats.

~~~~~~~~~~~~~~~~~~~~~~~

A few days later it was confirmed
that Evil's next race would be the
Travers Stakes on August 25, in a
little under a month. The Pacific
Classic, Groovy's next race, was
also coming up fast.

Marvin added to the sheet of paper
a few days after the race:

METROPOLITAN HANDICAP
WHITNEY HANDICAP

He had forgotten to add the Met
Mile before, so Marvin decided to
add it now.

Evil's career was fast coming to a
close, and Marvin wanted to ride
him once more on the racetrack
before Nick retired him. Maybe the
day before Nick would let him at a
walk.

It was August 3, and the Travers
was in 22 days. The Pacific Classic
was in 15 days, just a little over
two weeks. Marvin was looking

forward to watching Groovy race again. Another thing he wanted to know was how Groovy would handle the Polytrack surface of Del Mar, the racetrack were it was held. Groovy had not had much experience with the synthetic surface.

On August 5, Groovy had a full-out, six furlong work over the Del Mar surface. The official clocker caught him in a bullet 1:11 flat. It was an obvious sign that it didn't matter what kind of surface Groovy raced on, he had determination.

Evil was very mild these days. At the beginning of his four year old season, he was more aggressive and pushy, but now he was very quiet. Marvin hoped he would pass on his gentle disposition to his offspring.

About week after Groovy's work, on August 15, the chestnut horse had his final breeze before the Pacific Classic. He went three furlongs in :36 and 2/5 seconds, a respectable time. Back on the East Coast, Evil breezed five furlongs of his own in :58 and 4/5 seconds with the gag bit. Nick thought he had made a smart move, changing the exercise equipment. The Travers was in just under two weeks, and the closing preparations were beginning to be laid down. Nick scheduled Evil a rare blowout a week before the race, on the 18th.

That Saturday, Groovy would try to become the second horse in history to sweep the Santa Anita Handicap, Hollywood Gold Cup, and Pacific

Classic all in one year. The first
horse that did it was Lava Man in
2006. He was a five year old that
year too, but he was a gelding.

Some trainers in the country
criticized Nick for racing his
amazing colt in such close races.
They didn't think Evil could take
it, but Nick knew his horse better
than those other trainers did.

On August 16, Marvin was scheduled
to see a doctor about his arm. He
had not seen one in three weeks,
and he didn't miss it. Now, Marvin
just had a brace on his arm,
holding it in place, but the bone
was far from being healed. The
stitches had been taken out, and
Marvin had a big, ugly scar on his
arm were the doctors had cut his
arm open.

The doctor examined his arm
closely while he was there. He
thought the healing progress was
coming nicely and he said Marvin
would not have to visit again for
four weeks. Marvin was glad. He
hated having to bend his arm in
weird positions for all these sorts
of x-rays.

When Marvin got back to Saratoga,
Evil was pacing at the back of his
stall. After Marvin showed up, he
looked out the window at the stable
yard. Nick saw the horse's gaze and
came up with a solution. He was
going to let Marvin graze the colt
outside with a thick chain attached
to his halter. Horses could be very
unpredictable, especially
Thoroughbreds.

Marvin wrapped a thick chain around the noseband of Evil's halter and led him outside, where a lawn chair was waiting. Marvin plopped down on it and gave Evil his head. The black onyx-colored colt was enjoying the outing already. He dropped his fine-shaped head to pick at the grass. Marvin was glad it was sunny and dry, not wet and muddy. Evil liked his grass dry and crisp; he was picky. The beautiful horse grazed peacefully beside Marvin for half an hour, then Nick told Marvin to bring him in. He didn't want Evil to founder because of too much fresh grass.

The long awaited day of Evil's blowout finally dawned bright and sunny. The colt sensed the excitement of Marvin in the air as he put a few saddle pads on Evil's back, followed by a light exercise saddle. He was wearing his snaffle bit for this workout.

Nick was standing with Ray at the fence. Nick was going to let him ride today because he thought Ray was very good at "letting the horse out of control". The blond-haired jockey saluted Nick with his right hand and guided the colt out onto the track, to where he was eagerly awaiting to go. He was going five furlongs, one of Nick's favorite breezing and working distances.

Evil knew the rush was coming. He could feel it in his blood which was boiling so highly. As soon as Ray crouched over the horse, he rushed forward into a run so fast, so effortless, it seemed unreal. The Saratoga track was a moving brown mark against the ground, and the rail was a white blur as the colt thundered past. Ray could not see the track ahead of him anymore. The wind was stinging his eyes like a thousand bees as Evil roared into the homestretch. His black mane whipped his cheeks, and Ray wondered if Evil would sprout wings and fly away soon. The colt soared past the eighth pole and was home in no time. Ray stood in the stirrups and leaned all his weight against Evil's mouth. The champion fought him for a few strides, but then slowed to a slow gallop and gradually slowed the pace until he was at a walk again.

Marvin was waiting for him at the gap. "I don't think dad wanted to watch after the first furlong. He told me to keep the time to myself and the official clocker."

Ray sighed. "He was really flying, you know. He was absolutely flying!"

37

Marvin kept the time for Evil's blowout to himself, staying true to Nick's promise. The track clocker didn't believe it at all. This horse was a freak. The time was like that of a sprinting quarter horse with extreme stamina, only faster. That work had released some of the energy that had been mounting inside the powerful horse all these years. After the workout, Nick started calling him "the beast".

Later that day, after Evil's run, the Pacific Classic was going to post. Groovy had drawn the far outside, the tenth post. Nick did not think it would hinder him, but Eddie would have to keep him back further than usual, just a little bit closer than he did in the Hollywood Gold Cup.

Just half an hour before post time, Eddie was peacefully sitting on a couch in the jockeys' lounge. He would have to go out to the paddock in about ten minutes, so he quickly pulled on the red and blue-checkered silks of David and Sonya's farm, known as Adrenaline Stables. Eddie opened a fresh pack of gum and put a few pieces in his mouth.

Meanwhile, Victor was watching his horse from his wheelchair outside the stall of the receiving barn. His leg was not healed enough to be around horses yet, but he always tried to stay ahead of their commands. His leg had been broken just above the ankle when Groovy had spooked at a bolting horse and thrown him. It was simple fractured, not enough for surgery, but the doctors advised him to stay in the wheelchair for just a few more days, then he would get crutches. His leg didn't hurt, but it probably would start if he got up on it and tried to walk.

The call to the paddock came minutes later, and Victor watched

as another groom came up and led
Groovy out to the paddock. Victor
didn't follow on his wheelchair,
but instead was helped up to the
trainer's box by Nick's assistant
trainer. He would not go to the
paddock today to help with Groovy;
he was merely a spectator today.

It seemed like an eternity until
the horses were on the track and
warming up. Groovy's chestnut coat
shimmered like the sun as he
cantered along in the California
sunshine. The other horses looked
good too, but Groovy was definitely
the best-looking horse in the
field. After warming up for several
minutes, the ten horses began
making their way over to the
twenty-ton starting gate. The Del
Mar weather was typical—hot and
sunny, but Groovy thrived in it.

Groovy was loaded in on the
outside, and the horse breaking
from the rail was loaded almost
simultaneously. The horses between
them loaded soon, and the field
prepared for the break, in which
the traditional Pacific Classic
would be off.

~~~~~~~~~~~~~~~~~~~~~

Groovy broke a half-step off, but
still fired. Within a few strides
he was in a close stalking position
in fourth. The pace was very fast
to start, with the first quarter in
:22 and 1/5 seconds. Eddie felt the
horse waiting patiently underneath
him, wanting to make that sweeping

closing move and pass the leaders.
Eddie kept him in hand easily, and
he waited like a game of cat and
mouse. The horses passed the half
mile pole, and the leader was
fading fast. A few strides into the
far turn he was going in the
opposite direction, rapidly
slowing.

Meanwhile, Eddie saw his chance
to get a head start on the other
closers, so he began moving his
hands with the horse's reaching
neck, pushing more momentum into
his stride. Groovy took off from
there, passing the tiring
frontrunner and turning for home.
Another closer was coming fast, but
Eddie saw him coming and pushed
Groovy into a full drive at the
three-sixteenths pole. He was
widening down the stretch as he
came to the sixteenth pole and
finally the wire. He hit the finish
five lengths in front of the
closer, and he was not tired. The
chestnut horse had only broken a
light sweat as Eddie let him gallop
out a sixteenth. He slowed the
winner of the Pacific Classic down
to a walk after a few fighting
strides, but Groovy finally gave in
to the pull on his mouth.

Victor barely wheeled himself to
the winner's circle after a
struggle, but he made it. Groovy
had romped in the million dollar
race, already stamping himself as
the main horse for Evil to beat in
the Breeders' Cup Classic. Victor
knew his horse had a shot to beat
the greatest horse of all time,

which had never been beaten in
nineteen lifetime starts. It was
better than the great Colin's
record, who also went undefeated in
his career. Evil had won the Triple
Crown, broke the Derby record, won
the Classic that same year, then
came back in his second four year
old race to break the world record
for a mile and a quarter in the
Dubai World Cup. He had an average
winning margin of almost fifteen
lengths, and he had no intention of
being beaten.

~~~~~~~~~~~~~~~~~~~~~

Marvin watched on TV as Groovy was
led out of the winner's circle and
back to the testing barn, and after
that, his stall. The chestnut had
just established himself as an
actual contender in the Breeders'
Cup Classic.
After the post-race coverage was
over, Marvin went back to Evil's
stall, where the colt was brightly
looking at him. He was looking in
the direction of he track, and then
at Marvin. Marvin smiled lightly at
his horse. "You can't go out there
right now, Evil. In a few days, I
promise, you'll get to run. But do
you want to know something even
more fun? Before you retire,
somehow, I'll ride you again."
Marvin patted the colt on the
neck. "Someday..."

38

The day of the Travers post draw came up lightning fast, and Marvin found himself waiting as the man fished a number out of the box.

The young-looking man read the name and number. "I'm Not Evil has drawn post number four for the Travers Stakes."

After the rest of the posts were drawn, a four horse field remained. The only horse Marvin thought could get close to his champion was All for You, the horse that raced Groovy in the Sunshine Millions Classic. The only other comparable horse was Ewinar, the horse that ran second in Evil's Derby and had tried countless times to beat Evil, but had failed every time.

On August 23, Evil had his last breeze before the Travers. With the gag bit, he went seven furlongs in 1:23 and 3/5 seconds, exactly what Nick wanted for a change. The black colt was fighting Ray the whole way, but Ray kept a good hold on him.

Nick was very satisfied and knew the colt would be in prime condition on race day. He was all muscle and almost no fat. He ate a lot, but it all went to benefit his muscles. His single quart of oats was almost not enough to give him enough energy on race day.

On the eve of the Travers, Marvin sat in Evil's stall, feeding him some sugar cubes. The colt loved the attention, rubbing his head

against Marvin's shoulder, trying
to butter him up so he could get
more treats. Marvin didn't give in
very easily, making Evil beg a lot
for a single treat.

One horse had scratched since the
post drawing. The rail horse, a
longshot, had withdrawn due to the
forecast that the track was
supposed to be sloppy. It didn't
matter if the track was sloppy for
Evil - like his dad said, a good
horse could run on anything. The
scratch left just another three
horse field, comprising of Evil,
Ewinar, and All for You. There were
no three year olds this year. The
field came in three basic sizes-
Evil was huge, All for You was
average size, and Ewinar was tiny,
just barely fifteen hands. Marvin
knew that neither of them would
catch his superhorse.

Marvin could not go to bed that
night. There was something nagging
him, but he wasn't exactly sure
what it was. There was a weird
smell in the air, a smell of
danger. He went to Evil's stall and
checked on him. Nothing was wrong,
and the colt was deeply sleeping in
the back of his stall.

That was when Marvin heard
screams from along the backstretch.
He rushed out the barn door and saw
that another barn, a couple down,
was on fire. The roof was engulfed
in flames that sizzled and crackled
along into the insides of the barn.
Marvin didn't have time to go get
Nick. He had to help right now.

~~~~~~~~~~~~~~~~~~~~~

Marvin sprinted across the late night grass with a burst of adrenaline. Various grooms were outside, bringing some of the horses out. That was when Marvin realized that the barn burning down was the barn that stabled Ewinar, one of the other horses in the Travers Stakes tomorrow. He rushed into the smoke and flames, having no idea were he was going. Marvin saw that the tack room was not yet engulfed, so he collected a few bridles, exercise saddles, halters, and finally some lead shanks and threw them out the barn door into the grass a few yards away. He saw another groom pick up the tack and carry it off to safety.

Marvin himself grabbed a halter, attached a nylon lead rope to it, and went searching for horses that could be trapped. He heard what sounded like a mare screaming from one of the back stalls, so he went over there looking. There was a small gray filly calling out from her stall, begging for help. Marvin went and opened the stall door and haltered her. He didn't need to encourage her to trot along with him as they emerged from the smoke and flames unharmed. Ewinar was not outside, so he was still in the blazing barn. It was getting worse now. The smoke and flames were creeping down into the stalls, especially the front ones. Marvin grabbed another halter and lead rope and went looking for Ewinar.

The smoke was starting to get to
him. Marvin choked and gagged,
trying to expel it from his lungs.
He rushed on, looking for a horse
so very important to its owners; he
had to be somewhere!

Meanwhile, Nick had woken up in
their barn and noticed Marvin was
gone. He smelled the unfriendly
scent of smoke and checked every
stall in his barn. When he found
nothing, he went around the side
and checked his roof. Nothing was
there, but when he looked off to
his left, a barn blazing with angry
flames was a standout. Marvin would
not be anywhere else at a time like
this. He raced up to another groom.
"Is my son in there?" he asked
with urgency.

"The small, dark haired one?
Yeah, he's been in there for a
while, but he hasn't come back
out," the other groom replied. He
was holding a small bay colt that
appeared to be traumatized by the
loud sounds.

A fire engine arrived. It
instantly began spraying a powerful
stream of water into and on the
roof of the barn. The flames
resisted the powerful stream at
first, but gradually gave in to the
force.

Marvin had searched everywhere
for Ewinar, but the small chestnut
colt was nowhere to be found. He
finally shouted out the colt's
name, inhaling a lot of smoke in
the process.

A loud shrill whinny came from
one of the far stalls. Marvin

rushed over to it and saw that the
entire back of the stall was coated
in flames, but a horse was standing
at the very front. Instincts told
him it was Ewinar. The tiny
chestnut colt was going crazy,
rearing and kicking like a horse
that was never tamed. Marvin put
his hands to the stall door latch,
and it was hot. There was no one or
nothing around to help him open it,
so Marvin ignored the screaming
pain on his hand and opened the
stall door. He threw the halter on
Ewinar with amazing quickness, and
the small horse resisted the pull
on his head. Marvin twirled the end
of the lead rope by Ewinar's flank,
and the horse walked on. He began
trotting, forcing Marvin to jog to
keep up with him. Marvin never
looked back at the blazing flames
following him. The barn floor had
been littered with highly flammable
straw, and the fire was chasing him
and the Thoroughbred as they raced
away. There was a while to go, and
the flames were catching him.
Without thinking, Marvin led Ewinar
over to a pair of crossties. He
hooked them together at the middle,
stood in the middle, and vaulted
himself onto the chestnut. Ewinar
was not expecting this, so he took
off at a fast, crazy canter which
was hard for Marvin to adjust to.
Nevertheless, it brought them to
the end of the barn, and the grooms
outside were amazed to see a small
horse canter out of the barn with a
small boy on his back. He looked
like a silhouette in a horse

magazine as he slowed to a stop
right in front of his own groom.
Marvin slid off, exhausted by the
smoke and flames. Nick was there to
catch him as he collapsed.

39

Marvin woke up in his cot in the
barn. He glanced at his watch,
which told him that it was 7:30 on
Travers Day. He scrambled out of
his cot, trying to get to Evil's
stall, but an arm held him back. He
glanced behind him and saw that it
was Nick. "Hold on, there. You'll
have plenty of time to attend to
your horse later. I want to talk
about last night."
Marvin sat on his cot, expecting a
scolding for getting on Ewinar.
Nick continued, "You saved that
spunky little colt's life, putting
your own life at risk for a horse.
His owners are really grateful, but
you had me very worried.
I don't want you pulling a stunt
like that again, okay? About riding
him, I am not mad at you. I don't
think you would have made it out
alive if you would have been
leading him. " Nick paused for a
moment. "You can attend to your
horse now. "
Marvin thanked his dad and went to
the tack room to get his grooming
supplies. He heard Evil's long,
loud whinny, calling Marvin to his
stall. Marvin smiled as he led Evil
out of his stall and put him in

crossties. Evil loved the attention
as Marvin brushed his coat to a
dazzling shine.

He spent the remainder of the
morning glossing Evil up for his
last start at Saratoga. When there
was just an hour left till time to
take Evil to the receiving barn, he
was shining like the night sky.
Marvin was very satisfied with his
grooming, and so was Nick, who told
him that Ewinar was still racing in
the Travers that day.

The Travers would be Evil's
twentieth lifetime start, and his
last derby. The Travers was often
called the summer derby because it
was so prestigious. He had won this
race by a huge margin the year
before, and he was going to keep
his title, whether people liked it
or not.

Just two hours later, Marvin was
in the receiving barn with Evil. In
the stall next to him was Ewinar,
who was looking at Marvin keenly.
Nick had gone to hang out in the
track kitchen for a few hours while
Marvin and Evil waited.

Evil touched noses with Ewinar
when Nick came by for a final check
on Evil. Nick laughed as the two
horses touched noses, and then
turned away sharply, probably
realizing they were rivals.

Finally the loudspeaker called
the horses to the paddock for the
Travers. Marvin leaped up at the
sound of crackling and got Evil
ready. He was going to be the first
horse down at the paddock, as
usual.

As Marvin led Evil through the
tunnel, he was greeted by cheers
and whistles. Evil arched his neck
and trotted into the paddock, where
reporters, owners, and trainers
were waiting. When Evil was halfway
to his saddling stall, an overeager
reporter ambushed Marvin. "Do you
think your horse will win today? "

Marvin snorted at the very
question. "Do you really think I
would say that he would lose? "

The reporter turned away at
Marvin's reply. Marvin snorted
again. The only time the other
horses got close to Evil was in the
gate.

Nick saddled Evil perfectly, and
Marvin began leading him around
that familiar walking ring. The
jockeys had still not come out yet
after Marvin had been walking he
colt five minutes. Just a few
minutes before the bugler began
playing all the jockeys hurried to
their trainers, their faces red.
Marvin thought Ray's was the
reddest of all. He led Evil back to
Nick, who had asked Ray what had
taken so long. Nick told Marvin
there had been a controversy in the
jockeys' room. He gave Ray a leg up
and sent him on his way as the
horses were called to the track for
the Travers.

Ray had a feeling that Evil was
not going to run his best today.
There was something bugging him.
Was it the way the horse warmed up,
or was it just him? Ray hoped it
was just him. The horses approached
the starting gate after a few

minutes on the track. Ewinar was
the first horse to load. He
hesitated at first, but his jockey
swatted him on the hip with his
whip, and he went in. All for You
was next, and finally Evil went in,
and they were all set for the
Travers Stakes, the summer derby.

~~~~~~~~~~~~~~~~~~~~~

Evil broke from the gate a half-
step off, and the other two horses
were in front of him for a second,
but within two strides Evil was in
front again, this time by three
lengths. Going into the clubhouse
turn Ray knew he had been wrong
about the horse being a little bit
off. The colt was rolling along,
setting a first quarter fraction of
:21 and 4/5 seconds. Ewinar was in
second about eight lengths back,
holding off All for You. The two
horses battled it out for second
place as Evil increased his lead to
thirteen lengths.
The big black horse passed the
half mile pole fifteen lengths n
front, but that lead was decreasing
slightly as Ewinar tried to close,
closely followed by All for You.
Ray did not see them coming, but
Evil heard them. He tried to grab
the bit in his teeth and run off,
but Ray held the bit tight to the
corners of his mouth. The colt
battled on, still trying to get the
bit in his teeth. He shook his
head, finally wrenching the bit
away from Ray's grasp. He grabbed

it in his teeth and began to pull
away from the other horses. Ray
leaned his whole weight against
Evil's mouth, vainly trying to slow
his down, but Evil was determined
to leave his performance in the
Travers a lasting memory at
Saratoga. He rushed on, completing
the far turn and hitting the top of
the lane. Behind him, at the middle
of the far turn, Ewinar was pulling
away from All for You. The tiny
colt was determined to finish
strong.

Evil roared past the three-
sixteenths pole with a rushing
fury. His lead was increasing, and
he was almost a sixteenth of a mile
in front of the rest of the horses.
The colt thundered past the eighth
pole and came down to the wire. He
finished the Travers thirty lengths
in front of the rest of the horses.
Ewinar hit the wire in second, ten
lengths in front of All for You.

Evil dropped the bit a furlong
after he had passed the wire. He
was satisfied with his performance,
so he decided to quit. After all,
he knew that when the wire passed
by, the race was over.

Ray quickly took the colt in
hand, for he would run no more
today. Evil reluctantly slowed, but
at least he obeyed. Ray turned him
around and pointed his nose in the
direction of the winner's circle.

Marvin met his colt at the gap.
He seemed delighted with his
outing, and followed Marvin like a
puppy into the winner's circle, a
place all too familiar.

40

Evil came out of the race in
excellent shape. He was not lame at
all the next day. Nick decided to
take him back to Belmont for the
Jockey Club Gold Cup, which would
be his last start before the
Breeders' Cup Classic. Marvin added
to Evil's list of wins:

TRAVERS STAKES (again)

Evil and Groovy would race on the
same days from now on. The Goodwood
Handicap and the Jockey Club Gold
Cup were both on September 30. The
Jockey Club Gold Cup was a little
earlier scheduled than it had been
in recent years, but it likely
wouldn't affect Evil. The horse was
unbeatable.
For the remaining days of August
Nick let Evil enjoy his last days
at the Spa. Next to Churchill Downs
and Belmont, it had been his
favorite racetrack. He was now
going back to the place often
called by some the "Test of the
Champion". Belmont would be the
last track at which he ran.
Aqueduct had offered David and
Sonya a large sum of money to get
him to make an appearance there,
but Nick told them to refuse.
Rumors were spreading of Churchill
Downs about to make an offer, and
Nick would have to think about it.
All of the major victories of

Evil's career had come at
Churchill, like his first Breeders'
Cup Classic and his Kentucky Derby.

On September 2, Marvin loaded all
of Evil's tack in the trailer. Back
in the barn, Evil was patiently
waiting in crossties, wearing
shipping boots around his legs and
a light sheet. Marvin attached a
lead rope to his halter and led him
out to the trailer, where Nick was
standing eating a doughnut, waiting
to leave. Marvin circled Evil
around and let him look at the
track. "Get a good look at
Saratoga, Evil. This is the last
time you'll be here."

Evil gazed at the track wanting
to run on it again. Marvin finally
turned him and led him into the
trailer. He was to never see
Saratoga again.

~~~~~~~~~~~~~~~~~~~

Nick pulled the truck into the
Belmont stable yard, where a small
crowd was waiting for Evil again.
Marvin led Evil out of the trailer
to loud cheering and applause. The
colt pranced as Marvin led him to
the receiving barn so the racing
officials would know he was there.
Marvin temporarily settled him in a
stall until they sent him to Nick's
barn.

On September 6, Evil had his
first breeze since arriving at
Belmont. He went a mile in 1:35
flat under heavy restraint. Ray
said later that he was ignoring the

gag bit's power, but it was
somewhat successful in slowing him
down.

Word got back from California
that Groovy had blown out three
furlongs in :32 over Santa Anita's
dirt course. It was near a new
track record, and it was without a
doubt the fastest time of ten other
horses at that distance. Groovy
absolutely loved Santa Anita, and
he always ran his best there.

Groovy was already in perfect
racing shape on September 7, three
weeks before the Goodwood. The
Grade 1 handicap served as the last
major prep race for the Breeders'
Cup Classic in California. As the
Classic drew near, Victor, who was
now out of the wheelchair, had a
main idea of who would be in the
race. He drew up a twelve horse
field, which consisted of Groovy,
Evil, Maximum Strength, All for
You, Smagg, Powdered Snow, Simply
Sinful, I Had a Dream, Ewinar,
Hellothere, possibly the
Argentinian horse Calypso Crush,
and the Kentucky Derby and
Preakness-winning filly Monday
Madness. Calypso Crush was also a
turf specialist who might choose to
run in the Breeders' Cup Turf
instead.

Thinking of the Breeders' Cup
Turf made Marvin think of Happy
Boy. His most recent race had been
the Secretariat Stakes, in which he
had finished second by a length.
His last race before the Turf would
likely be the Joe Hirsch Turf
Classic, which was also at Belmont.

Happy Boy had had a successful
career since moving to turf last
year. He had come in second in the
Breeders' Cup Mile as a three year
old, and had since lengthened out
in distance. He had won the Charles
Whittingham Memorial Handicap
earlier in the year, along with a
few other turf races. He had run in
the Derby against Evil, but had
faded to last, for he was tired
from the blistering pace and he had
not liked the surface. He liked any
turf surface that was under his
feet, though. Marvin had watched
some of his races, and they were
impressive looking with his late
charges down the center of the
track. Happy Boy had also grown a
lot since Marvin had last seen him.
He had gotten taller, maturing at
sixteen and a half hands, and
wider, measuring at nearly two and
a half feet across at the chest.

The son of a former Kentucky
Derby winner was sent back from
California on September 15. He was
very muscular and handsome looking.
Marvin remembered why David had
liked him so much. The turf star
was beautiful. Nick was giving him
charge of the colt's grooming and
care until he was retired at the
end of the year.

On September 17, both Evil and
Happy Boy had a work. Evil was
going seven furlongs on the dirt,
and Happy Boy was going five
furlongs on the grass. Happy Boy
went first. His jockey, Caleb, was
aboard for the move. Marvin watched
as Happy Boy obeyed his rider's

commands flawlessly and took off after a quarter mile. Happy Boy was a turf stalker and had an amazing cavalry charge that could overtake many horses if he was close enough. He finished out the work in :58 flat, a great time.

Evil, on the other hand, fought Ray as he galloped along. He was going at an amazing pace, able to fight Ray's pull on his mouth. The black colt's sheer strength pulled Ray along, finishing the work in 1:21 and 4/5 seconds. It was, as always, too fast for Nick's taste.

The Joe Hirsch Turf Classic, Jockey Club Gold Cup, and the Goodwood Handicap were in exactly 13 days. As Breeders' Cup preparations began to slow down, the horses began to speed up. The Classic shotguns and the Cinderella turf horse all would race on the super Saturday of fireworks.

41

Marvin propped himself up in Evil's stall. The colt was dozing peacefully as Happy Boy, in the next stall, was watching him. Nick placed the two colts next to each other; Evil in stall 1, and Happy in stall 2. They were instant friends, no longer rivals as they had been in the Triple Crown preps.

It was September 20, and the races were in 10 days. The nation's excitement was building like a locomotive gaining speed, and that

energy would be released in just
over a week.

Groovy was reported to have had a
work the next day at Santa Anita on
September 21. Word got back that he
went a half mile in a bullet :46
and two. The time was once again
fastest of thirteen horses at that
distance. He had established
himself as the West Coast's premier
Classic horse.

The week before the post draw
dragged slowly, but finally came.
On September 27, post positions
were drawn for every stakes race.
For the Jockey Club Gold Cup, Evil
drew the 1 post in a field of just
two. In the Joe Hirsch Turf
Classic, Happy Boy drew post seven
in a field of eleven. Finally,
Groovy drew post five for a six
horse race in the Goodwood
Handicap. Nick knew the horse liked
to race down the middle of the
track, so the post was perfect.

On the night before super
Saturday, Marvin was standing at
the front of Evil's stall. He had
been thinking about doing it for
days now, but he was finally going
to fulfill it. He was going to sit
on Evil-not for long, but he was
going to ride him around his stall
for a minute or two. Nick was down
at the track kitchen playing cards
with a few fellow trainers, and he
would be back in about five
minutes, so Marvin had to hurry.

Marvin entered Evil's stall
quietly, but the horse still looked
at him curiously. Marvin took the
strong water bucket he had brought

into Evil's stall and placed it by
Evil's side upside down. The tall
colt turned his head slightly to
see what it was, then continued
drinking from his actual water
bucket. Marvin stepped up, testing
his weight on the small but durable
bucket. It held good, so he grabbed
a piece of Evil's mane and
scrambled on.

Evil snorted, now aware of the
rider on his back. Marvin leaned
down and patted the colt's neck,
reassuring him. Marvin made the
tiniest of clucking noises and Evil
stepped forward. He was riding his
horse again, for the first time in
months.

The ride was cut short, for
Marvin heard Nick chatting with a
friend across the stable yard. He
slipped off quickly and rushed the
water bucket back to the feed room,
where Nick kept the other empty
ones. Nick came strolling into the
barn, waving a bundle of cash in
front of Marvin's face. "Guess how
much I won!"

Marvin looked at the bills in
Nick's hand. "Fifty bucks," he
guessed.

Nick waved them again. "Nope, but
close. Fifty five."

Marvin waved his dad off and
looked for a new Racing Form.

~~~~~~~~~~~~~~~~~~

The watch read 4:30. Nightguards
were still patrolling the areas
around the barns, but the silence

was broken by a few horses
whinnying out for their breakfast,
including Evil. Marvin crawled
sneakily out of bed, creeping
toward the feed room. He scooped
out Evil's rations, took them to
his stall, and dumped them in his
stall. Happy Boy was up too, so
Marvin retrieved his portions. When
Happy Boy was finishing his oat and
grain mixture, Evil was already
staring out the barn door towards
the racetrack. Race day had come
once again, and the colt cherished
the fact.

The Joe Hirsch was a race before
the Jockey Club Gold Cup, and
Marvin didn't think he would have
enough time to cool Happy out and
then rush back to the receiving
barn to collect Evil, so Marvin was
going to let Tim lead Happy down to
the paddock for the Joe Hirsch. He
had been volunteering to groom
horses for other trainers while
Nick had been racing Evil at other
tracks, but since he had come back
to Belmont, he was working for Nick
again.

It was 5:30. Tim was not at the
barn yet to keep Marvin company,
and he was thirsty. He didn't want
to go out into the dark night just
for a drink. Marvin had always had
a slight fear of being outside in
the darkness of night and early
morning. The sun would rise in
fifteen minutes, but Marvin still
could not wait. He threw himself
out the barn door. Looking at the
towering grandstand across the way
gave him an even creepier feeling.

He stood at the barn door and fixed his eyes at the cafeteria, which seemed so far away. He heard a snort from Nick, which startled him into a sprint. Thinking about who or what could be behind him only lengthened his stride and quickened it. Marvin had that eerie feeling that you got when you knew that someone was watching you. He was tiring, but still, through the flight instinct that some people got when they were scared, he raced on. His feet pounded against the early morning grass, making a light, crisping sound. A nightguard watched as the rushing boy sprinted past him in the direction of the cafeteria. Marvin's shrinking energy finally diminished as he jogged into the track cafeteria. The door was open, but the only light came from the Pepsi machine that stood near the counter. He dug in his pocket and found a dollar, barely enough to buy himself a Mountain Dew. He needed the energy for the race back to the barn.

Marvin caught his breath, then chugged down the Mountain Dew. It quenched his thirst immediately and gave him a burst of energy. His watch read 6:12, and Nick would be waking up soon, wondering where he was. Marvin opened the door of the cafeteria and stood in the middle. He walked a little bit away and let go of the door. As soon as the door slammed shut Marvin was off, keyed up like Evil would be in his race later on in the day. The pop had provided him with short lived

energy that was rapidly giving out.
Then he thought of his colt and
remembered how badly he wanted him
to win the Jockey Club Gold Cup and
Breeders' cup Classic. Marvin ran
on, powered by determination. He
finally jogged up to the barn door,
exhausted. His mission had been
accomplished. As 2 Timothy 4:7
said, "I have fought a good fight,
I have finished the course: I have
kept the faith."

After Marvin had been at Evil's
stall door for a few minutes, Tim
showed up. He was usually dropped
off by his mom every morning and
was late. The young groom made his
way over to Happy's stall. "I
can't wait to get to know him. He
sounds like a great horse," Tim
commented.

Marvin reached into the stall and
scratched the colt on the nose.
"And he is. This is his last race
before the Breeders' Cup Turf."

Tim got a halter and led the
horse out. "He definitely is,"
Tim said as he put Happy in
crossties to begin grooming him.

Marvin smiled and got Evil out.
He turned him around and put him in
the crossties in the direction
facing Happy Boy. Then both grooms
began preparing their horses for
their last starts before the
Breeders' Cup.

42

On the other side of the country, in the very early morning, Victor was doing the same thing. He had the large chestnut horse Groovy in the crossties, preparing him for his own last start before the Breeders' Cup Classic. The older horse was enjoying the grooming, his head leaning against the crossties. Victor let most of his weight rest on his good leg as he groomed Groovy's red coat. He was almost asleep as he was groomed perfectly.

Victor didn't think there was much competition in the race. Simply Sinful had flown out from the East coast for it, but Victor thought Groovy was better. Evil had broken the bay colt's heart one too many times. Groovy, like Evil, was also a heartbreaker.

Back on the East Coast, it was noon. Marvin and Tim had covered their horses in blankets and loosely tied them in their stalls. Soon, they would go to the receiving barn for the rest of the day, till their races would be run. Tim was going to stay in the barn with Marvin the whole time and get to know Happy.

After Marvin and Tim downed a few glasses of chocolate milk and breakfast pastries, the boys headed back to the barn, where their horses were ready to go to the receiving barn. Marvin bridled Evil with care and precision, making sure every strap was in the exact place it should be. Tim bridled Happy perfectly the first time,

also doing a check-over. Both
grooms put halters on over the
bridles and followed the familiar
pathway to the receiving barn with
Evil leading the way. He never
liked any other horse in front of
him, not even when he was being
led.

The massive crowds had not all
found a way to the receiving barn
path yet, but a few individuals
were there, applauding the two
horses. Tim and Marvin smiled at
the spectators and whispered their
"thank-yous" as their colts kept
them going.

Once both horses were in their
stalls, the two grooms plopped down
in the stall dirt, each waiting for
that long-awaited call to the
paddock. A few claiming and
allowance races went off, then
finally, the loudspeaker buzzed and
called the horses to the paddock
for the Joe Hirsch Turf Classic.
Tim waved goodbye to Marvin and led
the big bay horse down to the
paddock for the prestigious turf
race. Marvin looked up at Evil.

"It's just you and me now,
Evil," he said.

~~~~~~~~~~~~~~~~~~~~

Tim had never led a horse down to
the paddock for a big of a race as
this. The Joe Hirsch Turf Classic
was one of the final big East Coast
prep races for the Breeders' Cup
Turf. Various winners had gone on

to do good things in that race. It was a race full of tradition.

Nick was waiting for Tim at the number seven saddling stall. He saddled Happy Boy carefully, admiring his looks in the process. The bay colt had to be the prettiest horse in the field. When all eleven horses were saddled, the jockeys in their colorful silks emerged from the jockeys' room. Caleb came and shook hands with Nick and Tim. Caleb had always had a reputation for being very quiet. But now he said in a heavy Bostonian accent, "He gets better looking every day…"

Nick nodded and boosted the small jockey up. Tim looked around and saw that the rest of the horses were heading in the direction of the track as the bugler played. He accelerated Happy to a trot and followed the rest of the horses to the place where a Thoroughbred always proved himself–the racetrack.

Caleb may have been quiet on the outside, but on the inside he was always talking. The bay horse felt good beneath him today, and he was moving with the movements of a horse that was ready to run.

As the horses advanced toward the starting gate on the turf course, a knot of doubt formed in Caleb's gut. The horse was acting too perfectly. Something had to be wrong. When Caleb felt something was wrong, he was usually right.

And he was. When the horses broke from the gate, Happy Boy broke a

step slow and didn't respond when
Caleb asked him to pick it up a
little. As they went into the
backstretch Happy Boy was laboring,
not running well at all. The smart
jockey waved his whip in front of
Happy's eye, trying to get his
attention. When the colt didn't
respond, Caleb had no choice but to
lash into the horse's flesh with
the whip. Finally Happy Boy
responded, eating into the deficit
from the lead. This was more like
the colt he usually rode.

The horses turned for home, with
Happy Boy still fifth. He was
battling, but not gaining very much
as Caleb continued to strike him
with the whip. He moved into third,
but it was too late to catch the
leader, who had opened up a three-
length lead. Happy moved into
second and flashed under the wire,
only two and a half lengths behind
the winner, who had gone wire to
wire in an impressive victory. Tim
led Happy back to the barn utterly
disappointed, but the real
excitement was building as the
Jockey Club Gold Cup would be off
in half an hour.

~~~~~~~~~~~~~~~~~~~~~~

Marvin was standing by Evil's
head in the receiving barn. The
call to the paddock would come very
soon...

"Horsemen, bring your horses to
the paddock for the $750,000 Jockey
Club Gold Cup. Bring your horses to

the paddock for the Gold Cup, " the loudspeaker boldly announced.

Marvin took control of Evil who had been standing in his stall for quite some time, bored. Marvin had taken the bridle off during the long wait, but it was back on now. Evil was going out to the track again for his twenty-first lifetime start. No one had ever collared him at any point in a race if the colt was serious.

The paddock was thirty-person deep on the outside rail. The inside of the paddock was full of mostly reporters. Marvin saw the one that had asked him the dumb question about the Travers a month ago. He chuckled when he saw that the reporter avoided him and turned to the other horse's trainer.

Nick saddled the horse as usual and sent Marvin along the walking ring. The jockeys were out earlier than usual today, so they spent a while standing with their trainers, discussing strategy, though it may have been pointless. Ray was standing silently by Nick when Marvin led Evil up. The paddock judge called for riders up, and the two jockeys were given a leg up onto their horses.

Marvin led the black horse out onto the track in front. The other horse in the race was a longshot whose owners claimed was super-fast and could outrun Evil. Marvin thought that was stupid. He handed his beloved colt off to the pony rider, who looked thrilled to be taking him to the gate.

Ray loved the horse at that
moment. He was warming up nicely as
the two horses headed in the
general direction of the gate. They
were fully warmed up after about
six minutes, and they began loading
earlier than scheduled. Evil was
the first to go into the gate. The
other horse caused the race to go
off at the normal time, for he was
giving the starters a hard time.
Every time they straightened him
out and walked him up, the colt
moved his hips to the side and
avoided the slot. Finally the
starters gave up on loading him
normally, so they blindfolded him,
led him around in a circle a
distance away from the gate, and
then walked him in. When they
pulled the blindfold off, the colt
threw his head up in surprise, but
he stayed in the gate.

When the shrill bell rang and the
gates opened, the longshot was left
behind. Evil gunned himself out
like a rocket, never having trouble
sorting himself out. He had the
lead by ten lengths when he was
turning into the middle of the
backstretch. The other horse's
jockey was already driving him and
going to the whip, but he was
already tired from the blistering
pace after three furlongs. As Evil
passed the half mile pole, the
other horse's jockey knew he had no
chance and now began easing the
horse up.

The black monster on the lead was
increasing his lead with every
stride, that long stride which ate

up the ground like a beast. It was
thirty lengths at the top of the
stretch, but it increased like dust
to a dresser in a closet. By the
three sixteenths pole it was forty,
and then forty five just a few
strides later. Ray knew the race
was won, so he slowed Evil down by
putting a strangle hold on him.
Evil hit the wire forty-eight
lengths in front after the longshot
horse had been eased up. Ray stuck
his fist in the air, for Evil was
going to be an undefeated horse
going into his final race.
  Who really thought he wouldn't?

43

     On the other side of the
country, Victor was leading Groovy
down to the saddling paddock. The
colt was in prime condition, and he
was prancing along. Victor led him
through the Santa Anita tunnel to
whistling and cheering. As soon as
Victor was in the paddock he was
ambushed by a group of reporters,
asking what he felt his chances
were to beat Evil. Victor snickered
and said, "The Classic's over a
month away. I'm worrying about this
race first!"
  The reporters took the hint to go
away, so they went and bugged
Simply Sinful's connections. Victor
shook his head and finished leading
Groovy over to Nick's assistant
trainer, Andrew. Andrew saddled him
quickly and sent him off around the

walking ring. Victor felt proud to
be leading such a racehorse around
the walking ring. Groovy's green
saddlecloth looked smart against
his bright red coat.

The jockeys suddenly materialized
at their trainers' sides as the
paddock judge called for all riders
to be up. Victor trotted Groovy
back to Andrew, who boosted Eddie
up onto the horse. Andrew looked up
at Eddie and said, "Do you know
what to do?"

"Yep."

"Good."

Victor heard not too far off in
the distance the bugler playing. He
pointed Groovy's nose in the
direction of the track. "Let's go
running," Victor said. He led the
horse through the tunnel again and
out onto the Santa Anita racetrack,
where thousands of fans were
cheering. The pony rider took
control of Groovy now, and Victor
stood at the gap, where he would
wait till the race was over.

Eddie never got sick of feeling
the short, packed stride of Groovy
underneath him. The chestnut was
feeling his oats today, Eddie could
feel it. The horses warmed up
quickly in the California sun, then
moved quickly towards the gate. The
race was a little off schedule so
far, and they wanted to send it off
as close to the estimated time as
they could.

There were six horses in the
race. Groovy had drawn post five,
on the outside. Simply Sinful had
drawn the two post, near the

inside. Eddie thought he was the
main threat. He loaded into the
gate without any problems, and
Groovy loaded into the outside
slot. The other four horses loaded,
and the field for the Goodwood
Handicap was all set.

~~~~~~~~~~~~~~~~~~~~~~

On the East Coast, Evil was being
led from the testing barn back to
his own stall. The Jockey Club Gold
Cup results were official, and Evil
was still undefeated in twenty-one
lifetime starts. Marvin added to
his sheet of paper:

JOCKEY CLUB GOLD CUP

Marvin knew that the other horse
never posed a threat. Evil would
now begin preparation for the
biggest race in his life; bigger
than the Triple Crown and the first
Breeders' Cup Classic. This was his
last race, and the competition
would be fiercer than ever in the
form of a single chestnut horse.

~~~~~~~~~~~~~~~~~~~

Groovy broke from the gate just a
half-step off, but he was right
where Andrew and Nick wanted him to
be. Eddie brought his firm hold on
Groovy's mouth and kept him in
fifth, a perfect stalking position.
Simply Sinful was out on the lead
and cruising. He had not been on

his beloved lead since before he
faced Evil in the Preakness the
year before. He was soaring on the
lead by five lengths, and no one
had challenged him yet.

The big chestnut horse was ready
to roll. He was getting more
impatient with each and every
stride he took. Groovy was like a
coiled spring, ready to release his
energy at the slightest signal. He
seemed to be asking Eddie, "Do you
want me to run? Do you want me to
run?!"

Finally, at the far turn, Eddie
let Groovy run. The chestnut horse
was running like he loved to now.
His strides were becoming bigger,
faster, stronger, and he was
catching Simply Sinful.

Groovy collared Simply Sinful at
the top of the lane.

He was moving effortlessly,
running with the bay horse for half
a dozen strides, hesitating just a
little; then Eddie waved the whip
in front of his eye, and Groovy
thundered past. He was flying down
the Santa Anita stretch,
lengthening his lead to three
lengths; to five at the sixteenth
pole, and finally six as he flashed
under the wire. Just Groovy had
just established himself as Evil's
main challenge in the Classic.

At the gap, Victor hollered for
joy as he saw his horse flash under
the wire six in front. He walked
towards the front of the gap,
waiting for Groovy to come back.
Out on the track, Eddie was pulling
Groovy up. The determined

Thoroughbred was slowing down, obedient to his rider. Eddie was pleased with the horse's performance. It was off to the Breeders' Cup.

Victor collected Groovy at the gap and led him into the winner's circle. After the pictures were taken, a young woman reporter approached Andrew. "So it's off to New York?"

Andrew smiled. *"He'll be there."*

44

It was October 1. The Breeders' Cup was exactly 33 days away. Groovy was scheduled to come to Belmont the next day, and Marvin had somewhat missed the horse. The gorgeous chestnut was a great racer, but Marvin had remembered that Groovy had liked to try to bite Marvin's arm off. He was still a beautiful horse, but he had an attitude.

The nation and world's spotlight was on the Breeders' Cup. It was not just on the Classic matchup and the final race of Evil and Groovy, but the other races as well. The Breeders' Cup was expected to be action packed that year. Every race had some juicy matchup or rivalry. The Breeders' Cup Turf along with the Classic was likely to be the most exciting race to watch. Instead of going in the Classic, the Argentine-bred Calypso Crush was going to the Turf after being

seriously considered for the
crowning event. He had won a few
races on dirt, but his owners felt
that he was better on the grass. He
would have to take on Happy Boy in
that race.

That next day Groovy arrived at
Belmont from California. Victor was
laughing so hard when he saw that
Marvin hadn't come looking for him
yet. The other groom was in Evil's
stall, reading a Racing Form.
Victor chuckled. Marvin was such an
analyst.

Victor led Groovy from the
receiving barn a few hours later.
Marvin was still analyzing the
history of one of the Breeders' Cup
races in Evil's stall. Victor
walked Groovy up to the door of
Evil's stall, right above where
Marvin was sitting. Then, Groovy
snorted, and Marvin looked up. A
chestnut muzzle was hanging above
his head, and Victor was peering
down at him with a huge smile.
"Hi, Victor," Marvin said.

Victor jangled Groovy's lead rope
to keep him from getting into a
potted plant just outside the barn
door. "Hello," he said.
Marvin pointed to the horse.
"He's still mischievous as ever I
see," he commented.

"He is. Is that the big black
beast I see behind you?" Victor
asked, nodding at Evil. It was a
dumb question.

"That would be him. Remember
Happy Boy?" Marvin said, referring
to Happy in the next stall.

"I do! He's gotten I lot bigger since I saw him last. I know he's doing well on grass and is running in the Turf, right?"

"Yes. He didn't quite respond in the Joe Hirsch, but dad didn't think he liked the turf course. It was a little messy that day."

The turf course *had* been messy that day. It had rained earlier in the week and the grass course still hadn't dried out. The mud underneath it flew out in great chunks, and Happy's hooves had likely gotten too much suction in it. The main track had been sealed, and it wasn't affected much.

Groovy was settled into the stall next to Happy Boy, two stalls down from Evil. The two horses had never really been friendly toward each other, and Happy Boy was going to stay in his present stall to separate them.

A few days later, on October 5, Groovy had his first gallop since arriving at Belmont. He seemed to handle the sealed course all right, but Victor wasn't sure. As Victor led Groovy back to the barn Marvin walked by. He shouted a message at Victor as he passed by. "Your horse is going to get whooped in the Classic!"

Victor shouted back, "Yours will!"

Marvin counterattacked, "Someone's gonna lose, and it won't be Evil!"

Victor laughed. "*You'd be surprised!*"

~~~~~~~~~~~~~~~~~~~~

Evil had a work the next day. He was going a mile with a tight but not unbearable hold. Nick wanted him to stretch without running too hard. Ray was aboard for the run, and every time Ray got on the results were the same. Evil ran too fast, going the mile in 1:34 and 4/5 seconds. The horse was unstoppable!

With every second, the Breeders' Cup got closer. It was October 10, and the championship day was in 24 days. The final field contenders were beginning to take place. All races but the Classic were expected to have fourteen horses.

On the 11th, the horse racing world was shocked when, out of the blue, the Kentucky Derby and Preakness-winning filly Monday Madness was pre-entered for the Classic. Many analysts and handicappers were expecting her to go in the Distaff, but not now. The filly's fans thought she had a chance to beat Evil.

Happy Boy was pre-entered for the Turf, and Groovy and Evil were pre-entered as separate entries for the Classic. Marvin was shaking in excitement of the whole thing, and he had picked a horse to win in every race.

The week of the Cup came up lightning fast, and Marvin thought that he had taken a trip forward in time. The post position draw was on the 30th, and Marvin found himself in a small room awaiting the rest of the drawing for the turf. The man at the front of the room drew Happy's name out of the box. "For the Breeders' Cup Turf, Happy Boy has drawn…" The man fished in a box for a moment, then pulled out a number. "Post eight," he announced.

Marvin looked over at Nick and Andrew and saw that they were nodding their heads up and down in satisfaction. Post eight was perfect, not too much to the inside where Happy could get boxed in, and not too wide.

Calypso Crush had drawn post two for the Turf, which was perfect for him. He was the kind of turf horse that could go a mile and a quarter in a swift pace and then still have enough energy left to sprint home the last quarter and hold off the closers.

The Turf posts were drawn, and now it was time to draw posts for the Breeders' Cup Classic. Marvin's heart was beating very fast, like it always did when officials talked about Evil's race.

The man drew a name out of the box. "For the Breeders' Cup Classic, Powdered Snow has drawn…post four."

Marvin saw Powdered Snow's trainer and owners nod from across the room in satisfaction. The gray colt had some speed, but not enough to go with Evil for a mile and a quarter. He was more of a miler.

Another two names were drawn, this time they were the names of

Maximum Strength and Ewinar. Marvin
was getting impatient as the
Pimlico Special horse Hellothere
drew post ten, and Simply Sinful
drew post five. Marvin couldn't
help but feeling a stab of sympathy
when Monday Madness, the filly,
drew the very outside eleven post.
Her owners shook their heads in
disbelief at the draw.

Finally Evil's name came out.
"For the Breeders' Cup Classic,
I'm Not Evil has drawn...post
seven. "

Marvin nearly went airborne in joy
at the lucky draw. The next moment,
he nearly cried out in vain when he
found out that Groovy had drawn
post six, right next to him. He
hoped that Groovy wouldn't attack
Evil in the gate. He was a very
territorial horse. Evil had always
had his own space, but what would
he do if another horse came at him?
Marvin hoped he wouldn't hurt any
unlucky horse.

~~~~~~~~~~~~~~~~~~~~~~

On the night before the Breeders'
Cup Marvin was handicapping every
race. It was an action-packed,
promising day, full of fast horses
and big purses.

The Juvenile Fillies had a lot of
promising two-year-olds. The baby
Marvin thought was the best was a
jet-black filly with a white star
on her forehead. The filly's name
was In Advance, and she had won all
of her three starts, including two
stakes races.

The Juvenile was also very promising. Marvin's pick was a light bay colt named Untouched Sky. He regularly posted Beyer speed figures in the 100 range, and he was also undefeated. The only colt Marvin thought could beat him was a tiny chestnut similar to Ewinar. He was actually a full brother to Ewinar, and his name was Cherry Popsicle. Marvin thought that was a weird name for a horse.

The Filly and Mare Turf was going to be one for the ages. It premiered the East Coast's best turf mare against the West Coast's best turf filly. The best of the West came through the filly named Cocktail Party. She had been beaten a few times, but that was on the dirt. Like Happy, she really loved the turf. The East Coast mare was a seasoned veteran by the name of Inside the Box. She had been beaten many times, but her trainer claimed she got better with age.

The Sprint was full of the fastest horses the nation had seen in years. Marvin thought Evil could have been entered in the Sprint and still won. The horse that was entered in the sprint was a horse with the uncanny name of Keyboard. He was capable of ripping off :20 and 3/5 second quarter miles in his workouts, and Marvin had never seen Evil run a quarter mile that fast more than once.

The Mile was one of the most wide open races. Marvin's horse was a chestnut named Earthly Force. He was unstoppable over a mile. The

colt had a deadly closing kick, but
recently had been faltering in
Grade 1 company. That was the
reason the race was so wide open.
Most of the horses were between
five and ten to one.

The Distaff division was left
with a gaping hole when Monday
Madness went to the Classic. The
only filly Marvin thought could
fill that hole was Winter
Evergreen. She was a pure white
filly that ran on the lead. She was
mostly able to keep it when Monday
Madness wasn't in the race.

Marvin had picked Happy Boy to
win the Turf. He believed in the
horse, but he thought Calypso Crush
was a tough competitor. Marvin
picked them to finish one-two.

Without a doubt, Marvin had
picked Evil to win the Classic. His
competition was stronger than ever
with Groovy in the race, but Marvin
felt his horse would always be
supreme on the track. The field
from the rail out was Maximum
Strength, All for You, Smagg,
Powdered Snow, Simply Sinful, Just
Groovy, I'm Not Evil, I Had a
Dream, Ewinar, Hellothere, and
Monday Madness.

~~~~~~~~~~~~~~~~~~~

It was 2:00 sharp. Marvin had
only been sleeping for three hours,
but he was supercharged with energy
from the excitement of the
Breeders' Cup. Victor and Tim were
still fast asleep, so Marvin didn't

want to wake them up. He went to Evil's stall, where the colt was dozing peacefully. Happy Boy was awake in the next stall, looking curiously at him. Marvin gave the bay colt a pat through the railing of Evil's stall. He sat down in the stall and watched his horse sleep. Evil looked so peaceful, Marvin didn't want to touch him.

His watch read 4:00. Evil was awake now, looking for Marvin, who had gone off to the feed room. The black monster saw him feed Groovy and Happy, and then disappear back into the feed room. He reemerged with Evil's single quart of oats and poured them in his feed tub. By 4:30, Evil had polished off his oats and was staring out at the track.

For the final time, it was race day.

45

Tim and Victor woke up just five minutes apart from each other, at 5:00 and 5:05. Tim went to Happy's stall, and Victor went to Groovy's stall. Marvin summoned his two friends to the tack room.

"Who wants to have a grooming party this morning?" he asked.

Both said yes and collected their tools from separate corners of the tack room. Victor put Groovy in the far crossties, Tim put Happy in the middle, and Marvin put Evil in the ties closest to the door. The three

boys shared a large trunk of coat
and hoof polishers as they groomed
their horses' coats. The three
horses, all a different color,
enjoyed their massages before their
last races. Evil's black coat
sparkled like black onyx, Groovy's
chestnut coat shone like a ruby,
and Happy's bay coat was rich like
chocolate. Outside the grass glowed
an emerald green by the shedrow,
and was slightly browning over
where some of the horses grazed.

The weather was shaping out to be
perfect. The sun rose over Belmont
Park on the morning of the
Breeders' Cup with no clouds
blocking it. The air was crisp and
cool but comfortable if you had a
sweatshirt on. It was forecast to
warm up to almost sixty degrees
around post time for the Juvenile
Fillies.

By 9:00, all three horses were
groomed up perfectly. Their hooves
shone with the hoof oil that had
been applied, and their coats were
shining deeply like velvet. Marvin,
Tim, and Victor thought it was
funny how all of their hair colors
matched the coat color of their
horses—Marvin's hair was short,
slightly spiked, but jet black,
Tim's hair was light brown like
Happy's chocolate coat, and
Victor's hair had always been as
red as a ruby.

The three grooms went to the
track kitchen for a quick
breakfast, then headed back to the
barn. All three of them wanted to
get their horses to the receiving

barn early, so they did a final brushing and then haltered them. Victor had told Marvin and Tim to leave their horses bridles off till the loudspeaker told them to get their horses ready. Before they left Nick's barn, David and Sonya dropped by. Sonya was wearing a large, flowery hat that almost made Victor burst into his loud, squeaky laugh. Marvin thought it sounded like a chipmunk's laugh. David came by and wished all three of the grooms and horses good luck. He looked just as nervous as they did, his face holding a look of concern.

~~~~~~~~~~~~~~~~~~~~

Ray and Eddie arrived at the track at 10:00. The jockeys' introduction was soon, and Ray needed to change into his silks for the Juvenile Fillies. Eddie didn't have a mount until the Filly and Mare Turf.

All of the jockeys were already in the jockeys' room, some playing pool and cards. Others, like the miniature Cameron, were sitting on the couch, waiting nervously for the jockeys' introduction. Ray joined in a game of cards until it was time to go out to the track. Eddie was the first to go out onto the track. The announcer spoke, "From Mexico, Eddie Loitaro!"

Eddie jogged slowly out onto the track waving his little flag. The small Cameron was the next to join him. He was from Canada. Ray was next. "From France, Ray Buna!"

Ray had never liked the jockeys' introduction, for it attracted a lot of attention. The rest of the riders loved the attention, but Ray had always been shy. Caleb, Happy's jockey, was the same way.

When all of the little guys were on the track the announcer cried, "Ladies and gentlemen, the Breeders' Cup jockeys!"

Ray was glad when it was over. He went back to the jockeys' room and plopped himself down in front of the TV to watch the minor stakes races earlier on the card.

~~~~~~~~~~~~~~~~~~~~~

Evil began the parade of the Adrenaline Stables' horses to the receiving barn. Behind him came Happy, and Groovy brought up the rear. There was a line of people applauding them as they made their ways down the path and into the barn where a horse must report several hours before its race.

Evil was settled a few stalls down from the last horse there. Happy was in the stall next to him, and Groovy was in the next. The three friends spent all their time chatting happily for the next several hours.

~~~~~~~~~~~~~~~~~~~~~

The Juvenile Fillies, a two million dollar race for two year old fillies, was about to be run. Ray was on the filly that had drawn the number nine post. Her name was In My Life, and she had only been beaten once in her four race career. The chestnut filly was warmed up nicely when the assistant starter loaded her into the gate. The favorite, an undefeated black filly named In Advance, was to her inside, in the eighth slot. When the last baby loaded and was set, the starter pushed the button and the Breeders' Cup Juvenile Fillies was off!

Ray took a snug hold on his filly as the field went into the first turn. The black filly was leading, and Ray remembered not to let her get too much of a lead. He encouraged his filly to move up to second, and she responded willingly. As the baby girls moved into the far turn the black filly was trying to run away, but Ray was giving her a hard time on his chestnut. The black filly's lead was reduced to a length turning for home, but then her jockey lashed into her with the whip, and she responded with just enough heart. The filly that resembled Ruffian was moving away again. Ray was scrubbing on his chestnut, but she could get no closer than a length to the black filly as she swept under the wire.

Ray stood in the stirrups and pulled his filly up. She had tried hard, but the run at a mile and a

sixteenth had taken a lot out of
her. Ray turned the filly around
and took her to the gap, where the
groom was waiting. He had a soft
look on his face for his filly, and
he thanked Ray for trying.

Ray went back to the jockeys'
room disappointed. He didn't have a
mount in the Juvenile or Filly and
Mare Turf, so he changed out of his
Juvenile Fillies silks and into his
Sprint ones. Ray plopped down on
the couch, still trying to catch
his breath from the hard ride he
had just given the filly.

~~~~~~~~~~~~~~~~~~~~~~

Marvin was polishing Evil's bit
with his shirt when he heard the
final results for the Juvenile
Fillies. His horse had come home in
front. He was one-for-one so far.

He lay around in Evil's stall
while Tim and Victor chatted
excitedly. Who knew an afternoon so
exciting could be so boring at the
same time? And who ever knew it
could take so long?

After what seemed like an
eternity, the loudspeaker crackled
and called the horses to the
paddock for the Turf. Marvin and
Victor wished Tim good luck as he
disappeared with the bay colt
following him. Only the Classic
horses were left in the receiving
barn.

~~~~~~~~~~~~~~~~~~~~~~

Ray didn't have much luck in the Sprint, Mile, or Distaff. All of his horses had lacked the response that they usually had, or they had faded in the stretch. Ray felt his bad luck was ominous today. As he walked out into the paddock for the Turf, he thought about his chances in the race. He was riding the third choice horse to Happy Boy and Calypso Crush. Both of those horses were very fast, and his horse was a frontrunner along with Calypso Crush. The favorite would fight him, but that might wear him down enough that he would fade. His horse had major stamina, and that was always a plus when you were going a mile and a half.

The trainer gave Ray a boost up onto the tall bay horse. "Try to pressure the leader as much as you can without wearing him out," the trainer said, pointing to the colt Ray was on.

The post parade was very short. The races were a little behind schedule, so they were trying to hurry up. Caleb was not a fan of this. Happy Boy needed at least an eight minute post parade to be fully stretched and warmed up for a mile and a half run, but they rushed on. The Turf horses loaded super-fast into the gate, and stood still for a separate second. Then the bells rang, and the Breeders' Cup Turf was underway!

Calypso Crush immediately went out to the lead. Ray followed behind him, a length off the lead.

His bay colt was doing a good job
of pressuring the leader right off
the bat. Ray looked back and saw
that Caleb, on Happy Boy, was
closely stalking him.

As the turf horses went into the
stretch for the first time, Calypso
Crush was already under heavy
pressure. Ray was asking his horse
to make the other uncomfortable,
and his horse was very obedient.
The leader's neck was already dark
with sweat, and he had run through
the opening half mile in a faster-
than-expected :47 and 3/5 seconds.
The horses turned into the
backstretch for the final time, and
Calypso Crush was still being
pressured. His jockey was asking
him now - not a lot but telling him
to run on. There were five furlongs
left - just under half the race -
and Caleb was starting to move his
hands on Happy Boy. The turf course
was to his liking today and he had
stayed in third the whole time, but
now he was closing the gap between
him and Ray's horse, who had
started to take Calypso Crush down.
The leading chestnut was tired from
the pressure, and was slowly
folding. Ray's horse took the lead
at the half mile pole, and he went
on for home as Calypso Crush faded
horribly.

Happy Boy was decreasing Ray's
horse's lead. At the three-
sixteenths pole Ray saw him coming,
but it was almost too late. Happy
Boy had switched into his powerful
drive that came like a freight
train down the stretch. Ray was

going to the whip and scrubbing,
but his horse couldn't hold off
Happy Boy in the final sixteenth.
The bay colt overtook him and
crossed the wire two lengths in
front. The normally quiet Caleb
stuck his fist in the air and
whooped for joy as Ray quietly
pulled his horse up in another
second place finish. His owners
were pleased with the colt's
performance, but Ray knew he could
have won.

He went back to the jockeys' room
and changed into the Adrenaline
Stables silks; he was getting ready
to ride in one of the biggest races
of his life.

~~~~~~~~~~~~~~~~~~~~~

Marvin and Victor were standing
in the receiving barn, bridling
Groovy and Evil. Groovy wore a
white bridle and blue and red-
checkered blinkers, which all
looked good on his chestnut coat.
Evil wore a plain snaffle bridle
that you would find on a kid's
pony. The loudspeaker crackled,
calling the horses to the paddock,
and Marvin attached a lead shank to
Evil's halter and led him out to
the paddock in front of Groovy,
who, unlike last time, was behaving
perfectly. Marvin led the colt
through the tunnel, where the
largest crowd he had ever seen was
waiting. Various individuals
whistled and cheered at him at the
colt pranced along. It was the
black giant's moment of glory.

Once in the paddock, Marvin saw a
crowd bigger than the one in the
tunnel. This crowd was about fifty
person deep starting from the rail,
and all the eyes were on him and
his colt. Marvin led Evil up to
Nick, who was waiting with a huge,
cheesy smile on his face. His dad
carefully placed a few saddle pads
on Evil's back and then folded them
back over the royal purple saddle
blanket, which seemed fit for a
horse like Evil. Looking across the
paddock, he could see that it
looked good with Groovy's chestnut
coat. The older horse was already
saddled and walking around the
ring. Nick carefully placed the
saddle on top of the purple
saddlecloth and fastened the girth
tightly. He strapped a surcingle
over it next for extra protection
against the saddle possibly
slipping. Nick sent Marvin and Evil
around the paddock for the final
time.

The jockeys strolled out into the
paddock, some chewing gum out of
nervousness. Ray slowly walked over
to Nick with a very frightened look
on his face. The trainer
reassuringly gave him a pat on the
shoulder as Marvin led Evil back to
Nick for the final time. Nick gave
Ray a small boost up onto the large
colt and a small nod. The bugler
began playing that familiar tune-
oh, that familiar tune.

Marvin loved that tune.

He led Evil out to the racetrack
for the biggest race in his life,
the Breeders' Cup Classic, his last

race. Groovy was being ponied in front of him. Unlike last year, Groovy had been perfectly behaved in the paddock and had not squished Victor.

Ray loved horse racing. It was the only sport in the world when a five-foot man could stand ten feet tall. On Evil, Ray was easily the tallest man at Belmont. Evil was fluidly moving along, floating above the Belmont track in a beautiful canter that ate up the track like a hungry person devouring a pizza. The filly, Monday Madness, was cantering along behind him, struggling to keep up with his long strides. The horses began making their way towards the Belmont starting gate, which was positioned almost on the backstretch. Belmont was the longest racetrack in America at a mile and a half long.

The first horse to load was Maximum Strength. The dark bay colt resisted at first, but the assistant starters eventually coaxed him in. All for You and Smagg were next, followed by Simply Sinful and Powdered Snow. Then it was Groovy's turn. He halted just short of the gate and stared straight ahead, looking at what he was getting into. Eddie tapped him on the hindquarters with his whip and the chestnut horse walked in.

Evil was next. He, too halted in front of the gate for just a moment, but he walked in eagerly afterwards. I Had a Dream, Ewinar, Hellothere, and Monday Madness all

followed soon after. Evil jiggled
the bit in his mouth as he waited
for the break. The Breeders' Cup
Classic field was set to do what
they were born to do-run.

46

Evil leaped from the gate,
outbreaking all ten other horses.
Simply Sinful followed him heading
onto the monotonously long
backstretch. The giant black horse
was running effortlessly out on the
lead by four lengths, with Simply
Sinful second and Ewinar third.
Eddie knew something was wrong.
Groovy was struggling on the
Belmont track as if it were some
foreign, slippery surface. The
chestnut did not hold himself
together. Up ahead, Monday Madness
was being rated in tenth as Groovy
continued to drop back. After they
had gone the first quarter mile,
Groovy was 35 lengths behind Monday
Madness, and Eddie wondered if the
horse was hurt. He started to pull
him up when the champion finally
began to sort himself out. Groovy
was handling the track now, and
moving onto the bit.
Out on the lead, Evil was running
effortlessly. The colt was leading
the eleven horse field by five
lengths, for Ray had a strangle
hold on him. That desire to run -

Ray would never control Evil's desire to run, for it burned so strongly!

Groovy was running well now. A half mile had been completed, and not very much race was left. Eddie knew that the West Coast champion would have to pull a Silky Sullivan to even have a chance of getting to the front. He was catching Monday Madness, the length deficit was now only ten. The filly's jockey saw the huge charge from the chestnut behind him, so he readied his filly to follow him. Groovy was in the bridle now, he was running like never before. His last furlong had just been ripped off in :11 flat. This horse was rolling, oh yes, he was rolling!

Evil was going into the far turn with a ten length lead on Simply Sinful. The last quarter mile he had run was timed in :23 flat, and he was cruising. Ray thought the race was won, but he did not see the chestnut freight trains rolling up behind him. Groovy and Monday Madness were flying, but Groovy was flying faster. Evil heard the rapid hoofbeats behind him and he took off. Ray let him, for he thought that Groovy would catch him.

Just Groovy moved to I'm Not Evil at the top of the lane.

The two horses were reaching for more ground as the long stretch loomed ahead of them. Ray looked behind again and saw that Groovy was at Evil's flank. He let out most of the slack in the reins and Evil exploded. The pace quickened

in an instant, and Ray thought he
could relax. But yet he looked
behind him and there was a problem.

Groovy was still there.

Eddie was scrubbing on him,
asking him for his all, and Groovy
was giving it to him. He was trying
to get revenge for his poor
performance in the Derby before
Evil's. The two raced as a team for
100 yards, and then the undoable
happened.

Groovy stuck his nose in front.

That nose became a head and then
a neck as they reached the three-
sixteenths pole. The roar and
tumult of the Belmont crowd was
deafening already. Ray smacked Evil
as hard as he could on the right
flank, but something went terribly
wrong.

There was no response.

As the horses barreled toward
the eighth pole, something deep in
the core of the black champion
snapped. His triumphs, his
dominance, Marvin, and all the
times he had run in front flashed
through the colt's mind. This
chestnut thought he was better than
Evil? That would never happen. A
single message went flying through
the horse's brain.

Never back down.

The eyes of the black horse now
burned with anger; his heart
screamed with fury, and his blood
boiled with wrath, for one horse
had violated his racetrack rule:

When Evil was on the track, no
other horse was allowed to pass.

Evil came back with a rush of fury and once again the lead was reduced to a head and then it was uncertain as the two horses' heads bobbed back and forth in almost perfect unison. There was a sixteenth left till the wire, and the horses still raced as a team. Either one would rather give up his life than lose the race! The screams of Belmont were so loud, it was almost a supersonic sound.

The sound was silent to Ray, Eddie, and the horses. All four were concentrating on doing what they did best-win. The two horses swept under the wire together in the most exciting photo finish in the history of horse racing. That stretch duel had just taken the world to the cliff's edge - to the pinnacle in horse racing.

~~~~~~~~~~~~~~~~~~~~~

Marvin could not believe it. Evil may have just been beaten. His beloved black horse had just given the race everything he had. Marvin knew it would happen, that if Evil was ever caught that he would come back. The photo sign was still flashing after Evil and Groovy had come back to the gap. Marvin caught Evil and attached the lead shank to his bit. The colt was blowing hard; he had never run that desperately. The final time was already flashing on the toteboard-a new world record time of 1:56 flat. Only true champions ran that hard for the one

thing they desired the most-to win.
The third place horse was Monday
Madness, for sure; but the winner
was still uncertain. When the final
photo was posted on the board along
with the results, the crowd roared
like never before. Marvin whirled
around to look at it, and then let
out a cry of joy.

Evil had won by the slimmest
fraction of a nose!

His perfect record was intact; he
was never beaten in his career.
Marvin high-fived Ray and led the
valiant Evil into the winner's
circle. Marvin watched as Nick and
Tim lifted the winner's blanket of
flowers onto Evil's withers. The
black colt sighed, enjoying the
attention. His ears were pricked
up, as he knew where he was.

Evil was in the winner's circle,
and that winner's circle never got
old.

47

Nick let Evil rest up at Belmont
for a week. The greatest horse of
all time needed a little rest after
he was retired, didn't he?

On November 10, Evil was flown
back home to Kentucky, where he
would be forever. Churchill Downs
had made an offer for a million
dollars to let Evil gallop in front
of the stands before their program
started on Monday. Nick refused the
money, but asked Marvin what he

thought. Marvin smiled and told it like it was.

"I think Evil would like a final gallop."

Marvin had one more mission to accomplish. On November 11, the night before the gallop, he approached his dad in the Churchill barn and asked him for the mount. Nick smiled and said exactly what Marvin had wanted him to say.

"You're already riding him."

Marvin smiled at his dad and gave him a hug.

That next day, at around noon, Marvin was boosted up into the light exercise saddle by Nick. His dad gave him the nod and sent him off. Marvin was so happy to be riding his beloved colt, but sadly it was for the final time.

Marvin emerged through the tunnel on the undefeated horse. He trotted and cantered Evil the wrong direction down the stretch to warm him up, then turned him around. He saw the Twin Spires beckoning to him, and he lowered himself in the saddle. Evil jumped instantly into a gallop, but it was a slow one, exactly what Marvin had wanted. He glided gracefully over the ground as the thousands of fans cheered him. Evil pricked his ears up as he crossed the wire for the final time.

After Evil had been taken back to the temporary stall, Marvin loaded everything that belonged to him in the tack room into the trailer. He bandaged up Evil and led him out to the trailer. Evil kept his head

turned in the direction of the
track, watching the first race run.
Marvin led the horse halfway up the
ramp and paused him. The horse let
out a loud whinny, so loud that it
echoed over to the grandstand and
around the whole area, for it was
the last time he would ever see a
racetrack.

That whinny would remain in the
hearts of many forever.

~~~~~~~~~~~~~~~~~~~~~~

Nick drove down the interstate
towards David and Sonya's farm.
Evil was resting in the back of the
trailer. Marvin sleepily gazed out
the window as his favorite
spiritual song, "Songs of the
Wayfarer" went through his head.
Marvin sang out the last phrase as
the truck turned onto the exit.
"I'm going home…"
Marvin closed his eyes as the
years of sleeplessness finally bore
down on him. He had not slept well
in a long time, and those years
finally threw Marvin into a deep
sleep.

~~~~~~~~~~~~~~~~~~~~~

Nick was shaking Marvin's
shoulder. "Marvin, we're home. I
need you to help me unload the
trailer. Take Evil to the first
stall in the stallion barn. He'll
live in that stall for the rest of
his life."
Marvin stumbled out of the truck
and opened the back of the trailer.

Evil was waiting for him, so he led Evil over to a post, where he tied him and took his bandages and traveling gear off. He put them in the tack room, then returned outside and gave Evil a big hug.

Marvin led Evil past the training barn, the breeding shed, the training track, and all the familiar surroundings. He would never run again, unless it was in his paddock. He led the big black horse to the first stall in the stallion barn, the one reserved especially for him every time. Marvin turned him loose in the roomy stall. Then he latched the stall door with a lock, which with all the other stall doors were equipped. Marvin left the stallion barn with Evil nickering after him.

~~~~~~~~~~~~~~~~~~~~

Marvin made his way to his dad's office. "He's settled, " he said when he got there.

Nick nodded. "Good. He's been officially retired now. He's no longer a racehorse. He's a stud horse, just another horse in the stallion barn. Just like on the racetrack, he will have to prove himself there. He will always be remembered as the greatest racehorse of all time, but he doesn't race any more. His job is different. We'll see how the breeding legacy plays out. His lifetime earnings equal a new world record of $14,013,720. He did it in just three years." Nick paused for a moment and then continued, "It reminds me of an old saying I once heard…"

> Though the sun may rise
> And the sun may fall
> Nothing will ever replace
> What has ended once and for all.

Marvin walked out the door back to the training barn. Even after what his dad had said, he was still surprised to find Evil not in the barn he had been in since he arrived there.
Marvin would definitely miss his galloping figure on the racetrack.

~~~~~~~~~~~~~~~~~~~~

That night, in the stall that would be his home for the rest of his life, I'm Not Evil was dozing peacefully. Unknown to the world, he had a dream. He was running in a wide, open grassy meadow at sunset. Chasing behind him in vain were all the horses that ever lived. Behind him were Man O' War, Secretariat, Citation, Ruffian, Kelso, and the other great horses of the past. They were struggling to catch him. The rest of the horses trailed behind them, a big moving lump against the sky which was full of fiery reds, oranges, and yellows. Above them was the deep expanse of blue that stretched into space and beyond. Alone, twenty lengths in front, Evil was merely a silhouette against the salmon-colored fading sky. No one was cheering him on as he lengthened his lead, but the colt didn't care. Evil was roaring away from them all; none had ever beaten him. The big black colt was running like he always wanted to-- free, with no one to hold him back. That's all he had ever wanted to do. The huge horse was flying now, he was opening up daylight on them. He led them on into eternity through the race that never ended as a horse that had *never* been beaten, a perfect racehorse.

Epilogue: I'm Not Evil at stud

Evil would go on to produce multiple Grade 1 winners at stud. His most successful sons were the great turf horse Omniault, and the Triple Crown winner Grand Jubilee.

Even though he sired these two outstanding colts, he left an everlasting impact on the racing fillies. One of his greatest fillies, Imperfect Night, won the Belmont Stakes at the age of three. She would later go on to finish second by a nose in the Breeders' Cup Distaff.

Evil never did sire another horse like himself, but Grand Jubilee was the closest he came. He was a one in every millennium horse, but his actions would never be repeated. Marvin never did stop looking for another equal caliber horse. He was truly great.

About the author

Amber Ooley is a junior high student at a Christian school. She enjoys soccer, football, and of course horse racing. She rides horses at a nearby lesson center and her favorite horse's name is Tony.